Rules for Becoming a Legend

Rules for Becoming a Legend

TIMOTHY S. LANE   VIKING

VIKING

Published by the Penguin Group
Penguin Group (USA) LLC
375 Hudson Street
New York, New York 10014

USA | Canada | UK | Ireland | Australia | New Zealand | India | South Africa | China
penguin.com
A Penguin Random House Company

First published by Viking Penguin, a member of Penguin Group (USA) LLC, 2014

LIBRARY OF CONGRESS CATALOGING-IN-PUBLICATION DATA
Lane, Timothy S.
Rules for becoming a legend : a novel / Timothy S. Lane.
pages cm
ISBN 978-0-670-01488-0
1. Basketball players—Fiction.   2. Gifted boys—Fiction.   3. Life change events—Fiction.
4. Family life—Fiction.   5. Sports stories.   I. Title.
PS3612.A54994R85 2014
813'.6—dc23
2013036974

10 9 8 7 6 5 4 3 2 1

Set in Melior with Noa display
Designed by Carla Bolte

for Tiffany Leigh, of course

Like all legends, the legend of Jimmy "Kamikaze" Kirkus starts as an actual event and grows bigger than that. It grows like everything seems to grow in the Pacific Northwest rain. Tall and tangled. Slick and tricky. Changing all the time. Eating and rotting and molting—but always growing.

Contents

Part One

Rule 1. Value Those Who Keep Your Secrets

· ·

Monday, December 17, 2007

JIMMY KIRKUS, SIXTEEN YEARS OLD—MOMENTS UNTIL THE WALL.

Look at this kid in the high tops. Purer kid you never seen. Pure in his intentions, pure in his eyes, and most important, oh top of the list for the 8,652 residents of Columbia City, Oregon: pure in his jump shot.

Jimmy Kirkus, alone in this gym. This old sweat-soaked gym people call the Brick House. This basketball cathedral tucked away to be forgotten—like the loose hair gathered behind Jimmy's ear before he shoots foul shots—in the hilly, green folds of his small town. Forgotten, that is, except during winter: basketball season. In those coldest months the Brick House really heats up. Pulls people from a fifty-mile radius to duck in from the rain and the fog. To scream and love their team. To stomp their feet in the detritus of past games: stale popcorn, sticky candy wrappers, and crumpled game-day programs. To GO, FIGHT, WIN. Ever since four kids from Columbia City High went on to lead University of Oregon to the NCAA championship in the 1930s—and earn the nickname the Tall Firs—this town has been all about the dribble, dribble, shoot. Basketball to Columbia City is mass to church: a weekly expression of faith.

And Jimmy Kirkus was once anointed savior.

Jimmy—look at him—it's like he's floating in the yellow light on the edge of the three-point arc. Outside the gym he's a fish out of water, but here and now, kid's in his ocean. Flashing out in sparkly jumps, splashing down ball after ball.

Something's wrong though. His eyes are filled to the brim. His nose is runny and his throat catches on every breath.

He goes and finds the breaker box. Turns off all the lights. There are far-off clicks from within the walls. *Goodnight, goodnight,* they say, and the whirring of fluorescent light slows and then stops. Then darkness.

The only thing lit anymore is the EXIT sign. Shines on and on. Enough light so he can still see the names he's written and rewritten over the years on his gray basketball. One is darker and thicker than the others. Three letters. Painful to see. He grunts and throws the ball. It sails over the bleachers but bounces off something metallic. Stubbornly, it rolls back and stops a few feet away. Won't leave him, not yet.

Right under the hoop is thick blue padding, so Jimmy lines up to the left, where bare red brick wall starts. He kneels into sprinter's position. Puts his fingertips on either side of the out of bounds line. It's his runway and he's cleared for takeoff. He explodes a few steps. Then slows, then stops. He turns around, hands on his head. Back at midcourt, every sound he makes—breath or step— echoes. It's like someone is in the gym with him, whispering something, and he can never turn fast enough to catch him.

He drops to the floor and does ten quick push-ups. He leaps to his feet. Once again into sprinter's position. Once again an explosion of speed for a few feet and then let up, slow down, stop.

He can't do it. He's crying now. Face is slick with water. The wetness catches the shiny red of the EXIT light. He's coughing and his nose won't stop running. He takes off his shirt. He rips it in two. Listen how he screams so the echoes of the gym rise up to join him. The cold air touching his chest helps. A little. So he takes off his shorts. Over his shoes. Just in his underwear he crouches to the gym floor. He's shivering worse than ever but he's breathing still. If kid's got nothing else, he's got determination.

Up onto fingertips.

Toes dug in.

There he goes. Away from being *Jimmy Soft* and toward becoming *Kamikaze Kirkus*. Squeak, squeak, swish, swish, away with the old and in with the new . . .

It takes him fourteen full-out strides at the fastest he can muster to get to that brick wall. He plans on meeting it with open eyes. But. Some things you can't plan for. Sweat for one thing. Automatic reflexes for another. He closes his eyes at the last second, puts up his hands—the coward. *Jimmy Soft*. His head does hit the wall, but not full on. It hurts, but not enough.

There's a weakness in him and he wants to shake it loose, bang it out. He stands back up. Dumb kid. Gonna try it again. Same spot he started from as before. Sprinter's position. Just twelve long strides this time. Eyes open. Brick wall coming. He does it. Keeps them open the whole while. Hands down at his side, helpless to help. Amazing, his eyes stay focused on the wall as long as they do. Cracks and textures of it. From four feet, from one, from six inches.

Crack.

Boom.

Light.

Let there be light . . .

Hit is something he hears and doesn't feel. Or the other way around? He can't tell. It scrambles his senses. Makes a shape in his head bone he thinks he can smell as metallic. He feels blinking white light rain from every eave inside his head. Like when his pops spent an entire curse-soaked Sunday cleaning out the gutters of their house. Everything that had ever been blown up there came down. Then, on accident, he knocked the Christmas lights down too. They blinked on their way to the ground.

It all drops. And so does he. A knife of hurt thrusting into the front of his head so big his skull can't hold it. Not even close. He rolls to his back and stares up into the blackness, vents some of the pain in a crying jag. There's a security camera somewhere in the Brick House, but Jimmy thinks with the lights killed, it's too dark to pick him up.

After three times into the brick wall, Jimmy moves slower, but he's figured it out. There is always a moment before he hits when he can still put up his hands. If he gets past this moment then bravery has nothing to do with it. The hit is coming. He gets good at getting past this moment. His head throbs and the blood hesitates at his eyebrows before mixing with sweat and running faster to his chin. Everything is red. He can't focus. He's singing to himself, a Paul Simon song of all things. He's tuneless and spotty with the lyrics. *"People say she's crazy, got diamonds on her shoes. Lose them walking blues."* A teenaged dude singing Paul Simon? Must be something *very* wrong with him.

Back at midcourt he spits bloody, mucus-filled saliva onto waxed wood floor. Lines up, runs again. Slips a few steps in and slides painfully on his bare chest. Worst Indian burn you ever saw. Turns the skin see-through to the blood and muscle beneath, some of his chest hair ripped off. Hurts in the same rhythm as his heart.

He stands up and tries to blink his vision clear enough to see the brick wall. He's only five or six steps from it. There's something wrong with his balance though. He sways. He coughs but vomit comes up. He tries to keep it down by closing his mouth, and it erupts through his nose. Mixes with the blood of his chin and then dribbles to the floor.

Oh damn, our kid's a mess.

He shouts up into the blackness. "With Dex Kirkus in the. Middle. Jimmy outside. The Fishermen, Fishermen are a lock for Clatsop title! And Jimmy Kirkus shoots. He shoots. He SHOOTS, he

SCORES!" He's crying harder. It's for everything. For Dex, his mom, and even himself. "Fucking sand toads," he murmurs, "all bitten up from sand toads."

He decides, fuck it. Runs from there. The wall is in the ether distance. He's determined to give it the beat down. Give it the knowledge. He runs at it, as fast as he can. A dogged trot, he's a pub brawler gearing up for a head butt. *This wall. This stupid, fucking wall.* He brings his head forward at full speed. Crunches into the red stone. Forehead, poor forehead, smashes the bricks and the cut grows bigger. Big enough to swallow. Jimmy falls for the final time that night. *She's got diamonds on the soles.* His brain too haywire to instruct his hands to save him. He smacks the back of his skull. Feels like frayed wires are trying to pass electricity inside his head. Explosion of sparks. Jimmy gone down.

Rule 2. Come from Nowhere

JIMMY KIRKUS NOT YET BORN—TWENTY-TWO YEARS UNTIL THE WALL.

Todd Kirkus drove Genny Mori way out to Area C on the jetty and parked. They were young and it was a Friday. Out here, past areas A and B, they had privacy—and the starry sky. This far down the alphabet the beach was too hard-chewed by the Pacific to get any tourists outside the occasional treasure-hunter. And at night? May as well been Todd's bedroom. The stars, meanwhile, were the excuse. It was how he got all his girls to come out here with him. "You've got to see the stars from the jetty. They're beautiful. It's like that swirly painting by the guy who lost his ear? You know."

After he parked, he climbed into the back of the minivan. "Check it out," he said. He clicked the rear seats down until they were flat and he stared up at his personal sliver of sky through the rear window.

Genny Mori was a notorious prude and stayed in the front, but Todd was wearing her down, as he was known to do. "I know this trick," she said.

"Oh come on, I just want to show you the stars." The line came easy. It was well used. "More space than you'd think back here, Genny-baby." And it really was big back there, and charming in a way, to be so warm and cozy with winter's ocean so close.

"I can see the stars fine from here," she said, though Todd knew it was a lie. To see anything from the front seat, she'd have to lean uncomfortably over the dashboard and then crane her head up.

"Genny-honey, come on." Todd was whining, but he liked her reluctance—the one girl in school who hadn't come easy. Bravely he pressed on. This was their fifth date. Usually by this point Todd knew his girlfriend's favorite positions and was plotting his exit strategy—so goes life for a high school basketball star in Columbia City. With Genny though, all he'd got was enough heavy petting to start a campfire.

Todd also liked that she looked different than everyone else. A full-blooded Japanese and simultaneously the hottest and strangest thing in town. Hot because she was a dusty, dark-eyed girl blessed with full lips and a sound little shelf of an ass perfect for eyes and hands to rest on. Strange because the Mori family, aside from the random Mexicans who worked their way through for fruit-picking season, was the one little splash of color in the Scandinavia-white gene pool of Columbia City. No, scratch "little splash," more like cannon ball.

Then there was the fact that she only had her mom around. A bond because he only had his dad. It was a connection that seemed obvious and trite on paper but meaningful in real life. He didn't flinch with Genny while talking about his home life like he did with the others. She knew the language, her own experience rhymed with it.

Todd heard Genny Mori blow out air and knew she was clearing her bangs from her eyes. It was a habit he'd learned to love in her. So cute. She started climbing back. "This van's gross."

He helped her crawl over him to the space at his side and squeezed her ass on the way. She slapped his hand for it, which caused her to lose balance and tumble face-first into those utilitarian seats. She squealed.

"Uh, I think there's something wet back here," she said.

Todd knew his van was gross. It had been a place of countless hookups, impromptu lunchtime parties, and was a moldering mobile gym locker to boot. He spent all his time in that squeaky gray van because it was the one place his father, a man everyone knew as the Flying Finn, wouldn't come.

"I'll get something nicer when I hit the big times," he told her.

So there it was, and he had been the one to say it. Everyone knew Todd was going to star in the NBA someday. He was that good at basketball.

"What car will you get?" Genny was on her side, looking at him, and he could tell she was trying to keep something out of her voice. Her breath was hot with the rum he'd brought them.

Todd traced her calves with his fingertips, all the way up to that gorgeous ass. "Something hot," he said. "Mercedes, or Porsche."

A pause filled the close air between them and Todd wondered what she made of him. Everyone in this small town had an opinion and he was almost scared to hear hers. Maybe she was one of these girls who were frightened of him. Thinks he's all bang, bang, boom, on to the next one. She wouldn't be exactly wrong to think this—his reputation for getting with girls was exaggerated, but only slightly—but she also wouldn't be exactly right. Worse, she could be one of those chicks looking to hitch a ride. Willing to roll around with him as long as it got them somewhere. His father was always warning about girls spreading their legs to become part of the target. Todd was in the position of not being able to reassure Genny if she was the first type of girl, and being entirely uninterested in her—beyond the night—if she was the second.

Then, as if she could read his mind, in a voice so soft it tickled him, "I didn't believe that letter to the editor about you." Here it was—what she thought of him. "It isn't true. You're good for the team."

She was talking about the anonymous letter that had appeared in the *Columbia City Standard*. The headline ran, *Could Freight*

Train Derail Fishermen Basketball?, and it had become this burrowing worm in Todd's thoughts ever since it was published back in November. Hadn't he already brought the Fishermen a state title as a junior? Wasn't he leading them to a second? If he ever found out who wrote it, there would be pieces of that unfortunate man all over town.

"Thanks. It's bullshit, you know?" Todd said, anger rising just talking about it.

"I never did believe it," she said.

He let out a breath, settled. "Why do you like me, Genny?"

"I never said I did."

"You're funny."

And he was on her, and they were going. She was a river, her mouth, her tongue, and it was all rushing into him with drunken fury. Todd was surprised to feel her move in enthusiastic, if not expert ways, to have her take a certain amount of control. It was like nothing he'd had with her before—worlds different from the tedious stroking she'd reluctantly given him up until then. It thrilled him, pushed him on. Naked and without a condom— because Todd never guessed it would actually happen with Genny Mori, not so soon—he stopped, poised on the edge.

Then Genny Mori said, "OK, just this once. But pull out?" A permission they would both look back on, sometimes, as a mistake.

A memory flashed into Todd's head. Fifth grade. Genny Mori in pigtails running to her father's car. It was raining and there were puddles everywhere. Mr. Mori—the town's dentist for the short while he stuck around—was shouting something to her in Japanese and she was ignoring him. Little Genny avoided every single puddle along the way. Her father yelled louder and still she gave him no mind. Todd imagined he was telling her to hurry up, and so she was taking her time instead. Skirting every puddle instead of jumping them, or stomping through. Rebelling. She had seemed so brave to Todd. Brave and sad. He wouldn't have been able to stand up to the Flying Finn like that.

Damn, Todd thought, losing steam in the present as he got lost in the past, *get it done now or it's not going to get done*. So he pushed in. Then it happened quicker and bigger than Todd thought it could, and he told her, shivering, "Well shit."

And she said, "That's OK, Todd."

So Todd said, "OK, baby," and he pulled her closer and held her long enough to feel the warm wet turn cold. He held her even when he wanted to stop just because of the way she said "That's OK, Todd." And really in that moment it all seemed just fine because he knew she thought she loved him, and he thought it might be OK because he could do whatever he wanted back then, even fall in love with this girl. Everyone from Seattle to San Francisco knew who he was. Scholarship offers, shit, those were a dime a dozen. Todd was NBA-bound and everyone knew it. He was bigger than U2. At least in that little green-and-blue patchwork quilt sewed with the seamless stitching of fog and rain we call the Pacific Northwest he was. Goddamn. Besides, who ever got pregnant from one time?

This was Jimmy's father as a young man: basketball stud, biggest thing to hit town since Fred Meyer's department store, and always headed for bigger, better things.

A month and a half later Todd Kirkus and the rest of the team rolled south on a yellow bus done up in streamers and washable paint. It had been a good season for Todd; he'd led the Fishermen to an 18-1 record heading into the playoffs. There was greatness in the air and Columbia City decamped to Eugene to witness their beloved Todd "Freight Train" Kirkus win his second state title and cement himself as the greatest Fisherman to play the game—even the legendary Tall Firs had only won one in high school, and had needed four great players to get it. Added to this was the heady assurance that Todd was bound for fame and riches. He was the top recruit in the country, famous coaches called him by first name, and it didn't seem too big a leap to imagine him endorsing sneakers one day. Native son done good? Naw, native son done gold.

On the bus ride south, Coach Kelly got teary-eyed as he addressed the team, standing in the aisle, holding the leather bench seats for support. "A big couple of days coming up, and—" He coughed. Paused, looked out the window.

"Hold it together, Coach," Todd called out. "Can't have you crying in McArthur Court, that's for the girls."

Coach smiled, looked down the length of the bus, let the laughter from Todd's joke roll off his back, and then continued. "Be sure to call it The Pit, boys." Coach Kelly's eyes sparkled in reverence of the University of Oregon basketball arena. "Always call it The Pit because, because—"

And Todd interrupted him by starting the team on the unofficial cheer, not letting Coach Kelly find his thought: *Three cheers for Columbia City High, you bring the whiskey, I'll bring the rye* . . . and on and on.

In the early rounds of the tournament Todd was as unstoppable as, well, a freight train. He got his shots in, clean and true; and when the defenses collapsed, he kicked it out to James Berg, a small, wily guard with a knockdown shot who only ever smiled when Todd pointed his way, slapped his back, gave him a high five.

James Berg was Todd's best—only—friend on that team where the other players were disgusted by his cockiness. The way he held up his hand after making a shot, bantered with the refs like it was all child's play, spoke of himself in the third person during postgame interviews and found scouts in the stands to nod at after big plays. James somehow saw through it to the funny, kind kid he met at the community pool one summer when they were both in third grade. They'd debated which trucks—Dodge or Ford— were the best. This alliance despite—or maybe because of—the bad blood between their fathers that had boiled up back when the Flying Finn had inexplicably beaten Berg for a position on the City Council.

Todd and James going against their overbearing fathers by be- ing friends was a sweet, early helping of revolt. James had been at Todd's side ever since.

. . . . . .

The wins in the early rounds came so easy, Todd usually sat out the second half, scanning the crowd for Genny and giving her looks. After games there would be a team meal and then he'd sit in the hotel pool, feeling weightless. Then, after curfew, he'd slip the assistant coach in charge of keeping watch and go out the ser- vice door. It was three parking lots, no roads, hurdling the hedges and crouching behind cars, until Tall Pines Motel—the place Genny was staying with her friend, Bonnie. Two twin beds. Todd and Genny on one, a pissed-off Bonnie on the other.

"Seriously, keep it clean," Bonnie would always say.

"I'm a gentleman, Bonnie. Always a gentleman." Then lights off and he'd squeeze Genny close, butt to pelvis, back to chest. Hands clasped on her belly. After a while he'd trace a fingertip down her side, around her butt, into the space between the legs. It tickled her, and he liked it when she squirmed. He'd be growing bigger by then, and do nothing to hide it. Then it was all starts and stops, whispering, "Do you think she's awake?"

Todd couldn't sleep with another person on a bed so small. By the time the very first rays of light were escaping the dark womb of night, he would be gone, closing the door softly behind him, back to the hotel room he shared with James in a string of rooms taken up by the Fishermen team. Walking upright and proud along the road—too early for anyone to see him and get him in trouble.

Then another team breakfast, another soak in the pool, and his father taking him out for lunch.

"You know who call me last night," the old man whispered across the diner table. "Larry Brown!" He looked around to see if anyone was listening, like this was a state secret. In an even lower voice, comical and growly, lacing his plate of half-finished home fries with white spit, "the coach for the New Jersey Nets!"

This kind of talk from his father sank Todd and his appetite. A man who could polish off whole herds of cattle at a single sitting, he only managed a few mouthfuls when with the Flying Finn.

"Well, we got a lot of offers from colleges too, old man," Todd told him.

"Let me asks the question." The Flying Finn held his fork up, as if the tines were the irrefutable proof to what he was about to say. "They *pay* you for the basketball in college? No, they pay nothing!"

Then it was back with the team for a pregame meeting, and later, off to The Pit for a game with whoever the Fishermen were going to roll on that night. Then the cycle would start all over. Four rounds of playoffs knocked back in a line, one after the other, and it made the fans, even seeping out into the general public, giddy drunk on the historical dominance they were seeing from Todd Kirkus and the Columbia City Fighting Fishermen.

. . . . . .

On the morning of the title game between Columbia City and a rough and tumble team of boys out of Madras, Genny Mori took a pregnancy test. She peed on a stick and found she was with child in the Tall Pines fluorescent-lit bathroom. Staying there without her mother, she was supposed to feel like an adult; a grown-up.

There in that bathroom though, she felt younger than ever before. There it was in faint blue liquid at the bottom of a glass vial: the pronouncement she would forever be linked to Todd Kirkus.

Never had she wanted to hear her mother's voice so much as just then; even if it was only yelling in a language she didn't understand, with a frustration that always seemed outsized. Genny never could relate to her mother—her temper, her perfectionism, her odd need to hide socks full of change around the house—but she still needed her.

Genny knew it would be a scandal once it got out. The Mori family was different in that white-bread town. They had moved to Columbia City so Mr. Mori could open up his dental practice across the street from the football field. On Genny's first day of lunch, the kids teased her relentlessly for bringing cold soba noodles. One little girl had even rubbed the back of her hand, thinking her dark color could be washed off.

She became acutely aware of her parents' differences from the rest of Columbia City. Dad and his shy, clipped way of speaking English, never making eye contact. Mom and her habit of sitting on the porch of their little house, sucking up *udon* noodles that never seemed to end, careful never to bite through one because of the bad luck, steam clouding her glasses. People avoided them, even little Genny could tell, and in the end no one came to Dr. Mori's dental office. It was a stress that showed red in his cheeks and caused fights at home until eventually he left when Genny was eleven years old. She heard all sorts of rumors as to where he'd gone. To run a food truck that sold teriyaki bowls to surf bums in California, to Las Vegas to check coats, to the empty steel-cold bellies of railway cars rolling east.

It didn't matter in the end, and Genny Mori decided to hate him instead of wonder where he'd gone. To make ends meet, her mother worked as a line cook at Ling Gardens, a Chinese restaurant owned and operated by a family of Dutch Americans, the Johnstons. They were happy to finally get a real Chinese in their kitchen, never mind she was Japanese. Sometimes, because her friends loved the $5.99 lunch special that included one main dish (chicken or beef), a side of fried rice, your choice of egg flower or sweet-and-sour soup and a never-ending soda, Genny was forced into coming to the restaurant while her mom worked the kitchen. Ate General Tso's chicken and greasy pork fried rice like everyone else. Chopsticks for a second, for a joke, then onto the cheap silverware, rice by the forkful. Sat with her back to the kitchen, shoulders dancing with the tingling premonition that this was the time her mom caught wind of her being there in time to come out in her hairnet, place a grease-burned hand on her shoulder, ask in that pinched up English to be introduced to her friends.

And yet her luck held. All through high school, through countless trips to Ling Gardens, Genny had avoided just such an embarrassment. She loved the pure shot of glee, one she would find hard to match in intensity later in life, she got as she ran out after her friends. Escape. Booth left behind, red balled-up chopstick wrappers and fallen rice kernels littering the table, bill paid for, but just barely, no tip for that week's shuffle-footed twenty-something townie who served them, out into the parking lot, blast that pop, disaster averted again.

Only once had it come up, and only because of Trevor Wooster— a *boy* brought into their normally girls-only lunch because Bonnie had a thing.

"Can you get us a discount?" he asked Genny Mori, like $5.99 wasn't already flirting with forcing the kitchen to use day-old rice, cut-rate meat, to make cost.

"What, 'cause I'm Asian?" Genny fixed him with her business eyes—a stare she'd become famous for among her peers; it had made Kent Jackson cry in seventh grade after he'd dared grab her butt—and sipped from her straw. When she took her lips away, she let the back edge of the plastic catch and flick spitty Coke across the table at the idiot. "This is a *Chinese* place. You know I'm *Japanese*, right?"

"No, that's not what I meant, I meant because," he wiped off his face. Everyone knew what he had meant, even Genny, but this was her way of skirting it.

"Let's just go, OK?" Bonnie said.

So they went. But the Genny Mori force field had been breached. Even though she talked like a Columbia City kid, could get anywhere with her eyes closed, cheered for the Fishermen since the moment she could speak, and was better at Spanish than Japanese, she was still, at the heart of it, a Mori. An outsider. That little pee vial would rock the boat. The beloved Todd Kirkus having a baby with *Genny Mori*? The outrage! The indignity! The nerve!

. . . . . .

On that same morning Todd Kirkus was found bleary, sit-down-just-to-think drunk in his hotel room. Something in the easy cycle of winning had been broken. He had spent the night before wandering the University of Oregon campus with minibar bottles of alcohol clinking in his pockets and a pack of cigarettes. Rumor spread quickly within the Oregon basketball community gathered in Eugene for championship week that Todd didn't get back to the team hotel until well after four a.m. With pressure mounting, Coach Kelly had no choice but to suspend him from that night's championship game.

Todd's father, the Flying Finn, an overwound man with a bobbing head, found the coach eating a burrito in the student commons six hours before tip-off. "You pulling the pug on Todd?" he yelled in his slightly muddled English. The Flying Finn owned a restaurant on Pier 11 in Columbia City, and he was known for shouting, "Order up, hot, hot, hot, order up," in that accent, loud enough for the entire restaurant to hear. He was a tall man with a slim, wiry frame on which his head, hands, and feet looked huge and extraterrestrial. His great dome was balding and his neck was as thin as a pipe cleaner, hardly seemed up to the job. Whereas the Moris were local controversy, he was local color— the Grand Marshall of the annual Scandinavian Day Parade.

Coach Kelly decided that the loud accent was decidedly less charming in this context. "You mean 'plug,' Mr. Kirkus?" A bit of hot refried beans dribbled down his chin. He wiped it off with the back of his hand. "You mean I'm *pulling the plug* on Todd?"

The Flying Finn hopped from side to side in anger over being corrected. He was a relentless promoter of his son. Filming every single game and sending tapes off to college coaches with masking tape labels that said things like, *The Best Ever*, or, *This WILL Change Your Life*, he was a fixture on the sidelines. Yelling for his boy to get more touches. Screaming at the refs to open their eyes already. The sight of his Adam's apple running up and down that skinny neck, pushing out his extraordinarily loud voice, gave Coach Kelly nightmares, literal nightmares. His wife often told him he needed better work/life balance.

"You know what I mean," the Flying Finn said. "You know what I's saying."

"He was caught drinking, Mr. Kirkus." Coach Kelly tried to stay calm but it was hard. He was uncomfortable. First of all he also desperately wanted Todd to play. He doubted the Fishermen could win without him. Second, the beans he'd wiped off on his hand looked like smeared shit. Coach Kelly was stone-featured and could have been handsome if he hadn't known he was so close to being handsome. As it was, he was hyper self-aware, and anything he sensed compromising his appearance bothered him to no end. "It's a team rule, Mr. Kirkus. It's against the law in fact. He's underage."

"After all my son does for you, you will pull the *plug*?" The Flying Finn emphasized "plug" heavily and Coach Kelly felt the mist of his spit settle on his face.

"Again, it's a policy, nothing doing." Then quickly, hoping he could pass it off as more normal than he knew it to be, Coach Kelly dipped his head down and licked the back of his hand to get the shit-seeming beans off. "There's no wiggle room on this."

"You lick your hand when you talking to me? What kind of thing is this? Some insult I don't know?"

As always, the Flying Finn was practically shouting, and this drew the attention of the other eaters in the commons. Coach Kelly's face heated up. He took a napkin and dried off his hand. "There were beans, and it looked like—well." His words curled in on themselves, as if heated from beneath. He stood up. "I need to get going, Mr. Kirkus. I'm sorry there isn't more I can do."

The Flying Finn called after him, "Who told on my son? I like to know that!"

Coach Kelly hurried out of the commons. He knew the answer to the Flying Finn's question of course, and it broke his heart.

......

It had all been so typical. She was sick in the mornings, her feet were swollen, and her sense of taste seemed to be flaring up around certain foods. She told Bonnie about it and her best friend said, "Maybe you're preggers."

So Genny said, "Stop being a bitch."

Then Bonnie said, "So says the bitch."

And they teased back and forth but the idea stuck. Genny Mori bought her home pregnancy test at Mike's Kwiki-Mart three blocks from their motel. It was behind the counter and she finally got the guts to ask for it in a lull between customers.

"I want that one there," she said, pointing to the one on sale.

The clerk's eyes darted to her forehead, as if he could discover her age stamped there. He bit his bottom lip. "Anything else?" he asked.

Genny glared at him. Noticed the tufts of hair at his ears. The tired folds beneath his eyes. "Cigarettes," she said. "Give me some of those."

He snorted, not as shocked as she hoped he would be. He rang her up, put the test in a paper sack. "You come back when you're old enough for those smokes."

Later, when she discovered she was pregnant, her fingers shaking and wet and gross—because when the hell do you ever practice pissing into a small cup without wetting your fingers?—she also discovered that what she'd always thought she'd do with a baby in her belly, she could never actually do now that there really was a baby in her belly.

A part of her even thought that getting pregnant might be a good thing. It wouldn't be long until Todd blew the lid off the NBA and she moved far away from the Oregon coast with its shiny, spiderweb fingers that spread into places they had no right to go, rotting everything—her father's confidence, her mother's happiness, and her, just her *her-ness*. The baby would bind her and Todd together, and she wouldn't be left behind. Something deep in her bones awoke and all at once a part of her wanted a family. And she wanted out. It still didn't seem like good news exactly, but it did have some of the same coloring.

Bonnie, seventeen and wide-eyed with the bigness of the news she carried in her rusted red Honda hatchback, drove Genny to the student Rec Center where the Fishermen were having their final practice before the championship game.

"Are you sure you should wear a seat belt?" Bonnie asked.

"Why wouldn't I?"

"What if we, well if, if we crash then won't the belt, like, squish it?" Bonnie squirmed in her seat.

"Jesus, and if I don't put the belt on we'll just both die?"

Red faced, Bonnie gripped the steering wheel harder. "I was just saying."

"Don't crash."

When they got there, they found Todd sitting in an alley behind the Rec Center on a cement bench with pale, clammy-looking James Berg at his side. Todd looked hangdog tired and the day was cold enough his breaths rose above his head: unmotivated halos. He was staring into his huge hands while James pecked him with little chirping comments like, *"You'll be all right. You're playing college ball next year, who cares? Maybe NBA!"*

Beautiful, news-heavy Genny Mori ran to her man. "What happened?" she asked.

Todd looked up. "Can't play tomorrow, Genny-baby. Got ratted out for drinking."

It was odd, to see Freight Train like that, his bigness somehow all but melted off. For a man of exaggeration—who once snuck a dead seagull into the briefcase of rival Seaside Seagulls' coach and ended up giving the whole team lice—his reaction to the suspension seemed wet, sad, and chewed. Small enough to fit in a gum wrapper.

Questions swarmed in her head. *Why had he been drinking? Was it with girls? Was it a depressed drinking? Who told on him? Was it with girls? Why hadn't he called* me *to party too? When did he leave my room last night? Why* did *he leave my room last night? Was it with other girls?* "Oh," she finally managed to say.

He shrugged his shoulders, looked up at James, and said, "Looks like you'll have to win the game without me."

James Berg lashed out. "All those guys are just jealous. Bet it was Kyle who told. But I don't know who it was. I really don't. They don't tell me *anything*. They think I'll just tell you. Which I would."

Todd waved off his friend.

Then Genny Mori broke into the conversation and said something she hadn't meant to say, not right then in front of James and Bonnie anyway, but what was she supposed to do when she had something so big and important *inside her* and they were still talking about a basketball game? "I'm pregnant, Todd."

"Oh shit," Bonnie said and backed up like she was worried proximity to Todd would jeopardize her safety.

Genny Mori bit her knuckles. So what if it had been a mistake to lay the news on him just then? It wasn't like she instantly regretted it. "Todd?" she said.

"Well, damn." Still looking into his big, useless hands. "When it rains, it—"

"Oh, Todd!" She hugged him and wished she could play it off as a joke. But who jokes like that?

. . . . . .

Todd hugged Genny Mori, latest in a long line of girls he'd dated in Columbia City, and for some reason patted the back of her head. Where did this leave him? Suspended from the team for his final high school game and suddenly stuck to make good with a girl he was kinda seeing. Like those cells balled up in her belly were some kind of magnet whose only opposite in the whole world was him.

She was weeping harder and he just kept on patting the back of her head. He wasn't even at the point of not knowing what to say—so shocked, he didn't even know he was supposed to say something in the first place.

James turned away, kicked something that was maybe on the

ground, ran his hand through his hair. "Jesus," he said. "This is fucking. I mean, Jesus."

"What's your problem?" Bonnie asked. She snapped wide the mouth of her purse and rooted around: a pack of cigarettes. She shook one loose, lit up.

"Hey, what the hell?" Todd said. Here was something. He pulled away from Genny, took a step.

"What?" Bonnie squinted at him.

"You know what. She's pregnant."

Bonnie laughed. Three bleats in a row. A terrible laugh and the main reason Todd had never flexed on her. That and a big nose. He assumed kissing would be a puzzle with a nose that big—one he didn't want to figure out.

"Come on, Todd," she said. "She's not *that* pregnant."

Todd looked back and saw Bonnie was right. Genny stood there, belly flat, body stacked, still hot. There was nothing in her appearance that foretold of the stretching, the swelling, and the ripping that would come. "Still," he said, quieter.

"Todd, it's OK." Genny put a hand on his elbow, tugging at it. Maybe she needed to wet his other shoulder now.

"It's OK? No, it's not OK." He backed off a step. "None of this is OK, OK?"

"He's kind of an asshole, so it's weird, because he's also kind of right," Bonnie took a deep inhale and let twin jets of smoke blast from her formidable nostrils.

"He's not an asshole." James stood up, came over to Todd's side. "He's not the one who's pregnant."

"That doesn't even make sense, idiot."

"Hey, screw you."

Genny started weeping again so everyone stopped talking.

"Genny?" Todd asked, big numb paw halfway to her shoulder.

"I'm just tired. That's all." She sniffed, ran her hand under her nose. "Bonnie, let's go. I just need to lay down, that's the only thing."

. . . . . .

Last night he'd left Genny and Bonnie's room at the Tall Pines earlier than normal. Back at the team hotel he found the Flying Finn still awake in the lobby. Sitting in one of the ugly green chairs, staring into space.

"You know the money they make in NBA?" the old man had asked.

"Dad," Todd said, wondering if his father was going to try and punish him for sneaking out, tamping down the blush of anger he felt at being pushed, again, in a direction he wasn't sure he wanted to go.

"Much money!" the Flying Finn said, too loud for the small lobby, for the late hour. "I will move to New Jersey too! It is pretty! A garden state! I will help! We have waited so long for this. It doesn't matter about championship game."

And that was the start of it. Old man wasn't concerned with punishing Todd for having snuck out; gangly dude might as well have had dollar signs floating in his eyeballs like a cartoon villain. Todd exploded, shouted right back. All those years of him trying to breathe the same air, sweat the same sweat. As if this were his struggle too. It escalated, and then dipped, and then escalated again. The front desk attendant trying to tamp it down. Making ludicrous shushing sounds like that could have the slightest effect. Ended in a bang.

"No son of mine," the Flying Finn warbled in a stripped down voice. "No son of mine. You walk away from a better life? No son of mine."

And Todd coming back, purposely cussing because he knew how it grinded his father. "It's *my* fucking life!" And then out, hands in the air, out.

JIMMY KIRKUS NOT YET BORN—TWENTY-TWO YEARS UNTIL THE WALL.

Under the breezeway, storming, looking for a wrecking, Todd came across one of the cleaning-lady carts, bejeweled in its lower deck with small bottles of hard alcohol. Gin and vodka. He stuffed his pockets. Gone, out, bye to everything, everybody.

And in the morning after, hangover pounding, the realization that he was suspended, it had seemed like the worst thing. But it wasn't. There was a baby he had made now growing in Genny Mori. Genny Mori. A Japanese girl. Pretty, nice, tough in a way he loved, but still not who he'd ever pictured himself with when he pictured a future of playing in the NBA. A kid? It felt like the heaviest thing that could happen to him. He wanted to be away, suddenly—far away.

"I mean, what the hell am I supposed to do with that?" he asked James, the girls now gone in Bonnie's rig. "If she's pregnant, I mean, really pregnant, then what am I supposed to do with that?" They walked through campus. It was a clear winter day and bundled students with high-hitched backpacks walked to class or lingered in groups around benches and stairs. A crispness so sharp it brought tears. Old brick buildings on all sides, confident, academic.

"You think she's going to keep it?" James asked.

"How should I know?"

James coughed, said in a quieter voice, "Well, you know she will, don't you?"

"No," Todd said, anger quick-triggered at having to repeat himself. "Like I just said, how the hell should I know?"

James stopped walking and so Todd stopped too. He followed his friend a little ways off the path, under a big oak tree. "Listen," James whispered. "You know she'll keep it 'cause with a baby, here's the thing, with a baby she's got you, right? Anyplace you get to, she'll still have you. You make a million in the pros, she's still got you and she's got half that money too. That's why she's keeping it, guarantee."

Todd slapped the trunk of the tree. Every layer revealed confined him more.

. . . . . .

So things sped up and didn't matter and mattered more than ever all at once. Didn't matter that the Fishermen won the title without Todd anyway, Freight Train watching from the stands, but it did matter how—on a last second shot by little James Berg, who was then carried off the floor. Didn't matter that Todd's teammates avoided him after the game, but it did matter that he became convinced it was James who'd told on him for drinking because of the way he hugged his father after the final buzzer sounded—Principal Berg—the old man seeming to comfort James, reassure James, rather than celebrate with him.

Didn't matter that later Todd sat alone in the parked van, keys dangling in the ignition, and drowned himself in mini-fridge shooters for the second night running while the Flying Finn fitfully slept up in the room. But Todd's plan did matter: to go.

He needed the sharp infusion only an open window and a speeding car could give. The team didn't need him, his best friend had turned on him, but now this girl did? Genny Mori. Dating for less than two months. It wasn't right or fair. He was never coming back. Gone, gone, gone. One after the next he killed the screw-top bottles, tossing the little bodies on the van's floor. Todd got soaked and then slammed the steering wheel, honked the horn. He groped in his pockets, pushing back against the seat, looking for the keys before he realized they were already in the ignition and so he slammed the steering wheel again, he started her up, stomped the gas. The engine leapt to it but he still had it in park.

Then he saw someone walking through the parking lot, hood

up. James Berg, conquering hero. Todd opened the door and stumbled out sideways, engine still running. He regained balance and turned to James. "You're a fucking champion, my *friend.*" Then he charged, swinging wildly as he went.

James stepped neatly to the side, gave him a hard push in the back. Todd fell hard, rolled once, and then lay still, breathing.

"Genny's looking for you," James said.

Todd didn't answer. It was after two a.m. and the world was an empty place colored with the yellow of parking lot lights. There was the noise of traffic from I-5, half a mile away. Then, closer, sirens.

"Let's go, Todd. You can't get caught drinking again." He sounded tired, and that galled Todd. All he'd done was play a basketball game. Why the hell should he be tired?

Cops coming and Todd had to run. Pregnant girl, disappointment, it all felt like symptoms of place, and he could remedy all by a few peeled off miles. He got to his feet and went back to the car. James was there, tugging at him, trying to get him turned away, but here's the thing about Freight Train: he was in the best shape of his entire life. A legitimate NBA talent with muscle in spades. James had no chance of holding him back, but he did slow him down. Got in his way enough so that by the time he was sitting in his van, trying to put the thing into drive, James madly punching the door and screaming for him to get the fuck out, a cop car pulled in.

Two officers climbed from the cruiser and Todd got out of the van. "Hey, guys," he tried, woozily.

"Shut up," James whispered.

It didn't matter that Todd was drunk—what's another MIP?—but it did matter that one of the cops was the safety officer assigned to the high school basketball tournament who Todd had joked with during the first few rounds. A man named Officer Jakes, someone Todd felt too comfortable with.

"Son," Officer Jakes said, "why don't you have a seat."

Todd laughed, tried to shrug it off. Became agitated when Officer Jakes told him to calm down. "Ah, come on Jakes, don't be a blowhard." Todd took a drunken swing and missed by a mile. Jakes pinned big Freight Train against the police cruiser while James and the people awoken by the noise, ghosting the hotel windows, looked on.

His partner that night, Officer Pasadena, said, "Lucky that kid was so greased or he woulda took your head clean—"

"Shut up," Jakes told him.

"What is this?" shouted the Flying Finn, suddenly out, in pajamas, screaming from the balcony.

"Fuck you," Todd growled and shifted his weight quickly to his pivot foot and tried to spin—a move that had never failed him before on the court—but he was drunk and underestimated his own weight. Jakes sloughed off, his wind knocked out, and Todd went too far laterally on his left knee. He felt it go watery the instant it happened. He cried out as the muscular tension left him and pain entered, a shot of it, as potent as anything. He collapsed. Officer Pasadena was on him roughly cuffing him next to the cruiser's wheel—an extra shove for good measure—and Todd knew he was past the point of recovery. It was the fear every elite athlete has on the edge of better things. His body, a willing partner up to that point, quitting.

Some things mattered and some things didn't. Genny Mori was pregnant and it turned out that mattered. Breathe. Todd had never expected it, didn't want it really, but it mattered. He married her and the Oregon fog settled down again.

JIMMY KIRKUS NOT YET BORN—TWENTY-TWO YEARS UNTIL THE WALL.

Rule 3. Neither Confirm Nor Deny

JIMMY KIRKUS, SIXTEEN YEARS OLD—MINUTES AFTER THE WALL.

The door to the Brick House opens and a head peaks in. It's the janitor, Mr. Berg—Todd's once-best-friend. He finds the breaker box, flicks the switches. The big, overhead light fixtures, with their wire grills grinning, whine to life. The glow is still too new and hazy for detail. But it's warming up, building brighter all the time.

"Holy shit," Berg says.

When James Berg first sees the body laid out bloody on the floor, naked but for shoes and underwear, the red light of the EXIT sign shining on him, he thinks the kid is dead.

"Holy shit," he says again. He's backing away. A murder? Over what, drugs? All that stuff coming into town. The new one is meth, people are saying. He's back into the hallway, moving toward the door to the parking lot. Whole body is telling him to flee. Whoever did this is probably still around. Addicts will do anything for money. Every noise he hears behind him is the attacker come back to bash his head in. Hand on the push bar to exit, Berg stops. Thinks. He swallows, it doesn't go down. He coughs because of this. He has to call the police. Right now, call the police. But he hesitates. He's a coward, not just rushing in. The kid back there could still be alive. He probably *is* still alive. Back through the dark hallway, back to the gym. Lights groaning as they work, slow to warm up. That body still not moving. What a sad ending for some poor kid. Shit, there'd be a media maelstrom. He takes out his cell phone. Three numbers to hit.

Then he notices something along the baseline. A gray marked-up basketball. Everyone in town knows that ball. That boy on the ground is Jimmy Kirkus. Berg rushes to him and holds his fragile head in his hands. Jimmy's chest still rises and falls. He's alive and the gym lights are getting brighter all the time.

Berg assumes Jimmy has been jumped and then the beating went too far. Didn't happen often in Columbia City, kids getting real violent with each other, but it wasn't unknown. *And after all he's been through?* It was a small enough town that whoever did it would be found by morning, if not sooner.

"Damn, Jimmy." Berg feels terrible for not just rushing in, getting to the door to the parking lot before he could think himself out of it, come back and help. *James Berg: Coward.*

"He scores," Jimmy sputters.

"Who got to you, kid?" There is blood everywhere. On the floor and also oozing and drying on the brick wall. Kid's face looks like a cut of steak.

"Huh?"

"Who jumped you? You been fighting?"

"No."

"Don't worry, I'm going to call for help." Berg has his cell out, pressing its bellybuttons, getting beeps. "Get the ambulance, the police and—"

"No!" Jimmy screams and then squirms in pain. "No, I was running. Just running."

With his eyes, Berg traces the blood from the wall to Jimmy, and then back again. *Couldn't be. No. Nobody could do that.* Then he understands why there's so much blood on the wall. A path of drippings up to it. Jimmy's done it to himself and that's the scariest thing.

JIMMY KIRKUS, SIXTEEN YEARS OLD—MINUTES AFTER THE WALL.

Berg helps him into his ripped clothes, hustles the kid to the cab of his truck. Jimmy goes where he's guided, a zombie. It's still snowing. Great twirling flakes touch down, individual masterpieces, piling up to be crunched through. Rain, this is, only frozen, memorialized. Berg shakes his head to clear the thought, focuses on the task at hand.

In the ride to the hospital, over the hill, right by Peter Pan Park, past Fultano's Pizza and the football field, past where Mr. Mori once had his dental office and past the new movie theaters, Berg keeps the radio jacked. Big news today: the Oregon State Athletic Association has decided to drop Columbia City High School down from 6A, the highest level, to 4A starting next year. The surprise isn't in the drop—the town has been hemorrhaging residents, and so students, for years—but in how far. Everyone assumed it would be 5A for the Fishermen. Now in 4A they'll be up against schools even tinier than they: Dayton, Burns, Milo. People are calling in, outraged or encouraged. They say OSAA should make it more like college—play in the division you're good enough to—not how it is, solely based on school size. Then there are others. People saying this will be good. Columbia City ain't what she used to be. Next year could be the start of something special. A run of titles in 4A.

Their last year with the big boys won't be easy either. This year's 6A division presents a uniquely demanding gauntlet. With Shooter Ackley out of Seaside, Ian Callert over in Canby, Danny Rubbe down in Cape Blanco—all NCAA Division I–bound athletes—not to mention Jesuit's factory of disciplined contenders, 6A is shaping up to be something to tell your kids about. Berg's got the windows down for cold air. He has to keep Jimmy awake. He knows that much. These call-in people with their outrage, they'll do it for him. *4A? This is a joke!* Whole town empty. The cold air isn't enough. He doesn't care what these people have to say. Only values the noise they make. *At least we know we'll kick butt.*

"What the hell were you doing, Jimmy?" he shouts over the wind and radio.

Jimmy's head lolls on the end of his neck. "Where we going?" he asks. Blood bubbles up on his lips.

"The hospital. We're going to the doctor. You've been hurt."

"I know." There's a gurgle in the kid's throat and Berg wonders if he should stop the truck, make sure Jimmy isn't choking on his own blood. Instead he presses down on the gas harder. Truck roars. The hospital is nearby.

"Don't tell, OK?" Jimmy says after a little while. The sound of his voice is barely audible over people pissing on over the pseudo issue of sports divisions. Kid sounds like his father, Todd Kirkus, from back when they were best friends and he was about to do something Berg wasn't sure about. *Bergy? Be cool. Don't tell.*

Tears come to Berg's eyes. "I won't tell. I won't."

. . . . . .

Two nurses come at them moments after they enter the ER waiting room.

"What happened?" the first nurse asks. Berg doesn't recognize her.

"Chris?" the second nurse shouts. "We need a bed out here, get us a bed." This one Berg knows. He can't remember her first name, but she's a Parson. She was a couple grades below him in high school, her mother was the English teacher. He used to drink with her brother. Bud Lights and bonfires.

"Where's Todd?" the Parson nurse asks. "James, where's his father?"

But the bed is there and Berg is pushed aside in the activity as the first two nurses and a tall, bald man who must be Chris, lower Jimmy onto a wheeled gurney. Sarah. The second nurse's name is Sarah. Sarah Parson. Berg feels an unnatural amount of relief to remember her name. With this, it somehow seems to him, every-thing will be OK.

Then a pale girl Berg has never seen before steps through the nurses and up to Jimmy just as he's about to be wheeled away. Young, still in high school probably. She bites her lip and reaches her hand out toward his head.

Sarah grabs her hand before she can touch the kid, holds it. "No, honey," she says, "not now."

"Is he going to be OK?" the girl asks in a shattered voice.

Jimmy just stares. Berg isn't sure he's heard her.

"He'll be OK," Sarah says and places the girl's hand back at her side.

"Carla?" It's the Reverend Ferguson. New to town, homeschools his kids. This girl must be one of his, Berg thinks. "Carla, come here now."

Chris, the bald male nurse, is pushing Jimmy's bed toward the door that leads into the ER. Berg walks with them. The door opens before they get there and some doctor out of Portland, because Columbia City can't seem to raise their own doctors—just janitors and Pepsi deliverymen—ushers the nurses back, already talking jargon Berg has no hope of following. Sarah stops, looks at Berg, and Berg stops. He can't go back there.

"Remember," Jimmy calls out.

Mr. Berg releases a breath he hadn't known he was holding. "What?"

"You won't tell?"

The doors are closing. Berg nods his head, not sure if Jimmy can see.

"We'll take good care of him," Sarah says, a calmness he could cry for in her voice.

Berg keeps nodding.

He turns back to the waiting room in time to see the pale girl wavering out of the sliding doors, the Reverend Ferguson holding her elbow. She's visibly weak. "That's Jimmy Kirkus," Berg hears her tell her father. *"The basketball player."*

Berg doesn't know what's wrong with the girl to be here so late at night, to be so pale and sick, but something surely is. He feels like he's seeing a different side to the town he's always known and it frightens him. This is a world populated by pallid, shaky girls and boys bent on smashing themselves out. He wishes it were any other night, and he was home, watching the *Late Show*, smirking along with Letterman. He sits in one of the gray chairs, picks up the courtesy phone, checks for a dial tone, places it back down.

Berg remembers running into Jimmy and his father, Todd, years before. They were in the Safeway parking lot around Christmas, buying a tree from the Boy Scout sale. Jimmy couldn't have been more than two. Such a sweet kid, he ran around picking up tree trimmings. Couldn't believe those were free. Sweetest kid. Lately though, kid's been different—no surprise there with what he'd been through. Whole world's weight on him.

So maybe, in a way, Jimmy *was* jumped back in the gym; only by himself and not some other kid. The sweet Jimmy snuffed out by the new one. Mr. Berg shakes his head. He doesn't like thinking about things in this way. Brings him close to a black hole in his mind. All the possibilities and none of them right. Trapdoors. Slippery slopes. He had hated college for that reason and chose work as a janitor for the way it shrunk the world down.

First he calls Van Eyck beverages, gets Todd's cell number from a sleep-voiced kid who perks up at the word "emergency." Hangs up on him quickly, lest he forget the number floating in his head, and dials Todd. Of course he does. He's the father of a kid too, isn't he? Jimmy Kirkus wasn't thinking straight when he told Berg not to tell. There are records and insurance claims to be factored in. Jimmy is a minor, who the hell did the kid think would check him out? The phone is ringing and Berg's shame is building. Not rushing right in, or coming sooner to have prevented it happening in the first place, these are things he adds to his own case against himself.

Todd answers on the fourth or fifth ring, the oceanic roar of driving in the background. Berg pictures him in his Van Eyck Beverages delivery truck, working the night shift as always.

"Hello?"

"Todd, it's James. James Berg?"

There's the background roar and a sharp, rhythmic clicking too. Blinker?

"It's about Jimmy. I found him in the gym. I thought he'd been jumped. But that wasn't it." The phone is fumbled, and in the ensuing scuffling, three bangs in a row, it sounds to Berg as though it's been dropped from a great height, though it was probably just from ear to lap. "Todd?"

"I'm here," he says so quickly Berg can't be sure the phone was ever dropped in the first place.

"Jimmy was on the floor and . . ." Berg doesn't feel guilty for telling, just guilty he hadn't called sooner, from the gym, from the car ride over, from twenty-two years before.

When he's done there is only breathing on the other end. No words, but what could James expect? This was about Todd's kid, not their friendship. Still, he can't stand it, he presses on.

"I wish I would've known he was still in there, in the gym— Coach Kelly should have told me. I would've never. Well, you know that. Listen. He's at the hospital now. I guess you'll have to come pick him up." There's a shifting sound, the pop of the truck door opening, Todd getting out. James pictures him pacing on the side of the highway. He hears a siren from far off, though he can't tell if it's on his end or Todd's. He looks up and notices the nurse,

Sarah, staring at him from the check-in desk, listening. He wants to say more, but can't, not with her there.

Then a click. Hung up on. Not even a scrap of gratitude, forgiveness, or acknowledgment. James throws the phone across the lobby. Cord yanks it short so it bashes onto the floor, receiver cracked. He looks up. Sarah's all owl eyes from where she sits.

The dial tone, dull but somehow urgent, bleeds out.

"I'll pay," James says. "The phone. I can pay for that."

. . . . . .

Look at our kid Jimmy, asleep in a hospital bed. He's dreaming beautiful things. Car window studded with water. Taillights smeared red across the windshield. Paul Simon singing on and on from the CD player about diamonds on the soles of her shoes. Mom and Pops looking back at him through the rearview mirror, and then at each other—like they still care. Dex playing his Game Boy and asking Jimmy to "Please, please, just get me past the fireball plant in level eleven." Watching the darkness outside the car from warm safety. A day he always wants to dream about, but never does. He's hovering, just on the dusty side of sleep, a great happy sadness welling within.

It's been a fitful hour of doctors coming in and administering tests with penlights and clicking sounds. And once, in the middle of it, a nurse with Mickey Mouse scrubs and a doctor with hairy spider hands laid him down and inserted him headfirst into a giant, whirring machine. The doctor had been kind, patted him on the foot and told him it was just a CT scan. Jimmy hadn't known what that meant, or what they were looking for with the machine, but he said, "OK, yeah," and listened to the whirring and beeps for clues. He figured with a machine that big, with mechanics so obviously expensive, it could see straight into your brain. Poke around and tell if you had hurt yourself permanently, but also, maybe, see exactly who you really were and what you wanted and who you wished to become. Jimmy isn't sure of what they found. This scares him. Like it's a test he might fail.

......

Gravity. That's the only thing that pulls Todd out of the parking lot—big Van Eyck truck taking up two spots—and through the sliding automatic doors and into the hospital. Emotional gravity. He was on the cliff, just an hour earlier, when James Berg called. Son. Hospital. He'd dropped the phone. Not that. He couldn't handle *that*. But then it wasn't that. And there was an easier grade down after all. Not the smash into flat-out oblivion he'd first seen. Jimmy was alive.

Otherwise he'd be too tired, too spooked by the empty future that had snapped into focus when he had assumed the worst to even make it this far. He would have walked away, truck left on the side of the road where he'd pulled off when James Berg called, blinking hazard lights. They would have found the truck—known immediately that it was his from the dead cow skull he'd glued on the dash—but never him.

Into the hospital and the first one up is James Berg. Out of a waiting room chair and at his side. Matching steps.

"Todd, he's going to be fine," James says. "Nothing permanent, I'm told. He'll be OK."

"Where is he?"

"Right through there. That's Sarah Parson, you remember her?" A nurse he vaguely recognizes, smiling, pressing a big, blue button that opens the doors into parts of the hospital you don't normally see unless you're bringing life into the world or sending it away.

"I just found him laid out, you know, on the floor. I think he did it to himself. I took him here just as fast as I could. I'm sorry, Todd."

Todd knows what's happening. He glimpsed down into the gap

where their friendship once was. Best friends. Until Berg had rat-ted him out for drinking. It seems silly now, but somehow, twenty-two years old, it's still fresh-black dug. Guy's trying to fix it all wrong though, like he always has. A gnat. Trying to fill it in with words. Be nicer, kinder, more understanding. Get lower, why don't you? What he needs to do—and Todd recognizes this even if he couldn't put the right words to it to say so—is just man up and tell him he's an asshole. Nobody made him do any of what he did that led to his initial, selfish spiral. He'd drunk, he'd fucked, him, Todd Kirkus. Just stand up and tell him like it is. Then maybe they could get on with it. Move some dirt.

"James, just go," he says, as kind as he can manage.

"Yeah, OK, but if you need anything."

More wrong. Todd waves him off. Picking up steam. He's closer in orbit now, crashing through the atmosphere, following Sarah Parson. James falls off as Jimmy—his son—a planet, rolls in. Emo-tional gravity.

. . . . . .

For the last half hour he's been left alone. It's quieter than before. The lights in the ER dimmer, there's a curtain pulled around his bed, and it's a delicious gray. He could stay in this color forever. He loves how everything is shades of the same.

Then his pops comes in, yanks wide the curtain, lets in the background light, casters screaming. He grabs Jimmy's shoulder, shakes him out of his half sleep. The whole bed moving. Jimmy's brain is a loose marble rattling in his tin-can head. Last night with the brick wall comes back to him. Pain. All is pain.

"You're dead, kid," his pops says. "Now get the hell up."

Jimmy whimpers as his father's low-down voice brings on a dif-ferent kind of hurt; now it's like his brain has too much water packed around it. No room to think. "It's too early?" he says. His pillow is wet. Somewhere, something is leaking.

JIMMY KIRKUS, SIXTEEN YEARS OLD—MINUTES AFTER THE WALL.

His pops whispers like air let out of a bike tire, "Getthehellup."

"But, Pops," he's almost crying. "It's too early."

"Too early? I gotta pick my kid up from Columbia Memorial, four in the morning, and it's too fucking early?" Todd sweeps Jimmy's thin hospital blanket off in one go.

Jimmy's robe is twisted, riding high, and he scrambles to cover his half-hard dick, listing solemnly to the side. He burrows his head into the pillows, clutching his junk with two hands.

Todd slaps a hand over his eyes. "Jesus, Jimmy."

The suddenness of cold air on his naked body makes Jimmy's head hurt. But everything makes his head hurt. He curls into a ball at the top of the thin bed and he's sweating, can feel his heart beating in his tongue and his temples. He needs a glass of water, he needs a week alone. Jimmy gropes for the blanket that has been cast off him in the dim hospital half light, one hand over his stuff, head still beneath a pillow. The fog in his brain feels as though it's draining from his nose. Strange. He sits up, sniffing, too confused to care what his pops sees.

"We got to go," his pops says.

"It's too early," Jimmy tries again.

"Too early for living too, since you already dead." His pops finds a wall-mounted exam light, flips the switch, and everything cracks into being. Gone, the grayness.

Jimmy winces in pain. Fireworks. A quick fear runs cold up his spine that he actually *is* dead and this *is* hell. He grinds his teeth. So hard they might come out. Groans again.

For the first time his pops is seeing his head. Those great tree-trunk legs buckle, Jimmy watches him reach for support, grab hold of the back of a chair. He breathes out bumpy. "And take care that bloody nose." His pops yanks the curtain back, casters screaming again. Jimmy puts a hand to his nose, it comes away red.

. . . . . .

Sarah Parson meets Todd Kirkus as he's leaving Jimmy's cur-
tained-off bed, headed toward the waiting room. She stands before
him and all manner of physics are violated when he slows and
then stops instead of just running her flat. He rears up, eyes flashing.

"Mr. Kirkus, it's the hospital's recommendation that Jimmy stay
put for a bit longer," she says, voice calm. She clicks her pen to
meter her words. A trick she learned in nursing school. "He
should be seen by someone, make sure he doesn't do it again."

Todd laughs, gruff, unfunny. "Oh, he's not doing that again."

"Still it's our recommendation."

Todd cuts her off—and this she hates. "Shouldn't a doctor be
telling me this?"

"Dr. Maron has been called away, but has asked that I speak
with you."

He leans in closer, breath thick with cheap mint. "Let me ask
you something. How many people you already called about this?
Prime gossip, all this."

Sarah has seen this line of thought coming. She knows Todd
doesn't recognize her from high school—what use could he have
for a short, pudgy girl who liked to spend her time in the library,
rewriting her favorite scenes from books, word for word, just to
see what greatness felt like—but she knows him, or at least his
type. Everything leads back to his or his son's persecution. So
center of the bull's-eye is he that he doesn't realize nobody's
shooting arrows. "Mr. Kirkus, it would be a breach of my personal
moral code, not to mention the hospital's, not to mention the law's,
to do any such thing."

"Can you keep him, legal?"

Officers Jones and Markham had already been through, cleared
Jimmy on any criminal counts, and Dr. Maron signed off on his

physical condition, so no, she couldn't, not legally. Still. She wished she could pull the brakes on the infamous Freight Train. No doubt he was going to try and ply his son with more "tough love," the exact same shit that got him into this mess in the first place. There were times Sarah Parson thought of moving to Portland, or Seattle, or even somewhere on the east coast for a chance at love, happiness, and adventure (Columbia City being a terrible conduit for all three), but the prospect of leaving the idiots of this place to themselves made her linger.

She stepped aside and Todd barreled past.

. . . . . .

There's a small eddy of calm in being behind the curtains again. It's enough for Jimmy's thoughts to get all the way through his swollen head. It's the day after and his pops knows. Blood pats down in Jimmy's lap. Sticky. He pinches his nose high on the bridge, and guess what? It gives him a headache.

Jimmy gets up. Shaky, he holds on to the bed. The pain meds have been useless and what little effect they did have is waning as they are spreading their wings, flapping, ready to leave him but not yet sure of flight. Every movement sets his body afire in hurt and he knows it will be even worse once the last of the pills have flown the coop. He puts on his shorts from last night. Feels the small territories of stiffness where his blood had dried. Sweatpants over them. No T-shirt anywhere in the bundle and there snaps back to him a memory of ripping it off in the gym. He whimpers and pulls his sweatshirt on over his bare torso. Then his winter coat. Last his socks and sneakers. This is a challenge. Down on one knee, wobbly-weak with the burden of balance, tying the laces. A pair of white sneakers go by, visible beneath the hem of the curtains, pushing something with wheels. If people's feet were portals into other lives, Jimmy would choose these. Simple, white, perfect for their world of hospital corridors and break rooms.

He stands up. Slow, steady. He pulls on his hood, careful of the radius of ache around the soon-to-be-famous wound. Puts that mess of black hair in check. Pulls the drawstrings tight, knots it in two bunny ears. He doesn't have that beautiful, straight-as-an-arrow Japanese hair like his mother and Dex did. It's got more of his pops in it. Curly shape at least.

He wonders how his pops found out, but then brushes the thought from his mind. It's a useless mystery to entertain. By now everyone in Columbia City must know; it's too little to hide a secret this big.

That's small town.

He leaves the curtained area and there's a nurse standing with her clipboard—someone he doesn't know. She looks up at him, smiles. "Jimmy, I'm Sarah."

He blinks at her, not sure how to respond.

"I think my mother had you in English class, Mrs. Parson? I was here when Mr. Berg brought you in. Quite the shock."

Our kid feels sick, sweaty, and ready to sit down. This nurse in scrubs printed with hundreds of fish all pointed the same direction is in the way. Big eyes ready to take everything in. She steps closer, reaches out and takes his hand. He lets her, though he keeps it limp. Hers is small, dry, but with an expert dexterity in her squeeze.

"Listen, it's never as bad as it seems, do you hear me? I can tell you that for a fact, it's never as bad as it seems."

Who the fuck is this woman? He's hurt, clothes stiff with his own dried blood, and she's giving him this? What if it's just exactly as bad as it seems? What if it's even worse than he's letting on? He takes his hand away and Sarah the nurse smiles. He's going to brush past her but she puts a hand on his chest so he stops and slaps down her clipboard. It clatters on the ground, outsized in its noise. She reaches down, all calm and easygoing like it was her fault. She straightens the papers and smiles at Jimmy again.

She tucks a card into the pouch pocket of his sweatshirt. "I'm a good listener."

He goes down a stubby hallway and exits into the waiting room. His pops is there, hunched over the counter, signing some paper. The nurse behind the desk has pushed her chair back a few feet, watches him over this gap. A tall Mr. Clean–looking dude stands back against a wall, arms folded.

Jimmy sits in one of the chairs. This room smells of coffee. Coffee in the morning used to be a thing him and his brother, Dex, joked about. They'd come shuffling into the kitchen, noses leading the way, bumping into things. You know, after that Folgers commercial. People waking up because of the smell of coffee brewing. Like shitty coffee could bring a family together. It used to crack them up till they were laid out on the floor, his mom being like, "Can't I ever get some peace and quiet?" and his pops just trying hard as hell not to smile in front of her.

The stink of coffee.

His pops is done with the papers. Comes to stand over Jimmy. He's got a flimsy cup of the hospital coffee and is machining through mint after mint that he pulls from a bag in his pocket. He cracks a mint in his teeth, and then takes a noisy sip. Must be an interesting taste. He always has a big bag of those green candies wherever he goes these days. Cracking them habit enough to keep his mind free of the drinking. There's a cabinet above the fridge stuffed with family packs. At about fifty a pack, Jimmy has it figured his pops goes through over two hundred candies a day. That amount of sugar could have killed an elephant. But hell. Couldn't touch his pops. Freight Train himself. If his mom were around she would have been bugging him about switching to sugar free. She could be like that sometimes. Working in a hospital and all.

"Let's go," his pops says loudly and Jimmy's head fizzes.

"Can't a kid get some coffee?" He wants to delay whatever his pops has planned for as long as possible. His heart pounds.

"You want coffee?"

"I always get coffee."

"Dead don't get coffee, and you already dead."

He didn't want coffee anyway, but this is too much too soon. Only been a few hours since the wall. He didn't die, did he? Can't this all just slow down? "Shit, Pops."

"Shut up. You run yourself into a fucking wall you don't get to speak neither." His pops is trembling, and Jimmy wonders, *Am I gonna get smacked? Right here in front of some nurses? Dial up child services. Old man's losing it.*

Instead the big man stomps over the waiting room tile and out the big automatic doors. That limp is there. Same as always. Bum knee. The *boom, creak, slide. Boom, creak, slide.* Jimmy follows him out the automatic doors and the wind is immediate. It's cold as hell and he feels stipple designs up and down the back of his neck. Jimmy turns back to the hospital waiting room for shelter from the wind and zips his winter coat to the top, pulls its hood over his sweatshirt's hood. The doors have closed again and he catches his reflection in the glass panes. Hood on and blood streaking down from his nose, bruise like a third, busted eye. Blooming, almost tropical in color and vibrancy, whitish bandages covering the epicenter. A beat-to-hell movie monster. Doesn't recognize himself.

It's five in the morning and Jimmy hasn't yet been called the nickname that will dog him wherever he goes: *Kamikaze Kirkus.* It'll come soon enough though. By this morning's first class, kids will be whispering the strange story of Jimmy Kirkus and the gym wall. Adults will be talking in hushed tones. It'll be on the lips of everyone. It will snowball, include the basketball feats of his childhood, the drama of his parents' lives, getting bigger all the time until it takes in things that have no relation to the things he actually did. Until it's about someone who seems nothing like our kid Jimmy. Until it's an avalanche.

And he'll never try and stop it.

Rule 4. Come from a Difficult Background

Saturday, December 1, 1990

JIMMY KIRKUS NOT YET BORN—SEVENTEEN YEARS UNTIL THE WALL.

A weekend morning and the world was their lumpy, king-sized bed. Room happy in its disarray. Todd's Van Eyck uniform flung over the door to the closest, a shed skin, while other things of all sizes—from a little girl's shoe to a woman's black stockings, strung out and runny on the windowsill—lay about. Comfort in the chaotic domesticity. Todd blinked his eyes, still somewhat sealed with sleep. He rolled over, slowly—his bladder full—and found Genny's hip with his palm. From this reference point he traveled northwest and found the beginning swell of her pregnant belly. Another baby on the way; a boy, Todd hoped.

"Quit it," Genny said. She waved back with her left arm and hit him in the side.

"Oof." A burning fullness swelled out from the impact. Todd hadn't peed the bed since he couldn't remember when, but just then, almost.

Genny leaned up, suddenly awake. "Are you OK?"

"My teeth are floating is what."

She laughed and lay her head back down. "I almost popped the balloon?"

Todd got up and shuffled through the drifts of his adult life— dirty laundry, coffee mug, small stack of bills—toward the bathroom. "It could have been bad for you, too."

"At this point, I wouldn't care."

The worst part of their house on Glasgow was that there was no bathroom attached to their bedroom. Todd had to scoot down a little hallway—always a chill here—and enter the bathroom via a swollen, likely to stick, impossible-to-keep-quiet door across from the pantry. It would take a miracle to use the bathroom without alerting the whole house that he was awake. And then it would be Suzie jumping up and down, singing whatever song she'd picked up from the morning's cartoons, demanding a detailed itinerary of the day's events. If not that then the Flying Finn would come in, probably just in his boxers, eating graham crackers or something, crumbs all over the place. They would be listening for the creak of that bathroom door, even if they didn't know they were. Todd had done the same thing when he was a kid and that room was Finn's.

Out in the living room he heard the purring click of the Wheel of Fortune spinning on the TV in the living room. Todd was absolutely certain *Wheel of Fortune* didn't play at eight a.m. on a Saturday. It had to be one of the Flying Finn's tapes. Todd wondered how the old man had persuaded Suzie to switch away from *Looney Tunes*, or whatever.

Todd reached out and turned the knob to the bathroom all of the way, anticipating the latch clicking. Next he stepped forward and put his bare foot at the base of the doorway, so that when he pulled, the clear section, near the bottom, wouldn't come out before the swollen section nearer the top. Next he gave the door little jerks, easing it out centimeter by centimeter until, blessed be thee of wood and brass, it came away quietly. Todd stepped in, sat down for his piss to minimize noise, and was back in the bedroom with no one the wiser.

The warmth around Genny was delicious, and the moment he settled in next to her he was able to regain the just-below-the-surface sleepiness that was the best part of waking up.

"Is the old goat watching *Wheel of Fortune*?" Genny asked.

"I think it's one of his tapes."

"Why would anyone watch a game show more than once?"

"His name is, legit I mean, the Flying Finn, so watching game shows on tape is basically par for the course."

"Legit, like it's legal?" She turned around to face him. She goosed his ribs so he shot out his arms and held her, brought her close, conformed to the curved shape of her body. "In a court of law?"

"You know what I mean."

Then the door burst open and Suzie came running in carrying something bleached white in each hand. "Look it, look it, look it!" she yelled.

Genny pulled away from Todd—the successful coup of sneaking into the bathroom all for nothing—and smiled down at their daughter. Todd rolled away, arm draped over his eyes, trying to dunk himself back under the waterline. "What is it?"

"Grandpa gave it to me if I didn't watch 'toons."

"Jesus," Genny said—and in this one word Todd heard the business end of his wife come out and was thrust onto dry land, totally awake. "Todd?"

He sat up and looked at what his daughter held. It didn't correlate with anything he recognized until he tilted his head to the left and saw the grin. His little girl, sweet chickadee of summer and light, was holding the skull and separated jawbone of a long-dead cow. "Whoa, Grandpa gave that to you?"

"Your father . . ." Genny was whispering savagely.

"It's for my white collection," Suzie said—the *ct* in collection coming out as an *sh* sound.

"That's great, baby, but do you know what that is?" His daughter, ever since she had been able to get around on her own, had gathered things together that caught her eye. This magpie tendency had become color-coded in the last six months and the habit only seemed on course to get more sophisticated going forward.

"Moo-cow's head," she said seriously. "He's dead now."

Then the Flying Finn was in the doorway with a jar of peanut butter in one hand, scooping out the last bits with the other. Todd and Genny still in bed, people coming in, this felt like John and Yoko.

"Mori"—this was how his father always referred to his wife— "almost no peanut butter."

"A cow's skull, Finn?" Genny said.

"Oh, so you want she's playing with the pink dolls!" He was mock-outraged, peanut butter caught in his whiskers. It was a joke between them. Whenever they saw little girls around Suzie's age, all trussed up in ribbon and lace, they conspired about where else a bow could conceivably be tied—around the knee, on each ear?

"Get your own peanut butter!" Genny yelled, halfway ready to laugh, but not there yet.

"Get out of our room, Dad."

"This was my room one time!" he yelled back, already on his way out.

"Go watch your reruns!"

"It's practice for when Vannah calls. Then you see the laughing, and it'll all be me!"

"Daddy, let's go to the beach! For collecting!"

Genny collapsed back into bed. "Can you take her? Maybe I can sleep a bit more."

"Yes, let's go, let's go!" his daughter said.

Todd kissed his wife on the cheek, tucked the sheets in around her. She smiled back, already sailing. "Wash the damn cow skull," she whispered.

. . . . . .

Beach was winter white. Bleached driftwood and white-capped waves. Blown-out sand sculptures formed around things washed up and forgotten. The littlest piece of trash, or stick, or turned-over cup grew in the drifts of sand until it seemed big enough to hide a creature. Some malformed thing waiting to scuttle forth and eat when the time was right. Passing rain squalls dumped parts of their burden on their journey inland, patterns in many-cratered pointillism.

Todd watched Suzie run in the sand, so small she seemed unreal, collecting the things she found in the basket she made with the front of her T-shirt. She had her blue jacket unzipped and it flapped in the gusts. When she turned a certain way, the wind flipped it completely up, and it looked like his daughter was hanging by the armholes as her jacket tugged her into the heavens.

"You stay close," Todd called out on that last day.

"OK, Daddy," she yelled back, not even looking.

He chuckled to himself. Little, pretty, Suzanna. A startling thing he called Suzie Q. Baby girl born so cute nobody was safe. Even the most checked-out teenage boys stopped to coo at little Suzie.

It was the last day Todd was fully happy. Oh there would be other days of pleasantness, surges of positive feeling, but this was the final time he was filled all the way up. He lay back in the sand and crossed his ankles, a practice Genny Mori said would give him varicose veins. She was always saying things like this. It was how she told him she loved him. He crossed them anyway and sighed. What a luxury. The people of Columbia City had finally started seeing him for who he had become rather than what he could have. They asked him questions about little Suzie instead of rehab on his knee. There were no illusions of a basketball comeback. No pipe dreams of an NBA star hailing from their town. Not anymore.

The beach was empty and surprisingly warm in that Oregon way—that is, only when the wind slacked for a moment. Todd thought he felt his spine aligning into a straighter form as he sank into the sand and the wind built banks of it at his side, working hard at covering him up. His little girl was safe, in his sight, scampering to driftwood logs, stealing the treasures caught in the little wet caves of their sides. His wife was home, pregnant with their second, probably studying at the kitchen table, going to be a nurse. Another child had been Todd's idea. "Suzie's lonely," he'd said. Life was in order so he let his blinks linger a little longer. A little longer still. Small curtains of sand ran over his nose. In a day or two, hell, he'd become just another mysterious shape hidden by the beach. It was hard work at Van Eyck Beverages. Loading case after case. And soon he was asleep.

Some time later—how much he didn't know then, but would spend many years trying to calculate—he jolted awake. He stood. Blood stuck in his legs made way for his head. His whole body was tingling, asleep or dead. He looked out and saw an empty beach.

"Suzie?" he yelled. And then yelled again. Nothing. He scanned the beach. Empty. He had the sudden thought that she'd been kidnapped so he rushed up the sandy dunes in the direction of the parking lot. His old gray minivan was there and nothing else. He felt his weak knee, watery with pain. He turned and was back on the ridge of the dune, looking down at the ocean and the sky and the harried little waves that came in. Gray, white, white. He looked far to the left and then to the right and it was the same. Gray, white, white. Gray, white, white. Then. Blue.

Her blue coat.

She had needed a new one growing as fast as she was, so they took her to Fred Meyer and she chose her own.

"Which one do you like, honey?" Genny Mori had asked.

Suzie ran down the aisle and stopped in front of a bright blue one. "Blue, blue!"

Todd came up behind her. "OK, blue, we get it, OK." He picked the tag, looked at the price, and then let go as if it were hot. "Jesus." He showed it to Genny.

"Think this is bad, just wait till high school." They shared a laugh at that. Not much, but no matter. Sometimes enough really is enough.

......

There was a big driftwood log shifting and half-caught in the water. The tide had come in a ways since they arrived and the ocean seemed intent on sucking that big log out to sea. There. Blue. Todd saw so clearly. A bright blue sleeve pinned by the log. It floated as lazily as the seaweed around it. He started running. There was her hand—small—sticking out of the end of the sleeve. So electric white it could have been plugged in.

Todd "Freight Train" Kirkus ran faster. The watery pain in his knee spread to his heart.

......

They had the funeral the next week—a rainy Thursday. The Flying Finn disappeared shortly after. Todd found all his tapes in the garbage, their gutted ribbons pooling, tangled, around them. Todd called the police and they found him three days later south of town, in Cannon Beach, walking along 101. He didn't want to come home, so they let him be.

Meanwhile, the Flying Finn's restaurant—Finn's Kitchen—out on Pier 11 was shut down, the lease taken up by someone opening a place called the Crab Shack. Todd sold his father's kitchen equipment in one lot. The buyer made out like a thief.

......

The memory stayed with Todd forever. As vivid as if it had always just happened. Her little blue sleeve in the water, the huge gray log lolling back and forth on top of her, playing or lustful. Close his eyes for a second and he had his own private hell. It left him broke-hearted and Genny Mori cracked-but-not-broke-hearted.

JIMMY KIRKUS NOT YET BORN–SEVENTEEN YEARS UNTIL THE WALL.

And that was the big difference between the two parents. Todd was shattered completely. The very conception of himself as a good man, a good father, destroyed. This void invited filling, and so Todd focused himself—with the coming of a new baby boy—on building himself back up from ruin into a workable, though paranoid father. Genny Mori on the other hand, because she wasn't there when her daughter died, because she had an easier time dissociating herself from the blame, only had her heart cracked. Badly, but still structurally sound. Over time she knitted emotional scar tissue over it to make do. And make do kept on until it was status quo.

It seemed to her in the first few weeks after Suzie died that she had lost a part of her own body as real as any limb or organ. Suzie was of her own flesh so that when she laughed, Genny felt it too. Then suddenly her little child, a piece of her, was gone forever. Things like her remembered laugh became phantom limbs that ached just as much and as real as any of her own.

An awful pact with life, she thought. You divide yourself so this little child can have a chance, but then it's not like any other part of the body. You can never keep this part of you close enough and safe enough. Life was a puller by nature, and it pulled and pulled and pulled until that little part of you, that little child that was the best part of you, was pulled away. And there was nothing you could do to really protect that little best part of you because even though it felt like a piece of you and looked like a piece of you, it wasn't you. And if Genny Mori was learning one thing, it was this: only count on what is truly you, because that's the only thing you have total control of.

And so with Jimmy on the way, Genny Mori withdrew as far into herself as she could, hoping the baby took little, or better yet, nothing of her because she didn't think she could stand to be divided, to be wrest of her own self again.

Her plan seemed to work with Jimmy. A little pale-skinned mouse of a boy who was more interesting than adorable. She was relieved and angry all at once that it had worked. Aside from size, the kid was all Todd. It was as though, through some biological impossibility, she had cuckolded herself.

Then, when Todd wanted another child, she agreed. When Suzie had been born, it brought them together in a way that patterned her skin in goose bumps—corny, but true—and so there was a hope that with more children, they could reclaim that space of being two people in love. And, if it didn't work out that way, it seemed Jimmy only got her slightness, and that wasn't so much to give.

Hot August, a chore to conceive Dex. A favor to the big, hulking man above her, inside her, everywhere. Everything close. Logic rebounding too quickly. She wanted it too, right? Then halfway through a mild May, Dex came. Huge like his father, he needed a C-section when he twisted in the womb and the umbilical cord wrapped. Left a scar on her belly. Braille she often read. And there was a problem she noticed from first sight. He'd taken in the womb when Genny wasn't looking. Here he was, dark like her father, eyes like her mother, and her own straight hair so black it was almost blue. "That hair comes from Japanese royalty," her mother used to tell her.

There was more. Dex had taken the way she smacked her lips while she drifted to sleep, as if it were tasty. He took her love of sly humor, her way of holding her fork as if it were a tree branch she was hanging from, and the little cough she always seemed to have in the morning. Also, she started to realize that while Jimmy hadn't seemed like her at first, she was coming out in him as he got older. He had her way of shaking his hair out of his eyes when it was too long in the front, her little curl in the upper lip that called his bluff when he was trying not to laugh, her love of staring out the window while it rained, and her crooked, double-jointed fingers.

She had been divided again. A part of her split into two boys, running full on into a life filled with sadness. They were like two arms she had no control over but still caused her pain when they flailed and bumped and bruised.

It's a terrible deal with life, she thought.

Heart cracked, she applied local anesthesia—delving into the practical. It just didn't hurt as much, if you kept yourself busy. She picked up extra shifts at the hospital, became obsessed with the small flower garden at the front of her house, dreamed of how her life would be if she had married differently, or never married at all. And then sometimes she just got dripping drunk off economy-sized bottles of cheap white wine. Ignoring her boys, her vulnerability, she confused the wine's fuzziness with the soft love she missed feeling from her time before, her time with Suzie.

. . . . . .

Maybe it was here, with the death of Suzie on the heels of a basketball flameout of epic proportions, old Finn Kirkus off wandering the streets, that people first started talking about the Kirkus Curse. Or maybe that came later. It was a long, leaky life. Many more chances for tragedy to seep in.

Rule 5. Be Betrayed

Tuesday, December 18, 2007

JIMMY KIRKUS, SIXTEEN YEARS OLD—EIGHT HOURS AFTER THE WALL.

His pops is already halfway across the hospital parking lot to the road by the time Jimmy's ready to go. Apparently the old man doesn't want to drive. Jimmy sees the Van Eyck delivery truck parked crooked, cow skull grinning out the window, and is almost relieved. These days he always prefers to walk. Jimmy looks back once more to the hospital, and then is off in pursuit.

The night is lit. Columbia City had its first and probably last snow of the season yesterday. A big deal. Snow's all dirty and used up now, but still bright enough to make everything glow in a soft, blue-white way. The town is sleeping and Jimmy and his pops share this world with nobody. This is frightening for the kid and he tries to scrunch deeper into his coat. The cold air tickles the inside of his nose with its freshness. He sneezes and it threatens to implode his head. He cries out and it sounds like a much younger self. His pops, though? Big man just keeps moving. Doesn't even stop to ask if he's OK.

He follows him on Exchange and after a quarter mile, turns on Alameda. Everything is frozen, at rest. They come up to Tapiola Park and Jimmy watches his breath rise. There's an outdoor court, place he'd sneak off to with Dex to shoot some midnight hoops way back in the day when they still had curfews. Pretty good place to play if you don't mind the steep little hills on every side. Be careful or you'll twist your ankle on a long rebound, swear to

57

God. Mostly Mexicans play there during the day. Guys who can't shoot but will outhustle you. Some of them playing in collar shirts and jeans. Beat you eleven to seven on a bunch of put-back points. No style, but sweat in spades.

Don't think back now, he tells himself, and is just able to snuff out a mental vision of headlights drifting right.

Besides, there's no time. Not when pops is full steam ahead. Jimmy's sense of dread is rising but it seems out of place with the stillness around him. Anything could happen with his pops at the helm, and none of the possibilities seem good. Maybe he'll send him off to military school, or a center for troubled teens, or some multiday hike in the woods where he'd bond with kleptos and arsonists; or maybe his pops is just going to keep walking forever and Jimmy won't know when to leave off, when to stop. He keeps on past Sudsy's Laundromat, Dairy Queen, and the baseball diamond where coach Steiner tried to get him to join the team and become the pitcher if basketball wasn't in the cards.

They turn on to Old Youngs River Highway and Jimmy knows where they're headed—to the high school. A memory jumps up, raises its hand, has the answer: *Today's the day they agreed he would start school again.* Jimmy shakes his head; it's not possible.

The river is just a few feet away. It's whispering threats all the time. That's the problem with river towns. A real heavy rain and who's to say it won't just swell up and swallow everything? Flood. It happened in 1938. A week after the Tall Firs won the National Title for the University of Oregon and came back to Columbia City for a parade. Rain so thick people got lost crossing the street. The parade was postponed as the rivers—Youngs on one side, Columbia on the other—drank their gluttonous fill and waded in their girth over the roadways and buildings on the lower ground. Water sluiced down from the hills, eager to be swallowed. Sections of houses sank as their foundations trickled away beneath them.

Entire docks washed out and the Brick House was turned into an aquarium. A single crab was found hanging in the basketball nets when the waters receded. Jimmy's seen the pictures. A town dirty and bedraggled. Straight wrecked and years out from being fully fixed again—but victorious with their native sons, the Tall Firs, National Champions. Every person in those old photos has a gleam in their eye, a question to the universe. *This your best shot?*

By the time Jimmy gets to the parking lot of Columbia City High, he's huffing, out of breath. He pulls back his hood and the cold air feels good on his wound. He sits down next to his father and stares at his hands. They come in and out of focus. He wonders where he'd be without them—possibly better off?

His father reaches out and pokes Jimmy softly on his cut head, right in the bandage covering the bruise crossed with stitching. It brings the urge to vomit alongside pain. He yelps. Remembers the gushy way it felt inside his head. Worse after each hit against the wall. Like he was turning himself into mashed potatoes. *Twenty-one stitches*, he thinks, *that's all it was, a lucky number.*

"You're dead," his pops says and it's hard to hear Freight Train's voice tremble like this. Man's supposed to be tough. "This sort of shit could kill you."

"Sorry, Pops. It's just . . ." Speech is hard to come by. Words rotten at the edges.

"What were you proving? What were you thinking? Gone crazy or something? That's what people are going to think—you're bonkers. They're gonna call Kirkus Curse on this one. Twenty-one stitches, Jimmy? That's my new least-favorite number."

"Was just seeing something and—"

"There's no way. Just no way." The man is crying now. Big, outsized tears pattering down in his lap. "There's just no fucking way, Jimmy."

JIMMY KIRKUS, SIXTEEN YEARS OLD–EIGHT HOURS AFTER THE WALL.

Jimmy tries to put a hand on his father's shoulder, but it's hard to aim and he takes it away after hovering uselessly in the air.

His pops stands up, louder now. "There's no fucking way." Words bounce off the outside wall of the Brick House, run full out across the parking lot.

Jimmy stands and big Mr. Kirkus wraps up his son tightly in his arms and Jimmy feels his flabby belly against him, the soft girth the man has put on in this last year, and the two sob together. It finally feels a little more right than it did the day before, the week before, the months. Seems closer to how it's supposed to be—kid crying, dad hugging. A dam broken, they shudder, the cold creeping in minute after minute to crawl up in their bones and crystallize in their blood. Tired and strained sobs. Thick and wet ones. All manner of sadness finally given voice.

Out of the snowy darkness, they hear voices. Jimmy and his pops step apart from each other, embarrassed. Like a kid and his pops got something to be ashamed of by hugging. They wipe their eyes with just their fingertips, as if there's something caught there, blinking like they can't see clearly.

"So Jimmy went nuts-o," somebody says.

This shocks our kid stone still.

"That's not exactly." It's Mr. Berg answering, but he's cut off.

"Running into a fucking wall? I'd call that crazy." Jimmy recognizes this as David, Mr. Berg's son. "Any day of the week, I'd call that crazy. Man, even in Afghanistan they'd call that crazy and they have fools blowing themself up over there."

"There's more to it."

Jimmy can see them now. Nuts how close they are. "No, no, no, I get it," David's saying, walking in the lead, head down. "Jimmy's an egg. Fragile. Got to be careful, or you'll crack the shell. I *get* it. I'm just saying: makes black lipstick seem like horseshit, huh?" Then David looks up and sees them. Jimmy feels David's eyes on his cut. He and this kid, they go way back, and Jimmy can't think of a worse candidate to see him like this. There's a scar just above his eye he got from David Berg. Dude looks like a Goth punk, but throws a rock like he's on the mound for the Yankees.

Mr. Berg, just behind, stops too. "Hi again, Todd. Morning, Jimmy."

"James," his pops says. "Morning, David."

David shrugs, plugs in some earphones, and walks past. Mr. Berg grimaces, and then nods his head once and walks to the gym door, unlocks it, and his son darts in. "David?" they hear him calling as the door creaks shut. "David, come back here."

Jimmy looks to his pops and sees he's studying him. Something in his eyes telling his son, *Look, this is just how it's going to be.* No sympathy. "Well, have a good day at school anyway," he says.

Jimmy looks at the school, then back at his pops. He's confused. Not thinking straight. His pops springing this on him? Bashed-up head, not even a backpack or school supplies. "Pops," Jimmy says. Yeah, they said today would be the day he'd start classes back up, but surely . . .

"Have a good day at school, Jim," his pops says louder, shortening his name like Jimmy's just another guy he works with.

Jimmy breathes for a moment. All his teeth feel loose. He's got to think about the words before he says them, otherwise they might not make it out. He remembers a time when they were all eating cherries, him, Dex, his mom, and his pops. Bought from a Mexican at a shed near the highway. They had been on a trip to a lake. Camping. All four in a row on the hot shoulder of the road, sitting in the gravel, watching the cars go by. Must have been the summer after kindergarten. Eating cherries and spitting the seeds. Fun to see who could spit the farthest. His mother getting drool all down her chin and his pops being like, "elegant as always," and then the both of them laughing. Jimmy had noticed that his mom said pit and his pops said stone for the hard seed in the middle of the cherries. Stone like rock or pit like hole. Pit from a story about a troll who lived inside of one. Stone like the things he and Dex used to throw to see who could knock a GI Joe off an overturned bucket first. Jimmy remembers how he wanted to ask his parents about this—stone or pit—but didn't because he wasn't sure how to express it. Nervous that he would do it poorly, or they would think him weird, and all of the dusty joy would blow away when his mom got silent and his pops made little comments out the side of his mouth like, "Real sense of joy in this family." So he hadn't said anything. Same as now. How to tell his pops that there isn't any way school's the right move today. This must be the old man's way of teaching him a lesson. Dumb. Head bashed up wasn't lesson enough for his pops, now make him do this? Asshole. The fluorescent lights, the tardy bell ringing, kids screaming, fucking around, asking him questions. All kind of questions. But old man thinks this will do him good. Old man doesn't know jack.

"Yeah, fine, OK," Jimmy says.

Todd nods once, presses a crumpled twenty into Jimmy's hand. "Lunch," he says, gruffly, and goes.

He watches his father, big Freight Train, limp off across the snowy parking lot just populating with early morning students getting tutoring sessions or extra practice. Muddy trucks pulling in with Confederate flags pinned to their ceilings. Beat-to-shit Civics or Corollas blasting Kanye West. Jesus walks. All of them cursing school for still being open on this icy day. Town hugged by water like Columbia City—rivers on two sides, marshes all around, and the ocean's shoulder visible always—hardly ever gets cold enough for ice or snow. Now, here it is, snow all around and *still* they got school?

They watch Todd Kirkus limp by. He's the man they've heard of, the guy whose black-and-white photographs still dominate the trophy case and whose name tags along with basketball records, like an annoying kid brother. The early arrivers turn their heads back toward our kid, squint their eyes. *Could that be Jimmy Soft? I thought he fled to Mexico.*

Class will start soon, but Jimmy isn't going. He hurts. Feels sick. He hates himself for the extra attention he'll have now. As if coming back weren't going to cause talk enough, last night he had to go and make it worse. He isn't even wearing his school clothes. A scrub in his crusty old sweats and sweatshirt. There's blood from the night before on his shoes. Pops could have at least let him go home to change. This is impossible, what his pops wants him to do.

Jimmy turns away from the school, walks to the track, and goes into the woods beyond the javelin pit. These are the paths he and Dex used to know so well from sneaking around town to each and every court, looking for a game. They were like street urchins of the woods, punks running the alleyways carved by deer and drunks, making their way to the courts and begging to be let into a game. Back then ball seemed like something important and meaningful. Hell, seemed downright holy.

Jimmy picks up the pace. He doesn't know where he's going, but he can't go to school and he can't go home. He fades into the bushes. He hopes he sees no one and more importantly, no one sees him.

. . . . . .

Even though Jimmy's left the school, he's still there, name on everyone's lips. It's too soon for details, but people still talk.

"Marcy at the hospital told me Jimmy Kirkus came in last night with blunt-force trauma to the head," Mr. Jackson says, holding court in the teacher's lounge. "Twenty-one stitches. Get this, came in with James Berg. Then, then, when I was coming in through the gym this morning, I saw Berg scrubbing down the wall. Put two and two together." He punches his fist into the palm of his other hand. "Bam. Jimmy Kirkus ran himself into the wall." Mr. Jackson pauses a moment to give enough space to the off-color thing he's about to say. "Just like he's a fucking kamikaze pilot."

JIMMY KIRKUS, SIXTEEN YEARS OLD—EIGHT HOURS AFTER THE WALL.

The other teachers are blank-faced, not getting it, or pretending not to. Twenty years ago being half-Japanese would be a just-under-the-surface topic of intrigue, and in some circles, scandal. Sometimes, it would openly boil out in racist comments. These days though, at least 10 percent of the student body is Mexican, and Jimmy isn't the lightning rod his mother was. And so this joke of Mr. Jackson's is so obvious, so on the nose, so blatantly offensive, that everyone is uncomfortable. Maybe in a bar, or at someone's Christmas party, this line could be delivered with a ducked head, embarrassed laugh, and sail on by. Not now.

Mr. Jackson forces out his own laugh. "Cause the kid's half-Japanese? You know. Kamikaze pilots?"

The other teachers did know, they did get it, and if Principal McCarthy wasn't standing behind Jackson in the doorway, listening to him basically fill out his own temporary leave of absence slip, some might have given him a pity laugh. A few dart their eyes to signal to Mr. Jackson that his boss is behind him, but the man doesn't get it and so jumps when McCarthy speaks.

"Mr. Jackson. That's quite enough," he says. The security tape of the Jimmy Kirkus incident has gone missing and he's in no kind of mood. And then, to top off his shitty morning, he has Sid Lang with him—caught the punk smoking this morning, fourth time this year—and he's on his way to make the exasperating phone call to his libertarian parents. Now he'll have to reprimand Mr. Jackson too. "You'll see me in my office in half an hour."

Fifteen minutes later, sitting in the office and waiting to be taken home for the day, Sid sees Michelle Roberts, whom he's always had a crush on, as she drops off the attendance for homeroom. "You hear about Kamikaze Kirkus?" he asks, and it's off to the races.

Jimmy's new nickname spreads. Smokers are putting rings around it, girls lipsticked lips, and the teachers are shooting holes through it with their stares, showing how inappropriate it is, and then whispering details and rumors with one another when they think no one can hear. Kids are already trying to get into the gym to see the stain. Secrets in small towns don't last. There isn't enough space for them to hide.

Kamikaze Kirkus.

Mr. Berg catches kids tracing Jimmy's stain on the Brick House wall with their fingers. He scatters them by clapping his hands. Spends the rest of the day trying to wash it off, again, but it remains. His eyes water from the chemicals in the air, and he wished he'd been there sooner. The stubborn stain that remains? That's a little Kamikaze Kirkus right there. That's the spot where basketball players, Fishermen and foes alike, will bounce the game ball against in warm-ups for luck. It will become a tradition. Go on for years and years. The Blood-Red Bricks of Jimmy Kirkus.

Not yet, though. Our kid's got a ways to go.

. . . . . .

The Flying Finn is alone in the wet woods. He wishes he could go home and see Todd, but something feels too big around his son, like he wouldn't fit in that life anymore. The Flying Finn shakes the thought.

This is his second stint being homeless. He's going on a year now. He knows how to survive and rule number one is to keep busy. He's found that if he slows for even a moment, a heavy dread will build up in his veins, weigh him down. So it's back to work. He's looking for the mushrooms he knows are safe to eat. He's out here, but he's not really out here. "Got ghosts in the knees," he whispers to himself.

This reminds him of when he first moved to town. Summertime, 1960. Bumble Bee was still canning back then. He worked precooking tuna. Fish dangling on big hooks. Burned hands, close smell. He couldn't stop for a second. He'd sink if he did. Then Todd born and his wife died in the process and he was moving even faster. Just stay above. By the time Todd was born Columbia City was in a serious rut. Bumble Bee plant closed down. Nowhere to work. He'd opened his restaurant by then. Working double shifts so he could keep his prices down, catch those shady after-bar drunks. The let-outs from the infamous triangle of bars: the Brass Rail, the Wreck, and the Driftwood. Town wanted to raze those bars for the shady characters they kept. But the Flying Finn had served them. Made it work. Scrappy, cheek-dirty cigarette bummers who'd clean him out of creamers and sugars: he started only keeping two creamers, two sugars on each table. A pain to reset each time, but better than the loss of cash.

He didn't stop moving then, wouldn't stop now.

. . . . . .

Carla Ferguson gets ready for her shift. Her hair a little out of style, her clothes a little out of date. She carries the cross of the home-schooled. Only reason she got the job at Peter Pan Market is 'cause she can work during the day when everyone else is at school. She ties her shoes, hands shaky. There's still a weakness in her muscles from last night. She doesn't know why she took so many pills. She told her father it was an accident and maybe it was. She begged to still go to work today—she wants to hear news about why Jimmy Kirkus was at the hospital last night—and finally her father relented. She pouts her lips in the mirror while she waits for her father to bring around the car. She pinches with her fingers to bring forth redness. She wishes she were allowed to wear lipstick.

Really, she feels better than she has in weeks. Here she is, caught up in it. Something is finally happening to her. She makes sure to pack her journal.

. . . . . .

Diane Kaiser—editor of the *Columbia City Standard*—has heard the rumors. Can't decide if this is a brief or a news story. If it was a suicide attempt, then it's a brief, with no name attached. If it's an attack, then it's a news story and she can tack Jimmy's name to it. There needs to be something about it in the afternoon's *Standard* though. Anything.

......

Coach Kelly stays home from school. He heard about Jimmy through a phone call from Mr. Jackson. He can't help but feel responsible, even if he was just trying to do right by Jimmy. He shouldn't have left him alone in that gym, he guesses. His wife doesn't help much. His ears still ring with her screaming. He took it all, filed it away into an ever-growing section of his mind called *I Should Have Known Better*. He can't see the next step. For the first time coaching basketball, a thing he's guided his life by ever since they discovered Lucy couldn't have kids, seems like the least important thing in the world.

......

"Who took the tape, Johnny?" Principal McCarthy asks the computer teacher.

"How should I know?" Johnny Opel—Mr. O the kids call him— is leaning back in his springy chair, two bites into his customary morning McMuffin.

McCarthy runs his hand over a nearby grease-shined keyboard, tickling the keys, and the machine beeps back at him. Everything in the computer lab is greasy because of Mr. Opel's morning McMuffins. It's disgusting, but there's no one else in town qualified to teach computers. "I thought only you and I had access to that room."

"I know I have a key. I don't know who else does."

"Put a new tape in, and change the locks. Let me know if anything else turns up." McCarthy wouldn't put it past Mr. Opel to have stolen the tape himself, but then again, given the man's tremendous slothfulness, there is no way he would have been at school early enough.

"Aye-aye," Mr. Opel says, the idiot saluting him ironically.

......

Johnny Opel can't believe his shitty luck. Being the computer teacher meant he was also in charge of the surveillance cameras placed in five spots around school. In all the seven years he's worked at Columbia City High, this is the first time he's actually had anyone ask to see a tape. The cameras are on a twelve-hour loop. Anything more than half a day old is erased by the future. He only checks up on the cameras once every two weeks to clean the lenses and make sure all is running. He supposes the last time he checked, he left the door unlocked.

He takes a pull on his Big Gulp, swishes the Pepsi around in his mouth, and finally swallows. He gathers Jimmy Kirkus—son of Todd, a guy who used to tell him he had a rock-star name when they were back in high school together—did something bad in the gym last night and now the tape is gone.

Of all the shitty luck.

......

Jimmy spends the day on those backwoods trails that connect the town in startling ways. Kid's so knowledgeable he could run a smuggling business. Through backyards and across the occasional road, but mostly in the woods, he goes from court to court like him and Dex used to. But it's different now. Colder than he remembered it being. When he and Dex ran them—in all kinds of weather too—they were too hopped up on the prospect of hoops to feel cold. Now, the temperature takes up most of his awareness.

Everything is dripping. The noise seems huge. He slips often, his mind still so fuzzy. He vomits ropey slime—Top Ramen he ate last night before he went down to the Brick House—and it slides into the fallen leaves, steaming wildly. Jimmy takes an orange leaf encased in ice and licks it to get the taste off his tongue. He slips again and mud streaks his sweats. Thankfully, he avoids landing in his own vomit. His knee will be bruised badly by tonight. Add it to the list. His head rings in pain. Headache? More like head*break*.

He wipes his hands off on the front of his sweatshirt and feels something there. He reaches in and pulls out that card the nurse gave him in the hospital. *Not as bad as it seems.* Jimmy laughs aloud. *Sarah Parson, RN.* Pretty for an older lady. Weird, how she's the daughter of his dumpy English teacher. Breath so bad you tasted it even before you smelled it. English class was the worst.

So this was her daughter. Do nurses have business cards? Jimmy doesn't know, but there's something in it that seems a reach. *Not as bad as it seems.* He rips it in two, and then he rips it again. Let's the flakes pepper the wet grass cupping his vomit.

He's talking to himself, under his breath. Just ordering my thoughts, not crazy, he tells himself. He really could hitchhike to Mexico. He imagines his life there like a beer commercial. Hammocks and hot chicks and lime crowning bottle tops—always dressed stylish, always headed to great waves or live music. Get away and stay away. Hell, they don't even play basketball down there—all soccer. He practices the Spanish Pedro has taught him over the years. *Cabrón, puta, señorita, mamá chula.* Pedro. Where the fuck is Pedro?

His imagination takes him to another place. He's older, coming back to Columbia City for a ten-year reunion. Slick clothes, nice car, hot wife. All the other things checked off. Basketball? Naw, he *could have* ran with it, but he decided instead to start a company/be a lawyer/write a novel. He's fit while Pedro's put on a few pounds and lost his hair. At the bar he orders wine. Something with an accent in the name. Later, he corners his old best friend, or, better yet, catches him hitting on his wife. Then it's all, *what the fuck*? But Pedro isn't cool about it, so bang, a punch in the gut . . .

Jimmy is shaken out of his thoughts by sounds. Dribbling and shouts. From the woods he spies people playing basketball in the middle of the day. People just shooting around. High school drop-outs and overweight men on lunch breaks.

And then he decides, all at once, a snap in his head that cracks his brain in two. *Fuck ball.*

. . . . . .

At school his absence is adding weight to the rumors. Everyone has a theory. Kid was high. Kid was deranged. Kid actually *was* jumped. And finally: Kid just did it so there'd be no question of him playing this year—the Fishermen's last in the talent-heavy 6A Division—and come back next year when he can push around the little guys in 4A, have an easier go. Jimmy Soft-cum-Kami-kaze Kirkus never was good with pressure.

. . . . . .

Principal McCarthy makes an announcement on the intercom. "For students upset by the recent events regarding a certain class-mate"—he sounds on the edge of tears—"Mrs. Cole will be avail-able during periods one, four, and seven in the guidance office, as well as all breaks, to talk."

Soon there is a line to see Mrs. Cole. All boys. She's blond and she's curvy and they swear to God that if you can get tears going she'll put your head on her epic chest and hug you till the lights blink. Sure beats geometry.

And all because of crazy Jimmy Kirkus.

. . . . . .

Mr. Kirkus gets home and sits on the couch. He allows himself something he's not had in all the months since the accident: time.

For so long he's been filling his head and his hands with whatever they come across that his real thoughts feel like ghosts to him.

He stares straight ahead, puts his hands in his lap, and watches the frozen leaves still left on the trees outside drip, drip, drip. The heater is pinging. The refrigerator whirs to life. He has the state of mind that all good athletes have. Complete concentration. It comes in those too stupid to juggle more than one thought in their head at a time, or those so highly trained that thoughts levitate. Mr. Kirkus started as the first and has become the second.

Then abruptly there are the memories he almost convinced himself were gone. They are huge and so skittish that if he tries to grab them, they'll flee, bury themselves claws-up in the sand, wait until he's weaker to strike. So he leans back into the couch and lets them come.

He feels silly. Not a man to cry and here he is, crying for the second time this morning with the names *Suzie*, *Dex*, and *Genny Mori* running through his head. They jockey for space, they elbow and shout to be heard. Then the phone rings. It's Teresa Hass from the high school.

"Jimmy didn't come to class today, Mr. Kirkus," she says in that nasally whine of hers. "I have in the record that he was due back today." When they were both in high school she used to always be snapping gum. Popped it like it was the punctuation on her sentences. She doesn't do it now on the phone, but Todd imagines it anyway.

He kicks over the coffee table. It skids and then stops. *Where the fuck did Jimmy run off to?* "Well, yeah, he's sick," he tells her. "So that's why he didn't come."

Before he was with Genny Mori, he and Teresa used to take lunches together and hook up in the van. It was how he got gum stuck on the hair around his scrotum one day. When he moved it pulled so painfully, he skipped practice. Pretended he had pulled a muscle. James had laughed himself blue when he heard the story.

"He's sick? Oh, I'm sorry to hear that, Mr. Kirkus."

She lets out a breath where Todd imagines the pop of gum. Gummy Hass, he and James started calling her after that day. Todd can't help it now, he is too drained from the morning he's had, so he laughs a little breathily as he remembers taking the scissors with him into the bathroom, giving himself a little below-the-belt haircut.

"Are you laughing?" Teresa asks. "I don't think that after all your boy put himself through you should be laughing. You should be getting him some professional help."

Todd stops because there it is. Gummy Hass already knows about what Jimmy's done. Hell, the whole town probably woke themselves up by hollering down phone lines like, "You're never gonna believe what that Kirkus kid did." Worst part is that at the heart of it, they're probably talking basketball. About how with Jimmy crazy, the Fishermen aren't gonna be any good this year. Last year in 6A and it's going to be a fiasco. Like that's the thing that matters the most.

"He's got a goddamned headache, Teresa, and NO, I can't god-damn speculate on if he's gonna play ball this season or not!"

As Todd recalls, Teresa hated him after he stopped their lunch-time dates. He had started going with another girl and then after that, Genny Mori. That's the way it always was for Todd—anyone who couldn't have him, hated him.

"I didn't ask about basketball, Todd. You're not the only one who cares about Jimmy. You should see the line we got here to see Mrs. Cole. Students are really taking this hard."

"The guidance counselor?" Todd's voice is thin and bitter.

"Kelly Cole? And I'll bet she's wearing a low-cut shirt too. Let me guess, it's mostly boys lined up."

"Todd, that's no way to talk."

"What're you vultures gonna do when there aren't no Kirkuses left? Huh?" And then more bitterly, "No way to talk!" He slams the phone down.

......

Later that day Teresa takes a concern to Principal McCarthy. The man is shocked by the accusation that what these boys are doing with Mrs. Cole is anything but profoundly mourning the almost loss of their dear friend. That is until he walks in on one counseling session to see that weird Pedro kid getting hugged fiercely into Mrs. Cole's enormous chest, his boner making a micro tent in his sweatpants.

Walk-in counseling is shut down.

The next three days Jimmy doesn't come to school. Teresa doesn't bother calling the Kirkus household. She just fills in the forms herself. *Absent—Jimmy Kirkus—headache.*

Rule 6. Have Something to Prove

JIMMY KIRKUS, FIVE YEARS OLD–ELEVEN YEARS UNTIL THE WALL.

All day Jimmy hadn't said a word to Mrs. Lilly or anyone else in the class, out of an instinct for self-preservation. Even when Mrs. Lilly promised Jimmy the honor of leading the lunch line he refused to speak. He was still spinning from the events of the morning. Father walking him to class, not saying a word. His mother at home sleeping off last night's shift at the Seaside hospital. Taste of strawberry yogurt and toothpaste mixing ugly in the back of his mouth. One squeeze on the shoulder and then the big man gone. People looking at his father, whispering to each other. The other kids all with their moms, or their moms *and* dads, getting three, four hugs. Some of the parents even camping out on the sidelines of the classroom during morning meeting, there just in case. Jimmy with no one. No just in case for him.

Speak? Naw that wasn't for him. Not on this first day of kindergarten. He needed every bit of himself and giving away words counted.

Then at lunch, as he pulled out a peanut butter and banana sandwich, an apple and a baggie of chips, the black hair clip he had taken from the many in his mother's nightstand fell out of the bag too. His mother's hair. Such a symbol of her. Every night she sat at her bedside table and combed her hair while the news of the day was grimly told over the radio. When it was all combed out she clipped it in place with clips—so many clips! To have one with

74

him was to have her with him, even when she wasn't, even when it was becoming clear to him that she didn't want to be.

The kids at the table laughed at his clip, at him. *Aren't those for girls?* So he threw it in the trash—a thin, rare thread that connected him to a deeper part of his mother, gone.

Then recess and salvation. Outside, he saw two classmates passing an orange ball—a basketball—back and forth. Of course he'd seen basketball played from the back seat of his father's van driving through town, flickers of it while flipping through channels on TV, but he'd never actually played it himself. If someone were playing it at the park his father led him into a new game, if it came on the tube, his pops turned the dial.

Right then though Jimmy was alone, and couldn't help but be drawn in. That ball, suspended briefly in the air, seemed magical—something worth chasing until he could hold it. Once held, it seemed big enough to anchor him, at least until he was home again. He was a year older than Dex, but more comfortable drafting off his wisecracking sibling than leading things himself. The background was a place Jimmy preferred. It was from there he was let into his mother's affections most often. From a quiet game played on the floor he could watch her as she talked on the phone, sucked salted *edamame* skinny, discarding the green husks until a small mountain crowded her plate, crossed off check numbers in her checkbook, one ear to the phone, painted her nails or watched daytime television—*Judge Judy* her favorite. Through this study from his blind of shyness he had spotted the rare flash of her smile on occasion, stalking across her face like the deer that sometimes high-stepped into their yard, trembling and ready to bolt. A thrilling peek into what it might be like to always be loved by your mother. And with boisterous, banging, always talking Dex in the picture, Jimmy's contrasting quietness went unnoticed all the more. Alone and trained for anonymity, basketball suddenly seemed like a tempting way out. Just shoot the ball, just pass the ball, just dribble the ball and you were doing it right. It seemed perfect and it overrode his instinct for shyness. He walked right up to boys he'd never met before in his life.

"Let me," Jimmy said.

The little blond-haired boy looked at him, shaking his head. "We aren't letting you, right Pedro?"

Pedro didn't miss a beat, as if it were all planned out. "Yeah, yeah! Come on, pass it to me, David!"

This boy was even browner than Jimmy, about the same shade as Dex. It made Jimmy like him even as he was being mean.

"You don't talk, so you're dumb," David said and passed to Pedro. "We only like people who talk."

"I can talk," Jimmy said. "Look, I'm talking."

They ignored him and his unassailable logic. Pedro accordioned his body down, and then unwound in a burst that pushed the ball up toward the hoop. He missed badly.

Jimmy felt itchiness in his nose and around his eyes. He might cry. All morning he carried an aching loneliness at being away from his pops and Dex, at seeing everyone else's mom come and drop off their kids, at the hair clip thrown in the trash, and now this? Also, he felt—no, our kid Jimmy *knew*—these two little boys were doing this magical thing wrong. He *knew* their playing was a sacrilege, even before he learned what a sacrilege was. Like farting in church, pissing in the pool, stepping on cracks and breaking grannies' backs. There was an itch in his bones to step up and show them. Correct it. But he couldn't because these kids wouldn't let him play. It hurt. He shifted his weight back and forth and stayed at the edge of the court while the rest of recess boiled around him.

Pedro and David kept missing badly. They shot blindly, trusting strength over aim. On one heave from David, the ball careened off the back of the rim—a "brick," Jimmy would soon learn—and flew right into Jimmy's hands.

"Hey!"

"Give it."

And. Well. Jimmy gave it all right. Hell, our kid was born with the *dribble, dribble, drive* pumping in his veins. He was a natural— he was *the* natural. So Jimmy shot two-handed, somehow still beautiful with no form, and the ball arced up and into the hoop, straight and true. Dropped so clean it took the bottom off all three of their little worlds, in different ways.

"Sweet," said Pedro. Jimmy noticed something for the first time on his lips—an accent.

"Bet you can't do it again," David said.

"OK."

So Jimmy teed off again. And he made it again. Our kid was lights-out. He dropped two in a row, and then extended the string to five, then seven, then eight shots in a row. With each shot he made, he got his change—another shot. A rhythm developed. Pedro kept yelling, "Give 'em his change!" and they passed the basketball back to Jimmy's tingling hands and he made another; but also each time he made a shot, David became more angry. Soon he was jumping up and down, screaming, "No fair! No fair, you're cheating!"

It wasn't clear how exactly David thought Jimmy was cheating, but he was red-faced and adamant. By the time the bell rang at the end of recess, Jimmy was squaring up for his last shot, his ninth, and David simply couldn't take it anymore. He ran headfirst into Jimmy's stomach just as the ball left his fingertips . . .

. . . . . .

Back at the Kirkus house, over on Glasgow Street, Dex sat beside one of the big front windows. His parents and Jimmy were the only stars in his sky, so right then, his pops at work, his mom flickering in the bathroom, drawing a bath, and Jimmy gone for his first day of school, the sky was dark. He tapped on the window. He knew eventually Jimmy would come back home, through the front door, and he'd see him first through this window. He tried to imagine the things that were happening to Jimmy at school. He couldn't though. He could only see the things that were really there. The tree. The sidewalk. The mailbox. So he just kept tapping on the glass, waiting for his brother. Tapped one, two, three. And again and again.

. . . . . .

Genny Mori lay on her back in bed. Today would be the same as the last—spend all afternoon putting the house in order with Dex underfoot, then head off to her night shift at the hospital just as Todd was getting home. Come home later as Todd was leaving, sleep through the morning and then do it again. All told she spent maybe twelve real hours with her husband each week. She complained to Bonnie, but then Bonnie had just said, "Welcome to real life," so she'd hung up on her.

And then there was the fact that today was Jimmy's first day of school. Todd had taken him on his way to work. Didn't even ask if she wanted to go. He was good like that, not putting guilt on her, not weighing in on what she should do, how she should divide her time. Ever since Suzie it had been like this. Fine. Just fine. But that was all. A small part of her wished he would push a little harder, demand a little more. It was too easy to hang back. She had started to feel Todd preferred it this way. Had he asked her to be there, she would have probably said no. Still, to be asked.

She'd be angrier if she hadn't just gotten out of a very hot bath. Genny felt the heat unfold off her in wave after paralyzing wave. Light-headed from the effort of getting out of the tub and walking the short distance to her bedroom, she could picture her heart beating in that particularly strutting way hearts have when seen on monitors in the hospital. Fingertips and toes numb, mind dipping and vision blurred, she gave in, fell asleep.

. . . . . .

. . . the ball splashed through the net as Jimmy and David tussled on the cement. Kids gathered around, taking up the universal chant, *"Fight, fight, fight!"* It was the last fight Jimmy Kirkus would win in a very many years.

Meanwhile, Pedro was hopping around yelling in his little accent that squished the *o* on each word, "WOW! WOW! WOW!" For he was the only one to witness the miracle of the Ninth Shot while Jimmy and David fought. For even as Jimmy was getting piled into by David's huge head, the ball was dropping through the net. An improbable, impossible, incredible, nine baskets in a row.

The Ninth Shot of Jimmy Kirkus.

It was Principal Berg who pulled them apart. Father to James and grandfather to David, he was a skinny, crooked old man whose interior spring had gone shoddy with age. Hunched and lilting slightly to the left, he gave the impression of constantly being suspicious.

Principal Berg bent at the waist until he was sure the boys felt his hot coffee breath on the tops of their heads. "Against the wall," he said. He pointed at Pedro, who had stopped jumping around, but still had his mouth wide open, like another "WOW" could possibly escape. "You too." While the rest of the students lined up to go back into school, whispering about the fight, Principal Berg made the three boys wait in silence. Silence was the best discipline trick he'd ever learned.

He tightened the knot of his tie. The incident had made him feel loose, undone. He buttoned his suit jacket. More trouble between a Berg and a Kirkus.

When the playground was empty, he finally spoke. "Well?"

Pedro went first. "He made nine shots in the row!" He pointed at our kid Jimmy, finger trembling. "And the last one, David hit him." Pedro patted his own head. "With his head. And he made it still!"

"He's lying, Pop-Pop!" David shouted.

Principal Berg ignored his grandson. He knew he should think the world of little David, but he couldn't get over it—kid was a whiner. Actually, he'd always taken a weird pleasure in denying David. He was sure it was evilness inside him and so he chose not to think about it.

Principal Berg eyed Jimmy. "Did you make nine shots in a row?"

"I don't know." Jimmy looked away. "I didn't see. He hit me."

"He made nine in a row," Pedro said with the firmness of a true believer.

"Pedro can't count, Pop-Pop," David said. "He speaks Spanish."

Principal Berg stomped his foot and the boys flinched. "Shut your mouth, David." He took a moment to gather himself, turned and patted Pedro on the head. "It's great you're multilingual."

Pedro ducked. "Huh?"

Principal Berg thought for a moment. "Do it again, Jimmy."

"What?"

"Do it again, make nine shots in a row."

So Jimmy picked up the ball and started shooting. He didn't make all of them, but he made enough, including two streaks: one of five and another of seven.

"Jesus," Principal Berg said.

Later in his office, he started making phone calls. He couldn't help it. And new news in a small town is lighter fluid on a barbeque.

. . . . . .

At Van Eyck Beverages, Todd "Freight Train" Kirkus accidently cut his thumb with a box cutter. As he took his time wrapping it with medical tape, he worried about how his son Jimmy was doing at his first day of school. He could feel his heart through the wound in his thumb.

The phone rang on the loading dock and Todd's boss, Ronnie O'Rourke, picked up. After a little talking, the pitch of his voice rose. He put down the phone and walked over to where Todd was loading up a truck for a solo run to Fred Meyer.

Ronnie slapped him on his broad back. "What say, Freight Train?"

Todd shrugged him off. "How's that, Ronnie?"

"Just got off the phone with Shawn, and she just got off the phone with Nell, who ran into Mrs. Lilly. People are talking about your boy Jimmy. He was wowing over at Grey School today. They're saying he's a basketball natural."

Todd had long known this was going to happen. He did. What kid in Columbia City could go to school and not play basketball? It wasn't death and taxes in this little town—it was basketball and rain. Still, gone were the hopes he could protect his boys a little longer from the game that would be anything but a game for them. Todd breathed in. Kept telling himself, *It doesn't mean anything. Stay calm, you knew it was going to happen. You knew. It doesn't mean anything.*

"Yeah," Ronnie slapped Todd on the back again. "They say he's a chip off the old block, or an apple not far from the tree, or . . ." He tilted his head slightly to see how far he could take this. Todd was grimacing, face in profile, so maybe old Ronnie mistook it as a smile, because for some reason he kept going. "Let's hope he's not *too* close to his old man." Ronnie nudged Todd with his elbow.

A kid from across the loading dock joined in, "Yeah, hey Todd—" but he stopped because he could almost see the anger dance off Todd's ox shoulders, heat on cement.

Somehow Ronnie didn't get it. Took the kid's half-said sentence as backup. "Let's hope we don't get another Kirkus letdown!

JIMMY KIRKUS, FIVE YEARS OLD–ELEVEN YEARS UNTIL THE WALL.

Columbia City couldn't handle that, although I bet old Diane'd get wet for the headline potential." He bent his fingers in the air in front of him like he was bracketing a newspaper headline. "Kirkus Curse Strikes Columbia City Again."

That was how they kidded at Van Eyck Pepsi Plant. Mocked one another about the old days. The time you tried to get the girl, drink the booze, win the fight, land the job, and you failed. It was their catharsis. Their therapy. A manly portal into talking about their feelings. The guys kid you, so you kid 'em back, and at the end of the day, everything is out on the table. No couch. No bill.

It wasn't that way with Todd, though. Ronnie remembered too late. It was never that way with Todd.

"Hey, Todd." Ronnie looked around the loading dock but got nothing. The rest of the workers avoided his eyes.

Todd slowed in his actions. Carefully he placed the last crate of Pepsi liter bottles into the back of the truck. He breathed out. Then in again. His shoulders flexed. He wasn't the lithe basketball player he used to be. Years of loading heavy crates into the back of trucks had stacked him up comically top-heavy. Arms so big they didn't lie flat if he put them to his sides but angled out instead, like he was about to curtsy. Chest a barrel, neck a series of thick cables. And angry, Todd seemed even bigger. The other men on the loading dock hurried to busy themselves. An alarm had been tripped in Todd's mind and they were picking up on it. *They're gonna use him*, it screamed. Todd started shivering. *They're gonna use my boy!*

Todd slammed the back door of the truck shut, kicked a crate of Pepsi cans off the edge of the loading dock. They dropped the three feet to the ground and skittered about the tires like fizzy demons. He leapt down after them, breathing hard, climbed into the cab. Engine took on the first turn and he was off.

Ronnie was yelling, stomping, spitting mad. "Get back here goddamn it, that's company property!"

And Todd floored the truck, middle finger out the window, whole rig tipping on his first turn, his daughter's old cow skull, his accomplice, grinning from the dash. He was gone, renegade.

. . . . . .

Jimmy came home but his pops wasn't there. Instead his mother, who should have been at work by then, was pacing in front of the bed, phone at her ear. She wrapped and unwrapped the cord around her arm. It made little white lines in her skin. She wore her nursing uniform. It looked impossibly crisp and clean. Her hair in clips and makeup perfect. Amazing. Dex was on the carpeted floor, watching her.

"I realize that, Mr. O'Rourke," his mother was saying. "But I don't think calling the police is necessary."

Jimmy crept up and kneeled in front of his brother. "Dexy?"

"Pops didn't come home," Dex said.

Something very bad happened, Jimmy thought. *Maybe he died.* In this moment his mouth went dry and he felt very small. Jimmy had a sister who died—he knew that—and it meant you never got to know them or see them.

There was a picture on his mother's bedside table of his sister, thumbs up and grinning, standing in a rain puddle, wearing a blue jacket with the hood up. It was behind the cradle for the phone, so when his mom hung up she blocked it out for a moment with her hand and sleeve. "Come on, boys, we better get your father."

"You know where he is?" Dex asked, face slack with relief.

Genny Mori ignored Dex's question and snapped to look at Jimmy. He was pulling threads from the carpet. "Stop that, Jimmy-boy. You know how carpet is?"

Jimmy didn't know and he didn't care.

. . . . . .

Freight Train drove across the bridge from Columbia City into Warrington. Past Fred Myers and over the next bridge into Hammond.

JIMMY KIRKUS, FIVE YEARS OLD–ELEVEN YEARS UNTIL THE WALL.

He looked out and noticed how sparkly the mud was at low tide. He remembered a story about a man who got sunk waist-deep into that mud when he was out clamming and the tide started coming back in. They couldn't pull him out without ripping him in two, but if they waited, he'd drown.

Past the Shipyard Bar and Grill, the green soccer fields and the turnoff for Camp Kiwanilong, he arrived in Fort Stevens State Park, skidded past the winter-deserted campsites and burst into the Area C parking lot.

His truck was the only vehicle in the lot. He listened to the crates of soda shift and fall in the back of the truck. Ronnie would dock his pay for each broken bottle on top of firing him. Todd didn't care. He was thinking of other things. It was strange to him how the swaying of the trees and bushes growing before the dunes echoed the sounds the crates had made sliding just before they crashed.

He sat in the cab and stared at the trees. Coming back to this place, this place where he had conceived and lost Suzie Q., this was his punishment. He had let her down, and now his boy too. He reached out for the keys to turn off the truck. Hands shook so bad, it took him three tries. *Just a beer*, he thought to himself. *Cool the nerves and then home.*

While Van Eyck Beverages exclusively bottled PepsiCo products, they also distributed a wide variety of beers and wines. Todd Kirkus opened the back of the truck, smelling evil sea, and broke a can off a sixer. He drank the first beer quicker than he meant to. Gone in a blink. He'd go home, soon enough, he just needed to clear his head of his thoughts, so he drank another. Ronnie O'Rourke and the town putting pressure on his kid already? Another. Jimmy was just a baby. Five years old. And another. Still into bedtime stories and all that.

He started to feel warm and that was no good. He wanted to be cold. So he took off his coat. He took a bottle of red wine from the back of the truck and knocked the head off the bottle on the bumper of the truck and drank from the uneven, sharp-edged neck on the way down to the beach. He cut his lip. He walked along the water's edge and it ceased being about cooling off.

He stopped when he thought he had found the right spot, but of course he could never be sure, the beach was always changing. Much better at moving on than he. Todd lay down in the wet sand, the waves touching his feet on each incoming breath of water. Jimmy had been born three months after Suzie died. And so however many years his son had was also how long he'd been without his daughter. A curse in the numbers. Todd stared at the sky. He drank, pouring the wine straight into his mouth from arm's length, only bending his wrist. Red everywhere.

The seagulls screamed at him and the ballooned seaweed, tangled under his head, squeaked when he moved.

That Pacific Ocean up Oregon way, don't kid yourself, she's as cold as they come. As the tide came in farther Todd went numb. He rolled to his side, more weightless with each incoming wave. What a wonderful feeling for a man so used to causing tremors. *She had sand everywhere*, he remembered. Her ears and nose. He had hooked it out of her still-warm mouth with his pinkie. The tide was coming in now. He opened his mouth to the salty water. He swished it, tasted brine. Still, it was not enough to take his thinking away from his head, so with his numb fingers he scooped in the soupy sand and felt the grains jam deeply into the gaps of his teeth. It helped a little. He tried to swallow. Tasted fishy. He coughed and gagged. The polyester uniform with the Van Eyck logo on the front of the jacket turned dark blue, almost black, with the wetness of the sea.

. . . . . .

The Kirkus family had only one car and it was parked down at the Van Eyck bottling plant. Bonnie couldn't give Genny a lift, she was already at work, and Caleb, the one taxi driver in town, was on a cruise in Mexico, so that left the neighbors. However, after years of feuding with the Flying Finn and then Todd over street parking spaces and responsible lawn upkeep, bridges had been burned. Genny Mori couldn't bear the looks these neighbors would give her along with a ride.

So this new take-charge Genny Mori started walking, two boys in tow. It took an hour and a half, but they got there. All on their own, too. Who knew how many people actually saw her—up over the hill, past Peter Pan Park, down the other side, past the post office—and why no one offered to give her a lift, but rest assured everyone in town heard about it before nightfall.

You see poor Genny Mori and her two boys? Todd can't even get her a car of her own.

I saw her up by Peter Pan. The little, chunky one, Dexter? Poor girl had to carry him. I thought she'd be squished!

After all the chances that man had. And her, she was always so beautiful and smart—different, but pretty too.

She could have had things better. But you know her parents couldn't stick so I don't know what to think.

At the lot the van wouldn't start. Genny Mori got it going by having her boys both push against the back bumper while she pushed from the open driver's side door. Ages five and four, hands already dirty. The car lurched forward when the engine caught. Dex fell down, started to cry.

"Shut up a second," Genny Mori said, leaning out of the van, engine revved. "We need to find your father."

And Dex, skinned knees and all, he shut up.

There was a surety in Genny's thoughts that she knew exactly where her husband was—the same place he always ran to. Still, she strained to keep it a deniable surety. Genny Mori hadn't yet lost all she had for Todd. There was still enough lightning in his bottle that she could hope for the shock of not finding him on the beach where their daughter had died. An electrical derivative formed from pity for what he'd witnessed and also guilt at her inability to feel as acutely as he had for the loss of their daughter rubbing together inside her. Also a hope that things were not as bad as they might be. She could pull up and find only sand and sea; and the only thing mourning would be the twisted driftwood left behind. Her husband could be waylaid somewhere with a flat tire—perfectly understandable, perfectly loveable. Not some man in a hurry to hurt, five years distant from the blow.

Still, at the edges, a black doubt that things *were* just as bad as she imagined. A slow-approaching cold front of anger that she felt for her husband. Their little girl never should have died. Their life would still be right side up, if not for him. It was a feeling she disallowed herself to feel—anger. Bonnie had told her that anger was the right way to feel. But no. Letting even just a little of that in would blow the hinges off the whole thing and she'd suffocate.

. . . . . .

Jimmy had rarely ridden with his mother behind the wheel and he was surprised at how fast she went compared to his pops. He and Dex sat in the middle bench seat, not saying a word. Their eyes itched and Dex's jeans were ripped where he'd skinned his knees. Their mom turned the radio on, whistling as she drove. Jimmy watched her lips move in the mirror, wishing he could be closer. Maybe whistle along, or become the actual sounds that started in her mouth and ended in the air. It was a game he and Dex sometimes played. Pretend you're a dog, sleep on the floor. Pretend you're a storm, go blowing through the house. Pretend you're a bird, fly from chair to couch. Why couldn't he be his mother's sounds?

She knew exactly where she was headed, exactly where their pops had gone missing. In around twenty minutes they pulled up

JIMMY KIRKUS, FIVE YEARS OLD—ELEVEN YEARS UNTIL THE WALL.

behind a Van Eyck Pepsi truck in the otherwise empty parking lot of Area C where their pops's truck was.

Genny Mori moved with a quickness Jimmy couldn't pin to her. She was different than the mom who was always on the phone or sleeping large swaths of the day away. She took out two Pepsis from the back of the truck, rare treats for the boys whose father refused to feed them sweets, and shut the sliding door by pulling on the tether. She had to hang with all of her weight to get it to come down, but she got it. She could have gotten anything. Out of nowhere she was amazing. In all his years watching her, he hadn't seen this. "Drink these," she said to her sons. "Wait here and don't go near that." She pointed to the broke-off head of a decapitated wine bottle. "Jimmy, you're in charge while I'm gone."

"OK," Jimmy said. As he watched his mother climb over the dunes toward the beach, he thought, *I like her best now.*

All their lives they hadn't been allowed to go to the beach on account of what had happened to Suzie, but it was still a presence. Only nine miles away, on the sunny days it shined on the far-off horizon out their kitchen window like lamplights bounced off tinfoil. On the windy days salt air blew through Columbia City and across their faces. Far off. A made-up place. Now to actually be standing near sand, the ocean's roar in the background, it was overwhelming.

If it were up to Dex, they probably would have stayed in the parking lot and ripped through the Van Eyck truck, getting sugar-sick on pop. He was like that. However Jimmy knew something was wrong—horribly, horribly wrong—to make this big of a change in his mom this fast, and he was going to see what. He did something out of the ordinary—hell, the whole day was wobbly anyway—and he took charge. Off he went the same way his mom had gone.

"Where you going?" Dex asked over the top of his Pepsi bottle, breath catching a whistle at its lip.

"For a walk."

"Mom told us stay; she said."

"OK, Dexy, stay here."

Jimmy went to the dunes. It was strange, to sink in the sand when he walked. He felt foreign in his own body. Used muscles he didn't know he had.

"Wait, Jimmy!" Dex yelled and started to run, but the bottle slipped from his hands and shattered on the cement parking lot. He stopped and watched brown soda fizzle at his feet. He started to run again, crying, to catch up to his brother. He fell many times in the strange sand.

......

Genny Mori Kirkus found her husband sobbing and rolling back and forth in the soupy tide. He looked to her in that moment a huge baby, face knotted up and red, fists pounding the sand. There was blood on his face and his thin hair was in his eyes. Black sand drooled from his lips. His pants, heavy with sand and sea, had come down, showing half his butt. Genny sat on a nearby log. She shook her head and laughed to herself. Was this how her mother felt when Genny's father split town? Why hadn't she got out before it was too late? What was it? Had she been scared or just lazy? What a choice. Funny, in a small, sour way.

She was tired. Felt destined to take care of this man for always. She was level, she was fine—it was he who had the binges and purges. He who needed the guiding hand. Maybe she didn't run around the house playing Cowboys and Indians with the boys, but she was consistent while he was one phone call away from breakdown. There was a sucking feeling in her heart for him and on one hand it depressed her, but on the other it proved she felt something still, and this relieved her. If life was not going to plan—no out from Columbia City, Oregon, for her—at least she still had the capacity to be devastated by the man she married. "Feel better?" she asked.

. . . . . .

Todd was too out of it for Genny's presence to be a surprise, and he said the first thing that came to mind. "You're drunk."

"Says the man eating sand. I think what you meant to say is, '*I'm drunk.*'"

"This isn't funny."

"Get up, Todd. Ronnie O'Rourke is missing his truck and your son wants to tell you about his first day of school. Rumor has it he's inherited your basketball skills."

Todd sat up, his back making a suction sound. The wind came in. Cold hit him hard, teeth chattered. It felt good to have his wife, his Genny Mori, sweep in, but he couldn't give in this easily. Something in him needed to push. "I guess you love this."

"I don't." Genny Mori looked off down the beach, the wind taunting her eyes.

"I guess our kid could be the best in the league. Everyone'll want a piece and he's only five." Todd wanted to be mean to her. He needed to be mean to her. "Maybe Jimmy makes it to the NBA. Maybe he doesn't let you down like I did . . . How much money you figure you'll need off him?"

"He's five fucking years old. NBA? I'm not the one putting pressure on him." Then, strange, Genny Mori started to cry. She pinched the bridge of her nose. "You don't think I miss Suzie too?" She slid her hand up and she was palming her forehead. "I wasn't here, you were. You were here with Suzie."

The name hit Todd hard, as did her tears, but mostly the blame. Something she'd withheld from giving, even when it had rightfully belonged to him. Here it was. He'd wanted to push, but not this much. He looked past her to buy time, and there he saw his two boys standing on the top of the dunes. When Jimmy met his eyes, his son turned and disappeared, sweet Dex not far behind.

"He saw me," Todd said, tears welling, but Genny didn't understand him. She offered her hand. He took it and stood. The wind picked up, making the cold so piercing, he felt bitten. He hugged her, and her warmth and the breathing of her body shocked him, as did her willingness to be hugged. In her ear he whispered, "It was my fault."

"Don't say that."

"She was wearing a blue coat."

"I know, I dressed her."

"I bought it for her."

"I know, I was there."

"It was too much money. But I bought it for her."

"I know. I know."

And he was happy that she knew.

They stayed like that, almost perfect, for three seconds maybe, and then Genny Mori pushed her husband away.

Cracked heart versus broken one.

"Come on," she said, "You're soaked and we got a lot to do."

Todd squeezed the cut on his thumb from earlier in the day. If he pressed hard enough, blood still came to the surface. He knew she was right, there was too much to do.

At home, Genny Mori drew Todd a warm bath and put the boys in front of a movie. She made him tea and left to go smooth things over with Mr. O'Rourke by bringing a pint of clam chowder from Norma's, his favorite. Mrs. O'Rourke watched suspiciously from just inside the door.

"The funniest thing, Mr. O'Rourke," Genny said, "Todd got two front flats while going the back way to Fred Meyer, and, you know how that back road is ever since the new highway opened, hardly anyone uses it. One flat, fine, he can use the spare, but two? I'm just glad I got there when I did."

Down the block, porch lights lit up, window curtains tugged to the side. Genny could feel people's eyes.

Who's that at the O'Rourke's so late?

It's Genny Mori, poor thing, come to beg for Todd's job.

Mr. O'Rourke's eyes told her that he too noticed people noticing. Genny saw how his temper melted with the shame of her standing like a beggar at his door, the salty aroma of the chowder and her pretty face. "Make sure Todd's ready for work tomorrow." He took the bag with the chowder inside. "And tell him I'm switching him to night shifts with the high school kids." He looked down the street and then back at Genny, speaking louder. "And I'm docking every single broken bottle."

. . . . . .

Todd listened to Genny come home, feed the boys, and tuck them in. He was under the covers, still shivering slightly. Finally, she came into the bedroom and changed into pajamas. Todd watched her and was reminded of what had attracted him to Genny Mori in the first place. She had a brain in her head and guts in her stomach.

She told him casually, "You got the night shift tomorrow. Ronnie O'Rourke expects you." She climbed into bed.

"Genny, my Genny," he said. She had been the one girl who hadn't come easy. He liked that in her. Meant she wouldn't go easy either. And then he acted on a feeling he hadn't had in too long. Draped a thick arm over her side, pushed his pelvis up against the cushion of her butt. His body all pins and needles. She squeezed his hand, not unkindly, and took it off her hip. "You need to talk to them."

So Todd went. God bless her, it was the best she'd ever be to him, for in his misreading of the mood, in trying to make a pass at her when that was the last thing she wanted, when he had been a blubbering child when she needed a man, he had leaned into the first punch of her fight to stop loving him.

Todd crept into the room Dex and Jimmy shared. Jimmy was awake, staring at the ceiling, his eyes lit up by the pumpkin night-light plugged into the wall.

"Your mother tells me you had quite a day," he whispered. He rubbed his hands down his face. Somehow they still felt cold from the ocean. "Something about basketball?"

"What were you doing, pops?"

Todd played dumb. "What do you mean?"

"In the water. You always say no playing in water."

Todd considered it. *What was the best way to do this?* A thought came to him. "Well, I got bitten."

"Bitten?"

"Have I ever told you about the Sand Toad?"

"No, not ever," Dex said—apparently awake and listening the entire time.

"Well, boys," Todd rubbed his hands together as if it would bring forth the story he needed to tell—and strangely, it did. "There's a certain kind of toad that lives on the beach. She's always cold and muddy. She can't jump very far or move very fast. She's ugly and smells bad too."

"Gross," Dex said.

Todd fed off the reaction. "Yeah, gross. Only thing special about a sand toad is she takes growing seriously. Big as a car."

"You're kidding us," Dex said sincerely.

"I'm not kidding you, I wouldn't kid about something like this . . . She's huge but it's very weird because she thinks she's small."

"What's she eat?" Jimmy asked, one eyebrow higher than the other, just like the Flying Finn.

JIMMY KIRKUS, FIVE YEARS OLD—ELEVEN YEARS UNTIL THE WALL.

"What's she eat?" Todd wanted to wipe that look off Jimmy's face. How'd the old man find a way in? "They eat. Well, seagulls of course. She opens up her big mouth—and it's just the same color and feel as wet, grimy sand—and she flicks her tongue. A trick tongue. On the very tip there's a part that looks like the tastiest bread crumb you ever saw. When a seagull flies down to get it, then, WHAM, the sand toad closes her mouth and dinner is served." Todd clapped his hands and startled his sons. He had them now. Oh boy, did he ever.

"But see, here's the thing. The sand toad isn't happy. She doesn't think she's special. She hates being cold and muddy and scared all the time. She hates sitting in the sand all day long and feeling small. Worst of all, she can't stand the taste of seagulls. She *haaaaates* the taste of seagulls.

"The one and only thing a sand toad wants is to be human. Be warm and eat all kinds of delicious food." Todd paused and dropped his voice into a whisper. "And there's only one way for a sand toad to change human. She has to get brave enough and bite three people on the foot. Then she'll change into a human herself."

"Bite?" Dex asked.

"Scary, I know. But it's even *moooooore* scary for her," he held up a finger, "because remember, she *thinks* she's tiny. She *thinks* she's going to be stepped on. With the first bite she'll be the same shape as a human. This takes, oh, three months. But she's still got the *skin* like a sand toad, wet, grimy, and gray; and she's still got the *eyes* of a sand toad, yellow and slanted; and she's still got the *tongue* of a sand toad, thing with a bump on the end just like the tastiest bread crumb you ever saw."

"And then what?" Dex, again.

"When she bites someone else, she'll lose the sandy skin and the yellow eyes, but she won't be able to talk because her tongue still has a thing like a bread crumb on the end. She won't be able to hide anymore because she's got human skin. So she'll go live in the forest or the bathrooms of a mall, waiting until she can bite one more human . . ."

Todd paused, let them squirm.

"And if she bites that last human, she'll be a full person. Smartest kind too. She'll make lots of money. She'll spend it all on food and clothes and heat for her house. She wants to get rid of the small and un-special feeling of being a sand toad. She'll pay a person to sit by her. This person's only job is to tell her how big she looks, how special she is."

Jimmy kicked away his blankets. "And you got bitten! What happens to people bitten? The bitten people? What happens to them?"

"They start turning slowly into sand toads. That's where sand toads come from. First their eyes go yellow, then their skin goes sandy, and then all the rest. That is unless the bitten person goes back to the beach every time something on him changes and gets some sand toad tears. If he drinks these then the changes stop."

The story lingered in the air. Todd stood, went to the doorway. "At least for a little while."

Rule 7. Never Flinch

JIMMY KIRKUS, SIXTEEN YEARS OLD—FOUR DAYS AFTER THE WALL.

It's in a shoebox in the very back of the closet. Underneath the limp, drifting hem of Genny's old wedding dress got at discount from Geno's—lace caught with jaundice now. This is the shoe box Jimmy's first basketball shoes came in. Todd hadn't been there when Jimmy opened them but Genny said she had never seen the kid so happy. Running circles, saying how fast his new sneakers made him, Dex trying to keep up. Poor little kid just wanting Jimmy to stop a second so he could confirm his suspicion that the shoes glowed in the dark. Poor little kid.

Todd Kirkus flips the box top and pulls it out. A yellowed newspaper clipping. He comes back to this more often than he'd ever admit. It's an anonymous letter to the editor that ran in the *Columbia City Standard* November 22, 1985. He reads it again now because he was with Jimmy three days ago during his low point, his black abyss. The thought of his son smashing his own head into a wall has kept Todd up these past three nights, going over Jimmy's life, his own, his father's—everyone ever connected to the kid—to try and figure out how something like this could happen. All that bullshit about the Kirkus Curse, was it real? Was his family destined for crash down, flameout? The newspaper scrap is an artifact of his mental dig. When it was published it wasn't the low point for Todd, not anywhere near it, but it was the start.

Maybe if he can remember himself from that age, when things started to go wrong, he can understand his son better.

Could Freight Train Derail Fishermen Basketball?

Todd "Freight Train" Kirkus missed a Fishermen preseason game against Clatskanie yesterday. He didn't have the flu, or a death in the family, or low grades—Todd Kirkus missed the game because he was playing for someone else.

The Knights are a tournament team based officially out of Portland, but they pull kids from all over the state. Their colors are red and silver, the very same colors as our rivals, the Seagulls. But who cares, right? They're just colors.

I'll tell you who should care: Coach Kelly, Finn Kirkus, and most importantly Todd himself.

I know people will say it's all about numbers, and he got more exposure playing in the Northwest Invitational than a preseason game. Well, I agree: it's all about numbers. Let's crunch them.

44, 12 and 11: that's the number of points, rebounds, and assists our Freight Train racked up on his way to being named MVP of the Northwest Invitational. There were a lot of college coaches and even some NBA scouts there to watch, but does it really matter anymore? Todd Kirkus is going to be able to play wherever he pleases, with or without the Northwest Invitational.

1, 1 and 11: That's the number of games played, the number of games lost, and the number of other Fishermen players who had to watch their run at a championship repeat pause for the Todd Kirkus show.

Todd "Freight Train" Kirkus is derailing Fishermen basketball and yet we still cheer him on. After all, not since the Tall Firs has Columbia City been blessed with such basketball success and we'll do anything to be a part of it.

JIMMY KIRKUS, SIXTEEN YEARS OLD–FOUR DAYS AFTER THE WALL.

The problem is, it's a crash we're going to get—because make no mistake, the selfishness of Todd Kirkus will only lead the Fishermen astray—when we showed up for, and deserve, something greater.

The Flying Finn had been livid when the morning paper came. Wanted to know just who the hell wrote this thing. In a small town where it almost seemed everyone's name could fit in Bic on the back of your hand, it was shocking to think there might be a stranger, a traitor, in their midst. It made Todd self-conscious. And while he was no stranger to his father's erratic outbursts of rage or jubilation or an odd, comical mixture of the two, this was something on a whole new level.

Shortly after slamming the paper down and breaking a glass in the process, but before chugging the remains of his coffee and choking on the grinds so his white shirt was spattered with brown splashes, and then ripping the collar as he tried to take it off, and then giving up halfway and keeping the tattering, spotted shirt on, the Flying Finn yelled, "I'm gonna tear the roof off! Give them a star player and they starts a witch hunt!" The Flying Finn went off in a storm to the *Columbia City Standard*'s office, looking much like the destitute man he was destined to become.

Todd stayed home, embarrassed by a father so vocal and public. And the letter to the editor? Was it really so bad as it made it seem? He figured the guys would have rolled Clatskanie without him. Little team from out in the woods. How was he supposed to know they'd choke? And what did it matter? Clatskanie wasn't a league game; it didn't even count for their official record. He couldn't be expected to do everything for the team. He had to look out for himself sometimes.

A couple of hours later, the Flying Finn came home looking exhausted and sad.

"What happened, pop, you find the guy?"

"Don't worry. Never worry. Anonymous letter means nobody."

And it occurred to Todd that his father looked a way he had never looked up until then. Old.

. . . . . .

So Freight Train reads the letter now to remember what it was like. One line sticks with him especially: *Make no mistake, the selfishness of Todd Kirkus will only lead the Fishermen astray.* It burns. He'd been one game away from proving them all wrong. But why should he have ever had to? He comes to a conclusion. In cases like his and his son's, the whole town is at fault. They're awful, despicable, child-abandoning people. 'Cause when you start telling a kid they're special and better than everyone else—and they aren't even your own kid—then hell, you're adopting them. You don't have any right to put that kind of weight on someone's shoulders. When they win, fine, but what about when they lose, and there's no faith left, and you leave them alone, drowning? That's neglect right there. They wouldn't have been in a position to take on so much water in the first place if you hadn't of convinced them they could make it rain.

For Todd, the whole town of Columbia City let his son down. They let him down. Todd has half a mind to pack the van, load up his school-skipping, self-destructive son, and be gone.

Instead Freight Train reads the article again, to figure out the secret code inside. He knows he can make things easier for Jimmy. He's sure the key's in there somewhere. Something that will let his poor son sidestep the Mack truck of attention bearing down on him.

And hell, he might be right. Anything that's not nothing is something.

. . . . . .

The first time Jimmy called Sarah Parson, RN, was yesterday, from a pay phone. She had answered on the fourth ring. He heard the sounds of people talking in the background.

JIMMY KIRKUS, SIXTEEN YEARS OLD—FOUR DAYS AFTER THE WALL.

"Hello?" she said. "Hello?" she said again, this time breaking into a higher pitch on the second syllable. Then she had shocked him by saying his name. "Jimmy? Is this Jimmy?"

He hung up on her. Now he's calling again. It's Friday, the fourth day in a row he's playing hooky from school and wandering the woods instead. Head's feeling better, though still mushy, still dull with pain. He's at the pay phone outside the Mormon church—or do they call it a temple? Jimmy doesn't remember, he just knows that when he sees them around town in pairs, so dorky in their shirt-and-tie getups, he feels comforted to know there are people even lower in the social hierarchy than he.

"Hello?"

He waits out a car tooling past, as if whoever was driving could eavesdrop from forty feet away. "It's Jimmy."

"Jimmy. You want to talk?"

"You said it's never bad as it seems."

"I believe that; it never is."

He's gripping the phone handle. Thoughts of Dex, his mom circling. Can't get the scene from wearing out the reels in his head. Imagines every detail as though it were happening to him. Can't stop. Then when he tells himself to stop, he's *still* thinking about it because he's purposely not thinking about it. Hell. "It's pretty fucking bad for me."

She breathes out. A beeping sound passes by in the background on her end and Jimmy imagines himself on a hospital stretcher, rushed to a new room, all hands on deck. Save his life. Back into the whirring machine. Mind reader. "Yes, Jimmy, it's pretty bad for you."

"You ever seen me play?" He isn't sure why he's asked this, but there it is, and he finds he can't wait to hear the answer.

"Play what?"

He laughs, like yeah right. Then her silence, so he says, "Basketball."

"I've never been one for the sports."

"You're screwing with me, right? *The sports?* You've heard about me, about me playing ball?"

"No, Jimmy, I haven't. I mean, I should have guessed it. I used to watch your father play and—"

She's cut off, a recorded voice asking if he would like to put in more money to extend the call. Naw. This is a good out. He hangs up.

Breathing hard, this reminds him of coming home after his first day of kindergarten, having discovered basketball. Flying up the sidewalk and through the front door. He had so much to tell. He'd been to school! He'd made friends with a boy who spoke two languages! He'd been in a fight! He'd been in trouble! And most importantly, the biggest thing of all, he'd learned about basketball! He had rolled the word around his mouth with the tip of his tongue. *Basketball, basketball, basketball.* But nobody was in the living room, the place his pops said he'd meet him to hear all about that first day of school. "Pops?" Jimmy called out. "Pops!" He ran through the dining room and the kitchen. Still no Pops, no Dex either. In his parents' bedroom he stopped. There was his mom. Come into a situation expecting joy? Anything but can lay you flat. Same here with Nurse Parson. Only opposite. Expect after-school-special-too-sticky-sweet and come away from it actually feeling better. What the hell?

. . . . . .

Later, from the cover of the trees, he's watching two men in Subway uniforms throw up half-assed shots at Peter Pan Courts as he dulls the edge of Sarah Parson, RN's words in his head. *I've never been one for the sports.* One of the guys shooting isn't bad. Clearly he's played a little ball in his day.

Jimmy hears the bushes behind him rustle. He's not scared though. Hell, when kid Jimmy and Dex used to creep for hours back and forth through the bush-whacked animal highways on their missions to find the beautiful game, they came across all sorts of things. Raccoons, deer, stray dogs, half-naked teenagers. He remembers one time coming up on a couple of kids, probably still in middle school—though they seemed huge to him then. They sat side by side, staring straight ahead. The boy had his left hand up the girl's shirt and was moaning, saying, "I got them."

Then Dex threw a stick. Crash. They both scrambled off the log like it had been a grenade, boy running ahead as girl called after him, "Hey! Come back!" She fought to straighten her shirt. Fucking Dex, always looking for an angle on a joke.

What if you like hard-boiled eggs and hatching has nothing to do with it? Then you think it's OK to count your chickens before they hatch 'cause you're only after the egg anyway?

So Jimmy isn't startled by the noise now. Whatever it is, he's seen it before. He turns and faces the bushes. Out comes an old man. He's back to wearing that green motorcycle helmet and is dirty as hell, but he's the same guy in the face and eyes. Look close, it's the Flying Finn.

"Grandpa, what the hell?"

"Jimmy, that you?" The Flying Finn's eyes are milky and his chin keeps shaking. "Jesus, you are the sight for the eye sores. I hear some the guys say you crazy, all the way around the loop, or the bend, or however people say this thing, and I told those guys, I's say, look who's calling who crazy, you crazies!"

Jimmy doesn't think his grandpa can even see out of those opaque marbles he calls eyes and this makes him almost sob. "Grandpa, I—Are you doing OK? I haven't seen you in—"

"Would you quit crying already? There's been enough of that for a whole long while. Only reason to cry now is if you lose a lovey, and I's lost plenty and yous lost none, 'cause you never get loveys. Are you a gay boy?"

"Grandpa, your bike's gone."

"Last thing I need is a kid telling me things I already knows."

"Where is it?"

"My coach stole it. A Swede bastard." The Flying Finn looks down at his hands turned to claws from scraping up food from wherever he can—always half-sprung into a grasp. Then his eyes water a little and he looks up with the same twinkle Jimmy remembers from back when the old man made him and Dex cut flowers out of Genny's little front-yard garden for his loveys. "You go into Peter Pan store and you buy old Flying Finn some eats. Huh? What you say for that?"

Jimmy's still got lunch money his pops gave him, so he comes out of the bushes in the middle of the day when he should be in class. Out from the wilderness. He walks across Peter Pan Park to the small market that's been selling sweets to the kids of Columbia City since back when the Flying Finn first came to town.

The two Subway workers have stopped playing basketball. They sit smoking cigarettes on a bench. When they see Jimmy, they stop talking. The bruise on his forehead might as well be green neon and in the shape of a pair of legs the way they're staring at it. Hungry almost. Jimmy hurries. His balance shifts, as it has so often in these days since the wall. He stumbles one step to the side, he worries he'll vomit.

"Hey there, Jimmy," one of them says.

Jimmy ignores him.

"Hey, Kirkus, they say you're crazy."

"Crazy." The other one laughs and then sputters his lips with his index finger, making loopy sounds until they're both just busting up. Jimmy guesses they're high. He hurries on to the store.

He picks up four boxes of Boston Baked Beans and three Moon-Pies, both favorites of his grandpa's, and heads to the counter. A familiar-looking girl behind the till has some sort of glitch in her operating system. Until she noticed him, she had been scribbling

JIMMY KIRKUS, SIXTEEN YEARS OLD—FOUR DAYS AFTER THE WALL.

away in a black leather journal. Big-looking words that she'd savagely cross out every other sentence or so. When she notices
Jimmy, she stops. She's biting her lower lip and her eyes flutter,
unable to choose what feature of him to focus on. Jimmy's a little
concerned. What he doesn't realize is this girl's just starstruck.
Being in the store alone with the one, the only, Kamikaze Kirkus.
She's the same girl who asked him if he'd be OK in the hospital,
but Jimmy can't place her, not yet.

He puts the candy on the counter but she doesn't move. "I'll just
buy these," he says, to get things going.

She finally snaps out of it and fumbles with the boxes and plastic packaged fluff. The scanner won't take the last box of Boston
Baked Beans. The cardboard is crumpled around the barcode.
She's sweating. The scan gun buzzes instead of beeps each time it
fails to read the barcode. The girl says, as though chanting a
prayer, "Sorry, Jimmy, sorry, Jimmy, sorry, Jimmy."

"Just scan one of those again." Jimmy points at the first two
boxes of Boston Baked Beans that went through fine. The buzzing
of the scan gun is giving him a headache. His focus floats. He
thinks he sees something scuttling out of the corner of his eye.
Sandy, cold.

"Oh yes, oh, YES!" she says and scans the first one. Beep. Right
through.

Jimmy squints his head clear and pays.

"Jimmy, are you worried, you know? About 6A? You not playing
this year because of that? Are you waiting for next year, when
we'll play at 4A? I heard that the teams in 4A are much worse."

It's her voice. Sound almost close to shattering. *She's the girl
from the hospital*, he thinks, and then, quickly after, *she's pretty*.

"I'm just . . . don't really play anymore." He hurries to get out of
the door before the talk continues, paper sack full of sweets tight
in his hand.

"Hey Jimmy?" she calls out.

"Yeah?" he turns back.

"I'm Carla."

"I'm Jimmy," Jimmy says, but then, realizing the redundancy of it, he gets embarrassed and quickly leaves. The bell above the door dings.

......

Then it happens—the gossip spreads. Not because Carla wants it to, or because she's a bad person, but because she is new in the small town she has moved to, and wants desperately to be a part of its social scene.

She would be a freshman in high school if she weren't home-schooled. In her spare time she often writes poems. She wrote one this morning about Jimmy, in fact, called "Oh Kamikaze, Why?" Her father is the preacher down at St. Mary's Star of the Sea Chapel. Her mother, when she's not teaching her and her brothers, runs the youth group. She's only been in town a year, but she knows all about Jimmy. He's a story she can't get enough of. She picks up loose conversations that are dropped in the aisles of stores or tossed over gas station pumps. She's pieced them all together in a giant, oral mosaic.

She can't believe she called out to him as he left. The sensation just before she did it was like something rising in her bowels. *Maybe I'm sick*, she'd thought. *No, not sick.* Just a little bit of reck-lessness bubbling up in her up-to-that-point carefully plotted life. She's heady.

Jimmy's this weird kid who hardly says anything—at least not anymore. There are rumors that he talks to himself now, just like the Flying Finn. People say he's turning into a ghost, roaming the woods, looking for the people he lost. Carla's heard it all. Her fin-gers are itching to call the friends she's made at youth group and finally *be* the start of gossip. Nobody had believed her when she

JIMMY KIRKUS, SIXTEEN YEARS OLD–FOUR DAYS AFTER THE WALL.

said she saw Jimmy in the hospital. This time they'll have to believe. It's *her* turn to tell *them* something they don't know. Something they can't deny. Say, "You're never going to believe who came into the store just now. Yes! Kamikaze Kirkus—he bought Boston Baked Beans and like MoonPies." So she dials.

Then whoever she calls, calls someone else, and the story shifts until it's, "Guess who went into Peter Pan Market and stole twenty boxes of Boston Baked Beans and ten MoonPies? Yeah, Kamikaze Kirkus. He's bonkers."

Baked Beans and MoonPies? Shouldn't he be in school?

He's a delinquent. He's over at Peter Pan Park right now, really losing it.

Might head over just to see.

Just to make sure.

Me too.

Poor Carla doesn't know it, but she's the lighter. . . . Doesn't really matter though. If it's not her, it'll be someone else. Kid Kirkus is gasoline.

Rule 8. Be a Bit Off

. . . .

Wednesday, October 15, 1997

JIMMY KIRKUS, SIX YEARS OLD–TEN YEARS UNTIL THE WALL.

Jimmy and Dex were out of the house, flying. They ran down Glasgow street, through the Barnes's backyard—careful of Sam the dog, his chain goes farther than you'd think—out on to Alameda and then into Tapiola Park. Across sloping fields where people walk their dogs and kids use broke-down cardboard boxes to sled the grass, digging big streaks of bruised green.

"Do you hear it?" Jimmy asked.

"No!" Dex said.

"You don't hear it? 'Cause I hear it."

"No, not yet, do you? Really, do you really hear it, Jimmy?"

Dex was bigger than Jimmy already, but slower too, and huffing to catch up. His brother's feet ate up distance with an amazing appetite, like Sonic the Hedgehog after some gold rings.

"They're playing! I can hear it!"

The basketball courts weren't even in sight, there was no way he could hear balls bouncing. And yet. "Jimmy, wait up. No fair, come on, wait."

In the year since they saw their pops wallowing at the beach in the soupy incoming tide, a lot had changed. Ronnie O'Rourke had pushed Todd into working night deliveries with the high school kids, a punishment. This meant Genny Mori started working the day shift with a recently hired doctor named McMahan. So here it was: when Jimmy and Dex came home after school it was to their let-anything-fly mom, instead of their too-watchful pops. All they had to do was be back to the house by dinner, and it was fine. Most days, Genny was too busy gossiping on the phone with her friend Bonnie to even notice the boys had left. Jimmy and Dex took in how their mom didn't particularly care if they were around and this drove them out all the more. Basketball gave them reason to ignore their mom before she could ignore them. We're not alone, we're looking for a game; we're not lonely, we're just waiting to be found. They ran to the outside world with its wide-open possibilities of revealing the beautiful game every chance they got.

They were almost there, one more grassy rise and then a long sloping spread of park to the Tapiola basketball courts. Dex *could* hear it by then, and he was amazed that his brother Jimmy had heard it so far back—the sounds of basketballs bounced, guys grunting in effort, calls of "*And one!*" and "*Foul!*"—and it only cemented further the mythical place Jimmy held in Dex's mind. He was shy in everything else, let Dex take the lead, except in this, except in ball, and Dex loved the game for this reason. With Jimmy on basketball, he was the little brother.

There were eight guys playing four on four. Two more sat on the grass, watching the game, laughing and calling out taunts. Also—*look!*—three basketballs not being used, lying beautiful, just waiting for Jimmy and Dex to grab hold, dribble and shoot at the opposite side of the court from the real game, ears pricked for any sounds of play coming back their way.

This was an every-day-after-school thing for these two brothers. They roamed unattended through Columbia City, looking for the paved squares of basketball heaven that popped up in city parks. Running secret trails, hopping fences, skirting drunks, all to get to the next court. Always the next game. In the past year since Jimmy had discovered basketball he'd converted completely, like how some come to religion. An instant, intense, before-and-after thing. There was something preordained in hoops. It was a fact that wasn't lost on the town: all anyone could talk about was how Jimmy was taking after his pops. Teachers, other kids at school, the bus driver on field trips, all had memories—first-, second-, or even thirdhand—of his pops playing for the Fishermen. To play basketball was to step into a role Jimmy felt—even at so young an age—written for him. A relief. With a little dose of context, he didn't need to worry about who he was because his last name was Kirkus. Kirkus = basketball. He'd got his brother to buy in too. So he and Dex were just two kids jonesing for a bounce, praying for the rain to hold off for just a little while longer.

People who saw them couldn't believe it.

The Kirkus kids? Naw, couldn't be them.

No, it's them. Little half Japs. Dark-skinned like their mom. There's not another like 'em in town.

You seen these kids around?

They show up at any court in town if there's a game going on. It's like they can smell it.

Where are their parents?

How these little kids watch games so patiently? They should be shouting, crying—you know, scraped knees and gum bubbles out their mouths. Not watching like this. Creeps me out.

Kindergarten and first grade? Damn. Don't sleep on them. I've seen them make shots you wouldn't believe.

Jimmy shot and Dex rebounded. Then, when the game came back down, they ran off the court, watched some sloppy play unfold, before someone missed, or made it, and the game went galloping off to the other end. Then it was Dex shooting and Jimmy on the bounds. Switch and repeat. Repeat. Until the lights went on, until the players, steaming from their workouts, zipped up their duffels, left. Repeat.

So it was Jimmy's turn to shoot. Dex snapped the ball back to him and he made a few in a row. Then there was a breakaway in the game. Someone picked a pocket at the top of the key and Dex wasn't quick enough to warn Jimmy. *"Run!"* Some knee-braced sweat-machine, all facilities focused on dribbling, running, not messing up in front of the guys, didn't see Jimmy in time. Ran our kid down. Scraped knees. Wind gone. Covered in this guy's sweat. Disgusting. The weight of him. Guy got up, and then pulled Jimmy up after him.

"What the hell, little dude?" the man said. He was someone Jimmy recognized. Then again, it was an odd occurrence when Jimmy *didn't* recognize a person in Columbia City.

Jimmy stood up, chest heaving.

"You OK?" The man put a hand on his shoulder. "Just breathe. You got your breath knocked out of you."

"Fat as you are, I'm surprised the kid isn't loose a lung!" someone said.

Jimmy looked back at where the other men were standing, arms making triangles as they held their hands at their waists. He started off the court with the ball he'd been using. *I won't cry*, he kept telling himself.

"Listen, I'm sorry, but you got to get out of the way. You could get hurt."

Jimmy kept walking, ball on hip.

"Hey, pass it," one of the guys from the sidelines said. "That's my ball, give it here, kid."

Jimmy rolled him the ball. Suddenly the other men were getting theirs as well. Basketballs zipped up in bags.

"Maybe enough for tonight," another guy said. "You need a Band-Aid or something?"

Jimmy did not. What he needed was a basketball of his own.

But how? Every time he asked their parents to buy him one, he was told there wasn't money to spare. And so basketballs became hugely expensive, precious objects in his mind. Still. It was the tipping point. His inalienable rights might as well read: life, liberty, and the pursuit of hoops.

. . . . . .

The next day, Jimmy got his chance. David Berg came to class with the brand-new basketball he got for his birthday, and Jimmy had an idea.

"This the one they got in the NBA," David told everyone. "Real leather and genuine size."

"You seen the glow-in-the-dark basketballs?" Jimmy asked. Imagine, being able to play the beautiful game even after the sun went down.

"Those are for babies. This ball's real."

Jimmy shrugged. "OK, let's play."

"I don't want it dirty."

"If it's the real thing, than let's play," Pedro said. "Me and Jimmy versus you and whoever you can think."

"You, you and Jimmy?" Ever since the Ninth Shot, Jimmy and Pedro had become inseparable. It was one thing to lose your best friend, it was another to lose him to your worst enemy. David practically boiled. "That's not fair."

"OK," Jimmy said, "We'll play you and I won't even shoot, only Pedro."

The small crowd of kids who had gathered sank into whispers. The story of Jimmy and David's fight was famous. A prominent footnote to the Ninth Shot.

"Um." Jimmy had him in a tough spot. If David played and lost with Jimmy not even shooting, he'd never hear the end of it. Then again, if he didn't play at all, he'd be tagged as a scaredy-cat, and never hear the end of that either.

JIMMY KIRKUS, SIX YEARS OLD—TEN YEARS UNTIL THE WALL.

"I told you," Jimmy said, "I won't even shoot."

Pedro interrupted him: "Ah, Jimmy, I."

"I won't shoot and if you win you can throw the ball at my head, hard as you want."

This was too good to pass up. "OK," David said.

They played with that beautiful leather basketball, just like the NBA guys used, and every time Jimmy touched it, he passed. Poor Pedro played valiantly, but he was a little bit slow, a little bit fat, and a lot a bit off with his shot. Jimmy stuck to his word. He never shot the ball.

When David and his teammate won, eleven to two, he had Jimmy stand a few feet away so that the rest of the deal could be completed. The crowd of kids hushed. Jimmy stared straight at David, never flinching.

David addressed the crowd. "It's like how my dad says. Even if you are the best shooter, you need good teammates too, and Pedro isn't any good."

"Fuck you, puta!" Pedro said.

The kids oohed.

"Shut up, or I'll tell on you," David said.

"Doesn't matter, your *abuelo* don't even like you."

Jimmy turned away from David to look at Pedro and David saw his chance. He whipped the ball straight at the back of Jimmy's head. The crowd watched breathlessly. Pedro's eyes widened, he wanted to tell Jimmy to LOOK OUT, but the words were stuck.

Then, just as the ball was about to hit our kid Jimmy square on the melon—quite a good throw from David, really—a miracle. Jimmy spun around a moment before it was too late and caught the basketball. The leather snapped against his palms, ball humming a centimeter from his nose. The crowd, God bless them, erupted in cheers. Jimmy smiled at David and said, "Thanks." Then he took off, running for the far end of the playground, Pedro whooping at his side, David in pursuit and all the other kids following, laughing and screaming at the tops of their lungs. A rain was just starting, finally acting on the threat the gray skies had been issuing all day. With a thrill, Jimmy felt the first drop detonate on his forehead. More touched down just after. He pumped his legs faster.

"No fair!" David shouted. "No fair!"

"Viva Jimmy!" Pedro yelled back.

. . . . . .

Dex sat in his kindergarten class. He hadn't said a word the entire first month of school—even more stubborn than Jimmy in his refusal to speak. The teacher would often look back on that speechless month with nostalgia, because after Dex started talking, he didn't stop.

Dex looked out the window and saw his brother running across the playground with the most beautiful basketball in the world held in his hands.

"Basketball!" Dex shouted. "My brother and a basketball!" His teacher dropped an armful of Play-Doh canisters. When they hit the floor the kid-dirtied globs jumped out in a dull rainbow. "My brother and me, we love basketball!"

. . . . . .

Back at the Kirkus household, big Freight Train, alone and lonely with those northwest winds knocking on the windows, the raindrops tattooed with the day's spectrum of light, burned his lips on the coffee he was sipping. He spit it out across the table and poured the rest down the drain. It was terrible. He noticed how many coffee grains were mixed in with the sludge at the bottom of his cup, and this made him very sad.

He wiped the table with paper towels.

. . . . . .

Genny Mori sat at the coffee counter in the hospital cafeteria. She was trying to ignore the persistent stares of one Dr. McMahan. He was a little guy, tanned and bowlegged. A large easy laugh and ready opinions. Great smile with deep dimples asterisking each side. He had eyes like galaxies being born, each time she looked into them they seemed to have changed. Well-formed hands that he used when speaking, to shape his opinions and ideas, which she found herself following even when she wished she weren't. He was always wearing the mask of whiskers coming in, a five o'clock shadow that Bonnie called a *five o'hot shadow*. He had these sticky little looks he'd paste on her at the hospital that she found later in her thoughts, long after she was home from work for the day. She fumbled with the sugar dispenser while he stared at her. Spilled sugar all over the countertop. She wondered if it was the same as salt, if she should throw some of it over her shoulder.

She should have.

. . . . . .

Down along the docks, on Marine Drive, the Flying Finn pushed a shopping cart. This was deep into his first homeless period. He wore a green motorcycle helmet and Todd's old, purple warm-up jacket. He had disappeared after Suzie's funeral, wild with grief and the pressures of his failing restaurant. Now he was too dirty, too bearded, too ragged for most to recognize. It was a hard life he lived, but not an impossible one. He'd learned about a few warm places in town to sleep—a grate on the backside of River's Bakery that spewed warm, doughy air was especially nice—and he never got too hungry because it was understood that if he knocked on the back door of Fultano's Pizza he'd get a medium cheese, no questions asked, and his son, Todd, would pay the bill.

Still, some days were better than others. A car full of high school kids out for lunch cruised past. They used his green helmet for target practice. All out of pennies, they threw quarters instead.

Clatter, clatter, plunk!

"You sons of dogs!" the Flying Finn shouted. "*Female* dogs!"

The car honked back happily.

All in all, $2.75 dropped to the street around him, and he sung as he collected the coins: "We will, we will, ROCK YOU!"

......

Coach Kelly was down in his health class, thinking about what a bunch of bums he had going into next season. Diane, the sports reporter at the *Columbia City Standard*, was scheduled to call him in a few minutes to talk about the Fishermen's chances in the upcoming season. What chances? What he wouldn't give for another player like Todd Kirkus. He would have literally, no exaggeration, given his kidney. Who needs two kidneys anyway? He went out to the hallway pop machine to buy a Pepsi before his students came. Instead of cola, out came a beer. A practical joke by some Van Eyck Pepsi deliverymen.

Ha ha, the joke's on them. It was just what Coach Kelly needed. He put in a few more coins, made sure that the next can out was Pepsi, and went back to his classroom. He poured the beer into his empty coffee mug and then crumpled the can and buried it beneath papers in the wastebasket. He sat at his desk and sipped, waiting for the call.

Diane's first question was "We can't be too good next year, can we Coach? Tillamook and Scappoose look awful strong."

Coach Kelly blamed the beer for how he answered. "You know, before we got Freight Train Kirkus, we were terrible. One stroke of luck can turn the boat around."

The next day the newspaper ran an article with the headline *Coach Kelly Waits on Next Star Player*. Coach was furious.

"That's not what I meant!" he shouted across the breakfast table.

"Then next time, be sure to say what you mean," his wife told him.

......

In his tiny house on Youngs River, James Berg and his wife were in exhausted reset after another fight. They hugged, weeping. He promised to find a better job, she promised to spend another week thinking about the letter she'd just received. When they met in college neither of them pictured themselves living on the edge of a river, feeling always wet, getting by from paycheck to paycheck on what a custodian made. She had been an English major with dreams of going on to get her doctorate and that would never happen in Columbia City. Too small, too isolated, the cloud cover a suffocating cap, but that very afternoon a break in the gray—an acceptance letter from the University of Washington's graduate program.

"Do you mean it?" he asked.

"Yes, I'll think about it for another week," she said. "But you and David could come up to Seattle. A new start."

"I know, but David has his friends here and his grandfather and—"

"Todd's here too."

Really, she'd already made up her mind to go, they both knew that, but it felt good to pretend for a while that she hadn't. Not for himself but for David. A small flock of raindrops expired on their kitchen window, pushed fatally off course by a gust of wind.

"Oh, wow," she said, walking away, "it's raining again, what a surprise."

. . . . . .

David couldn't catch our kid Jimmy before the recess bell rang. After all, what sort of a legend would it be if he did? Jimmy went into class, chest heaving joyfully, and he sat with the ball under his chair. Later, when Principal Berg called him into the office he said, "Bring the ball too."

The class said, "Ooh, you're in trouble."

The teacher said, "Quiet now."

Pedro said, "Viva la revolución."

. . . . . .

Principal Berg sat Jimmy and David in his office. David was squeezing out sobs. Berg wondered again if it was a sin to hate your own grandchild. And if it was a sin, how bad? All his life he'd struggled with the gap between how he knew he should feel and how he actually felt. He remembered his son's junior year, when Freight Train was still the hero, pushing around opposing teams and sending shock waves into the bleachers and out into streets beyond. All of Columbia City had bobbed with it, acknowledged that, *yes, this is US, this is OUR team.* A feeling that had strangely been absent during and after the championship game the following year when Todd was suspended for his troublesome drinking and James finally got the chance to be the hero. *Why hadn't James been enough?* He had found even himself missing the electric feeling of the first championship season as his own son held up the trophy for the second. What kind of father did that make him?

Principal Berg made the boys wait, as was his usual strategy, and took a framed picture from off his desk. He turned to look out the window and down to the street below. Fog choked everything. It had rolled in shortly after the rain. From his office window it was easy to imagine the school as a ship and the fog the sea. The photo was of the Fishermen championship team his son's junior year. He slid his thumbnail into the small crack between the glass and the wood frame, the boys watching him intently. He pulled up the glass and then the picture too. Behind it were yellowed newspaper clippings, two or three of them—letters to the editor he had written. They were thin and brittle and with one good breeze they'd be no more. He sighed and he could have sworn that he felt all of Columbia City sigh with him.

"Jimmy," Principal Berg said, "David tells me you stole his new basketball."

David stopped crying to watch how it would play out and Principal Berg took this the wrong way. Bratty little tattletale. He knew David had a hard home life with his mother and father always fighting, but why couldn't the kid have a spine?

JIMMY KIRKUS, SIX YEARS OLD—TEN YEARS UNTIL THE WALL.

"He threw it at my head when I wasn't looking," Jimmy said, solemn faced. "He threw it really hard," he added, softer.

"David?" Principal Berg asked.

With the attention turned to him so quickly, little David accidently answered with truth. "Yes, Pop-Pop, but it's no fair 'cause—"

Principal Berg held up one finger to stop the red-faced David's blubbering. Another thing that grated on him about his grandchild: the nickname Pop-Pop. He'd never chosen it, had never agreed, and yet David insisted. "So you tried to throw the basketball at Jimmy's head?" He tsked under his breath. He knew David had been swindled, he just wished it had been the other way around. Jimmy was this quiet kid who seemed to only ever think about basketball—basically an idiot savant. How had he managed to trick David? Principal Berg could have restored justice, got David's ball back for him, but he wanted to foster in the child a backbone. Some spunk. Perhaps this would make him try and get the ball back on his own, not always go running to the adults. He turned to Jimmy. "Won't you leave my grandson and me alone for a moment?"

So Jimmy left, basketball in hand.

. . . . . .

Later, when James Berg heard the whole story, he dropped his spoon in his bowl of soup. "Goddamn Kirkus," he said. He got up, intending to make a call, make things right, happy for the distraction from his suddenly wifeless household, but then paused. "It's just a ball, Davie. We'll buy you a new one tomorrow. Now come on, eat your Campbell's."

"No fair," said David. "I don't want another basketball. I hate basketball and I hate soup and I hate you." He ran up to his room, slammed the door.

James listened to the bang and then got up and dumped the rest of the soup down the drain. He called out for pizza that night. Pepperoni pizza might make telling David about his mother easier. The kid loved pepperoni pizza.

. . . . . .

When Todd came home from a long shift, his lip still hurting from the coffee burn, he looked in on his boys. There was Jimmy, curled around the basketball, sleeping the intense sleep of children. Wait, a basketball? Todd didn't know. He just didn't know. The house felt invaded, and somehow temporary. A wind could blow it down. The things you fear the most, and prepare for the best, are never solved or banished for good. They are in constant need of shoring up and will never be put completely to rest.

He went to bed and woke Genny Mori. Put his hands all over her. Rough, ready, somehow he persuaded her to have sex. Shared *this* with her when he couldn't share anything else.

"Doctor," she said in her sleepiness and Todd didn't notice.

. . . . . .

So Jimmy Kirkus had his basketball. It wouldn't leave his side for many years to come. No one could tell for sure how Jimmy knew to spin around at just the right moment before the ball hit him in the head. Kid was a natural, that was it. Had a sense. An intuition. The Force was strong in him. And on and on.

The Catch became a part of the Kirkus legend.

JIMMY KIRKUS, SIX YEARS OLD—TEN YEARS UNTIL THE WALL.

Rule 9. Blind 'Em

. . . .

JIMMY KIRKUS, SIXTEEN YEARS OLD—FOUR DAYS AFTER THE WALL.

Jimmy leaves Peter Pan Market with the Boston Baked Beans and
MoonPies for the Flying Finn crinkled in a paper bag, mind fizzy
on Carla. He's so distracted that he doesn't even consider going
around the block, coming back to his grandpa the back way,
avoiding those two hecklers, until he's halfway there and they've
already seen him. Turn now and he'll make it worse. The two Subway minions resume their teasing, "How'd you hit your head, huh
Kamikaze?"

"This kid is in serious need of a straitjacket, right, D? The order-
lies know you're out in public?"

Jimmy stops walking. There's something crackling inside his
body. A bigness he didn't know he had. "Shut up," he says.

He takes in the men. There are details he didn't notice before.
Like one of them is older by a few years. And the younger one is
punk for sure. Kid who normally wears black eyeliner, earrings,
and leather with conical, metal studs. But he looks silly today because he's wearing the green and tan Subway uniform so the only
way you can tell he's punk is from his black eye makeup and his
stringy, black hair.

And suddenly Jimmy sees it. It's David Berg and the bigger guy
is Ray. Ray Atto. Used to be a big shot on the team. Was a senior
Jimmy's freshman season. He's gotten fatter since high school.
Rounder. A certified townie. Find him down at Desdemona's the

second his shift ends. What an odd alliance. Just two years ago and a high school hotshot, Ray would have been shoving effeminate Goth David into lockers. Now here they were, teaming up to mock Jimmy.

"The fuck you say?" Ray says.

"Why aren't you in school?" Jimmy asks David.

David shrugs. Giggles. "Work study."

"What the *hell* you just say?" Ray persists.

Jimmy shakes his head. "Nothing." He keeps walking. He's got Mr. Berg's eyes on his mind. First thing he saw coming out of the ether after banging the wall was a set of those Berg eyes. He's surprised to see the same ones live in David's head.

"Hey Kamikaze!" Ray shouts.

Jimmy doesn't turn around but he feels the ball hit him hard in the back of his head. Jolts his vision like the DVD skips. He halts. The contact with the basketball, the leather and air, it touches him deeply. Into his brain, down through his organs. Reaches within his sore head, finds the switch for pain, and then rips it from the wall. Forces him to take account of it. No wonder catch this time, no miracle.

"You want to play a game?" Ray taunts. "Old time's sake and all that?"

Jimmy turns and picks up the ball. He can feel his energy run down through his hands and into the basketball. He spins it on a finger and warmth spreads throughout his hand, back up his arm. That newfound crackling bigness is in him again. It threatens to burst him at the seams. He can't understand this. When he was little, basketball was so easy Jimmy's come to see that time as the setup for his fall. Life can't be easy, that's his new theory. But even when basketball was easy, it never felt like this. He'd always felt small, in deference to the game. Now here he is, big old spirit springing up. The game a thing to use. If it's not this then it'll be

JIMMY KIRKUS, SIXTEEN YEARS OLD—FOUR DAYS AFTER THE WALL.

something else. And how strange, to feel bigger than a game that once seemed enormous. Still, he's got to play or he'll punch Ray or he'll scream like a lunatic. No, ball will be better. If it hurts, it hurts. He's felt worse. Just put Ray in his place, that's all he's got to do. "Yeah, let's play, OK?"

"Hey look," Ray says, and walks up beside him. "I'm a beat the once-upon-a-time Jimmy Kirkus." He lowers his voice, pretends it's just between them. "Buckle up." For those with a life not going according to plan, a game against the once great Jimmy Kirkus— Jimmy *Soft* as he's been recently known—can cure all. So look how Ray elbows Jimmy in the ribs when he reaches for the ball. The air seeps out. It hurts, but Jimmy smiles for the license the pain gives him. He's been knocked enough to do some knocking of his own. Finally.

"OK, let's play," Jimmy says again.

"Let's play, let's play!" Ray blubbers sarcastically. "That the only thing you can say since you hit your head, retarded? You're *still* Jimmy Soft." Ray thinks he knows the keys to beating Jimmy Kirkus, just like every other guy in the state. Knock him around a little and there goes his shot. It's common wisdom. Doesn't take much to rattle him.

Thing Ray doesn't know is that this isn't the same Jimmy anymore.

Of course Jimmy makes the shot to get the ball first. Kid can still shoot. Ray tents his hands before him, like all the kung fu movies he's seen on TV, and bows.

"This how they do it in your country, Kamikaze?" Giggling, like it's the wittiest thing ever done, he looks back at David on the bench. "Shao Lin!" he shouts.

"Just check," Jimmy says, passes him the ball.

Ray dribbles hard a few times, between the legs, behind the

back. Skills are still there for sure. "You know, only thing good came from Japanese is pork fried rice."

"That's Chinese, you dick." Never has Jimmy wished violence on a person as much as he wishes it on Ray right now.

"Whatever, same thing. This is a favor, me playing you. I could get the Kirkus Curse rubbed off on me." Ray passes Jimmy the ball. He had once worked at Van Eyck with his pops. Then he got fired for taking product home. Now he's stuck making sandwiches, minimum wage, at the Subway. Plastic gloves, would you like a drink with that? "Look, maybe with this head injury and all you'll just sit the fuck out this season, jump back in it once we're down in 4A, playing with the children. That's more your speed. Don't have to embarrass yourself."

Jimmy catches the ball and the game starts. Ray drapes himself over him, poking at the ball however he can, scraping with his sandwich-oiled fingernails. He rips another elbow to his gut. Jimmy absorbs the blow. Feels it push out all the air in his lungs. His head is rolling. He spits up a little. Bends over and brings the ball close to his hips. He feels the pain pulse out of his body, feels that crackling bigness inside him.

Look! Jimmy's smiling to himself again. He brings the back of his head up sharply into Ray's sternum. Ray grunts and steps back, surprised, Jimmy can tell. He isn't the same Freshman Jimmy who was thinner than a ghost and eager to please. Jimmy takes the space opened up and drives hard for the hoop. Dunks neatly for the lead.

Ray can't help himself, says, "holy shit," at Kamikaze's hops.

From then on, every point scored by Jimmy needs to go through Ray's body. A layup past the point of his chin. A turn-around jumper with a knee-jab into his crotch. A runner with an elbow into the soft, fleshy part of Ray's bicep.

JIMMY KIRKUS, SIXTEEN YEARS OLD–FOUR DAYS AFTER THE WALL.

Ray's wheezing so hard that he steps back to call time-out and find his lungs. Soon he's doing it every time Jimmy scores. The Flying Finn comes out of the bushes with our man Jimmy up seven to zip. He finds the bag of MoonPies and Boston Baked Beans Jimmy left lying on the sidelines. Rips open the packages and chomps down greedily until there's thin, brown-red paste covering his lips and dribbling down his chin. He's giggling and saying over and over again, *Thanks, Jimmy; thanks, Jimmy; thanks.*

And meanwhile, see, a strange thing is happening. The news that Carla ignited is spreading throughout town. From phone to phone it jumps. Text messages and voice mails. "You'll never guess." Kids in school are counting down the moments until the end of class, coordinating rides, whispering routes. Adults are making sure they're in the neighborhood so they can stop by and see. Peter Pan Courts are halfway to everywhere in Columbia City so it doesn't take long. Even before the game with Ray is half over, people are showing up. They come to see famous Kamikaze Kirkus breaking down, and instead they find some real round ball. The small lot for Peter Pan Market is completely jammed with cars. They're walking down to the court in small groups. Quiet, respectful still, but their chatter creates a rustling. They're mostly adults at first, like the mailman stopping mid-route, or gray-haired Officer Aight keeping peace and looking on from the hood of his car.

Ray holds up his hand for time, gathers himself, and in this action Jimmy remembers Ray exactly as he was in high school. The Great Ray Atto. He was all-league every year he played for the Fishermen. His face is so disguised in layers of the sweaty salami he sneaks into his fat mouth during his shifts at Subway that Jimmy didn't really see Ray as he used to see Ray until just now. That senior on the team when Jimmy was a freshman coming up. A used-to-be stud jealous over Jimmy's flash.

"Wait," Ray says. "I got to get back to my shift."

"Oh, come on, Ray," someone calls, "Let the kid finish you off."

"Finish me? I was just getting ready to—"

"Ready to what?" crows the Flying Finn, his Adam's apple hard at work pushing up words through that skinny neck. "Meaner basketball player I's never seen." The Flying Finn's rounding into fine form, to the old shouting promoter he once was with Todd. "Kirkus blood runs hot and strong. Hot and strong. Sorry Ray *Eat-Toe*, you don't got chances in hell." The Flying Finn runs around the court flapping his arms and growling though his teeth. Hopped up on MoonPies and Boston Baked Beans. Dangerous. Jimmy looks on, surprised to find he's not embarrassed by the old eccentric like he used to be; this is his grandpa, this is his family. Stand up now, stand up together.

The crowd—'cause now, see, there's enough people that it's a legit crowd—laugh with the Flying Finn, jeer for Ray to play on, and vibe on the general energy.

Jimmy sees them all seeing him and it's like a hug. An envelopment that pulls him tighter into himself, calms his flailing soul. He doesn't want to be soothed by it—fuck them—but he finds he can't help it. He hears them whispering to one another, feels that spark.

Look it here.

Who's that?

That Jimmy Kirkus?

Kid got big.

Head doesn't look as bad as they say.

Playing who? Ray Atto? No way. Just no way.

Moves pretty good, huh? Maybe he'll be ready to play this year. A real shot at 6A on the way out after all.

Look it. Look it now!

They laugh with and at Grandpa as he runs. He's a local celebrity—the famous Flying Finn. Mouth going nonstop, one hand on the top of his green helmet and the other clutched in a fist at his side. He circles around and around the court. Big skinny dude like a blow-up man at a car lot. Air running right out the top of his head.

"Ray *Eat-Toe*, you wake the Kirkus up in young Jimmy, so now you will beat him maybe? But only if you didn't have to get back to the work?" The Flying Finn keeps turning to the crowd as he talks, like he constantly needs to be reassured they are still on his side.

"Listen, old man, can't lose a job," Ray says, voice crackling. "My girl's pregnant. I don't wanna get fired and end up homeless and crazy just like you."

The crowd oohs and Grandpa howls and Jimmy says, "Well," but then something happens. Little David Berg, all grown up and punked out, priorities mixed, skipping school to work an extra shift at Subway, steps in and says, "Yo, Ray, I just called Tommy. It's cool if we stay longer." All eyes on David now. He wilts, speaks quieter. "So you can finish the game."

Ray hunches his shoulders like he's been handed down a death sentence—and really, he has. He's gonna be the footnote in Jimmy's legend. The first casualty of the comeback. Jimmy looks at David and wouldn't you know it, David smiles before he looks away.

Everything forgiven in a second? Hell, it could happen.

Jimmy scores the last four buckets to win right through Ray's sternum, and once, his neck. Blows Kamikaze inflicts on Ray just like he's been taking himself in every high school game he's played for the Fishermen. Little chippy stuff that might otherwise seem like dirty play, but in the realm of sport is lauded as playing tough. Hits that hurt, no doubt, but are discrete and precise enough the ref would probably never see, certainly never blow the whistle on. Jimmy's taken so many of these over the years, he gives them as a maestro.

For the game-winner, Jimmy dusts off some vintage touch. Right after he gets the check from Ray, he splashes down from almost half-court. So far out, he divorces from gravity. You keep this world, I'll take the next. Leaves the crowd gap-mouthed like fish brought to deck. His shooting arm extended up, hand pointed down, frozen in form—he's the hook.

Somebody shouts, "Hey Ray *Eat-Toe*, got something in your eye?" and everyone laughs, even Jimmy a little. Ray stomps forward toward the crowd, his fist cocked like he just might try and punch out every single person. Then he turns for a second like he'll take a swing at our man Jimmy, but Jimmy doesn't flinch like, you want me? I got more than you can take. The crowd jeers louder. Ray melts. Wanders off taking taunts, red in the ears, muttering to himself.

Jimmy laughs out loud and the people are laughing with him. Here it is, a joy in the game, the beautiful game. Used to be he was scared to mess up, now he's just loving the process. It could be this, or it could be a thousand different things.

After Ray, opponents step forth from the crowd to challenge Jimmy, and he beats every single one. Jacked-up tough and looking for a test.

School's out so the kids crowd into cars and the back pegs of bikes to come watch Jimmy beat any and every comer. It's the Friday before Winter Break and everyone's already hopped up on the short season of freedom from class to come. There's nothing holding them back. They'll stay out as long as they like. And who will stop them? Boys pinch girls and girls slap back. Someone is passing around a big bag of M&M's. Everyone, including the losers, tingle with the sense that *this* is special. Kamikaze scraps after every ball, smiling and laughing and grunting and sweating; sweating, swatting, and galloping. Scraping knees and elbows, forehead and lip, he plays on until he's in such a tornado of fury

JIMMY KIRKUS, SIXTEEN YEARS OLD—FOUR DAYS AFTER THE WALL.

and fun that he beats the Johnston twins at the same time. Two on one and it feels like they are the ones outnumbered. His stomach lurches and his head aches. He pushes past them. Just little things. And the kicker is this: Jimmy doesn't get scored on once. Unstoppable. He seems to levitate over the cement. He's in the zone. To the crowd he's moving with almost supernatural quickness; knows the future, gets there before it happens. To Jimmy though, it's effortless, everything slow; he's got all the time in the world. The basket as big as the ocean, it's harder to miss than make a shot.

It's one of those "Hey you ever hear about" things. Like *Hey, you ever hear about the time Kamikaze Kirkus ran his own fool self stupid into a brick wall and then three days later beat ten guys in a row, including the Johnston twins two on one? Yeah, those Johnston twins. They were all Cowapa League! Can you believe it?*

Hey, you ever hear?

By the ninth game, the Flying Finn is still running as fast as his failing lungs allow him around the court. Hooting like some wizened, stretched-out monkey. He's giddy. He's always known deep down in his immigrant bones that him, or his son, or his grandson, was going to be great.

The crowd wants to take from Jimmy again, and poor Jimmy, he's still willing to give. They cheer and he nods his head. He wants to keep going. Keep this feeling alive. He's feeding on a love he thought he'd lost. That desperate "I need you more than you need me" love that is so powerful and full of poison. And even with nine pickup games under his belt, he could keep playing. Growing stronger with each step. Feet lighter. He could go on forever.

Part Two

Rule 10. Get Help from Unexpected Places

Sunday, October 22, 2000

JIMMY KIRKUS, NINE YEARS OLD–SEVEN YEARS UNTIL THE WALL.

Jimmy was in the backseat of a luxury SUV, getting a ride to his ten-and-under tournament with the Johnston twins and their mother. Genny Mori had to work, as did, allegedly, his pops.

On the way to the tournament, Mrs. Johnston got lost in the large-numbered blocks of Southeast Portland. Everything looked the same. Huge grids of neon-topped stores, big glassy buildings, and too-perfect office parks. Jimmy sat alone in the very back, unsure of what to say.

"Don't look so serious," Mrs. Johnston said, eyeing him in the rearview. "We'll find it."

Jimmy smiled, didn't say anything, the car smelled of new plastic.

"Mom, Jimmy doesn't really, like, talk," said one of the Johnston twins—Jimmy could never tell them apart.

"Brian, don't be rude," Mrs. Johnston said. Her eyes cut to Jimmy again in the mirror. "We'll win the tournament. You're just like your father, Jimmy, I swear to God. Didn't think genes could pass down something like that, but . . ."

Jimmy put his head down between his knees. Breathed in and out. He was used to this. Whenever he was out with his pops, strangers came up to ask the big man if he was playing anymore, talk about how they remembered when. Been that way since forever. Pops always changed the subject, batted down the question with a big paw like Jimmy did when kids at school asked him how come Dex—a second-grader—was already taller than him. It made him proud that people noticed his pops, respected how he had once played, but then if it were really true, why didn't Todd tell Jimmy about it? Or teach him some of his basketball secrets? He hardly ever came to watch either of his sons play and Jimmy had learned not to ask him about his balling days. Pops would button right up. "I was OK," was what he'd say, then back to dinner, homework, bed. Other people's praise of Todd Kirkus up against the man's steadfast refusal to acknowledge it created a dissonance in Jimmy's mind he dealt with by settling on something in the middle. Sure his pops had played ball—who in Columbia City *didn't*—but people were probably exaggerating about him being a great.

It hurt, the feeling that everyone else knew more about your father than you did. Still, all those things they said, "Like father, like son," or "Apple doesn't fall far from the tree," made him full up, if only for a moment, an affection he somehow credited his father because he felt in on the secret. It was a shaky conveyance of love that went: His pops was once something, and he was like his pops, so he was destined to be something too, something his pops would be proud of even if the old man wouldn't say it. And so his pops loved him.

Bottom line, though, the topic of basketball was a dead space between father and son.

Mrs. Johnston trailed off and Jimmy played a game with himself: if he didn't take his head out from between his knees once, if he just stared at the gray carpet, until the Yukon was stopped and they were at the game, he would do well again. He would win the game and people would keep talking about how he was just like his old man.

When they finally found the gym, the game was five minutes in and our Columbia City boys were already fifteen points down. Jimmy and the Johnston twins rushed into the locker room, started changing. Jimmy unpacked his duffel, pulled on his uniform, listened to the crowd cheering, felt like this might just work. He could still get in there, will his team to a win. There was just one problem: Jimmy had forgotten his shoes.

Even from the locker room he could tell his team was getting beat down by the way his coach was yelling. It drove Jimmy crazy. He wanted to get out there and help. Our kid paced back and forth, tugging at his hair. If he couldn't do well here, then some chain would be broken, he was sure of it, bad things would happen.

The Johnston's mom came in, frazzled. "What's the problem, Jimmy? Get out there!"

"*Mom*, this the boys' locker room," one of the Johnston's said.

"Forgot shoes, Mrs. J," Jimmy said.

"Well, wear your street shoes."

Jimmy looked down to his feet, Mrs. Johnston followed his gaze. He was wearing flip-flops.

"Brian, give him your shoes."

"His feet are way big," Brian said.

"Jesus, how big, Jimmy?"

"Tens."

"What size do you wear, Chris?"

"You don't know?" Chris, the other twin, whined.

"Just tell me."

"Sevens."

The Johnston's mom tried to run her hands through her hair but they snagged—blocked because of the copious hairspray. Small-town fashion wisdom held that style and product were interchangeable. Her hair stuck up. "Small feet."

"I'm only eight."

"Well, so it goes with a father like yours." Then an idea. "Look,

Jimmy, I'll run out and get you some shoes. Tens? Boys, go out there and see if you can help in the meantime."

"Don't forget the ribbon!" Chris said. Ever since their coach's son had joined the army, everyone on the team had to tie red, white, or blue ribbon into their shoelaces on game day.

"Would you just focus, please?"

So Jimmy was left by himself, watching from the locker room doorway, waiting on shoes while his team got beat. Other team had this guy named Shooter Ackley. Some kid a year older out of Seaside. He was killing them and it tugged at Jimmy's stomach, his heart. So. So he went. Waited until coach called a time-out and then trotted onto the court barefoot, tapped one of the Johnston's on the shoulder and said, "I got it."

I got it. He got it? Who was this kid?

He started playing before the coach even knew he was in the game—wearing no shoes at all. Ran up and down, shooting, driving, passing. Tired the bigger Shooter Ackley out with his relentlessness. Confused him by showing no fear, attacking, attacking, attacking! Five toes vs. Nikes.

The ref, just a college kid looking to make some weekend cash, didn't notice at first. Then, when a parent from the other team— a tall, brittle mom with blouse and shoes that matched the color of her eyes—charged onto the court and yelled, "get some fucking glasses, ref; kid's not wearing shoes!" the poor ref was too tied up with issuing technical fouls to do anything about it. By the time he had everything calmed down again and the tall woman removed from the building, both head coaches ejected, he'd forgotten all about the issue that had started it in the first place—Jimmy's bare feet. The ref blew the whistle for the game to start and Jimmy promptly dropped a three. This led the opposing assistant coach to throw down his clipboard and stomp into midcourt during play where Jimmy's own assistant coach eagerly met him. Play was again paused as the ref set about calming down both coaches. By the time things were in hand, Mrs. Johnston was back with a cheap pair of Payless sneakers and Jimmy was ready to go.

And there it was. Even though Jimmy only played a little more than a quarter barefoot, it was forever dubbed the Shoeless Game. Jimmy torched the nets for thirty-five points and led his team to victory. Holy hell he had sore feet to prove it. Jammed toenail bled red, medical tape holding ice was white, blisters all over the soles of his feet blue. Forget the ribbon, kid was an American hero on his own.

I got it? Kid was well on his way.

You hear about *that*? The Shoeless Game?

. . . . . .

The Flying Finn certainly did and it gave him an idea. He needed money though, so he went and begged for a job at Norma's Chowder House. Norma, the owner, made him a deal. He could sleep on a cot in the supply closet every night and get $10 a day so long as he picked the parking lot clean every morning and was gone before the lunch crowd came.

Finn sat in the parking lot, happy with a job well done, every bit of trash that had littered the cement now in a plastic grocery bag tied to his belt, ten one-dollar bills crumpled in his pocket. With his green motorcycle helmet on all sounds he made—breathing, grunts, even licking his lips—came back to him as echoes. He picked his teeth with a splinter and it sounded like cannons firing. Triumph. He didn't realize it, but this was the first step in his journey back. He hummed that favorite song of his. *We will, we will, ROCK YOU.*

. . . . . .

By the time Jimmy got back to Columbia City from the Shoeless Game, word had already spread. It was October and everyone wanted to be Jimmy Kirkus for Halloween. Forget about Jimmy being a chip off the old block, he might just be a block in his own right. Dex wrapped him up in a bear hug, his mom tapped his head.

"You . . . are the champion . . . my fri-eennnnd," Dex sang, off-key.

Jimmy laughed, bit his medal like he was checking if it was real gold.

But when his pops got home, he wasn't happy. "What the hell, our kid doesn't get enough attention, he plays a game in NO SHOES?" A full head of steam, he glared at Jimmy. "What the fuck is that?"

"I forgot them," Jimmy said.

"You, for. You forgot them?"

"Nice language, Todd," his mom said. "Maybe if you'd go to a game once in a while you could."

"I could what, I could what, I COULD FUCKING WHAT?" And Freight Train steamed out the front door. "Now it's my fault?" His question rolled off the neighbor's roof. He picked up a pumpkin, one they were planning on carving later, and smashed it down in the front lawn. It exploded on the stiff, frosty ground. Then he came back through the living room, knocking over a dining room chair on his way to the bedroom. Everyone breathed shallow in his wake. Maybe they'd choke if they took in too much.

"Come on, boys," Genny Mori said quietly. "Let's go celebrate. Ice cream at Dairy Queen. I'm buying whatever you want."

"Triple-fudge banana split!" Dex shouted.

But something was wrong with Jimmy. He was breathing hard, quick. Something rising in him, he couldn't tell what. Everything in the whole day was inside his chest—no shoes, hurt feet, winning the tourney, his pops, and the pumpkin—and only breathing could keep it down. So he did more of it, and more. His head grew light. There were a lot of things in the world he didn't understand— why Salisbury Steak was on the lunch menu, how spiders got into every single room, how to grow taller—but his father's weirdness about basketball was top of the list.

"Jimmy?" his mom asked.

Jimmy was going to explode. He took his basketball and threw it after his pops with all his might. Shouted some wordless insult that came out as high-pitched as a girl. It knocked over a vase, which shattered on the floor.

"Oh," Dex said and looked at his mom.

Genny Mori sighed, took Jimmy's hand, and walked him to the door. "Let's go eat ice cream." He was too worked up to even feel a thrill at the rare gesture of his mom grabbing his hand.

. . . . . .

Todd heard the crash. Heard the high-pitched scream. He winced. *Genny.* He stopped pacing the room and lay on the bed. His anger leaked out to make room for growing embarrassment. The scene replayed in his mind. He wished he could change it. Tweak the character playing Todd until he seemed fatherlike. What was he to do, though? It was all for them.

When he was absolutely sure they were gone, he left the bedroom. The last two months had been tough. Raising Jimmy right, protected, was his repentance for the loss of Suzie, but once his son joined a team, he hardly saw him. He was always at practices or games. Dedicated like Todd had once been. The talk of the town. And now everyone was going to think Todd couldn't even buy his kid shoes.

He went into the living room. There was Jimmy's old basketball among shards of broken vase. Scribbles covered it entirely: whenever Jimmy learned a new basketball legend, he added it onto his ball. Todd picked it up. He felt stuffed full of sand and he had felt that way for a while. He was tired of it. He set the ball on the table and swept up the broken vase. The basketball watched him work. He picked it back up. He ran his thumbs over the names written in Sharpie. Little-kid handwriting in some places, but Jimmy had gotten older. Most of it was in neat block letters now. Clyde "The Glide" Drexler. Earvin "Magic" Johnson. Wilt "The Stilt" Chamberlain. Michael "Jumpman" Jordan. Anfernee "Penny" Hardaway. Gary "The Glove" Payton. Rasheed "Sheed" Wallace.

Todd left the house carrying the ball, ignoring the smashed pumpkin. Up the street away from Dairy Queen. He remembered this route from when he was a kid. The neighbors used to lean out windows and shout, "Hey Freight Train," and "Choo-choo!" Little kids followed him, begging for autographs, sure his name on a piece of paper would be worth money someday.

Todd took a shortcut through the Lanes' backyard. Just like old days. *Hey, Freight Train. Choo-choo!* He wondered when exactly it had changed. When the adoration rotted and turned to jealousy or disdain. Probably when his father started pressuring him to skip preseason games to play in Portland for a tournament team, the Northwest Knights. A good way to increase his exposure—play against some real competition. And all in all, he enjoyed it. It was nice to throw his weight around with some players good enough to push back, even if it was just a little bit.

It hadn't gone over well in Columbia City, though. Small towns carry and distort news like a cave does noise. *Could Freight Train Derail Fishermen Basketball?*

Nope, playing for the Knights hadn't gone over well at all.

. . . . . .

Jimmy, his brother, and his mom came home sticky with ice cream to find a little man sitting in a black car outside their house. The driver's side window was open, the engine running.

"Genny," the man yelled.

Jimmy noticed his mom light up red at the sound of that man calling to her, and though he didn't know what it meant exactly, he wished she hadn't done it.

"Doctor McMahan," she said.

"Looks like some poor pumpkin met his demise." The doctor made a sweeping motion with his hand over the guts of the smashed pumpkin laid out on their lawn. The engine tone shifted higher as it worked to stay running.

Genny forced a laugh, started walking toward the car. "You know kids and their pranks."

"Mom?" Jimmy asked. He didn't want her to talk to this man. He couldn't explain why. They'd just got back from eating ice cream until they were sick, Genny telling them a story about a turtle who held the whole world on its back, laughing when Dex then pretended to be a turtle, waddling between the Dairy Queen tables. It had been close to perfect long since Jimmy had any right to hope things could be that way with her. Now off she went, to this stranger.

"Jimmy, take Dex in." She bent down next to the driver's window.

Fine, but the house was empty and Jimmy's basketball was gone.

"Come on," Jimmy said, already running toward his parents' bedroom. Sometimes his pops hid the basketball, and his mom would bring it out a few days later, shaking her head and saying, "Look what turned up." Even though it was a firm rule not to go snooping in their parents' room, there was something different about today. The smashed pumpkin. His father's unleashed rage. Jimmy's hurt feet and how he had lashed back, breaking a vase, and then wasn't even punished, his mother leaning into the window of some strange man's car. Some sort of agreement had been broken, and until a new one was established, anything went.

"You look in the closet, I got under the bed."

"We're not supposed to," Dex said.

"Nothing'll happen." And to prove it, Jimmy took a step toward the bed. Dex breathed in. Jimmy exhaled out. "Trust me." He dove under in search of his beloved ball. Dex ran into the closet, laughing with the nervous joy of breaking rules.

They had made a bet while eating ice cream at Dairy Queen. A

bet on a game of basketball, of course. The loser would do the winner's chores for a week. They taunted each other while they looked
for the basketball. Then Dex stopped talking, and Dex never
stopped talking, so Jimmy climbed back out from under the bed.

"Hey, Dex?"

His brother was there, on the floor of the closet, scrapbook open
on his lap. "Jimmy, look it," he whispered. "It's pops."

"What do you mean?" Jimmy sat down next to his brother and
together they learned about a man with the same face and name
as their pops . . . A man who played basketball and he was good.
Damn good. It couldn't be the same tired-eyed, quick-tempered
Pepsi-delivery man who hated basketball—*that* was their pops.
But this younger man in the scrapbooked articles, tight jersey and
dorky too-short shorts, was somehow their father too. Freight
Train. All those people talking at Jimmy, they hadn't been making
anything up; Todd Kirkus had been good—dang good. A great.

Page after page after page of yellowed newspaper. Headlines
that their father's name dragged across the page. *Kirkus Powers
Fishermen.* Grainy photos of their pops. *Freight Train Rolls On.*
Frozen mid-jumper, mid-pass. *All Aboard! Freight Train Behind
Another Fishermen Win.* Young, fit, and fierce. Excitement coiled
in Jimmy's chest so he wanted to scream. His pops might as well
have been Superman.

"Jimmy, look it here," Dex said at each new, amazing photo.

". . . holy shit . . ."

Todd "Freight Train" Kirkus was his pops.

. . . . . .

Todd stood in front of the steel-rimmed hoop of his youth. Double-
rimmed, you had to have all kinds of touch or you'd be shooting
bricks all day long. It hadn't changed much. He pounded the ball
off the cement three times. He breathed deep and then took an
awkward shot, as if all the specific parts of his shooting motion

had been snapped off and then glued back together, cracks showing. He missed badly and laughed at himself. No one else was around. He jogged after the ball, felt like his organs were a bunch of loose change jangling inside him. He shot again, missed again. There was a prickle along his neck. He came under the hoop and made four can't-miss shots in a row. By the end of the string, he was laughing, breathing hard. His knee ached, but it was dull, nonthreatening. He shook his head.

"What the shit?" he asked himself.

Basketball was, amazingly, still in him. The more he shot, the more it came back. His baby-hook, his fade away, his one-armed outlet passes so strong and accurate he used to skim Billy Koning's pathetic goatee from half court without knocking his chin off just to fuck with him. All of it packed away deep, under some fat and age, a little slower, a little sloppier, a little weaker, but still there. And then there was more. There was the joy in his chest at playing a game simply for fun. Good, solid joy that wouldn't soon be toppled. Same thing he'd been watching on Jimmy's face as the kid grew to love the game. All other troubles sloughing off in the effort. Active meditation. *This* was what it could be.

Todd walked home drenched in sweat and giggling like an idiot, his muscles were tired but they sang out. *Not forgotten, it hasn't all been forgotten.*

When he got through the door, Genny Mori was on the couch, turning her hands over in her lap. Had she been crying? She jumped up. She was excited to see him for the first time in he didn't know how long. Ran into his arms even though he was sweated clean through his shirt and smelled terrible.

"Well, *hello*, baby," he said.

Todd tossed the ball on the couch to catch her. She looked back at it, and then up at him, and then she pinched his sweaty T-shirt and it all clicked together. He'd been playing basketball.

JIMMY KIRKUS, NINE YEARS OLD–SEVEN YEARS UNTIL THE WALL.

"Wow," she said, her other problem forgotten, for a moment.

"Funny, you breaking the vase. Kind of . . ."

"That wasn't me, it was Jimmy."

"Jimmy?"

His boys weren't outside, or in their bedrooms. Then he heard voices—"Jimmy, look it," and, "oh shit!"—from in his room. He came through the kitchen, motioned for Genny to be quiet with a finger to the lips. Pushed open his bedroom door, a hand, Genny's hand, on his back. Exhilarating. There were his boys, on the floor of the bedroom. Then Dex leaned back and he saw. The scrapbook about his playing days the Flying Finn had made so long before. Yellowed newspaper and magazine articles, relics of a more promising time. The boys looked up at him with new eyes.

"Well, boys," Todd said.

"Pops?" Jimmy asked.

"Freight Train!" Dex said.

Todd didn't punish his boys for snooping. Not that night. He didn't shy away from questions about his playing days either. For the first time, he answered every single one.

. . . . . .

Later, just before bed, Jimmy began what had become his nightly routine to make sure that the names on his basketball didn't get worn away by all the bounces off sidewalk and blacktop. He traced over all the legends he had written on that ball he got from David Berg three years before. Re-blacked them with Sharpie so they'd last another afternoon.

Lastly, he added a new name, bigger and thicker than the rest. So big it was impossible to miss.

. . . . . .

A week later, a package arrived without postage or address. On the front was written: *For Jimmy Kirkus who is in need of shoes.* It was signed, *The Flying Finn.* All in orange crayon, all in lower-case letters. Inside, packed deep among crumpled-up balls of months-old copies of *Columbia City Standard* were a pair of the brightest basketball sneakers Jimmy had ever seen. So neon they might burn his fingers if he held them too long. So many air bubbles there wasn't enough oxygen left in the room to breathe. He put them on while Dex kept trying to give them a touch. Jimmy pushed him back with his elbow, said, "Quit it."

Genny Mori came home to see Jimmy running full-speed circles around the living room, feet blurring in the bright, high-end sneakers, laces flapping everywhere, Dex huffing to catch him.

"New shoes!" Jimmy yelled.

"Come on, let me touch," Dex said.

His mother scratched her head, still in her nurse's uniform. "Jimmy, I don't know."

Jimmy stopped running abruptly—kid could stop on a dime even back then—and Dex collided into his back and dropped to his knees so he could caress the smooth, white and neon-yellow shoes.

"Ooh," Dex drooled. "Nice sneaks."

"Dex, stop touching the shoes," his mom said.

"Don't know?" Jimmy sensed a trap.

"Who gave those to you? I don't know if you can keep them."

Jimmy wasn't one to cry, but just then, almost. "Someone called the Flying Finn?"

His mother burst out laughing, a rare, prized sound in Jimmy's world. She waved her hand. "You can keep them. Keep them." She shook her head.

"They're smooth," Dex said. He looked up to see how his news was received. He was ignored so he went back to the shoes.

"Who's the Flying Finn?" Jimmy asked.

"I think they glow in the dark." Dex had his hands cupped

around the toe of Jimmy's left shoe and he was peering into the small cave of darkness he'd made. "Yeah, they glow in the dark."

His mom smiled at him. "He's your grandfather, Jimmy."

This caught Dex's attention. "Pops said he was," he lowered his voice into a whisper, "a *sand toad*."

Again that laugh from his mother, and Jimmy wished he could figure out the secret to it. "Your father says a lot of things." She turned, started walking back to the bathroom for her customary postwork bath. "Keep the shoes, Jimmy." She called over her shoulder, "Keep the shoes."

Jimmy cheered, kicked off Dex, and started running around the room again to see how fast he could go. Look at the kid in the brand-new shoes!

Dex resumed his chase, yelling, "Jimmy, they *glow*, your shoes *glow. In the dark*. Stop. I can show you. They glow in the dark!"

Rule 11. Be Bold

Friday, December 21, 2007

JIMMY KIRKUS, SIXTEEN YEARS OLD–FOUR DAYS AFTER THE WALL.

Look at our kid Jimmy on Peter Pan Courts, taking all comers. Scene could have lasted all night. People laughing and joking. Pulling out little bags of chips, flasks of whiskey, packs of cigarettes and gum and passing them around. It's dark by now. A celebration. Could have gone on till the break of dawn. Bad luck finally banished from the land.

The moment gets sucked dry though because Freight Train shows up. Mood black as a thundercloud, he chugs through the crowd. He seems bigger than ever before. People move away as he approaches. They're smart to do it. He'd run them down, he's so locked into the tracks. Talking stops. Laughing stops. They feel the cold of this winter night as a gate-crasher to the party.

He'd heard about what was happening on the radio, of all places. Some guy calling in to that ridiculous local talk show, *The Weather Report*. Host, Chris Fogg, thinks he's some sort of Rush Limbaugh.

Todd Kirkus pauses at the edge of the court. His son has just beaten the Johnston boys two on one. Same kids he played with in his "Shoeless Game," as they call it now. What a thing. Todd wonders if this night at Peter Pan is going to be like all the rest: something to talk about. "OK, Jimmy," he says. "Time to go."

Jimmy blinks at his pops. Confused. The headache, the nausea,
push in to be felt again, sharper for the suddenness of their return. He shouldn't be playing ball this soon after the wall. Doctor's orders. The crowd whispers to each other. Spell broken. This
wasn't a different world after all, just a dirty, cement court lit up
by artificial lights.

Jimmy follows his pops back through the crowd and the Flying
Finn follows his grandson. The people let them through, but they
all crane to get a glimpse of Kamikaze Kirkus now that he's away
from the lights and in the same darkness as them. First one holds
up a cell phone for its glow, and then another, trying to better see
the Miracle Man who's just recaptured their imaginations. Soon
the whole crowd has their phones out. And the magic's back. It's a
rock concert with no lighters, only blue phones. A convention of
alien fireflies. A hundred stars fallen from the sky.

. . . . . .

Carla is there, watching Jimmy. She balances from toe to toe, desperate for a glimpse. Her shift at Peter Pan Market is long over and
her father can't find her in the throng to take her home. She doesn't
want to be found. Not until she's ready. She is sweating in her
armpits and tingling in her hips. She's a teenager, truly, right at
this moment, for the first time in her entire life, and whoa, you
better clear out.

She can help him, she's sure. She can be the thing he needs.

She pushes forward. When Jimmy walks by she reaches out her
fingertips, but doesn't touch him. She doesn't think it matters somehow if she actually touches him. She swears he'll feel it anyway.

. . . . . .

Someone is reaching out to touch his arm, and Jimmy snaps.
Quick, he grabs their hand before they can touch him. He needs
to initiate the contact because suddenly he's so weak if anyone
tapped him first he might topple over and never get up. The hand

caught, he squeezes and bares his teeth in a tight smile. She screams—he can tell it's a girl by this—and the people around her laugh nervously. Jimmy feels animal and injured, powerful and dead tired all at once. He sees the face of the girl. The girl from the store. *Carla.* Her hand in his. She'd asked him if he was worried about 6A. That's how people knew him now. A liability. Fragile with the cracks already showing.

"Watch it now," someone says.

"Jesus Christ, Jimmy," his pops says.

Jimmy lets go.

"It's OK," Carla says and disappears into the crowd.

Gone, he thinks, *there she goes, gone.*

. . . . . .

The Kirkus men walk to the van, the crowd, the town, the universe buzzing, *Look it, now, at our man Jimmy!*

Fans, if rich in anything, are rich in forgiveness. Hell, they can be fooled up and down the block, be brought to their knees by the star player who was supposed to be a savior but was a flop. They can get two-timed, subjected to doping and prostitute scandals, rants about how the fans of the rival city are better, hotter, louder—and then, in the very next moment, cheer that same scoundrel they just booed. All it takes is a few made shots. A few won games strung together. With some pizzazz and a bit of hope a fan's willingness to forgive is boundless.

Jimmy is astounded by this forgiveness. How it's being heaped upon him now. With the van in sight he knows he'll make it and so he lets their love build in his chest. He just made it rain on ten opponents. The Nine Games of Kamikaze Kirkus. His pops is angry and staring down anyone who dares to look, but Jimmy's got these clear eyes and this slack jaw, these open hands and these racing lungs. In-out, in-out. He's sick and hurting and on top of the world all at once. This is a feeling he hasn't had in two and a half years. He'd almost convinced himself he'd never feel it again. Didn't like it anyway. Didn't need it. But now that it's back, he's soaking it in. He likes it. He needs it.

. . . . . .

People in the crowd move only as much as truly necessary to let three generations of Kirkus men through. Then, there in the back, something is happening with the younger kids. One shows another. A grainy video on a small cell phone screen. That security tape from the gym, after hibernating for three days, is waking up. Some techie kid who'd stolen it figured out how to change the tape into a digital file. He sent it to one friend, being like, *don't send 2 no1 else,* and of course that friend sent it to another. And another. And another.

It's spreading only among the young people, Jimmy's peers, for now. It is dim and gritty and without sound, but it's incredibly compelling all the same. There's this shadow, shot from above. It's Jimmy. He's lining up, and then running, running, running. The actual wall is beyond the bottom of the frame, but because everyone knows what's there, knows what he did to himself, the hit reverberates all the same. Whoever sucked that video off the tape has cut it so Jimmy runs at the wall over and over with no break in between, wobbling and stumbling more with each charge. Then the video zooms in. Just a digital blowup on a freeze-frame of Jimmy's face as he looks into the security camera. It's pixilated and out of focus but the black that is smeared on his face is unmistakable.

This video is a huge secret that all of the kids delight in keeping from the adults. They pass it cupped in their trembling palms, one friend to the next. *Look at my fire.* The video will haunt them. They'll hash and rehash in their minds how the hell it could come to that. Imagine themselves in that cold gym with that brick wall. It will make them fidgety and scared. However, they'll still be pulled back to it time and again over the following years of their lives. They'll search it out on the Internet far into adulthood as the coda on a cocktail party story. Video and story a compulsion they won't be able to keep themselves from. On the surface it will be a gruesome tale with legs enough to hold anyone's attention, but there, just beneath, will be nostalgia for a time when first kisses were elating, the future was wide, and Jimmy Kirkus went wild. What if a tale really was as tall as it was told? What would that mean for all those other young passions remembered in impossibly vivid color? What would that do to the life lived now?

It's spreading. Jimmy's legend. Inking itself more perfectly by filling in the negative spaces.

· · · · · ·

Nobody wants to lose sight of the Kirkus men and this beautiful, expanding, insane, terrifying moment. Each and every person boiled and reduced down so they are just fans again. Not postal men or pastors, not high school kids or stay-at-home moms, whether eight or eighty they are the same. Just fans. Willing to believe, waiting to be converted.

Finally someone shouts and then others join in, as if trying to pin down the moment before Kamikaze Kirkus leaves them to beat their numb hands against their legs, remind one another of what they just saw, and invariably fall short in describing with words what they'd just felt.

"Way to be, Jimmy."

"Good seeing you, Kamikaze."

"You haven't lost a step."

These really are fragile apologies—all of them—only using different words.

· · · · · ·

Carla's father has finally ventured into the crowd to find her. He is suspicious of any gathering that isn't his own. He feels them to be sacrilegious and sinful in a way he can't fully explain, and feels

JIMMY KIRKUS, SIXTEEN YEARS OLD–FOUR DAYS AFTER THE WALL.

silly whenever he tries. A worrier to begin with, he's been in over-drive since Carla came in complaining of a stomachache. She admitted without him even asking to taking the pills. Some pain medications from his root canal. His mind is there again. He's suspicious. Has she gone back on her promise to never, never, never do it again?

"Carla!" he yells, ignoring how people look at him. "Carla, please!"

When he finds her, his relief is enormous and he assumes she feels the same. He puts a hand on her shoulder to steer her back to his car, to tell her it's all right. She has a bedtime to keep. He doesn't trust these other young people. All hips and lips and cigarettes, as far as he can tell. They homeschool Carla for a reason—all this Kamikaze Kirkus stuff, it's sick. Typical of a public education.

She shrugs him off though. He can feel her contempt of him in the heat coming off her shoulder, in the cut of her backward glance. She's not scared to be here—she's enjoying it just as much as everyone else in this insane town.

"Leave me alone," she says.

"Goodness, Carla!" he whispers back.

. . . . . .

Just before they get into the van, Grandpa starts flapping his elbows and high-stepping his knees. Classic Flying Finn. "Anyone and everyone wants to face Kamikaze Kirkus best be warned." He twirls around in place, hooting all the louder. "Can't be stopped, won't be stopped! From here to Galilee, nobody can beat Kamikaze!"

"Goofy bastard," someone shouts back to him.

"Braggart son of a bitch!"

"You idiot, Finn, you must be high."

"Yes," he yells. "High!" Not getting the reference. "I *am* the Flying Finn after all." Laughter from the crowd.

Todd grabs his father roughly on the elbow. It's been almost a year since they've had meaningful interaction, but there will be no heartfelt reunion. "Get in the fucking car."

They get in the van, Todd slamming the driver's side door so hard it pops back open. "Shit," he says and closes it proper. He starts her up. She squeals awake and they drive away.

. . . . . .

Jimmy listens to the Flying Finn hum the old song that he's always singing—*we will, we will ROCK YOU!*—as his pops turns on the heater full blast. Jimmy's in the front seat, next to his pops; the Flying Finn's in the back bench seat, arms out on each side as though he were making moves on two loveys at the same time. He's filthy in street-heavy clothes, motorcycle helmet cocked back on his head. The heat in the car unlocks his body odor. Todd cracks his window, keeps glaring at the Flying Finn through the rearview mirror.

"Why you got to do that? Adding to it. Like they don't get enough of us already, you strutting around, just giving them more. Phone lines'll catch fire tonight, believe that. You don't think Jimmy's got enough? He needs more of this whole." His pops bangs the steering wheel. Makes the car drift toward the center of the road. *Bam, bam, bam.* Jimmy's pressing himself up against the passenger-side door. The window crank digging his ribs. "He needs more of this shit you keep shoveling on?" Todd's getting more pissed as he goes. Red kind of angry—hard to cool off without burning something down first. "You pushed me so goddamn hard, Dad, that I broke. I broke. In front of the whole town. And now Jimmy too?"

The Flying Finn is still humming, choosing not to answer, and Jimmy turns his tender forehead back and forth against the window. Sweaty from the game, aching, it squeaks against the glass, cool with the outside air. This helps place him. *I'm here, in this van. I made it.*

JIMMY KIRKUS, SIXTEEN YEARS OLD—FOUR DAYS AFTER THE WALL.

"But it wasn't for me; it was for you," his pops is going on. "Hey. Look at my boy. Look at Jimmy. It was for you." His words are wet by the end of it and his pops leans forward and wipes the steering wheel with his sleeve.

Grandpa stops humming. "How you feeling out there this night, huh, Jimmy?" A whisper almost.

Jimmy wants to be honest and also strike a blow. Miraculously he finds the words to do both. "Good, Grandpa."

"You know why them peoples so quick to cheer you on, Jimmy?" The Flying Finn whistles out now, slow. Tests the interior of the van to see if his words will survive. When Todd doesn't pounce on them, he continues. "Cause you like magic, that's what you are. A long time ago, magic was everywhere you looks." His pops re-adjusts the rearview mirror to see the backseat better. "Least people thought. Now we know everything so there's no reason for magic. Not no way. Not no space. The cell phones, the Internet, no ghosts in the machines.

"But maybe. Just maybe kid like you or your pops comes along. Do stuffs people don't think possible." He leans forward and reaches out his gnarled hand and pulls on Jimmy's hair. It's the starter cord on a lawnmower inside his injured head.

"Grandpa, what the hell?" Jimmy slaps his hand and the Flying Finn lets go.

Todd keeps driving, his anger still there, just barely contained, and Jimmy can feel it about to slop over.

"Maybe if a kid can beats ten people in a row with no giving the points to none of them, there's space enough for a little magic still. Maybe they'll get better lives next year, or the year after that. Find lucks with the loveys. 'Cause yous just like them and look how good you are!" He laughs now. Ups the pitch of his voice to sound like someone else. "You heard about Kamikaze Kirkus beating both those Johnston boys by hisself? Magic . . ." Grandpa sighs, back to himself, and Jimmy can read his tiredness in that exhale, a letdown from the rush of the Boston baked beans, MoonPies, and basketball. "Life's always better with magic, wouldn't you say, Kamikaze?"

. . . . . .

This is too much for Todd. He pulls off the road, almost tipping the van with the sudden yank on the steering wheel. The car stops and shivers in its place. "You don't call him that name. He's Jimmy, that's all he is. I bet you want him to rush back in? Like those people who say he's got to prove himself in 6A? He's played them all before, coming up, and ran circles on them. Even with what happened his freshman season, he doesn't have to do nothing for no one and his name—god*damn* it—is Jimmy."

"Todd, you know, every star needs good a nickname as you had."

"No son of mine." He slams the steering wheel again. His voice trembles with rage. "No son of mine." He's gritting his teeth. He's remembering that night wandering the University of Oregon campus, lost and looking. His father had said the same words to him. *No son of mine.*

"Get out," he tells his own father who's been homeless almost a year with sightings of him as far south as Ashland. "Get out of my fucking car."

But the Flying Finn is already moving. He looks tired. So tired. There is a tug inside Todd, but he fears himself evil because it's easy to ignore.

"Sleep well, both you," the old man says, holding the sliding door open.

The exhaust from the idling engine wafts in like a ghost looking for haunting. Smells poisoned and good. Todd could breathe it all night. There's the cold of the night, too, muscling in late.

"Thanks for food, Jimmy. I's hungry." He slams the door shut; he's already shivering. He blinks his milky eyes.

. . . . . .

His pops puts the car into drive and starts off down the road. Jimmy is unsure but sure all at the same time. They drive in silence. He's trembling now, same as his pops. Some of that crackling bigness from the basketball court before is back inside him. Two blocks back, Grandpa is stumbling in the side-view mirror, still visible. Green helmet looks too heavy, a weight that's squishing his self down into his greasy shoes.

Jimmy punches the dashboard. Busts through the gray textured coating. It's yellow foam beneath. It's been enough. He's tired of his pops making him do what he thinks is best. Pops's life turned out a wreck, why's he get to steer Jimmy's too? Plus there's something in what his pops said about proving himself at 6A that Jimmy's been chewing on. 6A. Division with Shooter Ackley out of Seaside, Ian Callert over in Canby, Danny Rubbe down in Cape Blanco—all going to be NCAA Division I athletes. A bumper crop of talent rounding into fine form. Talk is already brewing about how the state tourney will be one for the record books. Jimmy doesn't want it, not yet he doesn't. But if he doesn't have it this year then next year it will be gone. He'll be up against the also-rans, the semi-goods. Why is his pops so pissed the Flying Finn is aware of this stuff? Shouldn't he be too? Shouldn't Jimmy? "Stop the car," he says. "We're bringing Grandpa home."

"You listen to me," his pops starts, rage threatening everything about him, but it's not enough, not anymore. Jimmy slams his left leg down next to his father's and hits the gas pedal. The car lurches forward, engine flooded in gas, trying not to drown.

His pops has no choice but to hit the brakes. Van makes a terrible noise. Smell of melting and metal. Tires squeal. Then Jimmy takes his foot off the gas but his pops is still stomping the brakes and the van is stopped. His pops's head cracks the steering wheel. He isn't wearing his seat belt. There'll be a bruise on his forehead tomorrow for sure. Like son like father. Jimmy's brains slosh around in his skull. How boring. He doesn't care about his pops's mood. He wants to lie down. He could sleep for ten years straight. He could die. He opens his door and vomits milky stomach acid onto the sidewalk. Then he turns back to his father, eyes open, unflinching.

. . . . . .

Todd looks at his kid. *When he get eyes fierce as that?* His head pounds. He can't imagine himself ever standing up to the Flying Finn like this. Or rather, not unless he was drunk. What is it in this kid, a sign of the times? The rap on the head? The rap music in the ear? He touches his forehead where the steering wheel hit. He might be bleeding. His eyes bulge. He feels his anger deflating around him—Jimmy's eyes popped it—until it's big and floppy, fits him poorly. It's a puddle he's splashing in. He's embarrassed by everything. He looks away from his son.

"You could of got us killed," Todd finally says, feeling deep inside that he should say something.

"Well, good thing you hit the brake."

Todd cuts eyes back to his son. This comment, to him, shines light on every corner of how Jimmy's changed. Kid's got deeper hallways, little trapdoors, secret rooms, and all inside him, hiding a man who could come out tough, or angry, resilient, or looking for a score. He's got to be careful. He'll have a hand in this.

When the Flying Finn catches up to the van, he has a small cough in his lungs as if ball bearings are loose in his throat, eating away at him on each breath. He climbs in, and for once, has no words to say.

The three men drive the rest of the way home in silence, and Columbia City colludes—dropping a thick curtain of ocean-laced

JIMMY KIRKUS, SIXTEEN YEARS OLD–FOUR DAYS AFTER THE WALL.

mist over their route. Sticky, beading rain glues together cars and houses, trees and telephone poles, until all shapes are parts of even larger shapes. Behind the curtain are hideous monsters made haphazardly from the normal parts of Columbia City's life. This magical rain gathers on the van's windows in covens of liquid until they are too heavy and race down with abandon. Todd burns through as much of the rainy soup as he can with his yellowed headlights and hunched forward he drives on.

Rule 12. Get Up When Knocked Down

JIMMY KIRKUS, FOURTEEN YEARS OLD—THREE YEARS UNTIL THE WALL.

Todd Kirkus looked up from the afternoon's *Columbia City Standard*, cleared his throat, and proceeded to surprise his whole family. "I guess the Fishermen are playing tonight," he said. He snapped shut the paper and stood from his chair. "Maybe we should go."

"Scappoose Indians?" Jimmy asked.

Todd looked to his son. Of course Jimmy would know exactly what team they were playing. He probably had the schedule memorized. "Yeah. Want to go?"

Kid looked him up and down, like there could be a trick in it. "Um, OK?"

"Todd?" said Genny Mori. "Whole town's going to be out."

He looked at his wife, annoyed that she didn't think him man enough to handle it. Also that she was showing it in front of his sons. He tried to brush it off, affecting a light tone. "Who cares; let's go. We'll have to get going, though. Probably missed first quarter already."

"Wait, really?" Dex asked from where he lay on the couch, dropping potato chips one by one into his mouth. He sat up a little and the next chip bounced off his lower lip and down to the floor.

"Dex, goddamn it, throw that away," Genny said.

"Whoa nelly, easy there, easy," Dex said in a cowboy accent.

"It's like I always say, if we had a dog, he'd just eat this up. Dropping chips on the floor is a *protest*, Mom, you ever hear of *that*?"

"Just get your coat."

Dex picked up the chip from the floor, blew on it, and then, just to get his mom revved even higher, popped it in his mouth— three-second rule—and stomped off, Jimmy following.

"Can't our family ever just be in peace?" Todd said, peeved.

"You tell me," his wife said.

. . . . . .

And so Freight Train took his wary family to the Brick House. It was the first time he'd been back since high school. They were late and had to wait for a stop in play to find their seats. Shoe squeaks, the smell of gym—Todd closed his eyes. Tracked the feeling as it reached his toes. Not relief, exactly, but a close cousin. The whistle sounded. When he opened them, play was stopped. A Fishermen time-out. Heads turned. People poking neighbors and pointing. A whole gym's worth of eyes. First one person clapping, and then another. Popcorn coming to full heat, it became one sound. Only sound. The crowd threatened to pop the roof right off the Brick House.

These were young kids who'd only heard of him in story and parents who remembered him play firsthand. Old classmates, fans, teachers, and teammates who had one of the best nights of their lives back when Todd led the team to the first championship and all of Columbia City went delirious. Two-for-one drink specials at Desdemona's, free soft-serve at the Dairy Queen. Dancing in the streets and car horns gone hoarse from being leaned on. These were the same people laid flat when Todd was suspended from the team the day of the championship game the next year. Their boy done good crashed up on the rocks of alcohol and injury. A hero wallowing, an ugly sight, Freight Train spent the years since trying to be as scarce as can be. Finally here he was, cornered with the whole town giving praise. Refs clapping too, players and coach on Scappoose looking on, calm, giving the moment the respect it deserved, the game could wait. People shouted, "Hey Freight Train!" and, "Go choo-choo!" Just like the old days. Hell, it was something to see. They still remembered him for all he'd been sixteen years before.

Todd nodded his head, bit his lip. "OK, now," he said, "all right." Waved his hand, like *You're too kind.* Crowd even louder. Feet stamping bleacher seats. The old chant: "*Hey, hey—down the lane. Hey, hey—it's Freight Train.*" Water in his eyes. Noise didn't stop until the Kirkus family found seats. And then when they sat, it settled down, but for the rest of the game, people kept stealing glances.

Todd felt as if he were floating. Jimmy, Dex, and even Genny Mori were balloons.

. . . . . .

On the way home, Jimmy's mom gave up on being bitter for a little bit and his pops was talking ball. Stories about his glory days that he rarely told, and never with this energy. There was a light rain. It studded the windows with water. For a night at least his mom didn't care she'd got pregnant with a doomed little girl and married too soon to a sure thing that turned out to be anything but. His pops forgot that he became a townie, a Van Eyck PepsiCo lifer, who had let his daughter die and screwed up his basketball chances.

"Let's play that tape you like so much," his pops said. He rubbed his mom's knee.

"Which one?" she asked, surprised. He usually preferred silence to anything else—and, he didn't really like that either.

"Paul Simon." Jimmy saw the way he smiled slyly in the rearview mirror, and it made him smile too. "Whose gonna get that girl diamonds on her shoes? Lose them walking blues?"

JIMMY KIRKUS, FOURTEEN YEARS OLD–THREE YEARS UNTIL THE WALL.

"You know what I like," she finally said, and laughed and it was all so odd, and peaceful and dark, that Jimmy felt a soft sleepiness drift over him. He felt young in the best way. He felt young and protected. Finally.

"You guys live in the Stone Age," Dex said. "Get a CD player already."

"Shut up," Jimmy whispered.

Dex shrugged, and as the music started, Jimmy watched the rain. Then his brother poked him on the shoulder, whispering.

"Hey, Jimmy, you gotta beat this fire plant for me. Level eleven."

Jimmy took the Game Boy. "Yeah, sure."

A, over, A, down, A, B, A. No problem. Got Luigi out right quick. Couple of Italian brothers dodging fire-breathing plants. Jump the problems till there weren't any problems left. Both of them blessed with real vertical leaps. They'd probably make pretty good two-guards.

"That's the tough part," Dex said when he took the Game Boy back.

"Yeah, that's the tough one."

Paul Simon sang on and on. Diamonds and shoes. *People say she's crazy.* Mom and Pops sometimes looked back at them through the rearview mirror. Dex played his Game Boy, kept his snide comments bottled up. The whole town had stopped everything for his pops. It had been amazing and unexpected. Filled him up. Filled his whole family up. Brake lights of other cars lit up raindrops on his window. A better night-light he'd never known. Jimmy closed his eyes—he could *swear* he felt the Earth turning—and fell asleep quick and easy.

......

What happened was the day before the Scappoose game Todd had switched shifts at Van Eyck to help a coworker out. He'd worked the night before, and then did the day too. Basically eighteen hours of work with a nap in between. He got home before the boys were even out of school; around the time he would typically be leaving for work. He parked the van in the usual spot, in their little inlet, behind the pine. Thick branches hid the van. He had the window open, arm out. Engine ticked and cooled. Air—through some trick in the jet stream—warm enough on this day to bathe in. He reclined the seat. He felt worn in the best way and so he lingered there. He drifted to sleep.

Dex's voice—teasing Jimmy—was what woke him. He peeked out the window, wiping dried spit from the corner of his mouth.

"Man, if this whole ball thing doesn't work out, you can go make toys for Santa."

Through the leaves, Todd saw Jimmy hanging from one of the maple limbs. He had soup cans tied to his shoes. He swung back and forth slightly, shaking the limb, trying to stretch himself. Recently, his son had become terrified of staying short and taken it upon himself to help nature out. In the last month, Todd had caught him walking around on his tippy-toes, making himself sick by drinking whole cartons of milk, whispering over and over to himself, "I will be tall, I will be tall, I will be tall."

"Shut up, Dex," Jimmy said, out of breath.

"Or cookies in the tree house? I hear Keebler's got an opening for a good elf."

"Yeah, yeah, keep talking."

"I would, but you're so short I ran out of things to say." Dex pulled out of his pocket a wrinkled page from a magazine. He held it up to Jimmy. "Look, it's cute."

Even though it was too far away to see, Todd knew exactly what it was. A month ago, after Jimmy led his team to a second undefeated season in a row and then was named MVP of an elite Nike basketball tournament, *Sports Illustrated* had published an article entitled *Jimmy Kirkus, The Next Larry Bird?* In the photo

Jimmy stood with his marked-up basketball on his hip. He didn't look much like Celtic great Larry Bird. In fact, with the hoop towering behind him, it was painfully clear just how small he was. He looked better suited for a spelling bee than a hardwood court. Dex had drawn a little elf hat on Jimmy's head in Sharpie. Written *Santa's Little Helper* in cursive over the top. He'd been tormenting Jimmy with it ever since.

Jimmy dropped from the tree. He undid the soup cans from his shoes and threw them one by one at Dex. "Shut the. Fuck up." His brother danced away. Then Jimmy stormed about ten feet off, dropped to the ground, and started doing push-ups.

Todd watched, fascinated as Dex took in his brother's rage. One thing about Dex was he simply couldn't handle it if Jimmy was upset. He walked over to the small pumpkin patch that sprouted on the edge of their yard every fall since Jimmy's famous barefoot game five years before when Todd had lost it. The pumpkins reminded him of basketballs—being blown up by the earth, turning from green to orange. Over the years he was always finding them mysteriously smashed just when they were the ripest. *Goddamn teenagers.*

Dex picked up one late bloomer—now half rotten and slimy—and lifted it over his head. Todd was worried he was going to walk over and bring it down on Jimmy. He went for the door handle.

Then, instead, Dex called out, "Hey Jimmy!"

Jimmy looked up. Todd could see his older son's smile already growing.

Dex slipped his voice into a pitch-perfect imitation of Todd from that day he'd smashed the pumpkin in a fit of rage. "You played without shoes? I could, I could, I COULD WHAT?" Dex threw the pumpkin down where it exploded into an orange, goopy mess.

Jimmy started laughing, and Dex continued stomping around. A big, huffing caricature. Todd felt the urge to scream. Spring open the door, shock his boys, *I've been watching the whole time you little bastards.* Then he stopped. Embarrassed already. This was who he was to his sons. Blowing up now would only make it worse. He'd chewed on it all that day and the next. Then an idea sprang to him while he read the *Standard*'s sports page. *Columbia City Fishermen Face the Scappoose Indians, Tonight at the Brick House.* It was something unexpected from him—he could be better, he could surprise them all.

. . . . . .

Taking his boys to the Scappoose game couldn't have gone better. As the winter and then spring waned and summer shifted in for its brief turn playing Columbia City, it was clear the standing ovation he received at the game had changed Todd Kirkus. He was more open, laughed easier. He even reached out to his father— who had first spurned Todd's help repeatedly when he took to the streets after Suzie died, and then, years later when he had been set up sleeping in the supply closet of Norma's and tried to come back home, been rejected in turn by Todd. In the intervening years Todd and the Flying Finn had seen each other on the periphery, but hadn't spoke more than a sentence or two. Then in the summer before Jimmy's freshman year, finally, Todd invited him over to officially meet his grandsons.

The first time he came, white hair ironed down the sides of his great dome, lost in a thrift-store suit made for a shorter, fatter man, the boys didn't believe it.

"Good afternoon," the Flying Finn said in a careful politeness that was laughable. "I's gonna come sooner but it's so long to walk. I'm the Flying Finn, I'm Grandpop."

"I've seen you down on the road," Dex said. "With the green helmet."

The Flying Finn grinned his big jack-o'-lantern grin, same one he used when he used to pretend he liked eating brussels sprouts just so Todd would give them a try, and snapped his fingers. "That's my hat!"

"Are you sure he's our grandpa?" Jimmy asked.

Before Todd could answer, the Flying Finn had both boys in headlocks and was pulling them out into the yard. "I's your grandpop, I'm so strong!" he was shouting. It was a game they used to play often when Todd was small. Strongest Man in the World. The Flying Finn threw first Jimmy and then Dex out into the grass. "I's just so strong, I's the strongest man in the world."

"Man, you *are* crazy," Jimmy said as he stood up, wiped at some of the mud now streaking his pants.

He looked at Todd for help and Todd shrugged, smiling. "He's the strongest man until you prove otherwise." It was strange seeing this version of his father playing at joy. Todd saw that the years out on the streets had got their knocks in as they passed by. Finn was missing three of his bottom teeth on the right side. There was a scar from above his right eyebrow running to just below his cheekbone. He moved in a glitch-heavy way. Steps down seemed to give him trouble. And yet still. Here he was, the crazy fuck, wrestling.

Jimmy turned back to the Flying Finn, red-faced. "There is something seriously loose in your head." Todd could tell his kid was being pushed out of his comfort zone with this. He wasn't entering on his terms. There were no rules or boundaries and he hadn't practiced his moves ad nauseam beforehand.

"If you looks where I am, you only sees where I's been, 'cause I's so fast, I'm the Flying Finn!"

Still, Jimmy would not bite, tried to play it cool. "Man," he said, rubbing at the grass stains on his jeans. "You got them all dirty."

It took Dex to get things started. "You're not that strong, and you're old, too!" he took a running charge at the gangly suit hanger, bulleted him in the chest, and they fell in a mess of limbs, Dex mostly on top but it was hard to tell with the flapping suit coat.

"I's not old, I's so strong!"

Dex was laughing and trying to get the Flying Finn pinned, but the old man was full of tricks and before long he was on his feet again, strutting back and forth, crowing, literally, like a rooster. *"Cock-a-doodle-do!"*

"Come on, Jimmy," Dex said.

Jimmy looked at Todd once more, and Todd nodded his head. He wanted his boy to get messy.

"All right, OK," Jimmy said, and this time both boys pummeled into their grandpa. All three fell into the muddy grass laughing and boasting about their strength. Todd went back in the house, shaking his head in joy. *Just like that . . .*

. . . . . .

Those visits from the Flying Finn were hard though. Todd had to willfully not think about the day of Suzie's funeral every time the old man came, which of course made him think of it all the more. He remembered how they were all dressed in black—even the Columbia City sky was dark with thunderclouds rolling in from the ocean—to put to rest this tiny box, painted white. It seemed too small to hold anything of substance. That box. Especially an entire person, especially a little girl who had hidden depth enough in her smile to hold a happiness so big it swallowed up two accidental parents.

At the funeral, Todd folded his arms high and tight on his chest against the wet, Oregon cold. He was shaking, vibrating, like at any moment he would come unraveled. Genny Mori beside him, slack and out of it. Eyes blurry, unfocused, but put together in a neat dress. The Flying Finn in a suit, old, dusty, and elegant. A used-to-be black, some of the color burned off. Todd turned to his father. Old man acted like he knew everything else under the sun, he should know what to do now for God's sake.

"Dad?" Todd spoke overloud. "Dad, what do I do?"

The Flying Finn turned away.

"Todd, stop it," Genny Mori said. She was huge, pregnant with Jimmy, and concerned he was going to make a scene. That was Genny in a nutshell, anti-scene.

Todd grabbed his father's shoulder and turned the old man around. It wasn't difficult. Todd was still solid and the Flying Finn had more or less turned to paper. He expected to see tears in the old man's eyes. But there were none.

"Tell me what to do."

"Get the hold on yourself."

"Tell me."

"Nothing-nothing-nothing." Voice a pile of dried-out wood shifting on itself.

Todd had the man by both of his shoulders. The priest was watching. *He* was crying at least. The Bergs, father, son, and pregnant new wife were there, even though no one asked them to be.

"Todd," Principal Berg said. "Come on now."

"Todd . . ." someone else. James? "Todd, buddy, come on. Come here."

Todd kept squeezing his father. He could feel the structure of the old man's bones beneath his hands. He felt like he could crumple him entirely. Fold him into a paper plane. Let him fly.

"Todd, honey, let go," Genny Mori said in that whisper that meant, *Other people are watching, you're embarrassing yourself.*

Then the Flying Finn said the thing that Todd had to willfully un-remember every time the old man came over to visit: "She lucky to die so young, see none of this bad place."

Todd let go of this man. He didn't understand. This man wasn't his father. Not the same man who pushed so hard for him to be the best basketball player he could be. The man before him was a fraud.

"Lucky?" Todd turned as if he were walking away, Genny turned too, but then, with a quickness that electrocuted his bones, a speed that the Flying Finn had so long honed in him for basketball, Todd turned back and pushed his father in his chest. Old man flew back and slid across the wet cemetery grass. In the process, Todd's knee popped. He buckled to one side, limped around cussing.

On his back the Flying Finn looked up at the sky. Storm was threatening for real. He was breathing fast, shallow breaths. "I can't get no protection!" he shouted. "Even my own flesh and blood."

Principal Berg walked over. "Here," he said, and offered him a handkerchief.

"No, you the worse of the lots. All of yous." He scrambled up, his back a cake of mud and grass, and ran off in a slippery trot that would have been comical in other circumstances.

Todd meanwhile became concerned with finding out who had been in charge of setting up the burial. "They did such a fine job," he said between sobs, "I want to give a tip, they did a fine job."

"Who's in charge here?" James said desperately, trying to help. "Who?"

Todd looked at him, closed his eyes, and sat in the grass.

. . . . . .

Now, with Todd allowing the Flying Finn to visit, the old man took his second chance seriously. Each day before he came, he washed with palm-cupped water in Norma's restaurant bathroom like the giant, bony, wingless bird he'd become, humming to keep his mind off the cold. He showed up at the house reeking of antibacterial hand soap, skin pink, almost red, because of how hard he'd scrubbed.

On these visits, the Flying Finn did most of the talking, Jimmy and Dex did most of the listening, and Todd sat way back in his chair, watching.

"You know why I called the Flying Finn?" He liked to ask the boys. "It's the soccer team. In Finland. I's the fastest son of the dog of the whole bunch." He puffed out his boney chest. "Move my feets so you only see where I's been, and there he goes like he's a flying Finn!"

Sometimes Todd interjected. "Oh, you made that up yourself."

"Me? No! It was the fans. My fans."

"You never had any fans."

"Yes, I did and they called me Flying Finn. I already told all about that."

The Flying Finn stayed for hours on his visits, wearing out his welcome, but the boys were nice to him, even as their mother strangely ignored him. He cracked them up. He used the bathroom to "Conduct Official Business," and ran the water full blast the entire time, singing, "We will, we will ROCK YOU," at the top of his lungs while he stomped his feet from where he sat on the toilet—classic grandpa. And then on his way out of the door, the Flying Finn asked Jimmy and Dex to help him pluck the flowers from Genny's garden. He was always in love with one waitress or another at Norma's Restaurant. "FLOWERS FOR MY LOVEYS!" he'd yell at the top of his lungs. And then, in a nudge-nudge whisper, he'd tell the boys, "Maybe you twos will be lucky to have a lady like my Lovey. She has Jesus tongue."

"What?"

"Tongue move so good you say, PRAISE JESUS!"

If Genny Mori caught him picking flowers, there was hell to pay.

"You get back here Finn, those are my tulips!"

"Too quick for you, Mori!" the Flying Finn shouted back, running down the sidewalk suit coat flapping. "I need tulips to kiss the lips!"

. . . . . .

During that summer, fighting the mood of nothingness that descends on small-town streets for three months each year, people went out of their way to shake Jimmy's hand, offer him a free slice of pizza, an ice cream cone. Next year he would be a freshman and all expected him to carry the Fishermen back to glory. Dex thought it was hilarious. He liked to stir the pot by shouting, "The great Jimmy Kirkus is here, live and in person. Five bucks a handshake, ten an autograph."

"Damn, Dex, I'm not signing anything. People are going to start asking you to put your money where your mouth is."

Dex thought on it a second. "People shouldn't be putting money where their mouths are. It's disgusting—you know where money's been?"

Sometimes Pedro would chime in, "We got two for the price of one. That's right, two Kirkuses today, so act quick, supplies are limited!"

The truth was, Jimmy was hopped up on the attention. It filled a need he hadn't known was there. He liked the way the girls smiled at him, how the boys gave him confident high fives. It didn't seem to matter that he never had anything to say, hated holding eye contact. And all this because of ball. If he could just never let them down, then all the love would keep coming. It was a simple equation and though it seemed ridiculous, for our kid Jimmy, who'd only experienced basketball success so far, it was entirely plausible.

. . . . . .

Toward the end of the summer, Todd let the Flying Finn move into the house. He was staying longer and longer on each of his ever more frequent visits anyway so it made sense. He slept in the pantry. It was barely big enough to fit the green cot that Genny Mori put in. He slept among jars of jam and cans of vegetables. Some mornings he'd emerge, chin stained with jam or peanut butter, complaining of stomachaches.

"Goddamn it, Finn," Genny scolded. "You can' be eating all night, making a mess of it, sticking your fingers straight into the jars."

"A midnight snack is how they say this," the Flying Finn responded. "It's so very common where I come from."

"This *is* where you come from, you old goose," Todd said.

Sometimes Jimmy and Dex would come down early in the morning, their mom already gone for the day, and find the two men sitting in the kitchen, be looking out the big, river-facing windows, talking about old times. Drank pot after pot of coffee while they waited for Todd's shift to begin in the afternoon.

One morning Dex asked for coffee too.

"Ah, you'd hate the taste," the Flying Finn said. "Asides, it'll stump your growing."

"It's *stunt*, not *stump*," Todd said.

"I don't believe it. You pulling on the foot?"

"Grandpa, I'm already tall," Dex said.

"Ha-ha!" the old man cackled. "I think you right. You're too tall! So go, drink coffee. You a tree, not a stump!" Then he gripped Jimmy's shoulder. "But you stay off the stuff. You're too short!"

On those mornings, Todd and the Flying Finn spoke as though the boys weren't there. Of where he went in the years after Todd lost his knee, future, and Suzie Q.—"*South, south, south. Figured I didn't need much if I were warm at night!*" Why when he came back to town he'd worn that ridiculous helmet—"*I was afraid someone would see me. Then there is the answer! I find a green motorcycle helmet that covered my ears, my eyes. A disguise!*"

Other than Suzie's funeral, the one thing they never spoke about was the night Todd went wandering off drunk before the state championship game. But it was there, just under the surface and the boys had no clue about any of that.

. . . . . .

That summer, the Flying Finn learned about the Tour de France. During the day he'd take over the TV for hours so he could see if Lance would win.

"Goddamn that's my sport!" he'd shout above all the normal household noise. "I was never one for my hands or my feets, but in my legs, I got the class."

"Isn't the Finnish thing like bobsled or something?" Dex asked.

"Goddamn it! It's in our legs. We show them smug Euros!"

"The Finnish *are* European."

"Just listen to your grandpa when he talks!" He threw the remote at Dex, chunked him in the side of his big head. The Flying Finn clapped. "Get me a bike, get me a bike and I'll show you!"

"Ouch, Jesus," Dex said, rubbing the spot. "You're insane."

At the local thrift store he picked up used bits of cycling gear until by the final few days of the tour, he was watching in a hodge-podge cycling uniform that advertised about a hundred different companies and seemed composed exclusively of neon Spandex. Hopping up and down in the living room, the big, glowing, skinny man—made all the skinnier by Spandex—watched Lance Armstrong win the tour again.

"Just get me a bike, you knuckleheads, I'll show you, I'll show you so good."

When Jimmy and Dex found a rusted old Schwinn in the thick blackberry bushes behind the elementary school one day, they took it to Pedro's house that always smelled of motor oil and fried food. His uncle Flaco fixed it up in no time.

"What you need a bike for, Jimmy?" Pedro asked.

"It's not for me."

JIMMY KIRKUS, FOURTEEN YEARS OLD—THREE YEARS UNTIL THE WALL.

When the Flying Finn saw the bike, he broke down crying.

"You little bastards," he wailed, "You can't just let an old man live proud to his boasts? It's all I gots after all!"

"But Grandpa," Jimmy said. "We wanted to see how fast you could go."

Then the Flying Finn leaned in close to the boys and whispered, "It's sorry to say, boys, but I never learn how to ride."

So there were the Kirkus boys, running next to the Flying Finn in his neon biking gear and his bright green motorcycle helmet—both with a hand on the bike frame somewhere to prop up his terrible balance, while he screamed and giggled. Pumping his legs, knees angled out, like a maniac.

"I feel like flying," the Flying Finn yelled.

. . . . . .

Meanwhile, for Genny Mori, the house started to feel like a foreign country she didn't have a passport for. She could find ways in, sure, but it was always with the fear that she'd be discovered at any point and deported. All boys and then her. All old stories, and somehow no mention of her. A whole decade of Todd slowly shutting down to her, but somehow still this light for his loudmouth father? She started lingering at work with the one person who always seemed to be around, Doc McMahan.

The affair started because Doc and his wife lost a child that summer. Happened after a long, painful fight where the little girl put up with all kinds of stuff little girls shouldn't have to put up with. Tubes down the throat, needles, and blood samples. An autoimmune disorder Genny Mori hadn't heard of before. They started meeting up after work to trade notes on grief. Commiserate and laugh over the stupid things people said in order to show you that they cared. *I'm so sorry for your loss. I was shocked when I heard. You have our condolences. We'll keep you in our prayers.*

Doc McMahan and Genny Mori laughed over the responses

they wished they could say. *Me too. So was I. Thanks, but no thanks. Was I in them before?* She appreciated that he let her be angry when she felt like being angry. Not like Todd who either exploded right back at her, or told her to cool off, think about it from the other person's point of view. For Genny this was the thing about Todd. She was never entirely sure he was on her side. With McMahan she could let loose. There was no doubt.

And in talking about Suzie with this wet, little man with the beautiful eyes, something happened to Genny Mori that should have happened fifteen years before. Her heart broke where before it had only cracked. Here was someone else who had lost the most important thing in their life without any fault of their own. So instead of building from the ruins with her husband when it had happened, she did it much later in a beachside condo with little, tanned-dark Doc McMahan. She found all sorts of reasons to believe he was the right man come along. Finally.

Tough luck for her, that one.

McMahan didn't actually live in Seaside, the small town where the hospital was, just down 101 from Columbia City; he commuted there three times a week. Whenever he talked about his life in Portland, all Genny saw were differences she had no hope of competing with. Back in Portland was his wife and their two other kids. Soccer practices and community softball. Potluck dinners and hikes in the Gorge. Big games and barbequed meat. The wife worked as an account manager at some ad agency. They had a huge house in the right neighborhood. They could afford to eat extravagant Saturday brunches at restaurants with two, sometimes three, accent markers in the name. They traveled to Europe when the kids were on break. He owned a small sailboat—the reason for his constant tan. However, on days McMahan worked in Seaside, always three- or four-day stints strung together, he stayed at a condo he owned on the beach.

This condo made the affair too easy to start and too difficult to end. Genny Mori would swear it off and then find that she had left something of hers at the condo. She would return to pick it up and then . . . One Thing, and Another—they liked to play follow the leader.

McMahan was such a welcome relief from Todd, the only man she'd ever slept with before in her life. Todd Roll-Over-You Kirkus. Todd Get-It-Done-Then-Saw-Some-Logs Kirkus. Bang, bang, snore. A man who had put on the pounds since high school and became soft in the middle. Meanwhile McMahan was ropy with the muscle of an active leisure life and a dedicated personal trainer. He was affectionate in just the right way. He always made sure she was taken care of first. He liked to laugh in the bedroom. Wasn't offended when her body made strange noises, when a weird gasp escaped her lips. He seemed determined to consume every part of her. In his eyes she was the sexiest thing in existence, and so she began to feel this way too. He said he liked the way she tasted and smelled. She could see that he was telling the truth by how eagerly he traveled down, and so she became relaxed and started to come on a regular basis for the first time in her life. And yet he was always with her because she let him. He never pushed the issue, which made her want to push it for him. Jump all over him. He was sweet, but passionate. He always asked, each and every time before he entered, *May I?* but he also had ripped a fair amount of her blouses in frenzied backseat hookup sessions that seemed almost comical in their headlong passions. He was the perfect mix.

And then there was the afterward cuddle. A concept she hadn't even believed existed outside of movies before McMahan. She described his affections to Bonnie as teacup cuddling. Small, fragile and taken in small sips as if someone were watching and might ding him for bad manners. Pinkie up. Hip goes here, hand goes there.

"Sweet Jesus," Bonnie said. "Who would have known the little guy had it in him."

"I know."

"It's like he stepped off the cover of a romance novel."

"He's nice."

She was able to see him two to three times a week—evenings worked fine with the boys at practice or going to Pedro's house and Todd still in night-shift purgatory—time she spent sweating with McMahan in his expensive condo, under his expensive sheets, crying about their lost kids into expensive tissues. He cultivated in her the belief that there was still a chance for her life yet. He liked to talk about the future. She could study hard, go to medical school, become a doctor too. They could run away and open a clinic somewhere tropical. And why not? It seemed her family needed her less than she ever dared to think. The Flying Finn just had to move back in, and it seemed everything was fine—everyone except Genny Mori. What was to stop her?

. . . . . .

As to what Doc McMahan saw in her? It came to be a million things—how Genny Mori was compassionate about his recent loss, laughed at his jokes and listened to his opinions—but interest always starts with just one thing.

"If you'd have told me when I was eighteen that I'd be with Freight Train Kirkus's girl, I'd have called you insane," he told her over smoozy-lit dinner at his condo. "I played against him in high school. People thought he was such a big deal."

"You're with me because I'm Todd's wife?" He saw her anger swelling.

"No, no." McMahan's face lit up red, he could fell it. "It's just life is *extremely interesting*. How it all ends up, you know? You never think it'll go where it does. I'm with you because it's impossible to not be. I'm with you because I care very deeply for you. You are my obsession. Truly. I love you, Genevieve, I do."

Teacup loving.

. . . . . .

One day, while the Flying Finn took a fitful nap in full biking gear, Todd and his boys shot hoops at Tapiola.

"So you were gonna go D-1, huh pops?" Dex asked.

"I had some offers," he said.

Jimmy whistled. "Oregon?"

"Oregon, OSU, UCLA, even some East Coast schools." Todd smiled. "The NBA. Larry Brown called your grandpa about me. He was coaching the New Jersey Nets back then."

"And your knee went out?" Dex asked.

"That's about it." He paused, shot the ball. Another drain. The net swayed.

"You got in a fight, Pops?" Jimmy was looking at Todd's feet. "With a cop?"

Of course his kid had heard the story. Columbia City, she liked to hear her own voice. However there's truth, and then there's what you're willing to believe. Todd bet on the second. "Where you hear that? I blew out my knee at practice, and that's all she wrote." If Jimmy pressed, if he really pressed, Todd would tell him the truth. First his son had to prove that's what he wanted.

. . . . . .

For the rest of the day, our kid Jimmy tried to come to terms with the fact that his father's knee injury had happened *on* the court, not off like he had always thought. Sure, Jimmy knew about injuries. NBA players had them. Knocked them out for a few games, sometimes knocked them out for good. It hadn't seemed real though. Like *really real*, if that made any sense. And with the knowledge that it had happened to his pops, it *was* real. Really real. It was a strange thought because the game he loved had only ever given him good, solid things. Got him and Pedro a spot at the popular table even though he rarely spoke with girls and had nothing to add to the jokes or talk on music and movies. It gave him a language to use with Dex—a kid who had no trouble being cool and popular and at ease. It had brought his pops back into his everyday life, blinking like a mole in the sun.

So can we blame the kid for being shocked that the beautiful game also brought dark things with it? Hell, even though our kid Jimmy was set to enter high school in a few weeks, he was still a little kid in many ways. Finding out that his pops busted his knee playing the magical game was like fleecing him of the invincible wool all young people think grows around their lives.

Our poor Jimmy.

Later, as he ran along the river walk, easily putting distance between himself and Dex, he was so caught up in the thought that basketball took as well as gave that he grew careless with his feet. He tripped. His hands were quick enough to brace the fall, but they slipped in the gravel. He smacked his chin. In his cloudy vision after the hit, he swore he could see the sandy-skinned movement of something scuttling off. Something huge. He felt pain in his ankle.

Walking back home, Jimmy leaned on Dex and kept his weight off the gimpy ankle. The whole way, Jimmy mumbled his delirious complaints. "I'm gonna grow sandy skin, tongue bread crumb. I need white tears. Tears from a sand toad."

"You're talking crazy, Jimmy. Sand toads? Come on."

The next morning Jimmy still felt dizzy, his ankle sore, and when he tried to shoot, he was off. Nothing would go in. What a muddy and cold feeling for the kid. In the next few days his ankle healed and his touch came back—but it was too late, in some ways, for Jimmy. Our kid Kirkus had seen the other side of the coin and it was frightening and viral and taking root in his chest, spreading everywhere.

Rule 13. Don't Talk Much, or, Talk Too Much

Monday, December 24, 2007

JIMMY KIRKUS, SIXTEEN YEARS OLD–SEVEN DAYS AFTER THE WALL.

Christmas Eve. Joy to the world. But Santa was a stinker and there appeared a terrible gift on the Internet. A blog titled *The Missteps*. Its first and only entry actually went live on Saturday, December 22, but for the first day and a half of its existence, it was largely ignored aside from a comment by hoop_star_45 who wrote, "damn . . ." By midday of the twenty-fourth, inside the Oregonlive.com high school basketball chat room, purpleperson128 posted: "You remember Jimmy Soft, now I guess Kamikaze Kirkus? Check it:" with a link to *The Missteps*. Suddenly the blog post jumped in hits. The comments below the first from hoop_star_45 exploded downward. Everyone had an opinion about Kid Kirkus and the Nine Games.

The Missteps

Kamikaze Kirkus and the Grand Trick
Columbia City High School Junior, Jimmy Kirkus, aka Kamikaze Kirkus, has the entire town buzzing. Two disappointing seasons into his Fishermen career, and everyone is eating out of his hand again. Yesterday at Peter Pan courts, Kirkus beat ten opponents in a row. This included such luminaries of Fishermen basketball as Ray Atto and the All-League duo, Brian and Chris Johnston, at the same time.

However, this apparent resurgence of our long-lost star is the absolute worst thing that can happen to Fishermen basketball, especially in our final season at 6A. If Coach Kelly allows Kirkus back on the team, prepare yourself for another downward spiral with Jimmy, or should I say Kamikaze, piloting.

Jimmy has been anointed Chosen One since grade school. I remember first hearing about him after the Ninth Shot when he was just a kindergartener. A shot from a kindergartner? We had taken it too far even then. But let's look at the facts. He was a standout in grade school and middle school. A fine thing, but plenty of kids with a little coordination do well in those leagues. Then he had one full and disappointing season of Fishermen basketball. Then last year, with him sitting out for understandable reasons, we posted a respectable 13-13 record behind the blossoming of the Johnston brothers. So far this season, and it's still only December, we're 3-2 sans Kamikaze. Why risk tarnishing our swan song in 6A with a risky bet on a shaky kid?

Many people are saying 6A is the strongest it's ever been this year. Don't you think Jimmy will be in a little over his head?

Quick history lesson for those young people who think Jimmy's new nickname is so cool: back in World War II kamikaze pilots were the guys who flew their planes into battle ships. They destroyed themselves and the ship too.

Kirkus is a good kid who's gone through some terrible things, but as a fan and lifelong resident of Columbia City, I can't in good faith put any more hope in him—and neither should you.

Last night Jimmy Kirkus may have beaten ten other young men. However that wasn't the greatest feat he managed—he also pulled the wool over our eyes.

It's Coach Kelly who calls Todd about the blog post.

"Todd?" is the first thing he says when Freight Train answers the phone.

"Yeah, coach?" Todd knows it's him right off.

"I just want you to know that this whole *Missteps* thing has nothing to do with me or any of my staff." A let-out of breath. "I don't know who it is, but it sounds like that letter to the editor from back when you were playing? Look, I just wanted to let you know. I'd never be involved in that sort of thing with Jimmy, especially since. Look. It's not any of us, I'm just saying."

"Thanks for reaching out, Coach," Todd says, having no clue what the hell he's talking about. He takes down the blog's address and then hangs up. They have dial-up Internet at the house but it's nothing Todd really messes with. He got it for Jimmy to do stuff for school, although only thing he ever sees the kid getting into when he passes by is ESPN or Nike and one time the shot, belly-button up, of a naked woman, oiled and glistening with huge breasts.

After what seems like an unnecessary amount of screeching noise, Todd manages to get connected, info card from the installation guy clutched in one hand. He taps out the address with his two index fingers. *Missteps* pops up. The blog's format all simple. No photos and done in purple and gold. Hard to read with those two colors bordering the text but the content tips Todd in. He splashes down in the words and comes back up dripping with anger. He clicks madly about the post, looking for any kind of name he can associate with this piece of shit that's hammering on his son. He wonders if it's the same person who wrote that opinion piece from years before. Certainly the same tone. He suspected who it was then, and if he finds that his hunch is right now, one big fatty sun-glassed head was going to roll.

Fifteen minutes after Todd Kirkus reads the blog post he's down at the high school, storming through the winter-break-emptied halls, looking for the computer lab and Johnny Opel. Whoever had answered the phone when he called Opel's house—sleepy-voiced, female—said he'd be down here. Merry Christmas. Opel, guy who graduated same year as Todd and Genny and went bouncing around town working gas station jobs while reading fantasy novels at the pump. Then, boom, computers, Bill Gates and soon, the Internet. Johnny Opel was sucked in. Started his own business called Dr. Wires, helping people with their computer programs, going in and killing viruses, driving around a stupid van he'd painted himself with a computer that had slanted eyes and a wriggling line for a mouth, thermometer jutted from its lips. Eventually he'd become the computer teacher at the high school and Dr. Wires shifted into a weekend business. Todd guessed the pay working for the school was steadier.

He found the computer lab on the first floor, nestled among the senior lockers, a room he remembered as being Business 2 when he was in school. He'd once made a business plan for the class with James Berg about a lawn care company whose main pull was that Todd and James would work with their shirts off. Dumb-ass high school stuff.

Todd ducked into the room, trembling. Johnny sat in a large cushioned wheelie chair, using a full table for a desk. Before him were three different monitors all sitting at different heights and angled to face him like inquisitive eyes of the same alien animal. His head jerked up at Todd's presence.

"Hiya, Todd."

"Looky, it's Johnny Opel." Todd was trying for casual, not an easy thing for him. He felt that if he were smaller it would come off better, but there was no way around the fact that he was huge. Tall and boxy in high school, he'd only packed on around his equator in the years since. Especially this last year. His hands in tight orbit between food and mouth. Eating somehow doing a trick on his thinking. Sounds, mostly. That's what he thought about. Had they screamed? Had the breaks?

He closed his eyes, slowed himself. He could do this, seem

calm. He didn't want to spook Johnny Opel so bad the guy didn't help him. "How you been? Still here, I see. No Bermuda vacation plans for you."

"I sunburn too easy." He took a slow sip of an enormous 7-Eleven bucket of pop.

"Hey, you know back in the day we always used to say you had a good name to be a rock star. You ever try that out? Being a rock star?"

The wrong thing to say. In school Opel been obsessed with Kiss and wore his hair long. Got pushed around some because of it.

"No I guess I haven't tried being a rock star, Todd."

"Oh, well, too bad. You would make a good one." Then, trying to take some of the weight out of the conversation, backpedal, "I tried to be a basketball star once, you saw how that worked out, ha ha."

Johnny sighed. "What's up?"

Todd ran a hand through his hair, paused to itch at the back of his skull. "Well, I guess you've seen this thing on the Internet? A website called, I guess, it's a web blog or something, called *Missteps*?"

"Oh, that. Yeah, I saw it."

"I was hoping, because you got Dr. Wires and you're the computer teacher, you could tell me who made the damn thing? Or at least take it down maybe."

"I don't know, Todd."

"Opel, it's not really for me though, you know? It's about my son, he's a quiet kid, like not really one to use what he got from playing basketball to lord it over other people. Different from me, you know? Look, I was an asshole, I get that. In high school, the worst. But this isn't for me. Jimmy, he's already had a tough go of it lately." Todd sank Johnny Opel with a stare that said what he hadn't said— *You know, about him and the wall and everything else.*

Already Opel was typing. "I don't know what I'll be able to do about taking it down. This blog is hosted by Google and they're pretty tight, really, for a public, free setup. We can send in a complaint, and they'll shut it down in a couple of days themselves. But what I can do now is post a link as a comment directly to the administrator, and he'll have to click it to approve or not, which will then get his ISP and I'll be able to get his physical location, you know. Or proximity. Like where his house is."

The whole explanation is beyond Todd and he has the distinct thought he's forgetting what's being said even as it's being said. He noticed something in Opel's eyes just before he'd cut them to the screen. Must be strange for him to see the former king of high school groveling.

While he works, Todd paces the room ringed with computers all showing the same rushing stars screen saver. He touches the mouse of one computer and it murmurs to life. Desktop a blown-up image of Columbia City High School's mascot, the Stomper. Big old fisherman with one foot forward, ready for a giant step into the future. Dopy nose and droopy eyes, Todd remembers how he was always a little embarrassed to be seen with that logo on his jersey while the other teams rocked things that could kill you. Cougars, lions, bears.

"Damn, guy already responded and, he's at, looks like the address is . . ." Johnny says. He looks up from the screen, hesitating.

"Yeah?"

"I guess it's old man Berg." Johnny coughs and takes a pull of his Coke. "At least I'd give it a ninety-eight percent probability it is."

Well god-fucking-damn. It's not how he thought it would feel. Knowing this. No blow-the-circuits-out anger. What Todd feels, really and truly deep into his bones, for the first time in his life, is old.

. . . . . .

Meanwhile, Jimmy's in his room, lying on his back, passing his ball up to the ceiling, where it bumps softly and dislodges paint flakes, thinking about what his grandpa said in the car. Magic. His basketball giving the people a little something to take with them. This thought almost bails out a bankrupt love. Almost. It still doesn't seem different enough from when he played to be perfect and anything less was failure. He can't slip back into basketball being his only counterbalance. That weight, he's found, is inconsistent.

He's noticed, thinking about his past, that there are moments that seem small in the before but grow big in the after. This thing the Flying Finn said about magic? Maybe it's a giant in the after. Seeing his mom lean into Doc McMahan's window, face red, back when he was nine? That's a redwood. The fact that his father keeps a dead cow skull glued to the dashboard of his work rig? A mountain. His grandpa a periodic bum? An ocean.

He needs to parse this out. This could be important. He's all buzzing. Then an image of Carla. Scribbling at the counter. A journal? Like a fucking after-school special, he laughs to himself. That's what it was like. Joke Dex would have loved. *Just write down your feelings, Lucy, and things will be OK . . .*

Jimmy is surprised Carla's number is in the phone book for some reason. Aren't they new to town?

A man answers. "Ferguson residence."

Jimmy pulls himself to it. This isn't natural. Butterflies on speed chipping away all manner of vital things on his insides. "Hi, may I speak to Carla, please?"

"Who's calling?"

"It's, well." Jimmy knows no one would want their daughter talking to him. His nickname is suddenly Kamikaze, after all, destruction. He says the first thing that comes into his head. "It's about Jesus?"

A let out. A sigh. That was a good move. "I'm a preacher, son, maybe I can help."

"It's just, see. Carla was talking to me about it . . . I was kind of hoping we could talk more."

"Who is this?" He asks again. Softer now.

"I'm embarrassed. Maybe I should go."

"No, hold on."

Scuffling, murmured words. Voices back and forth. A pause. Then clicking, scraping. "Hello?" It's Carla.

"Hi."

"Hi." Long draw-out on the *i*. She isn't sure who he is.

"It's Jimmy." He sits up. "Jimmy Kirkus? I saw you in Peter Pan."

More noises of the phone being brushed against something. A closing door. "Hi. Did you call me about Jesus?"

"I'm not scared of 6A."

"What?"

"You asked me, if I was scared? I'm not."

"But you're like, not on the team."

"Still." He's got the phone cord up around his feet so that he almost trips when he walks over to his window. Rain—again—and condensation on the glass. He draws a smiley face into the window fog. "You were writing? At the counter? What was that, like a journal?"

She giggles, nervous. "I guess it's something like that. It's *so* embarrassing. Don't tell anyone."

"Like your feelings?"

"Like my day. Or. Sometimes poems, or whatever."

"Can you write me one?"

"A poem?"

"Yeah."

"Oh, I don't really do that anymore." Voices in the background, the door being opened. "I gotta go," she says.

"Do you believe me?"

"What?"

"Do you believe me, about not being scared."

"I gotta go," she says again and hangs up.

He finds a notebook, opens it to a blank page before him. Write it all down, what a fucking waste of time. He jabs his pencil into the page, rips down and to the side, then throws his pencil across the room. It bounces off the wall—eraser end hitting—and then belly flops on the floor, its tip cracking off. He leaves it there and takes a pen from the cup bristling with writing utensils at the desk his pops set up for him in Dex's old room when he started homeschool lessons. He dots around the first line. It's the path of a bumblebee.

Jimmy grips the whole pen in a fist as though he were grabbing a bar to hang from. He etches into a new page, letters sprawling across three or four blue lines, IT'S THE FUCKING STUPIDEST THING IN THE WORLD TO WRITE ANYTHING DOWN. One whole page to get those giant-lettered words out. Breathing hard. Then, he keeps on with the next page, this time switching his grip to normal but still using big letters. LAST NIGHT I, he stops, goes back and crosses this out. Starts below it. NO MATTER IF I, again a stop, a cross out.

He stands up, paces the room, comes back and sits. *This writing it down thing isn't going to help anything, and I'll tell you why.* And he does.

Rule 14. When You Shine,
Don't Apologize for Your Sparkle

Tuesday, December 6, 2005

JIMMY KIRKUS, FOURTEEN YEARS OLD–TWO YEARS UNTIL THE WALL.

Jimmy started his freshman season under pressure you wouldn't believe. Already the college recruitment letters were coming in. Big envelopes with glossy tri-fold brochures brimming with positive stats, past players, and hints about Jimmy's eventual spot in campus hierarchy. *This is where the athletes eat . . .* The *Columbia City Standard* picked the Purple and Gold Fishermen as the preseason favorite to win the state title with little Jimmy at the helm. A day before the first game of the season, the paper ran a photo of him posing in his new Columbia City Fishermen jersey. He stood, arms folded, just enough to hang the uniform on. The headline read *The Second Coming . . . of Kirkus* and the article pushed its column legs all the way past the fold. News on distant wars, local elections, and a tax to fund repairs to the Mengler Bridge were all squished shorter that day, their headlines hardly getting breathing room under Jimmy's feet.

Neither of his parents made it to his first high school game, a matchup against the Tillamook Cheesemakers. The Flying Finn would have made it, if at all humanly possible, but no one in Columbia City would give him a ride and he'd failed his most recent driver's test in spectacular fashion: turning the Driver's Ed car the wrong way into the Warrington Bridge turnabout and driving straight into a bush in the center circle to avoid running head on into Officer Humphreys's police cruiser. No matter. Jimmy scorched the nets for 52 points in the Cheesemakers' gym. Capped it all off with a half-court buzzer-beater. Dex and Pedro stormed the court with the rest of the fans who had traveled, but they couldn't find him. Jimmy had promised to take the booster bus back with Dex and Pedro but his teammates had other plans. He was already swept onto the team bus, riding the shoulders of the upper classmen.

"Shit," Pedro said, "Jimmy was gonna ride back with us."

"You gonna cry?" Dex put Pedro in a loose headlock. "He just hit a half-court buzzer-beater, course he needs to go on the team bus. Can't be on the *booster* bus," Dex lowered his voice to a whisper, "These crazed fans would eat him alive!"

"You know, I got a tío who scored the winning goal for Mexico in World Cup against Uruguay."

"Damn, you got a tío for everything."

"I got a tío for your mom, you racist puta."

"I got a foot for you ass."

"I got a . . ." and on and on the boys went.

. . . . . .

After Jimmy hit that game winner in Tillamook, the seniors piled him on their shoulders. "Guys, I'm supposed to . . ." Jimmy yelled. "Pedro and Dex and me . . ."

They wouldn't listen, too hopped up on winning the game. Joe Looney, big slob of a guy, led the excitement, yelling, "We got our Mighty Mouse!" Everyone was excited but Ray Atto. It was his senior season after all. He had been the leading scorer two years running before Jimmy Kirkus came. Leading scorer on a losing team, but leading scorer still. Ray had finished the game with four points and five fouls. Worst output since middle school. He sulked to the bus with a towel over his head. What *was* he, if not a basketball stud?

On the bus ride home the rest of the team, all upperclassmen, erupted in the Fishermen cheer. It was a cheer that had been

JIMMY KIRKUS, FOURTEEN YEARS OLD—TWO YEARS UNTIL THE WALL.

around since before Freight Train. The coaches didn't exactly condone it, but wouldn't exactly stop it either.

"Three cheers for Columbia City High, you bring the whiskey, I'll bring the rye, send the seniors out for beer and don't let the sober FRESHMAN NEAR"—all fingers pointed to Jimmy, laughter rolling. *"We never falter, we never fall, we sober up on pure alcohol, watch the ro-yal faculty go stumbling down the hall! MORE BEER!"*

That night, in the back of the bus, junior cheerleader Naomi Smith sat next to Jimmy. He felt his heart in his hands. He trembled. She scooted closer to him on the cracked leather.

"You need more room?" he asked her. "I could give you more room."

She giggled. "You're funny."

A groupie! Jimmy realized all at once as she kissed his neck and trailed her lips downward. She gave him head that night as the bus rumbled home. It was something he and Pedro had joked about, but never thought would happen to either of them. Jimmy hadn't even puzzled out the mechanics fully. He was shocked that she was willing to put her mouth there. He worried over if they ought to use a condom. When he was almost there, she sat up and nibbled his ear and he came into his sweaty game jersey. He kicked the seat in front of him in ecstasy. Joe Looney roused from sleep long enough to say "corndog." Him and Naomi busted up laughing. Jimmy, exhausted, leaned back with Naomi's head on his shoulder. He knew his life was going to be, well, gravy from then on out.

. . . . . .

The next few games went much the same. Jimmy broke off audacious bushels of points as if there were perforated lines on the future—some cut-here directions that made the amazing things he did come off so easy they seemed scripted. Ordained. Word spread quickly through the league that our kid Jimmy was for real. Opinions floated around about the best way to stop him. Full-court press? Dedicated doubles? Traps? Nope. Six games into the season—all wins—and our kid averaging just over 29 points a game. Give him a breath's whisper and he'd dagger the shot every time. Just ask the Tillamook Cheesemakers.

Fifty-two points!

From a little, skinny, freshman kid?

Holy God!

Opposing coaches planned Jimmy Kirkus specials. Defensive schemes and setups that would do something, anything, to slow the scoring machine. It turned out little helped against Jimmy, as he was a gifted passer. In the seventh game of the season the coach of Clatskanie subbed in new defenders to guard Jimmy at every whistle. Fresh legs and whenever he got past half court, a double team. Still, nothing doing. Kid Kirkus dished out twenty-three assists that night, a school and league record, and still managed eighteen points. Fishermen won in a blowout.

After the game in Clatskanie's echo-heavy gym Coach Kelly, at the top of his lungs, shouted, "Way to go Jimmy! Making the rest of these bums look like stars!" He was joking of course, but . . .

Ray Atto, on his way past Coach, said, "So we're bums now?"

"Now, Ray, come on," Coach Kelly pleaded. "Not how I meant it."

Jimmy lingered after his teammates filtered from the gym to say hi to Dex and Pedro. He waded through the remaining fans still buzzing around slapping him on his shoulder, asking him to pose in their photos. He was newly weary about his best friend and brother. How could they fit into this time where he made the big shots and was carried off the court, a hero?

"You pass too?" Pedro said sarcastically. "How's that?"

"Yeah." Jimmy laughed.

"You were looking sharp, kid!"

"Sharp enough to cut," Dex said.

"Sharp enough for a knife to be fucking jealous," Pedro chimed in.

"Thanks, guys," Jimmy said, hoping to stop their routine before they really got into the momentum of it. A back and forth they found funny, but he never was comfortable jumping into himself. A lot of shouting and obscure references. Who can say the weirdest thing with the most bluster. It brought stares.

"Hey, Jimmy, the Wildwood sisters rode the booster up with us." Dex chucked his brother on the arm, gave him a wink. "Pretty cute, serious, so what you say we talk to them? After all, you're the great Jimmy Kirkus and their last name is Wildwood. They can get wild on our wood!"

"Yeah, yeah, Jimmy, you can be our in," Pedro said.

"There's only two, Pedro, so do your math," Dex said.

"What?"

"He's going to be *my* in, not yours."

"Man, you're still in eighth grade. Why they want to get with a child when they can have a man?"

"'Cause at least I *look* like a man. You don't even got hair in your armpits, squeaky."

Jimmy ignored them and watched Naomi walk by. Ray Atto was walking with her, whispering in her ear, flexing on her, but hell, she couldn't deny what had happened on the bus ride back from the Tillamook game. Even though it hadn't happened in all the away games since, it was *undeniable*, that was the word. They had history together. Maybe love? Something to build on at least. *Anything* could happen. A girlfriend?

"Hey, sorry guys," Jimmy interrupted their argument, "Coach wants the team to ride home together."

"Damn, Jimmy," Pedro said.

"Jimmy?" Dex asked.

"Sorry." Jimmy trotted off. He turned back to them, shrugged his shoulders, trying to make a joke of it, "When you're a star, your time is not your own." It came off lousy, he knew, and yet he still felt freer being rid of them.

. . . . . .

"Your brother's acting like a pendejo," Pedro said.

"Learn English, hombre."

"'Pendejo' means asshole, asshole. Study up."

"I know what 'pendejo' means, pendejo. I walk around with you all day, don't I? You're like the picture next to the word 'pendejo' in the dictionary, just you're walking around." Dex grabbed Pedro in a headlock and gave him a noogie.

"I'll kick your ass when my growth spurt hits!" Pedro yelled.

"Yeah, yeah, write me in a million years when that happens."

Back on the booster bus, sitting between old Mrs. Craig knitting a purple and gold blankie and this kid Wilson who once wore a tinfoil suit to prom, Pedro called over the aisle to Dex. "You ever heard Coach Kelly make the team ride back together?"

"How the hell should I know?" Dex said. He looked out the window. He was jammed into the side of the bus by a large guy eating two corndogs—one in each fist—that he had bought at the concession stand after the game when all perishable food was half off. A little tray of ketchup balanced on his belly. Dex recognized him as one of the gas station attendants at 76. "I'm not on the fucking team am I?"

"Watch your language, young man," the fat guy said. With his words he spackled Dex with little bits of corndog.

"Dude, you're double-fisting. I think that's the sign of a problem eater. Your heart says help."

The fat man burped a disgusting odor in response, something

between the heaviness of bad meat and the tangy spike of bodily sweat. He didn't bother to turn away. Dex gagged and the bus rumbled along. The giggles of the Wildwood sisters, sitting up front with a couple of sophomore boys, wafted over the seats, poisoning his mood further.

. . . . . .

Meanwhile, over on the team's bus—headed the same place, separated by just a few cars but worlds apart—Jimmy was the last to board. The only seat left was near the front, across from Coach Kelly. He heard Naomi and the other cheerleaders laughing from the back. Ray Atto's voice seemed to be the loudest of all, a bray that rose as it closed in on the punch lines to his raunchy jokes.

The whole ride home, Jimmy had to smell Coach Kelly's breath as he went on and on about how successful the season would be.

"Seven games, seven wins. That's even better than your father, Jimmy!"

He reeked heavily of the garlicky pizza he'd eaten sometime between the game ending and boarding the bus. It was strange because Jimmy couldn't remember Coach ever leaving the locker room while they were all showering and changing. Made him think of Coach Kelly bolting down the pizza in one of the bathroom stalls, worried that if anyone knew, he'd have to share. Sitting with his heels perched up on the toilet's edge so no one could tell he was inside. It was the sort of joke that Dex would have made.

. . . . . .

The *Columbia City Standard* ran another basketball feature, this time on the Fishermen's first seven wins. It featured a huge picture of Jimmy flashing through the lane. The Flying Finn cut it out and Genny Mori paid for the frame. Finn took the framed page with him to whatever room he was in. It sat in a chair across from him while he ate his lunch, it watched from the couch while he rode his bike set up on a spinning stand, it fogged up, frame growing warped, while he took his famously long showers.

. . . . . .

It had been a certain kind of torture throughout Columbia City that the first seven games of the season had been away. The eighth of the year, homecoming against archrival Seaside and the all-state wing that suited up for them, Shooter Ackley, was circled on every calendar. Even Todd and Genny Mori made plans to watch the game together. Trying to get someone to cover your shift? Forget about it. Jimmy Kirkus was coming home.

JIMMY KIRKUS, FOURTEEN YEARS OLD–TWO YEARS UNTIL THE WALL.

Rule 15. No Press Is Bad Press

Wednesday, December 26, 2007

JIMMY KIRKUS, SIXTEEN YEARS OLD—NINE DAYS AFTER THE WALL.

It's 5:30 and everyone is tuned in to KMUN. A call-in talk show with a crazy host. Chris Fogg. Guy who regularly produces can-you-believe-he-just-said-that audio clips. A forum where opinion is shaped for the entire town. Something not to be missed.

> *I'm Chris Fogg and you're listening to the Weather Report on KMUN Community Coast Radio. Let's hope Santa brought you all the good stuff you'd been hoping for. New TVs and stockings full of chocolate bars. Probably not, though. Probably you're all sad from this tinseled day of cheer and ready to blow off some steam counting it down to New Year's!*
>
> *I've got a big one to start off. Our sponsor Les Schwab is giving free beef again with any new set of tires. You know how I feel about free beef. You can't beat free beef. So even if you don't got a car and you're just getting new bike tires, go get some free beef . . .*
>
> *Hey, and speaking of beef, looks like Jimmy Kirkus is back into basketball! He put on quite the show at Peter Pan Courts. There's video of Jimmy's ten-opponent smack-down all on the YouTube, but I suspect foul play! A Christmas gift? A Christmas hoax! The shots are grainy. Gray. Who knows? Couldn't some prankster have Photoshopped that YouTube? Can't be real, can it?*

So Jimmy Kirkus. He's got a nickname now. Kamikaze. It's way better than Jimmy Soft, which, I'm sorry, could give the wrong ideas to the ladies! I like Kamikaze. It's close to the kid's heritage. Sort of rolls off the tongue. Kamikaze. Means "a divine wind" in Japanese, my producer tells me. Which, as some of you know, is me. And Google. Me and Google. I produce my own show. But, moving on . . . I'm sure you've all read the blog, this Missteps thing—the pot has been stirred!

Anyway, we're taking your calls for the top half of the Weather Report, so give me a jingle, let me know what you make of Jimmy Kirkus playing ball again, him running into a wall and if Coach Kelly should let him back on the team! Let's get the conversation going here on the Weather Report.

Hello, Chris? This the Weather Report? Jimmy Kirkus should be booted off the team. He can't. I mean, just coming back whenever he feels like it. Like I was saying to the guys at work, you gotta commit one way or the . . .

I had Jimmy back when he was in third, no I think it must have been fourth grade, and he wrote this most beautiful little poem about a caterpillar becoming a butterfly. I think it speaks to what this poor kid is going through. Metamorphosis. Becoming that beautiful butterfly and . . .

He doesn't deserve the purple and gold . . .

The kid is reeling. Can't anyone see that? I mean, I swear to god people are blind. He's what, all of sixteen? This is not a grown man playing professional basketball, this is a high school kid. Does nobody get that? Oh, I forgot, just because . . .

JIMMY KIRKUS, SIXTEEN YEARS OLD–NINE DAYS AFTER THE WALL.

Hello, hello? This where Fultano's pizzas? I want one cheese, and, ha ha, two orders of . . .

It's embarrassing, I'll tell you that much right now. Seaside's got Shooter Ackley gunning through the league and we're so goddamn, oh, excuse me, Chris. Didn't mean to cuss on your show. But we're so desperate to put up a fight last year in 6A we gonna get a frickin' head case suit up for us? We that desperate? God bless the kid, but we might as well go trolling for street people. I mean he's got issues. Kirkus Curse. That blog thing was right. Less we hear of Kamikaze Kirkus, the better . . .

You weren't there, Chris. You might as well stop calling him Jimmy, 'cause that wasn't no Jimmy. That was Kamikaze, just like his nickname say. Can't deny it if you were there. He's a player, boy, he's a player again. All people calling in who weren't there should shut it. 'Cause if you were there, then ho-ly . . .

He needs help. Have you seen the video? There's a part of him missing . . .

. . . . . .

Carla turns off the radio. She leans back into the big, run-down couch that is as ugly as it is comfortable. A present from the parish. Her father and mother and siblings are out for the night service. She's begged to stay in. Told them all that she was feeling ill. And maybe she is. She *does* feel a little warm.

Her dad was all, "Carla, honey, are you sure?"

And she snapped. "It was an accident, OK? I had a headache and I took too many, and it was an accident! Gosh!" They'd slinked off after that. Taking too many pills and being admitted to the hospital has given her more power than she's ever known.

She gets up and checks her e-mail. There's a new one come in with subject line: *HOLY FUCKING SHIT*. Her face blooms hot when she reads that. She curses herself and urges the blush to die. How's she ever going to fit in if any cuss turns her into a tomato? She checks over her shoulder even though she knows she's alone. There, at the bottom of a litany of comments from the people it was forwarded to before, is a QuickTime video. She clicks it before reading anything.

It's Jimmy and the wall. Just as she's imagined it from what people have said. When Jimmy disappears below the bottom of the frame, it is as if she feels the hit. Every time he comes back on to camera, it's a little slower, a little more wobbly. His blood shows up black on the monochrome security footage and this helps dull the reality, a little. Then again, there's so much of it that when she imagines it as its true red, she feels faint. She remembers his head in the hospital, and then later, at Peter Pan, his hand. Him on the phone. His voice didn't hold what she sees in this clip. Was whatever drove him to this still in him?

Seeing that grainy video wakes up something inside Carla, something she has to get out. She fights it for a moment, this urge, and then lets go. If she doesn't scratch, this itch will bug her all night. What she wants, more than anything, is to just tag on some generically shocked line similar to the others, just to get her in the game, and be done with it. Have the easiness the other kids she sees around live their lives by. A by-product of continuity, she assumes. But she can't do this. What she's just seen is too heavy to just flip off down the road. She's cried at Dove soap commercials before, so this, this needs something more.

Plus, he asked her to write him something, and he's cute, kind of. So, whatever.

She gets out the stack of *Columbia City Standard* newspapers her father collects for sermon ideas. She's looking through headlines.

JIMMY KIRKUS, SIXTEEN YEARS OLD—NINE DAYS AFTER THE WALL.

When she gets to one on Jimmy, she runs her finger through the article until she finds a word she likes, something that has enough weight in it to make this all seem more real. Then she carefully cuts it out. Then back to the newspaper. Soon she has enough. She arranges them on a white page, pins each in place with a bit of tape. It's a poem, of course.

She sits back in the couch. There was a time, when she was younger, that she didn't think of her family as the red flag they've become. She didn't smell the mustiness on the hand-me-down clothes that the other kids seemed to be able to pick up at great distances. She didn't mind her mother's crisp, just-so hairstyle, and thought her father's jokes were as funny as he did. Then something happened and she could see herself and her family how others must see them. A collection of ill-fitting, well-intentioned but not-to-be-taken-seriously spiritual vagabonds who would be rotated back out in three or four years—off to some other poor town to start all over with an awkward coffee-and-cake morning hour in a pink-aquarium room somewhere in the church basement, smelling strongly of papier-mâché from last year's divinity play.

So for Carla, even more than other kids her age, fitting in is the big goal. She doesn't do well with the scattershot questions of beginning relationships. Little chip-offs of her self as she answers poorly, or says something stupid. People are scared of her earnestness, her immediate care. It takes months to ease past that. Get down to who she really is.

. . . . . .

Jimmy's in bed. Halfway through Christmas Break. It's raining outside. Too warm for snow, too cold for anything else, gray everywhere. Columbia City's painter's pallet smudged for sure. He has to avoid his pops and the Flying Finn and all their leading questions for seven more whole days before he can go back to school, ignore everyone, and just think. After the Nine Games, wandering the woods doesn't feel right, but home isn't exactly a sanctuary. All his pops and grandpa want him to do is talk. Like him talking is the only way they'll know if he's all right. It's too much. He's quaking and stuffs the edge of the pillow into his mouth. He hasn't showered in days. He smells sour. He's crying. Howling. A great emptying out that he tries to bite off on the edge of the pillow but it keeps coming. He doesn't feel an end inside him. Cars are imperfect machines. The risk that comes from getting from one place to another seems a bad one. And for a stupid pay-off. Shallow. The world is a shitty place. For as good as he'd felt at Peter Pan Courts, it's all gone now.

Last week he met twice with Mrs. Cole at her home, Pops waiting in the running van. Both times it was she who broke down weeping, swept him into her chest and gripped the back of his head, saying all the while how it would be OK. With time, all would heal. Strange, but both times he felt that just talking was helping.

His pops knocks on the door. "Hey Jimmy?"

Jimmy coughs. His pops heard him crying, for sure. "Yeah?"

"Can I come in a sec?" Even his pops thinks if he's left alone he'll start slamming his head into a wall again. Like he can't wait to do it. Like it hadn't been a last resort.

"Whatever." His voice is still husky from crying. He wishes it weren't, it would make lying about how he's perfectly fine easier.

"Hey, buddy." His pops looks around his room. It's a mess. Jimmy in a tangle of sheets with dirty laundry flung about. His pops takes out another one of his peppermints. Cracks it in his teeth. Everything must taste the same to him for how often he eats those. Like peppermint must be the flavor on everything for him. Sweet even when he doesn't want to taste sweet. "You OK?"

"I'm fine, pops. Coach call?" And while Jimmy doesn't care

about basketball, or rather isn't sure if he does, he knows this question will set his pops back so he asks it. Because of the Brick Wall Incident, the school isn't sure he should play, his pops isn't sure he should play, even Coach Kelly isn't sure he should play. And Jimmy himself? Well, that's what all the thinking, and crying, is about. How much does it actually matter if he plays against the best? It's a game. A stupid one. And yet.

"No, Jimmy. Nobody called."

Jimmy knows what's coming. He just directed the conversation there after all. But all he wants is to sleep all day. He rolls over in his bed so he doesn't have to watch his pops give whatever variation of the Basketball Might Not Be for You speech he's worked up to today.

He manages to ignore the first bit, but by the end, his ears can't help themselves. "But look, you shouldn't be waiting around. Could be better you don't play? Whole town's nothing but vultures, I can tell you that firsthand, why you want to play for vultures? A good life doesn't have to have basketball in it. Right?"

"Right."

"Right?"

Jimmy rolls back to look at his pops. "But. I still maybe want to play. So . . ." And it's true and not true at all, and how is Jimmy supposed to make his pops understand both those things?

. . . . . .

Looking at Jimmy in the eyes sends a chill through Todd. *Those black hole eyes*, he thinks, *Jesus*. Same eyes as when he told him to turn the van around. Get the Flying Finn. He couldn't say no to him then.

He sees in his son an echo of what he himself has battled ever since Suzie and the beach. This recognition makes him all the more desperate to snap the kid out of it. Depression is insidious because it clouds the ability to look upon oneself, take stock. If Jimmy isn't careful, he'll wake up and half his life will be gone.

A floor up, the Flying Finn drops a tin bowl. It clatters loudly. Todd imagines pancake batter spilled everywhere. The Flying Finn giggles wildly. "Order up, hot, hot, hot." Todd doesn't want to be stuck cleaning up again. He has to get up there and catch the old kook before he skips the house for the day to avoid the chore. He knows he should be patient, stay with his son. But hell, the whole thing is shot through with holes. Hardened pancake batter, coating the cracks in the floor, no thanks. It would be easier if he could just have some time away from looking after his son, if he could just get a break. He can't. He has to keep constant watch. In the couple years before the wall, he'd let his focus drift. Jimmy coming home with random cuts on his forehead, knees skinned through ripped holes in his sweats. Boys being boys. Not anymore. Those all added up to something terrible. Now he needs to keep track of all the information he can get from his son, do the arithmetic fast, and get out in front of the equation. "Well, look, the reason I came down is 'cause this girl Carla, you know her?"

Jimmy narrows his eyes. Todd sees the gears stick, and then roll again. His son is remembering. He's noticed how his boy's mind catches like this since the wall. Sad to see. A side effect of blunt-force trauma to the head, maybe.

Jimmy's body becomes looser. He sits up. Wavers. "Yeah."

Todd smiles, a human reaction coming from his boy. Red-blooded. A girl. "She dropped this off." He holds up the poem. "Any idea what this is?"

"No, I—" Jimmy says quickly, a hand on his forehead.

"It's a poem."

"Well, give it." He's already swinging his feet off the bed.

"Come up to the kitchen, it'll be on the table," Todd says,

turning away, happy with the hook he's set. "Grandpa's cooking breakfast."

. . . . . .

The poem is more a list of words than anything—"dazzle," "genius," "points," "rebounds," "crowd," "record," "Jimmy Kirkus"— but after each pasted-on word Carla has drawn a dotted line to a bubble on the margins. In each bubble is the date and title of the article the word came from, a sort of bibliography. Carla. He is thirsty and drenched all at once. Puzzle pieces, every organ inside him. Like they need proper placement and she has the diagram to show exactly where each one is meant to go.

Some of the words are highlighted in yellow with a second line sprouting from them, leading to a definition:

Col-li-s-ion

noun

1. an instance of one moving object or person striking violently against another : a midair collision between two aircraft.

It's a detailed web of words that Jimmy imagines as a diagram of Columbia City's collective mind and how it thinks of him. He's got a cold sweat. There at the kitchen table, he thinks he can figure it all out, crack the code. He rereads the poem five or six times in a row. He realizes he's taking this too seriously. But that's his way. He remembers in practice back in freshman year, when Coach Kelly was done with the drills and the scrimmages, he kept the gym open for the guys to play around. Joe Looney liked to guard Jimmy just so he could post him up on offense, yell, "Mouse in the house, mouse in the house," get the ball and dribble his comet dribbles, BANG! BANG! BANG!, backing Jimmy up with his sizeable ass, the whole team cracking up. It was a joke, for laughs, and yet Jimmy couldn't get it. His teammates would yell to him,

"Jesus, just take it easy, Kirkus," but he would try everything he knew to stop Joe's rumble to the hoop. Pushing back with all his strength, going for the steal, trying a defense move he saw Ron Artest do in an NBA game Dex used to call "pulling the chair." And when Joe would score, Jimmy felt a failure. Cussed himself out. Threw the ball down, stormed off. He couldn't take it easy. He couldn't slow down. Same as right now, with these words. No way they're as important as he's making them out to be, but he can't stop. He finds he likes it this way. Good to admit that.

He doesn't know exactly what this girl—this amber girl, Carla—had in mind when she made this poem for him, but he remembers asking her for it. Now he needs to do something for her, something in response to show how he really is.

. . . . . .

Later Todd Kirkus is out on a jog along the River Walk. The Flying Finn is back at the house with his bike propped in his old a spinning stand, watching a taped Tour de France, trying to get back into shape. This latest stint on the streets has left him pouchy, poorly fitted. He and Todd have split shifts so Jimmy is never alone. Now's Todd's turn to be out and there's a freedom sprouting inside of him to finally be away from that morose house, and he feels guilty because of it.

It seems his son wants to start playing again. After everything, it's still in him. And if he fails? Gets out on the court again, carrying the water for everyone's dreams, and he freezes up? Starts missing shots, turning the ball over, living up to that shitty little nickname they've all been calling his son—*Jimmy Soft*—what then? That chant. *"Dad-dy's bet-ter!"*

It's just rained and his shoes make little wet slaps on each step. Todd's running faster, Columbia River out to his right, a big barge delicately navigating the sand banks. There's a class of people in Columbia City, barge pilots, whose job is to motor out to the ships taking containers of gypsum or coal up to Portland, and pilot them through the sand bars. Obstacles they know like the backs of their hands because they navigated them before. They make clear over a hundred grand a year, Todd's heard.

Now it hits Freight Train that he's been going about this in the wrong way. Ever since he had his boys he thought that to protect them would be to keep them away from basketball. Really, what he should have been doing is teaching them ways to thrive. Balling was a given, but how they did it wasn't. Todd turns around and heads home. Faster now. Really pushing it. Feet pound. If Jimmy is going to come back to basketball, Todd will make damn sure he's ready.

Rule 16.
If You Crack, Crack for the Whole World to See

Tuesday, Jan 24, 2006

JIMMY KIRKUS, FIFTEEN YEARS OLD—TWO YEARS UNTIL THE WALL.

Todd Kirkus wanted to see his boy in action, but hesitated because the last time he was in the Brick House play had literally stopped for the fans to cheer him on. He didn't want to take any of the attention away from Jimmy, so he made a plan with Genny Mori to come and go swift and unseen. Hell, even Dex thought his pops was working that night. After he met his wife out front with the game in progress, they'd go in the back way and watch from a secret spot he had discovered in high school. A little balcony where the lights were set up when the gym served as a theater. Then his little Jimmy would make him proud and Todd and Genny would leave before the final buzzer. Home making dinner before his kid even left the court.

Todd parked in the very rear of the jam-packed parking lot under a dead light. He felt a giddiness at being secretive. He waited inside the van for his wife to be dropped off by Bonnie. Todd wondered if they ever talked about him. Was he ever the reason for those little giggles they shared over the phone?

Then he saw Genny Mori in the passenger seat of a black luxury car he didn't recognize. Driving was this little, handsome man with a vague smile, somehow overdone and undercooked all at once. The man dropped Genny at the back entrance of the gym. Then the black car slid away, smooth.

When Todd came up to her, she was startled out of checking her lipstick in the foldable mirror she took with her everywhere.

"Jesus, Todd!" Her face was clenched in real fear. Then this melted as she studied his face. She playfully slapped him. "You scared me," she grabbed a hold of his shirt and pulled herself toward him. She gave him these little bird kisses up and down the side of his face. Her breath hot cinnamon. "Can't just sneak up like that."

"I didn't mean to," he said, stunned.

She kept kissing him, up and down his face, even while he talked.

"Whoa, so many kisses."

She answered him between kisses. "Well. You. Scared. Me." She was probably a little drunk, but that wasn't out of the ordinary. She sometimes went out with Bonnie after shifts—*but she hadn't been with Bonnie.*

"You kiss a lot when you're scared? I never knew that about you." She was nervous and he was annoyed. Some little man driving her to the game? He could call her out on it, bring it all to a boil right here, right now, no matter who got scalded in the process. But. Still there was a universe where it was all explainable, where that little man was nothing more than a ride to the game because Bonnie had been sick or tied up at work or stuck with a flat tire. If he didn't confront her then that universe still existed and his wife was faithful and these little kisses were little signs that things were all right.

She kissed him one last time, pressed hard into his cheekbone, and he could feel the edge of her teeth pushing through her pillow lips.

"Let's go inside."

"So you're finally getting me into the famous Kirkus Love Den?"

Todd didn't laugh. An older him and a drunk Genny Mori. "I guess so."

They managed to sneak in unnoticed and up the stairs but when they reached the little balcony they weren't alone. James Berg. Todd's stomach clenched, but he couldn't go anywhere else. Instead, he nodded to him and James nodded back. Genny Mori noticed Berg. "James, how are you?"

"Fine, Genny, you?"

"Drunk."

Todd unfolded two metal chairs and placed them by the low handrail as far away from Berg as he could get them. The gym was packed. Fans wore their purple and gold for the Fishermen or their silver and red for the Seagulls. Todd gritted his teeth as the band broke into a sloppy but energetic "Sloop John B." The crowd clapped along.

On the court, Jimmy was ten points into another phenomenal night—Fishermen-faithful well into their favorite chant, *"He's our fresh-man, he's our fresh-man"*—when the Seaside coach called a defensive switch. He put the heralded Shooter Ackley on him. Shooter was the same kid Jimmy had run circles around back in the Shoeless Game only he had grown. Tough bull-moose sophomore with adult frame stacked thick with the preening, always-flexing muscles of someone obsessed with the pursuit of them. He was quick too. Good enough lateral movement to mostly stay in front of Jimmy, and when our kid really turned on the jets, enough savvy to anticipate, harass, pester the advantage away. Already pissed off at the ten points Jimmy had dropped, he defended him first with his body and second with his hands. Wasn't about to let Jimmy get anything easy.

First possession after the defensive switch—an inbounds pass—Jimmy turned to start up the floor only to find Shooter, strangely, huffing alongside him, chest up into Jimmy's shoulder. This was something new. Teams didn't usually try and pull this on our kid, he was too fast. So Jimmy decided to make him pay. Behind the back, change of direction, all out speed. Weird though, Shooter seemed to know this move was coming, came right up into Jimmy's shoulder again.

"You *small* for a superstar," Shooter said in his ear. "Aren't you scared of getting hurt?"

Jimmy passed the ball to Matty Kemper on the wing, kind of forced it. Kemper barely got a hold of it.

"Careful, Jimmy!" Coach Kelly yelled from the sideline.

Jimmy ran to the wing. Their two posts, Joe Looney and Marty Cole, were doing a little screen and pop set up. Jimmy was happy to be out of the play. Shooter lagged off him a little, but still, kept talking. "Yeah, it's best you pass. You ain't used to me."

Seaside got the rebound and on the way back down the court, Shooter demanded the ball. "I heard about your pops and his knee. If I was you, I'd be scared of breaking mine," he said. Then he knocked Jimmy in the gut and drove past him for a bucket. Nodded his head, like, yeah, that's right. Jimmy looked to the ref, begging for a call. Nothing.

On the way back down the court Shooter continued, "Don't that run in the family? Weak knees? Don't you Kirkuses truck in some kind of curse? It'll hit you, you know that right? Just a matter of when."

"Hey man, shut the fuck up," someone called from the Fishermen's bench.

Shooter held up his hands like "what, me?" but kept jawing. Something was happening to Jimmy. Memory of his fall on the river walk. Thought of how his pops lost his whole basketball career. The Sand Toad. He was small. He'd never grow. The game giveth and it taketh away. Shooter wasn't letting him get anything easy. Hounding him every step. Jimmy started to sweat. An unsure feeling soaked him, left him shaking. Changing him from the inside out. Jimmy took a shot. He missed.

. . . . . .

Todd tried to take the anger spawned from his wife being dropped off by some curly-haired little puke and James Berg being in his secret spot and press it onto the silver and red of the Seagulls, the enemy. Coach Kelly used to tell him he wasn't a failure unless his team lost to the Seaside Seagulls.

But no. What the hell did he care about high school rivalries anymore? Was that why James Berg was watching from up in the shadows? Some lingering, beating heat against the Seagulls? No. It was more than that now. It was about his son. It wasn't about beating Seaside, it was about beating everyone. Or no one. Just so long as Jimmy was happy. That was all he cared about—and he was happy to realize it.

Todd watched his boy, his little Jimmy, get knocked around something fierce by that tough kid from Seaside called Shooter. *Did some asshole actually name his son Shooter?* Suddenly, he could see that Shooter was in Jimmy's head, under his skin. His son hesitated before his shots, flinched easily, and was often confused. There was defeat in his eyes. Ironic because Freight Train had given that same look to plenty of players in his day, doing the same sorts of things Shooter was doing now. Got opponents to the point where they admitted they were beat even before they made a play. His son was playing like the type of player Todd used to call soft. Looking to the ref for bailout calls rather than stepping up. And what the hell was Coach Kelly doing, keeping him in the game? Kid should've been nailed to the bench for the way he was playing. No special treatment. He felt his ears turn red. He was embarrassed that James was there behind him, seeing Jimmy choke; but then, there was more. He was embarrassed that James was seeing him and his wife at this particular moment.

"That Seaside boy sure is strong," Genny Mori said. Todd looked at her and was about to say something when she stood up and pointed at a man walking in front of the packed bleachers below, looking for a seat. "I know him," she said, "from the hospital." She cupped her mouth and shouted down from the balcony. "Doctor McMahan, Doctor McMahan, over here!"

James Berg shifted in his chair, coughed. Todd looked at him briefly—*same fucking face*—then turned back to Genny Mori. He grabbed her elbow. "There's no room up here." She was giving away his secret spot.

"Would you quit it?" she whispered viciously. "He's alone and needs someone to sit with."

People in the crowd began to look up at the balcony. The whispering started. "Todd Freight Train Kirkus was there to watch his son stink it up!" The gossip was brewing. Todd gripped Genny Mori's elbow harder, about to yank her back into her seat when he recognized the man as the same one she had gotten a ride from. Todd let go.

Pretending there was a universe where everything was OK between him and his wife was getting harder. Why would Genny or the little man even want this if they were doing something shadowy? It was confusing. Maybe there really wasn't anything to worry about. Then again, maybe it was a thrill to sit together in front of the man behind whose back their love lived. Give him a solid *fuck you*.

Genny Mori sat back down with her cheeks burning and a big smile stretched across her mouth, rubbing her elbow. "What a coincidence," she said.

"A fucking coincidence."

"Relax, Todd, he's a basketball fan."

By the time Doc McMahan found his way up to the balcony,

even the Seagulls' fans in the gym had caught on that Jimmy's famous father was in attendance. They started a new chant. It shook Todd's already reeling mind.

"Dad-dy's bet-ter!"

"Dad-dy's bet-ter!"

"Dad-dy's bet-ter!"

Todd's face flushed. *What in the hell is a freshman kid supposed to do with that?*

. . . . . .

Shooter played rough and was called for a few fouls, sure, but it was a better-than-even trade so long as he was able to carve out a spot in Jimmy's head. And he did. Shooter kept whispering aloud Jimmy's worst doubts. Used all the ammo he'd gathered from trolling the Oregonlive.com high school basketball chat rooms. Jimmy's arms felt watery. Eyesight blurry. Coach Kelly yelled louder from the bench and the refs called fewer fouls. The game became rougher. Something was wrong with Jimmy's shot. It wasn't going in. He couldn't understand it. This was the thing he'd always known how to do. Ever since kindergarten. Simple, easy, him. But. Not anymore. There was a hitch to it suddenly, too much thought in the mix.

Soon Shooter didn't even have to knock Jimmy around, all he had to do was taunt and our kid would miss.

"Your baby bro's bigger than you."

Brick.

"Your Grandpa sleeps on the streets."

Whiff.

"Your daddy was better."

Air ball.

Jimmy clanked wide-open looks. Botched easy floaters and even missed a breakaway lay-in when the nearest Seagull was half the court away. His mouth was dry, but at time-outs, he couldn't swallow water.

JIMMY KIRKUS, FIFTEEN YEARS OLD—TWO YEARS UNTIL THE WALL.

He noticed Dex and Pedro in the stands. Laughing, high as kites, they'd smoked weed for the first time just before the game. Jimmy knew because Ray Atto had caught them behind the Brick House on his way to the locker room. Came in and told Jimmy how his baby bro liked to "puff-puff-pass that shit." During one time-out, Jimmy saw Dex and Pedro giggling with a couple of freshman girls and all he wanted was to be where they were, be *who* they were. But no. Fuck them. They were a part of the problem too. Pedro wasn't any kind of friend—always drafting off him. And Dex, kid didn't work hard to be good like Jimmy did, just *was* that way. He wasn't a baller, this wasn't his life, he didn't know how it felt. And now, look at them, just laughing their asses off. Not even *seeing* this. One look from his bro, that was all he needed. But no, Dex and Pedro were leaving. Off to concessions again for something else to ease the munchies. Stoners.

"Jimmy, come on now, pull it together," Coach Kelly shouted above the chant, above the noise of the crowd.

Jimmy snapped out of it. "OK?"

"OK!"

The whistle blew. Time-out over. Jimmy went back on the court to face Shooter. Legs trembling.

. . . . . .

McMahan found his way up to the balcony. Sat down like it was just a coincidence, like *Wow, I just showed up and DID NOT give your wife a ride here.*

"Sure nice to meet you, Todd," Doc said as he leaned across Genny Mori. "I was going to have to watch the game by my lonesome."

Todd reached out and shook the man's hand. Small and damp. How the hell could people trust this guy to do surgeries? He used words like "lonesome." "Got a kid playing?"

"Nope, just a fan of Jimmy's."

"So you just like watching adolescent boys sweat?"

The Doc giggled, uncomfortable. "Funny. Hey, I got a little something extra in my soda if you care to . . ." He held out his paper cup with the blue PepsiCo logo on its side. Todd had probably delivered that cup, one in a box of hundreds, to the high school. A single delivery in a long line of other deliveries. A life of deliveries. Work heavy on the back, light in the pockets. And now here was *this* guy—caramel leather shoes so soft they were in danger of melting onto the floor, chunky watch catching light, silky, well-fitting clothes—here in this hot, dust-mote gym.

"He doesn't drink anymore," Genny Mori offered.

Todd tilted his head and took in Berg out the corner of his eye. *Everyone thinks they know my problems.* And while it was true, he'd stopped drinking since that day wallowing in the sand for Suzie so long before, it wasn't as official as his wife was making it sound. There was room to wiggle. The poke had come with the word "anymore." How it suggested a problem to this complete stranger. "I'll take some just the same," he said.

"What?"

"Sure, why the hell not, Genny? I'm here to see my boy play some ball."

"Why the hell not!" The Doc laughed loud and fake. A bark, really. "Why the hell not! I love this guy."

Todd wanted to punch him. He took the cup and downed it in three looping swallows. Same fire as always but an almost immediate hit to the senses, his tolerance shot. How wonderful. He noticed Genny cut eyes at the Doc.

"A real pro!" the Doc said sarcastically and took out his flask and a bottle of Pepsi.

Todd mixed a new drink, heavy on the whiskey. Then, before he handed the flask back, he took another big swallow. "For a kick start," he said.

JIMMY KIRKUS, FIFTEEN YEARS OLD—TWO YEARS UNTIL THE WALL.

Alcohol warmed him like he remembered. Like how shower water pressed heat behind your eyes. He drank and tried not to talk. He knew eventually the whiskey would make his legs light. He looked forward to that. And they drank, all of them silent, and watched Shooter Ackley and the Seaside Seagulls take basketball away from his son.

. . . . . .

Back on the court doubt spread to every part of Jimmy's game. His passing became sloppy and then his defense was all shot up. Our kid was unraveling in front of a Brick House packed to the gills with fans expecting another Todd "Freight Train" Kirkus. Instead they were getting a choke artist.

Coach Kelly put in Ray Atto, their once-star, to play alongside Jimmy. He drew a foul on his first possession. Made both free throws. The Fishermen-faithful applauded.

Joe Looney said, "That's how we do it, Ray, that's how we do it," but he was looking at Jimmy when he said it.

On Ray's way back up the court he yapped, "Quit being a pussy," so close to Jimmy's ear he felt the spit land.

Then, on the next Fishermen inbounds, Jimmy got the ball. He dribbled it up the court with Shooter in front of him the whole way, smiling cruelly. Sound piled on. The crowd overpowering. Nobody stopping it when it should have been stopped. Jimmy could weep. Couldn't anyone see what was happening? His lungs couldn't take in enough air. Too much, all of it. He went to make a pass and Shooter jabbed, feinting a steal. Jimmy overcorrected and threw the ball out of bounds.

"A little off . . ." Shooter said.

Joe Looney raised his hands like, *What the hell?*

"Shit," Ray yelled. "Fucking shit, Jimmy."

The fans groaned. Shooter's words pinging all around inside Jimmy, springing leaks. Boos rained from the bleachers. He was soaked. There was a pressure on his nostrils, he was crying. Face all crumpled up, breaths stuttering. He ran and picked up the ball from under the hoop.

"Is he crying?" he heard someone ask.

"No," Jimmy shouted, pulled up the neckline of his jersey and wiped his face, pretending it was sweat.

"It's OK, Jimmy, we'll get it back," Coach Kelly shouted. "Get in there and get it back." Jimmy nodded and threw the ball to the ref. Then, instead of going back into the game like Coach Kelly was screaming for—everyone was screaming, noise so big—Jimmy left. Face red, nose snotty, it was abundantly clear he was crying now. He ran into the locker room and didn't come back.

. . . . . .

God, Todd thought as he watched his boy run off, *it's all too much, isn't it?* He had to do something, but he couldn't focus, not with the Doc, his wife, James Berg, and the whiskey besides. He needed to go see about Jimmy, but was scared of leaving Genny Mori alone with this man.

"Jimmy left?"

"That Shooter's tough, Gen," the Doc said. "I'd need a break too."

Gen? Since when did anyone call her Gen? "What the hell you know about basketball?" Todd shouted over the bedlam erupting in the stands as the game continued.

"I played for Country Christian when I was in high school," Doc said. He tried to sound nonchalant about it, but it was hard in the loud gym. The Doc yelled to be heard, and the pride came out in higher decibels. "Nothing much. Got All-League my senior season."

What an insignificant fact in this moment. Then Todd remembered bumping McMahan's team from the state tournament. Must have been first round. The Doc a quick, little guard with a deadly shot. The Country Christian Cougars had all these polite fans who forgot their manners as the game went on. Todd only played the first quarter of that game because after that, the Fishermen were up big. He'd gotten some flack in the papers for taking off his shoes as he sat on the bench, kicked back and relaxed. James Berg ended the night with 33 points. They joked it was his team now.

"Oh, shit," Todd said. He took another drink. *Where* had *Jimmy gone?* The paper cup of whiskey and Pepsi was flimsy, waterlogged. "I remember you guys. Knocked you out the tournament. Country Christian Cougars, *roar, roar,* how come you didn't like, how come you didn't get Jesus to help you win that game?" He downed the rest and refilled the cup from McMahan's flask.

A pause. A small beat McMahan let drop so Todd would know it wasn't a joke to him. "You were too good," he said sarcastically, face red.

Todd hated the weakness he saw in this little guy. The sniveling. The giving up before you try. *You know what happens when you start to feel that way? You turn to cheating. You tell on him when he's out drinking and he just needs to think. You go behind his back to get playing time. You were supposed to be my best friend! Just 'cause you were too weak to hang with me, you cheat.*

"Todd," Genny Mori said sternly. She saw the anger rising in her husband and this sobered her.

"What?"

But when McMahan went to take the cup from him, Todd slid his hand down its slippery side and tipped the bottom of it so it spilled on the little man's lap.

"Jesus," McMahan said.

"Now we're talking!" Todd said.

McMahan stood up and took half a step at Todd. The cup skittered and rolled. "I—"

Todd was ready; a slight flex in his huge frame was all it took to scare the Doc off. Beneath the flab there was still some power.

"I—these—just got these pants." He rushed off to find the bathroom.

"Todd," Genny Mori said again. She got up to go after the Doc, but at the top of the steps, she turned back.

"How come you did that?" she asked, one hand shaking as it pointed at him.

Todd heard her as *How did you know?* So he said, "An accident."

Which she took as *Go fuck yourself.* So she said, "You're the accident. This whole thing's an accident."

And he knew she meant *Right back at you.*

There it was. A fissure opened between them, between their history as man and wife and their future as separate entities. Everything just under the surface, everything almost accused and almost admitted to. One more step and they'd tip into the fall there was no comeback from. Todd waited for her to say more; surprised it would happen like this, but not so surprised it was happening.

But, what's this, they both balked when they could have pushed the other in first with a "You're cheating on me" or an "I don't love you anymore." There would be no fall tonight. Genny stood before him a beat longer and then turned away. Todd would always remember how only one hand had shook, the other calm.

And then Todd picked up the paper cup and crushed it and threw it at her back because he'd just forced them to go off and be alone when that was the last thing he wanted.

In the bleachers, realizing that Jimmy wasn't coming back, the game in hand, the Seagulls started a new chant, *"Na-na-na-na, na-na-na-na, hey, hey, hey, GOODBYE."*

Todd turned on James Berg, who was now standing. In two

JIMMY KIRKUS, FIFTEEN YEARS OLD—TWO YEARS UNTIL THE WALL.

steps he was nose to nose with his old friend. "You still love this?" he asked.

"No, Todd, I—"

"You better fucking love this."

James's face crumpled a little. He bit a knuckle. "Go fuck your-self."

Todd reared back, took aim, and then let into a mighty swing. James easily avoided it, just stepped back. Todd spit, he had him cornered, and was about to charge. There was liquid in his head, sloshing around, hitting the levers and buttons of his rage. Then he paused. Something was going to break tonight, but it wouldn't be James. Todd turned and went to the railing.

. . . . . .

Jimmy changed into street clothes. Nobody had come after him into the locker room. What was that? He was the only reason his team had won their first seven games and not one person looking? He crept out of the locker room and underneath the bleachers. It was filthy, gonna get his new shoes—spotless Penny Hard-away's—dirty, but he didn't care. Among crumpled programs, and spilled puddles of pop, he scanned the crowd between peo-ple's feet, watching as the game went on. Then, way up in a little balcony, he saw his pops. Huge, bloated man swaying. Someone in the crowd caught sight of him. The chant changed back to "*Dad-dy's bet-ter!*" Jimmy, weak and sad and he didn't know what else, stepped forward to get an angle. His pops was shouting something back at the crowd. His thinning hair swept down over his forehead. Sticking in clumps. Guy didn't look like a legend. Looked like he might die of a heart attack.

"What's he saying?" someone above Jimmy asked.

"Shit if I know," someone else answered, but it didn't matter be-cause the final buzzer sounded and his pops was getting louder. Todd "Freight Train" Kirkus was yelling "*NO I'M NOT.*" Crazy grandpa, choked night of basketball, crying on the court, and now a dumbass father making a scene? Brought to mind that day seeing his pops in the sand for some reason. Big man eating the tide. Pathetic.

Jimmy always knew he was small, but under all this weight, he felt it in a way he hadn't ever before. For the first time in his life he truly hated his pops.

. . . . . .

For Berg it was tough to watch his old friend like that, even if Todd had just tried to take his head off. Leaning out over the railing, shirt come untucked to show his pasty flab, screaming down a bunch of high schoolers out for fun.

"NO I'M NOT!" Todd was yelling, almost weeping, to the bewildered people below. Old fool was going to lean too far. So Berg was there. Grabbing him around the waist and setting him back down in his chair. Todd still had that doctor's flask in his hand. He looked up at James with a crooked smile, best friends again for an instant. "You scored 33 points against Country Christian," he said.

"Yes," James said, laughing, almost crying too, "I did."

Todd finished the flask wetly and then pointed to McMahan's leather bag. "The Doc's," he said. He picked it up and made for the exit. James followed him down to the parking lot.

. . . . . .

Once outside, Freight Train found Genny Mori crying by the van. The Doc was already gone and Freight Train rolled straight at her.

"You fucking shit-head," she said as he got closer. "Why are you like this?"

"A little fun?" He dropped the Doc's bag at her feet as though it were proof.

"You're not in high school anymore. You don't drink, remember?"

"You're goddamn right, and you're not single, so why the hell did the good doctor come all the way to Columbia City for a high school game?"

JIMMY KIRKUS, FIFTEEN YEARS OLD–TWO YEARS UNTIL THE WALL.

"Well."

"I saw you."

People watched from open car doors and rolled-down windows. The gossip web of Columbia City was already tingling with this electric new development.

. . . . . .

Genny Mori's eyes gave it away, in how they darted to the corners, measured routes of escape, picked up on the Doc's bag. "He gave me a ride," she said, flinched. "No one else could. I didn't tell you 'cause I knew you'd act like this." She paused. Enough? Had she given him enough to pretend? Lie to himself that nothing was happening?

"That wannabe has the hots for you."

Genny Mori laughed, relieved he was choosing to go along and she could be angry with him too. "Wannabe? He's a *doctor*, Pepsi Man. And you ain't no big star anymore."

Someone in the dark laughed. They were a spectacle, a show.

"You're goddamn right," he said and stepped forward, but by then James Berg was holding his shoulder from behind. Had him stumbling back until he was pinned against his own van. Genny Mori didn't know it, but she was getting treated to a replay of the scene that had wrecked Todd in the first place. That night he'd drunkenly tried to flee Eugene after the state tournament his senior year. The first domino in the fall-down of their lives.

. . . . . .

Todd stopped struggling and the people around them hurried up starting their motors and closing their doors. Pretending hard they hadn't been listening the entire time.

The police were on their way, sirens already wailing down the road. Todd stopped struggling, and as cinematic as it seems, it started raining. That's just the Oregon coast for you. Soft at first, the sky unzipped and let its stuffing out. Genny ran the short distance to the passenger side of the van, skirting the puddles carefully, taking her time, just as she had when Todd watched her, years before, in fifth grade. He remembered how her father had yelled at her. How brave and sad it had seemed for her to be deliberately taking the long way.

Once again he promised himself he would be better.

. . . . . .

Days later, Genny Mori was off from work and sitting at the kitchen table, drinking a huge mug of green tea. She had read that it was full of antioxidants. Could extend the life. Her mother had drank it religiously. The older she got, she found, the more she picked up the habits of her parents.

Todd was asleep, or pretending to be. Ever since the parking lot he'd been sleeping more than usual. The Flying Finn was out in the living room, on his bike, headphones in and grunting. He'd stay there, she knew, until she left. They used to have a relationship strung together by acidic jokes, flung back and forth. No end to the sarcasm. Ever since he'd moved back in though, he avoided her like he had said something terribly rude when he was drunk and was now too embarrassed to cop to it. She was only too happy to return the favor.

Once again her thoughts returned to Jimmy. His night on the court with Shooter. People were saying he had a case of the yips. When she asked Carl at work to explain it, he started into a whole thing about some baseball player and—this was about basketball, though. She didn't get it. But what she did get was that Jimmy suddenly wasn't very good at basketball, and that it had gotten to him, deeply. She felt his pain twisting inside her—a relatively new development—and she wanted to help. She was stuck on the how of it. She had purposely walled herself off from her sons for so long that now she didn't know what to do.

She suspected it was like when wives came into the hospital

beat to shit by their husbands. Genny and the other nurses would patch them up and send them home. Then they would call the husband and tell him to please come down to the hospital to pick up the wife's wedding ring she had accidently left behind. When those asshole husbands got there, they'd have "lost" the ring and delay in finding it. This gave those women enough time to pack their things and move into a shelter. Of course Genny never knew if they actually got their bags packed, got out the door. That was up to them. Her help stopped at giving them the opportunity to have that choice.

Maybe she could help Jimmy in the same way. Buy him time, an opportunity.

The bedroom door opened and she heard Todd pad down the short hallway to the bathroom door. It gave a terrific shriek when he opened it—why hadn't they ever fixed that in all these years?—and she stood up, hoping to sneak out. Maybe window shopping downtown, or a walk along the river. But, just as she was passing the hallway to the bedroom, there was her husband standing by the open bathroom door, comically huge. Slack-jawed, pale, scratching himself.

"Genny?" he said.

"Yes, Todd?"

"Do you remember that day? I don't know. We were in grade school I guess. It was raining and your father was there to pick you up." He shuffled a step closer. "See I had a dream of it, just now. And your dad was yelling at you in Japanese to hurry up."

Genny Mori did remember that day. Her father wasn't telling her to hurry up though, he was telling her to keep her shoes dry. He was always so worried about shoes getting ruined by the rain. And so she had taken her time, skirted each puddle, careful not to dunk her shoes.

"But you, see you didn't hurry up," Todd was smiling. "You just took your time. I always liked that about you."

Was this how he said sorry? It wasn't enough. "Yes, Todd. My dad liked to yell at me. Just like you do."

And she left.

. . . . . .

Meanwhile word on Jimmy spread.

Worried about the kid with the killer shot? Don't bother. Just knock him around a little bit, just talk in his ear for a while, and shit, he can't hang anymore. Runs off to the bathroom like a little girl.

Nothing like his pops, huh?

No, nothing like Freight Train. Now that cat could roll. Jimmy Kirkus? He's afraid to take a hit. They call him Jimmy Soft now.

JIMMY KIRKUS, FIFTEEN YEARS OLD—TWO YEARS UNTIL THE WALL.

Rule 17. Trust in a Miracle

JIMMY KIRKUS, SIXTEEN YEARS OLD—SEVENTEEN DAYS AFTER THE WALL.

Video clips of Jimmy's exploits at Peter Pan Courts rack up hits across the country. Fans cut and recut the footage to make highlights, putting different songs to it, making some shots in slow motion. One version racks up more than five hundred thousand hits on YouTube.

Meanwhile, in a more clandestine distribution, the grainy footage of Jimmy in the gym, running at the wall, picks up steam as it's passed from one student to another. Finally, somewhere in the process, it gets e-mailed to Principal McCarthy. McCarthy ramps up his investigation into the stolen security tape. The entire AV club is put into detention—a first. He sends home a flier to parents, offers a reward, corners suspicious kids in the hallways. Decrees that any student caught watching the footage will be considered an accomplice. And because of his efforts, seeing the footage is all the more important for every student in school, and also for the parents at home. It becomes a rite of passage.

Talk of Jimmy flies through town. Aside from the overarching issue of whether Kamikaze even wants to play himself, there is the shuffling of feet regarding whether Jimmy will be allowed to play, and it is all infuriating. This tough new version of Jimmy with the feathery throwback shot is intoxicating. He's obviously a baller again . . . so . . . put him in, coach.

It's up to Coach Kelly, high school principal McCarthy, and Superintendent Berg to make the call. People say McCarthy's in, Superintendent Berg is out, and Coach Kelly's on the fence. At least that's what Coach Kelly needs everyone to think.

In truth, he was in the crowd at Peter Pan Park that night. He's racked up hits from his computer too. Reloading Jimmy over and over to prove to himself that it really happened. The Nine Games. And conversely, the inky shadow to that gleaming display of greatness, he watches the clip of Jimmy and the wall almost as many times. Sickening to know what Jimmy went through once he got past the bottom of the frame. He thought he could hear the crack of skull on brick even though there was no sound with the clip. Sickening and sad, and yet, he couldn't stop himself. He'd right-clicked the video, downloaded it to a folder named PLAYS, which his wife would never open. Whenever he had a chance he watched it again. And again. A weird admiration for the kid rising in him alongside the ache in his heart. He unplugged the Internet cable whenever he was about to watch. He was convinced that otherwise someone would find out how many times he'd seen it and send him to jail. Like there was some FBI agent on the lookout for such a thing.

He sees the obvious ways Jimmy has changed since freshman year. He is someone called Kamikaze Kirkus now who has a full seven inches, forty pounds, and grit-teethed toughness over the Jimmy Soft version who had first drifted into his dreams. The night Coach Kelly stupidly left the kid behind in the gym to shoot on his own sticks in his mind. Oh, how he'd argued with his wife after they heard the news. Jimmy Kirkus bashing himself silly against a wall in the Brick House.

"You left him behind, Paul?" she'd demanded, the thick wooden spoon she was using to mash the poor potatoes held out in front of her, their guts dripping.

Coach Kelly flinched. Although he wouldn't even admit it to himself, this woman he'd been married to for over twenty-five years was beginning to terrify him. He was increasingly an older man, and he didn't trust his soft hip if she were to make a charge at him. A large part of his latent dream to get the hell out of Columbia City on the wings of coaching a prodigy of Jimmy's caliber, was that among the flotsam he'd rid himself of would somehow be his wife. He hadn't fully thought that part out yet, but he knew there was no way in hell she was going to leave Columbia City. She was born there, and she'd kill to die there too.

He'd missed his chance to escape on the coattails of Todd all those years back with the drinking scandal and the busted knee. A handshake deal with the University of Oregon disintegrated. If Todd played for the Ducks instead of entering the draft—something Todd had assured Coach Kelly he didn't want anyway—then there'd be a spot on the Ducks coaching team for Paul Kelly. Then there was no telling. He'd work hard, work smart, move his way up. New suits every night. Taking chartered planes to away games.

When Freight Train's knee went out, so did the air on his plan. But maybe, just maybe, with this new version of our kid Jimmy, he'll be able to work something out anew, catch a ride to a college bench on Jimmy's success. Sure he is older now—in his sixties—but it isn't too late.

Then, as soon as the thought bubbles up, it's popped by the context. Only reason Jimmy's like this is because of how low-down his life—and basketball—had gotten him. Jimmy knocking himself silly, it twisted Coach Kelly's gut. There wouldn't be any coaching bench for him other than Columbia City's, and that is exactly what he deserves.

Then a thought comes to him. To see Jimmy off the court was to see a kid made up of negative spaces. People saw him walking with jocks, so they called him a jock. People saw him with messy hair, so they said he slept too much, he was lazy. People noticed his quietness and so mistook him for slow. People filled in those spaces that Jimmy didn't seem to be able to fill in on his own. Then, to see him on the basketball court—when he was playing well—was to see him for him. He defined the pace of the game, he exercised mastery.

Thing was—and Coach Kelly was a terrible offender on this count—only thing people really cared about when it came to Jimmy was ball. He remembered with a cringe the relief he felt when Jimmy had missed the team's after-season pizza party. Kid had been useless to him once he became Jimmy Soft. Now Coach Kelly is seeing it is much the same with Jimmy himself. When ball isn't clicking, the kid has no chance to be himself.

Coach Kelly sees it clearly. Jimmy Kirkus needs basketball, just a little while longer, until he's able to do what his potential set him up for, and then he can be done with the game forever. Coach Kelly promises himself that. Let the kid go. But first, knock the cobwebs off the idea that Jimmy could be great—just *prove* that he is—and then he'll have a chance to fill out those negative spaces on his own, become who he needs to be. Whoever that is.

. . . . . .

Coach Kelly finds Kamikaze Kirkus down on Tapiola courts one clean-skied afternoon at the tail end of Christmas Break playing an elbows and knees game of ball with a bunch of Mexicans. As Coach walks across the soggy grass, he hears Jimmy's awkwardly accented Spanish drift over the play. *Benga, tío, benga, cabrón.* He's laughing, playing simple sweat-it-out ball and this delights Coach Kelly. Odd how his mouth waters. As if this moment were edible. He swallows. That night at Peter Pan was no fluke, no hoax. Jimmy's back and better than ever.

When the game finishes, Jimmy trots over. "Coach?"

"Jimmy. God. You look good out there."

"You coming on to me, Coach?"

JIMMY KIRKUS, SIXTEEN YEARS OLD—SEVENTEEN DAYS AFTER THE WALL.

Coach Kelly is taken aback. Sure it's been many years since he was able to catch all the references his players make, but still this is strange coming from Jimmy. Coach is used to him being so earnest, so obedient, and yes, if he allows himself to be honest, a little dim too. This comment has the smacking of snotty. Inappropriate. It's something he could have expected from Todd so long before, or even from young Dex, God bless him, but not Jimmy. Then again, this Jimmy standing before him isn't like Todd or Dex at all. He's not even like himself. It's a difference in the inflection. A full stop between some words as if he's tasting them before spitting them out. It's in his afterward stare. That dark look that just won't turn away. Like there's something heavy to bear and he's done with it and now it's your turn.

"I'm wondering how you feel," Coach Kelly says. "After everything that. You know. All that's happened to you."

Jimmy shifts his weight but never breaks eye contact. "Didn't *happen* to me, Coach. I did it to myself."

Coach Kelly coughs. Again, he's caught off guard. He is beginning to feel the same sort of nebulous fear he so often feels at home with his wife. Did Jimmy blame him for what happened? "If I'd've known, I would have stayed. In your . . . well, time of need. I would have been there for you. I just thought, you know son, that it might be a sort of therapy, to well, you see, I was a gym rat back when I was a boy and I know when I was going bonkers from some tough day, then there'd be nothing I'd want more than to get into the gym and . . . therapy. I thought it would be a sort of therapy for you. Or I would have stayed. I never thought that you'd hurt . . ." he trails off. The kid makes him nervous, at the heart of it. He's so big now. Coach Kelly remembers a rumor going around: *Bob's Market got broken into a couple nights back and the only thing taken was two dozen eggs. There were shells leading down the sidewalk. Kamikaze got so he needed food so bad, he just . . .*

This isn't going at all as planned. Jimmy stares at him for quite an impolite amount of time, and Coach Kelly hates it, but he breaks eye contact first. He'd read you should never do this because it reveals you as a subordinate. It was an article on dog training, but he's always thought it applied to humans too. From behind Jimmy, an older Mexican guy who has sweated through his collared shirt, calls out—the *j* soft—"Yimmy, you play next game?"

Jimmy waves him off and a new game starts without him. The only person on the court Coach Kelly recognizes is a kid from Jimmy's grade. Kid who used to come to all the games and sit with Dex, obviously high on something. Called Pepe or Pedro or maybe even Manuel. He's one of those potheads Coach Kelly catches from time to time cranking all the showers to full blast in the locker room and smoking marijuana in the steam. Pedro, he thinks his name is. But maybe not. But definitely something with a P.

Finally, Jimmy answers with a sick, slow smile. "You were right. Staying behind in the gym was therapy, is all."

Coach coughs. "Be that as it may, Jimmy. I mean, whatever it was you think hurting yourself was. I don't think anyone would agree with you that it was. Well. Therapeutic. Irregardless, the reason I came to find you today is because I want—"

"'Cause your team's two and three and floundering? And now you want me to play, maybe pull you out of the gutter? 'Cause the 'blossoming' of the Johnston twins is a no go? 'Cause you *need* me to get where you want to go? You need Jimmy Soft, huh Coach?"

A joke. *Ha ha.* There is sweat on Coach Kelly's brow even though it is freezing outside. He wonders, *Does Jimmy know about the pact with Todd so long ago? Coach and star player package. Does he know about that?* He raises the volume of his voice. He's almost shouting. "It's because I want to see if you're ready. Listen to me," now the coach is hitting his stride, those feelings from the night before are back in his bloodstream. He can truly help the kid. He knows he can. "I don't care if you never play ball again outside this year. Next year you'll do fine. 4A? Easy. Everyone knows that. But this year is your last chance to go up against 6A. Guys playing in 6A this year? They'll be in Sprite commercials in five more. You'll regret it if you don't play against them. I'm being honest on that. So, see, this year, *this year*, it's all I ask of you."

Coach Kelly expects Jimmy to interrupt him again, but Jimmy stays quiet. Clearly the kid is picking up the tone in his voice. Or maybe the kid hears something he himself has been thinking. Coach clears his throat. He's talking too loud. The Mexicans have stopped their play. He feels a dribble of sweat trickle from his armpit down his side. "I know firsthand what all this can do to you. It's tough. Here's the thing, though, we all think you're great. The whole town does. And you'll be fine if you play next year. There will still be recruiting letters. College coaches will call. The secret is out. You are a great player. But if you don't go out there and show what everyone suspects now, *this year*, against the best of the best—that damn Shooter Ackley and all the others—you know what's going to happen? Ten or twenty years down the road you'll look back and wonder, just think, what if? Everything you ever do will be compared with what you could have done."

Coach rubs the stubble on his neck. Jimmy's staring at him, wide-open eyes, and there's something almost unhinged in it. *This kid might have something knocked out of whack from that night with the wall.* Jimmy shifts his weight.

"So anyway, here's what I suggest. We get you back on the court. You do what we all know you can do. You win a state title. Then, after that, you do whatever you want. You walk away from the game, or you don't. I won't say one peep either way. But at least then you'll know what your choices are. You call the shots."

Coach Kelly can see Jimmy wants back on the court with the Mexicans from the way he keeps glancing behind him. That cement rectangle is his safe zone. *Kid needs counseling.* He makes a quick promise to himself to guide the kid toward therapy if he ever gets him back on the team, his wife's idea. Someone more qualified than Mrs. Cole.

Then Jimmy pounds his famous ball against the concrete two, three times. "I'll play, Coach." Jimmy pats him on the shoulder. "I'll play." And then he trots onto the court, yelling nonsense taunts he's cobbled together in Spanish at the players. Pepe, or Pedro, or whoever the hell that kid is, giggles like a hyena, eyes red with fault lines. *Kids these days, high all the time.*

Coach turns to leave when he hears Jimmy call out.

"Hey, Coach Kelly?"

"Yeah?"

"Gracias."

Kid Kirkus wants to play.

. . . . . .

Later, Coach Kelly tells Principal McCarthy and Superintendent Berg that he has sat down with Jimmy for a real heart to heart, counseled the boy, and Jimmy is ready to become a contributing member of Fishermen basketball again. In fact, Jimmy's participation, in Coach Kelly's humble opinion, will be therapeutic.

Not surprisingly, Principal McCarthy gives his approval gift wrapped in a tearful pat on the back, saying, "You do so much for these kids, Paul, really above and beyond."

It's Superintendent Berg's approval that Coach Kelly is nervous about. The man is famously strange in his feelings toward the Kirkuses. He remembers when he coached his boy, James, same years as Freight Train. Little athlete who could shoot, but the real gem in his play was his out-and-out hustle. Superintendent Berg was always pushing for more playing time, more touches for

JIMMY KIRKUS, SIXTEEN YEARS OLD–SEVENTEEN DAYS AFTER THE WALL.

James. It was hard though, what with Freight Train being a true star. What was Coach Kelly supposed to do? James was just born the wrong year, destined to be eclipsed by his best friend.

Seeing Superintendent Berg consider Jimmy's fate reminds Coach Kelly of that cold, cursed morning before the state finals when James Berg and his father came knocking on his hotel room door. James looked like he'd committed murder—hands shaking and skin almost blue—and maybe he had. His father was behind him, standing straight, staring righteously, terrifying—and this was before his promotion, he was still just a grade school princi-pal then. When they told him that Todd had been out drinking, Coach Kelly pleaded with them. "Let's just wait, let's just think this through." But "No," Superintendent Berg said, "I've already called the *Register Guard* and the coach for Madras." So Coach Kelly got up. Had to. Put on pants. Be the adult and get out there and discipline. Thinking, *This is ridiculous, he's the best player, why they want to get rid of the best player night before the big game?* And then he saw it, clear as anything, the naked ambition to get James Berg more touches in the championship game, show-case him for any college scouts watching, and it infuriated Coach Kelly.

He stormed down the hall and into Todd's room, hoping with everything in him that the accusation was false. But. Freight Train was on the floor, naked. Smell of booze almost overwhelm-ing. Reporters were going to be there soon. *Oh, Jesus, son.* Phones were already ringing. Todd "Freight Train" Kirkus was big news. So Coach Kelly did what he thought he had to do. Suspended Todd. Faced up to the ridiculous Flying Finn with refried beans smeared on his face. All because this jackass, this Superintendent Berg, wanted more touches for his own kid.

Who cares that they won anyway because of timely shooting

from James? The whole thing still gives him acid reflux. He's felt for almost twenty years like an accomplice to Brutus.

So here and now, with an easy choice that will be understood by everyone, Superintendent Berg has the chance to keep another Kirkus off the court. Say it's the best for the kid that he doesn't play. And Coach Kelly knows he'll do it. Ban Jimmy. He just knows it. It won't be the final say in the matter, but it'll logjam the whole thing. There'll be petitions to get signed, a whole new level—maybe even state—of authority to get involved. Drag it out further when that's the last thing that Jimmy needs. The season will be through before anything is decided.

Coach Kelly knows he's going to get a no so he's already rising from his chair to storm off when Superintendent Berg opens his mouth.

And then the man says, "Well, if you think he's ready, then let him play," and Coach Kelly trips over his chair. Bangs his knee pretty good. Yells out in what Superintendent Berg and Principal McCarthy assume is pain.

. . . . . .

Out on Tapiola Park Courts Todd Kirkus readies his son to play basketball again. Word has come down that Jimmy Kirkus will be let back on the team in two weeks' time, and Jimmy wants it. Hungry for it. Todd has his work cut out for him. He's going to make the kid invincible.

He teaches Jimmy to constantly check the position of his body. "You must always, always be ready, son." He shows him footage of Michael Jordan in his prime, every muscle in his lean body on the verge of firing. "Michael Jordan was the greatest to play the game because nobody could get the jump on him."

He measures Jimmy's vertical and then builds wooden boxes, five in total, to simulate each stage in his leap. Jimmy has to stand on these boxes, one after the other, and make nine shots in a row—"in honor of the Nine Games, the Ninth Shot, son," Todd jokes—before he can move on to the next one. "This way, no matter what, you can shoot when it's clear to shoot, just wait until the right time during your jump."

While they practice the Flying Finn rides his bike in tight circles around the two, taunting Jimmy in just the way Shooter Ackley did. "Yous got a crazy grandpa, yous gonna break your knees, yous too small!" Jimmy learns to tune out everything but his body, the ball, the cement, and the hoop.

Todd makes his son run. He runs and runs and runs. He humps the hills and sprints the level roads. He jogs circles around the track and then off through the trails in the woods. Going, moving, always breathing. *If you want to be the best, you need to always keep moving.* So Jimmy keeps moving. Running miles and miles each day, his lungs expanding so they are powerful, so he only stops when he wants to—his body has no say.

Lastly, Todd works on his reflexes. He creates a game. Whenever Todd claps, Jimmy has to cup his hand into an *o* and spy his pops before his pops spies him. The advantage is with Todd, of course, as he's the one clapping. For every time that Todd spies his son before his son spies him, he gives him a weighted jogging bracelet that Jimmy must wear for the rest of the day. In the beginning Jimmy is so bad Todd has to put soup cans into the kid's pockets when they run out of bracelets. He is sore in the mornings from the weights he carried the day before.

By the end of the second week though, Jimmy is so laser quick, it's Todd who's eating his dinner with multicolored bracelets striped up each of his arms.

"This is some real *Rocky* shit, pops," Jimmy says.

"'Eye of the Tiger.'" Todd starts humming the intro, closes his eyes, punches the air. And what's that there? A smile between Freight Train and Kamikaze?

. . . . . .

Jimmy's almost there. Jimmy's almost ready.

Meanwhile, after everyone else has gone to bed, Jimmy stays up late in his bedroom, working on diagramming his mind. He meant for it to be one page, just like Carla's poem to him, but it's grown since then. He's about fifty pages through an eighty-page spiral-bound. Little snips of memory, glued-in pictures of sneakers he used to want, job ads for things he might do when he grows up, photos of his family—Suzie, Dex, Mom, Pops, and the crazy Flying Finn who thinks every photograph is a chance to show off all his teeth in an insane growl. He scribbles in small memories and feelings. Goes back to earlier entries to annotate what he had written with a different colored pen.

One night he wants an answer to a question that's buzzing in his head. He needs someone older. Can't talk to his pops and the Flying Finn is a clown. So he calls Sarah Parson, RN, instead. It's her cell and she's walking somewhere, wind brushing the microphone on gusts.

"Jimmy!" she says. "Been a while since you called. Thought you picked up a girlfriend or something."

"You ever think about where you go when you die?" Jimmy asks.

"Jimmy . . ."

"Like, is it a good place? And if it is, then it's fine to like, be happy again, right? 'Cause then they're happy, wherever they are."

"I've seen a few people die in the hospital, Jimmy, and let me tell you, it's neither as good or as bad as people make it out to be, it just is."

Next he calls Carla.

JIMMY KIRKUS, SIXTEEN YEARS OLD—SEVENTEEN DAYS AFTER THE WALL.

"Hello?" her voice is soft, tired. He imagines her under the covers, in bed. He imagines her speaking across a pillow to him.

"You ever think about where you go when you die?"

Rustling. Maybe she's sitting up. It is a strange question, and coming from him, will just make him seem even weirder.

"I mean, just wondering," he adds.

"No, I don't think about it." Then she breathes in. "Maybe we'll never die. Maybe we'll be the first people to never die."

Jimmy laughs—she's trying to be funny, he guesses—but what she said also makes him feel so much better.

Rule 18.
If Push Comes to Shove, You Do the Shoving

Friday, March 17, 2006

JIMMY KIRKUS, FIFTEEN YEARS OLD—ONE YEAR AND NINE MONTHS UNTIL THE WALL.

Coach Kelly loaded his team onto the bus for the annual post-season pizza party at Fultano's. "Come on, come on!" he shouted.

It was raining, and the players were pissed off. "What we got to celebrate?" Joe Looney asked aloud. Then he tilted his head up like he was talking to God. "Huh? Why is a 7 and 13 record reason to celebrate?"

"Oh zip it," Coach Kelly said.

On their way to the bus, Ray put an arm around Jimmy. "Hey do me a favor," he said. "Grab my jacket? It's in the gym. Bottom bleacher seat."

"Sure, Ray, sure," Jimmy said, voice so low it may as well have been groundwater.

"What's that?" Ray said, overloud. "Speak up, Freshman."

"I'm going, OK?" He turned, headed back to the gym. Ray fucking Atto. Since Jimmy's meltdown against Seaside, the Fishermen hadn't won another game his freshman season. He was labeled as a soft player, and his nickname came to be Jimmy Soft. He was benched, and Ray, with his slow-down, draw-fouls, ugly style of play, became the focal point of the team.

Jimmy, meanwhile, became scared of his own shadow. Hell, he was scared of the thought of his own shadow. The flash, the buzz, the glamour were long gone. Other teams, all thanks to Shooter Ackley, had him dialed in. Put a little body on the kid, whisper in his ear, and boom, he couldn't find his shot. Jimmy Kirkus wasn't so hot after all. Worst part of it all was Jimmy knew it and blamed himself. He did errands for Ray and the other upperclassmen without a second thought because everything in this world seemed penance.

As Jimmy scoured the bleachers he thought about this last week of practice. Whole season down the drain and most of the other players just messing around for fun. He'd been pushing himself, though. Over-practicing, if anything. And he was doing what he thought he should do. Getting on himself for every missed shot. Yelling, throwing up his fists, cussing. And none of it helped. He was still too jittery to make even simple passes, his shots inelegant knuckleballs pitched toward the hoop. His touch was gone and now all his extra practice, all that being hard on himself, hadn't amounted to anything. He'd been benched the whole season. He was sore and slow and everything hurt, and Ray's jacket was nowhere to be found. When he got back out to the parking lot, the bus was gone.

......

Jimmy wasn't angry at being left behind. By that point he was used to it and he'd slipped into a state of mind that told him he deserved everything bad that happened to him. Half-frozen lunchroom chicken fingers, Mr. Jackson's bad breath, and the never-ending rain that soaked Columbia City at least nine months out of the year: all a direct result of him losing his basketball grace.

Jimmy was so down on himself, he didn't wonder why there was no jacket where Ray said there'd be one, he just felt he had failed at finding the jacket like he failed at basketball, like he failed at life. He didn't get that it was both better and worse than that: he was just the butt of Ray's cruel joke, excluding him from the end-of-season celebration.

With nowhere else to go, Jimmy walked to Pedro's house. He couldn't bear going home to his pops and Dex and the always jabbering Flying Finn. When they asked him why he wasn't at the team's pizza party he'd have to tell them he was left behind. That he was so forgettable, the team didn't notice he wasn't there. Then his pops would do something embarrassing in the new sloppy version of himself. Ever since the game against Seaside, the man was a stereo with a broken volume knob. Always at ten. He'd taken up drinking again, which was the main thing, but he also didn't seem to care about what anyone else thought. Would openly glare at people in public he thought had wronged him, park his van diagonally across two, three spots at the grocery store, not shower on the days he had off—coffee on knee, eyes pinned to the gray horizon across the bay, as if something better would come out of there, but if he blinked, he'd miss it forever. Tell his pops about this and the man might drive down to Fultano's and make a scene.

As Jimmy walked he slipped into what was becoming a familiar routine for him. He imagined the Seaside game going differently, his streak as basketball golden boy continuing. He imagined a scenario where he was taller, stronger, and tougher than Shooter. Pushed him around all over the court. Then, back in the locker room, in this imagined world, he smacked Ray Atto in the mouth. The idiot would start crying, ask Jimmy to let up. And then later he and Dex and Pedro would go cruising to the beach—he could drive in these fantasies—and they had girls in the van, and they had a bonfire, and someone was playing the guitar, and he could feel that exhausted, emptied but somehow also filled up feeling of hooking up with a girl again.

On the way to Pedro's, Jimmy ran into the Goth crowd behind the baseball field. There was David Berg and all his freaky friends. Jimmy hadn't had much contact with David since they were little kids. It seemed David had spent the years after the Ninth Shot and the Catch seething about one thing or another. Tinkering with little computer kits, taking apart radios, blasting out speakers. He had those slightly buggy eyes you see when people who never take off their glasses finally do. A puffy, sleepy vulnerability the lenses usually sharpen. Strangely, though, David Berg had never worn glasses a day in his life, at least not as far as Jimmy remembered.

David still played sports because his dad and grandpa forced him to but between classes or at lunch, he snuck to the corners of school where Mr. Berg would not see him and put on a different sort of uniform. Black T-shirts with silver spikes embedded in the collar, thick, black eye makeup, and inky leather chokers. Fuck the jocks. A freak uniform, Jimmy heard some people call it. Even during his junior varsity games David managed to apply eye makeup in the locker room during halftime. Drove his father and grandfather crazy in the stands when he came back onto the court looking like some effeminate rock star in gym shorts. Some kids called him Faggy Berg. Rumor had it that he spent his time trying to conjure the devil, listening to Swedish death metal, and huffing things out of paper sacks or loose air-conditioning tubes. To Jimmy it always seemed David was ill-fitting no matter his environment. He couldn't fully believe the hard edge, but he respected his willingness to be different.

"Hey look, it's a jock," David said. It's the loudest Jimmy had heard him speak in eight years. Also, there was something strange in his voice: a giddiness that pegged him as high.

"A jock," said one of his friends.

"Never seen a specimen outside its natural habitat."

"Some sort of pygmy variety," a fake British accent, "extremely rare."

It was strange to our kid: The jocks considered him a freak, the freaks considered him a jock, and the nerds and stoners didn't seem to consider him at all. Where'd that leave him? Standing here alone, facing this crowd of kids who hated him for something he couldn't even be, close to tears once again.

Then a skinny girl named Kelsey with golden eyes—almost yellow, strangely—and a cigarette hanging between her fingers that she jabbed to punctuate on everything she said, started making gorilla noises and the whole blacked-out crowd laughed and closed in. "Get it? Get it? I'm doing his mating call!"

Ray Atto and Joe Looney were famous for tormenting the Goth kids—or any outcasts for that matter. Their morning routine included busting into the bathroom the Goths favored and pissing all over the radiator. The corner of school they'd managed to carve out for themselves forever smelled of burned pee.

"Wait," Jimmy said. He wanted to tell them that he'd never done anything like what Ray and Joe had done. In fact, most of the guys on the team wouldn't talk to him anymore and frequently slathered his underwear in Icy Hot. "Hey, wait." He was closer to them than they thought.

One picked up a rock and threw it at Jimmy. Then another. Mob-think. Jimmy flinched and stared at David. David stared back. Then all of them were hurling rocks. Jimmy danced back, avoiding the poorly thrown stones—maybe they should have gone to gym once in a while—but he didn't run, stayed in range. There was a heady inevitability to it he couldn't break from—wouldn't break from. The prospect of being hurt felt like something to be leaned in to. A cleansing.

"The famous Jimmy Kirkus is all alone."

"He's Jimmy *Soft* now."

"Hey, yeah, Jimmy Soft."

"You think it's 'cause he can't get it up?"

Big laughter all around. More stones, suffocating and too clouded to see through, to move past. Why *didn't* he run? He didn't owe it

JIMMY KIRKUS, FIFTEEN YEARS OLD—ONE YEAR AND NINE MONTHS UNTIL THE WALL.

to these cigarette-stub kids to stay around and be the outlet for their closed-circuit pain. Calling him Jimmy Soft, what did they know? Still, he hesitated, the signal to flee all jangled up, the circuits gone haywire. Fight or flight and Jimmy was stuck in the limbo between.

"Um, dude," Kelsey with the almost-yellow eyes said, pointing her cigarette, "I think he's too stupid to run."

They laughed.

"Makes sense," David said. "He *is* a jock, after all."

"Hey, wait, just wait," Jimmy said.

If Dex had been there, he'd have knocked every one of those suckers' heads off—including the skinny chick's. But Jimmy was alone and didn't fight back, didn't yell; he just kept slowly backing away. He was soaked and he felt tiny. His weakness only spurred them on. Finally one of the jocks cut down to size. They caught him. Hands and feet, too many to count, pushed him, kicked him, punched him. Jimmy blocked what blows he could out of instinct, but failed to swing back. Finally he squirreled away. Ran a few yards and turned around, heaving. The Goth group fanned out. Surrounded him. They were closing in for round two.

A real dread was knotting in his chest. All the strands of his circumstance tangling bigger and bigger inside of him, taking up the space usually reserved for the work of vital organs. He was still standing, still alive, but he wouldn't have guessed his heart or lungs had anything to do with it. He felt a cold trembling as even his body betrayed him. No more full breaths, but tiny sips of air instead that did nothing. He could see in their collective, pot-clouded eyes the real damage and hurt coming. He regretted not running before.

"Hey, David," he muttered. "Come on."

"Jimmy, you're an asshole," David Berg shouted. He picked up a big rock, weighed it in his palm. His aim had always been good when it involved Jimmy's head. Jimmy didn't turn away. Too bogged down in soreness, in sorrow. It hit him over his right eyebrow. A slow bleed. He let out a soft, high-pitched whine.

"The fuck was that?" someone said.

. . . . . .

Mr. Berg had been clearing out the winter scrum from the baseball clubhouse when he heard the yelling. Through the back window of the dugout, he looked up and saw the group of Goths, his son among them, surrounding Jimmy. Made Mr. Berg sick to see. Then he saw his own David throw a huge rock. Looked like it landed straight on Jimmy's eye.

He dropped the rake. "DAVIE!" he bellowed. He came running around the edge of the dugout, full speed up the little hill where the Goths liked to gather and fly their freak flag. They turned and saw him barreling toward them. They scattered into the woods, yelling, "Fuck you, old man," confident that their number would hide who'd actually shouted the words.

Jimmy also took off running when he saw Mr. Berg—up the street while the Goths ran the opposite way, melting into the trees. Berg stood on the hill, looking between Jimmy disappearing one way, David the other. David stopped at the tree line, bit his lip as he stared at his father, held out his hands, like *what*. Then he turned, disappeared, howling like a madman.

Berg coughed something up, spit it out, and then ran after Jimmy. He was never going to find his son in those woods anyway, and even if he did there wouldn't be four clean words out of his mouth. Respect for your elders, yet another thing he hadn't done a good job of imparting.

. . . . . .

In the backseat of McMahan's tinted-window car—because they hadn't been able to wait until the condo—Genny Mori surprised herself by coming faster than normal. She shivered with the force of it and bit his fingertip, a feeling of expanding on making her insides as big as the whole world.

"Ouch," he said in shock. He pulled his finger from her mouth, shook it in the air. She had drawn blood. They both laughed.

"Don't get blood on me," Genny Mori said, shying from his hand. "He sees blood on me, he'll know."

"It doesn't really matter, darling, he must already know."

Genny Mori pushed McMahan back. This was a big deal, a real marriage, and his casualness belittled it, piqued her dread of an eventual come-clean, knockdown, breakup, to her and Todd's twenty years together. Calling her "darling." That whole scene in the parking lot with Todd, that shouting, all those people making their own guesses, it hadn't meant anything to McMahan.

He didn't know what it was like to live with a man drunk and drowning at the same time. And Todd did already know about them, Genny was sure, somewhere deep down within himself. He just didn't want to face it. What a painful sight. Suddenly he was a guy who watched daytime TV, tallboy on the knee, enraptured by decorating schemes. Then a whip around the house, some desperate mission to get rid of every expired can of food present—sure of the deadly poison each one held. A man who both she and the Flying Finn began to avoid as deftly as they avoided each other.

And then there was the simple fact of her pride: that she didn't want to be seen as a slut, but now there it was, the whole town thought it. And still, it was a joke to McMahan. His wife was clueless, they were going on vacation to Mexico in a month, and here she was simmering in the looks being poured on her wherever she went. What they were doing, the wrongness of it, was on both of them, so how come she was the only one to carry water for it? She didn't think of herself as stupid, and yet, how come she hadn't seen this coming? "Get off," she said.

"What the—?"

She hit him on the chest, tried for his face but he barred her arm. Those beautiful eyes of his awash in a terror like he'd just got in too deep. She loved his fear of her hinted-at craziness. She played it up, huffing little whelps, scratching his forearm. He couldn't skate over this so easy, she needed to implicate him.

"Genny, Genny, what is this?" he asked.

She stormed from the car, all disheveled and nowhere near decent. Shirt half undone, hair all sticking out, reaching forth, itching, daring, to tell whoever saw her of what she'd been doing in the back of the car.

He rolled down the window, stuck his head out, and pleaded with her. "Come on, where're you going? Come back."

And maybe she would, eventually. She'd stick his bleeding finger in her mouth, taste the metallic shades of him, and they'd ramp up for round two. For now though she was stamping across the deserted parking lot, kicking through puddles, not caring about her shoes.

......

At the same time, back in the Kirkus house, Dex doodled on his homework. He drew pictures of what it would be like when he got to high school. He'd be seven feet tall by then, he was sure, and he'd clog up the middle so tight his bro could create a different kind of atmosphere out there past the three-point line. Dropping in antigravity shots, hoop as big as the ocean.

Splish, splash.

Jimmy'd be happy then. Dex was sure of it.

Dex squeezed his pencil too hard and it broke. It drove a piece of splintered pencil wood into his thumb. He squeezed his thumb so that it bled more freely. It dripped onto the drawing. It covered up the head of the seven-foot version of himself. He started to weep.

JIMMY KIRKUS, FIFTEEN YEARS OLD–ONE YEAR AND NINE MONTHS UNTIL THE WALL.

Then he heard his pops come into the room. "What's the matter, for God's sake?"

......

The Flying Finn glided his bike around and around the high school track. His friend Ralphi was yelling at him. He went faster and faster until his lungs felt like they were going to burst. On the back stretch of the track he could see the river, coursing as always, about fifty feet away from eating Columbia City High whole.

He decided to do one more loop and pumped his legs harder. Best shape of his life and he was pushing sixty. He was a neon spandex blur. Faster and faster. On the back turn, just before he was going to see the river again, something in the steering column caught. He couldn't turn. He ran off the track and crashed his bike into the woods. The same woods that Jimmy would later wander. The Flying Finn was buried in bushes, yelling every cuss he knew. "God-darned ghosts and bitches!"

"You idiot Finn!" Ralphi shouted.

"You bastard Swede!" the Flying Finn called back.

......

Coach Kelly leaned back in the fake leather bus seats and sighed. He was full to bursting with pizza and cola. Jimmy had skipped out on the pizza party, and that relaxed him. First time since that game against Seaside he felt totally at ease with his team. That kid just didn't want basketball bad enough when it counted. In practice, running lines or working on his form, he was all effort. Anything resembling a game though, and the kid froze up. In baseball they called it the yips. In basketball they may as well call it the jimmies. He'd always known there was something off in the kid. A little too quiet for his liking. Good riddance.

Coach Kelly joined in on a verse of the team song. "Send the seniors out for beer and don't let the sober FRESHMAN near!"

Todd "Freight Train" Kirkus sat on a stump in his backyard. He'd just walked in on his youngest son crying like a girl and bleeding on his homework. *What the hell?* The whole universe was inside his belly, wanting to be filled. Or drowned. He was drinking beer. Drinking the beer killed the hangover. They used to call it hair of the dog back in the day when he was still tipping it up.

He threw the empty can out across the lawn, some small amount of unaccounted for beer spewing out of it. His life was all these loose ends and what could be done to tie them all together, where could he start? The relationship with the woman he partially blamed for his flameout was a disaster. Even if Genny Mori hadn't admitted to cheating on him with the Doc, he knew something was up. He knew he hadn't acted right, but when he had worked toward an apology, she'd turned it on him. *My dad used to like to yell at me too*? Damn. Gum on the shoe. Low-down and getting lower.

She *had* been nicer to him these last couple months. Nicer, but chaste. A pat on the shoulder, his laundry folded, a dinner packed for his night shift. Nice in a way meant to convey distance. Duty done, obligation fulfilled, suspicion squashed. And him along with it.

. . . . . .

Jimmy showed up at Pedro's house with blood leaking down from the cut above his eye, heaving and out of breath.

"The fuck happen to you?" Pedro asked.

"Nothing . . ." Jimmy huffed.

"Someone get you?"

"Just nothing, OK?"

"You got that pizza party?"

He studied Pedro's greasy face. He didn't want to tell him about the run-in with the Goths. Pedro had started bumming cigarettes

JIMMY KIRKUS, FIFTEEN YEARS OLD–ONE YEAR AND NINE MONTHS UNTIL THE WALL.

from them at lunch. Was making in-roads. Jimmy couldn't be sure how he'd respond. "Fuck basketball."

Pedro smiled. Snapped his fingers. "*That's* what I'm talking about."

"Wanna do something?"

Pedro bit his lip. Then his face lit up. "Sure, follow me, sensei."

Jimmy and Pedro crawled into the space below Pedro's sagging house among the spiders and the mice. "Just wait, listen," Pedro said, snapping the lighter flame to the end of a twisted little joint. "Gonna be worth it."

They were right below Pedro's older brother's room. He had his girlfriend over for a visit. They were going to get high and listen to them have sex. It would be Jimmy's first time smoking and he hoped there was as much altitude in it as everyone said. If he was quitting basketball, then what the hell did he need his lungs for?

But the joint wouldn't light. And in the darkness under the house, Pedro mouthing all over that crooked little bit of lumpy paper, Jimmy felt like there were cold stones stacking in his stomach. The wait was getting to him. Here he was, about to smoke, and all he could think about was if anyone saw him now, his day would get even worse. He shifted side to side. Couldn't get comfortable. A spider bit his neck, he felt like they were all over him. Pedro cursed, mice squeaked, and Pedro's brother was taking his sweet time sealing the deal. They heard them up there, laughing and talking. The air was getting heavy with the reek of lighter fluid. Then the image of them came to Jimmy in a flash. They were there just to *hear* someone fuck. Pathetic. He remembered Naomi on the bus. Her warm mouth. He climbed out of the crawl space. Pedro came out after him, soggy joint stuck behind ear. They both blinked in the sun, knees dirty.

"They're about to do it," Pedro said. "Swear to God. You can hear the floorboards creaking and everything. Rose, she's *scream-*

ing the whole time." Then he lit his lighter, held up the flame. "Plus, once I get this going . . ."

"And I bet it's going to be the coolest thing *ever*."

Pedro blinked. "You don't have to be an asshole."

"I'm not going to sit around getting bit by spiders just to *hear* something. You ever even touched a girl, Pedro?"

Pedro's face sluggishly registered hurt, and then anger. "Hey, you only got with Naomi like once 'cause you used to be *some-body*. And now. Now you a loser who can't even get off the bench."

Here it was, the chance to push back, and Jimmy sprung. "Yeah, well, fuck you, JV, you didn't even make the team."

"'Cause I didn't want to, Jimmy *Soft*!" Pedro stepped up.

"Shut up, pendejos!" Pedro's brother yelled from his room.

Jimmy took a swing, missed, and Pedro awkwardly palmed his face. Took off the thin scab above his eye. Dirty, brownish blood all over his palm. Jimmy was grabbing his shirt, trying to rip him to shreds. Everything, all of it, made him want to kill his best friend. Little red-eyed hyena. What had he ever done for Jimmy? Hadn't been there for him when he was stinking it up, had stopped coming to games entirely.

"Jimmy Kirkus," Mr. Berg said from the sidewalk. There the janitor stood, panting, still in his coveralls. Pedro and Jimmy let go of each other. Pedro dropped to the ground, looking for the lost joint, and Jimmy walked away. He brushed past Berg on the side-walk, cut bleeding again. It leaked into his eye and he blinked furiously.

"Hey, you OK?" Berg called out after him, still out of breath. Old man must have been following him.

Jimmy didn't answer. What the hell did Berg care? He should be punishing his son instead of hounding him. Everyone should be doing something else besides hounding him. Blood stung his eye. *The fuck's an eyebrow for if it doesn't keep the blood out?*

JIMMY KIRKUS, FIFTEEN YEARS OLD—ONE YEAR AND NINE MONTHS UNTIL THE WALL.

Everything was letting him down just as he was letting everyone around him down. He couldn't play ball, OK, but Pedro couldn't say the right thing, his pops couldn't stay sober, his mom couldn't be home, his grandpa couldn't be normal, and Berg couldn't mind his own business. Jimmy was the verse and the universe of the chorus in the same low-down blues song. No matter how he tried, he couldn't break the beat. He made it home and went straight into his room.

Rule 19. Let Their Imaginations Run

Tuesday, January 22, 2008

JIMMY KIRKUS, SIXTEEN YEARS OLD—THIRTY-SIX DAYS AFTER THE WALL.

All around town there's only one thing to talk about—the amazing Jimmy "Kamikaze" Kirkus.

You seen Kamikaze Kirkus lately? They say he's changed.

Well, blunt force to the head, that'll do it for ya. I mean have you seen the video? Not the one at Peter Pan, the other one. Of the, you know, the night it happened? I didn't mean to. It was in an e-mail. Just popped up. And brutal. If he's a little slow, then God bless him. After what that kid's been through, to be a little slow in the head . . .

I've seen him. He's different on the court, sure. All the time sliding on the floor after every loose ball. Like he's trying to fuck it but doesn't know how, tell you what. Tough as nails, this kid.

But he's different besides that.

He's quiet. He doesn't talk to no one but that Mexican stoner kid, and not even him much—which is good. I'm not saying anything against Mexicans, but would it kill him to talk with some other kids once in a while? This is a tight community. We got to stick together. Jimmy doesn't get that. Acting like he's the only one in the world. Ignoring the good people who got him here.

It can't last. One thing about the Kirkus family: they can't handle pressure. It's that Kirkus Curse. Old man running around with a shopping cart and green helmet every time it gets tough. And then his son, Freight Train, being a boozehound and all—trying to run away from his poor, pregnant wife. The Kirkuses can't handle pressure, you ask me. Only a matter of time before Kamikaze snaps again . . .

My Matty says Kamikaze won't even sit with anyone on the team bus. He sits up front by himself. He's always reading up there. He ignores Coach Kelly even. It's rude to ignore your coach like that. He won't say a word to the poor man. And the coach? He just takes it. Like it's all OK. I just, it's too much. I thought a kid from Columbia City would be raised better. What happened to manners? Either one of my boys behaved like that and I'm telling you . . .

And I know there's a lot been said about Coach Kelly leaving him alone in the gym that night, but how was he supposed to know Jimmy was a nutcase? I used to drive him to games. I was out buying him shoes during the Shoeless Game. I never noticed he was crazy. Who runs himself into a brick wall? How could Coach have known . . .

They say he bled a lot. I guess Mr. Berg was up all night when it happened and he still couldn't get it all off. Scrubbed with every kind of chemical. Don't see how it's possible. I say you put a little lemon and baking soda and, poof—but who listens to me?
I guess you can still see the stain, Jimmy's stain, on the bricks. Every home game, I look, and sometimes I think I can see it too, but what with my eyes these days. Who can tell if what I'm seeing is what I'm seeing . . .

. . . a little lemon juice and baking soda, I'm telling you . . .

Some dudes, swear to God, they touch those bricks before games when no one's around. I saw Brian Johnston do it. His brother too. Don't tell nobody I told you. Brian says it gives them luck to touch the bricks. Like some magic. Those blood-red bricks of Kamikaze Kirkus . . .

Did you hear? The kids are touching the bricks. Yes, those bricks. Before the games? I can't believe it. I mean, really. It has to stop. It's sick. It's like a cult or something. And after that security tape spreading. It's Masonistic, or whatever the word is. It has to stop, they don't know what they're doing. I don't get it. If you ask me . . .

Well I for one could give a rat's ass what the kids are doing, they're piling on the wins so fast. Bricks or devil's hand—it don't matter. Oh boy the Fishermen are on a roll this year! Just try and stop us, just try.

. . . . . .

The Kirkus's phone is ringing all the time. Strange men are seen around town, little BlackBerry earbuds glowing red, talking non-stop, eating Slim Jims from the 7-Eleven, chewing gum like it did something bad to a family member. These are the scouts, or the agents, or the college coaches all here to see this phenomenon, last name Kirkus. All trying to plant their flag in Kamikaze's mind. He could be the kind of talent to transform a team, capture the wild imagination of a city, whip it into a froth.

There had been murmurs of this kid long before of course. And then murmurs of his downfall. They don't care. Or at least they'll tell Jimmy they don't. Scouting sports is a high-risk, high-reward proposition. You only have to get it right once in a while for the slot machine to light up, ring out, make the night, the season, the next four years.

JIMMY KIRKUS, SIXTEEN YEARS OLD—THIRTY-SIX DAYS AFTER THE WALL.

For a whole season, basketball produces a certain brand of satisfac-
tion for Jimmy Kirkus. Not the wild joy from when he made the
Ninth Shot, or the Catch, or played in the Shoeless Game. Not the
powerful abandon kind he felt while beating ten straight players at
Peter Pan Courts in the Nine Games. It is more careful and calcu-
lated than that. Jimmy enjoys his basketball now because he knows
he's doing it well, and he knows the freedom that doing it well will
grant him. He leans into hard fouls, messy collisions, rough rebounds. And he wins. Convincingly. Nothing left to doubt. Even in 6A.
Even against the best of the best. Jimmy Soft? No, you must be thinking of someone else. He comes home at night, mind free of the looping obsession he once had with the beautiful game: nit-picking his
memory for times he could have done better, more, different. Instead,
he watches TV, surfs the net, plays the Xbox his pops sprung for.

And of course, he calls Carla.

"I'm writing you a poem," he says. Laughs.

"Oh, shut up." Carla doesn't know if he's joking or serious.

"Let me take you out."

"I've heard bad things about you, Jimmy K." Since the Nine
Games, Carla has moved up in rank among the group of girls she
sought out for friends. She is a regular in their trips to DQ. Gossip
over Blizzards, Diet Cokes. She likes talking with him on the phone,
sure, but treats him in person, whenever they run into each other,
like all of the others, cautiously and with a minimum of words, like
if she spoke to him in person, the weight of her voice would be the
straw that broke him. On the phone, though, they're good.

"Oh that? No, see, everyone's heard about that. That's nothing."

"I'm not talking about *that*." She giggles. He imagines her as she
must be, cord tangled around a finger, toes pointed as she lies back
on her bed. Pink. Stuffed animals. "I heard Naomi Smith used to
give you"—here she drops into a whisper—"*blow jobs* on the bus."

"Oh, Jesus," Jimmy laughs. "That . . ."

Ultimately, Jimmy Kirkus hopes that finally becoming the best
prep basketball player in the nation will free him from the terrible
label of Potentially Great Player and deliver him into a new realm
where he can be whoever the hell he wants. Next year the Fishermen will play below, in 4A. People will asterisk any success by
saying they aren't going up against the best. Not this year though.
Jimmy's going up against a bumper crop of transcendent Oregon
talent—and coming out on top.

. . . . . .

Jimmy's pops and grandpops go to every home game his junior
year. They never go inside the Brick House, though. Jimmy never
lets them. They don't like it but they obey his wishes. He's in the
driver's seat these days. The two men sit outside in the parking
lot, engine running when it's too cold, while the rest of the town
works itself into a tizzy inside the Brick House. They listen to the
games on the radio. Keep tallies of Jimmy's stats on notebook paper. Watch couples come out of the gym to steal kisses, old men to
steal smokes. Sometimes they don't stop talking, other times they
never start.

The Flying Finn complains. "After all I done for this kid . . . I's
the one to buy the shoes and give the tips . . ." he says. "Who are
we to listen to a kid anyway?"

"Just listen to the game and shut up, old man, you're banned
from the Brick House anyway." This had come about long before.
Something to do with a stuffed animal and pantyhose.

"I like to see them try and keep me out!"

But they are both smiling—happy that Jimmy is speaking up
and happy that he is playing well. They are never allowed to make
the drive to away games, so just being in the parking lot of the
Brick House has juice. They can almost see the old, red gym flex
with the energy from within. On especially dynamic plays, the
rapturous cheers of the Fishermen Faithful can be heard all the

way outside, competing with the tinny version playing over the van's speakers.

. . . . . .

Sometimes, on his way into a game, Superintendent Berg will stop by Todd's window, knock on it. Todd will roll it down, smell the exhaust, wave to frightened Mary, the old man's new wife, standing just over Berg's shoulder.

"Seems to me all the Fishermen need is Jimmy."

"Yeah, well, you never know."

After they leave the Flying Finn will use the same joke he always uses after these encounters. "Why don't you two just put the ring on and kiss the lips? You *loves* each other now."

"Don't be intolerant, you old goat."

What happened after Todd found out the identity of who was behind *The Missteps* blog, and right around when Superintendent Berg, Principal McCarthy, and Coach Kelly were deciding if Jimmy should play, was he drove straight to the big, white house on the hill where Super Berg had moved after being promoted from principal to superintendent. Todd parked his squealing van at the bottom of the drive. He went to the back door and rapped three times. He noticed the shed door cracked open. He peeked the fancy riding mower inside. He wondered, *Does Superintendent Berg mow his own grass?*

The old, flabby man answered the door, but opened it no wider than the crack the security chain allowed. Through that small gap, wearing yellow-tinted John Lennon glasses for some reason, a desperate grab for youth through fashion Todd guessed, Super Berg spoke.

"Now I've already called the cops, Todd, so don't do anything crazy," he said, the darkness of the big house behind him pairing with the outside daylight to create an odd glow in his eyes. "I've only ever tried to be a father figure to you. It's more than most men would have done."

"You wrote that opinion piece back when? And now this blog too?"

Super Berg scoffed, didn't bother denying. "Todd, it was for your own good. How can you not see that? You really are egotistical."

"What do you know about Jimmy being able to play or not? He's *my* boy."

Super Berg snorted. "Now, Todd, you really think Jimmy is ready to play again? Be under that pressure? His emotions are obviously too fragile. As a father, you should be thinking about this."

Todd laughed sadly. He looked at the chain keeping the door open just a crack, nothing more. He understood that this man, the father of his one-time best friend, actually thought that he could hurt him. It was beginning to seem funny, how far off this town was in their perception of him. Made him want to be violent, this expectation of violence. It was ironic, or some other college word. He coughed. Turned halfway away. Maybe he should just slam back into the fucking door. Shake the whole house, rip the security chain out, tear off the siding, and go around to each window, one by one, and punch out every pane. Of course he'd been thinking about whether Jimmy was up to being on the court again. It sat perched at the top of a list of things keeping him up at night. Here's the thing, he didn't know what to do. His son wanted to play again, that was a fact, and for once he was going to listen to what his son wanted rather than do what he thought was best.

Todd turned back, hands clenching, unclenching, like his heart was his hands and they were pumping blood. "Well, even if he shouldn't play, that's for me and Jimmy to decide. Nothing to do with anyone else. Your blog brought everyone else into the conversation."

"No, Jimmy and the wall, Jimmy and the goddamn Nine Games did that. Here's what's the matter with you, Todd: When the attention's on in a good way, it's just dandy, but when it comes around, you can't handle it. Look at you and James. You threw a fit when he finally took just a *little* bit of the spotlight."

"You think I took away from James?" Super Berg was pushing it. Todd's throat tightening up, but he didn't want to care. "I loved James, like a brother. He's the only one kept me feeling like a person, you know? He's the only one didn't treat me different." Todd took a step closer to the door. Super Berg flinched and the security chain snapped. "I could've been drafted by the New Jersey Nets, you know? Make a million dollars. I didn't though. I was going to play ball for the University of Oregon Ducks. Bring James and Coach along." He laughs, sadly. "I didn't want to take anything from James. At least I don't think I did. I was just a kid. Remember? You didn't have to go and tell Coach Kelly on me. Could have just asked. Or told me. 'Get James the ball more so scouts can see,' and I would have. I would have passed up every shot so he'd get his. Swear to god."

"Todd, I don't think this needs to be—"

Todd punched the door frame and Berg flinched again. From somewhere in the house a withered woman's voice called, "Honey? Honey?"

Todd stepped back, rubbing his hand, already regretting that he'd let even this little bit of violence seep out. "I'm sorry, Mr. Berg, I'm so sorry," he said. He turned away, walking back to his van. He'd messed this up too.

Then, a break. He heard Super Berg call out. "Todd, wait!"

Todd turned. He called up the driveway. "I'll be better to James. And you be better to Jimmy." He looked down, examining the knuckles of the fist he'd just used to punch Super Berg's door frame, smiling. "You know on Jimmy's birth certificate, it says James. He's named James. I named him for my best friend. Because listen. Even though my whole basketball life ended that night, I didn't drive. I didn't crash, I didn't die, or worse yet kill someone. After losing Suzie, after knowing what that's like, I couldn't have lived with myself if I'd driven that night and hurt someone. I've been alive these years to meet my three beautiful children all because of James."

Todd got in that old van that vibrated so much while running it could burst at the seams. He knew he'd gotten to Super Berg. Jimmy, his son, would be allowed to play. He peeled off.

JIMMY KIRKUS, SIXTEEN YEARS OLD—THIRTY-SIX DAYS AFTER THE WALL.

Rule 20.
When You Do Talk, Have Something to Say

Summer, 2005

JIMMY KIRKUS, FIFTEEN YEARS OLD—ONE YEAR AND FOUR MONTHS UNTIL THE WALL.

Being at home all day was simply unbearable. Jimmy couldn't be sure, as he hadn't talked with him since the fight with Pedro, but he was fairly certain Dex hated him. His little—*big*—brother acted like he didn't exist and every chance he got, he ran off with Pedro. Left a hole Jimmy was too proud to just point-blank ask about. Like *You sided with him over me?* Meanwhile, the Flying Finn spent June going on incessantly about calories, hydration, and training for his senior cycling circuit; his mom was always in the process of just leaving or just coming home; and his pops was increasingly becoming a drunk poltergeist banging around the house, always knocking something over in the next room, denying he'd done it, shouting stupid things like "WE'LL SHOW THEM," an embarrassment.

So Jimmy needed out. He needed to get out of the house, but away from the basketball courts. Couldn't be Jimmy Kirkus, didn't want to be Jimmy Soft. He saw a help-wanted ad in the *Columbia City Standard*. Phrases like "Must be able to lift forty pounds" and "Large amounts of lawn maintenance" appealed to him. He imagined himself with a bunch of guys, drinking pop after mowing fields. All of them laughing at some joke, the same joke, together, the setting summer sun alighting on their shoulders. Nudging each other with their elbows. Iconic. He applied for a job working the seasonal crew for the school district under Mr. Berg. Berg didn't even call him in for an interview. He was hired.

The reality of the work was a bit different from what he'd imagined. Each morning he and a crew of middle-aged men and one college-aged guy home for the summer met Mr. Berg in a small room at the back of the high school to be assigned their tasks for the day. While they waited for Berg to show up the old guys traded stories of hot girls. Who fucked who where and how. Who saw who sucking who and when. Stuff that always started with "Hey, I probably shouldn't be saying this but," and ended with "And I was like damn!" Jimmy started to tell his own story about Naomi once, but stopped halfway through when he noticed how quiet the room got. Wouldn't go on no matter how the men pressed. So they filled in the blanks for him and he felt disgusting. After that it was all elbows to the side and "Jimmy knows what I'm saying." He was better than all these men. Fucking go-nowhere townies.

Then Berg would come in and everyone stopped talking. He ticked off their tasks for the day. Weed-whacking, waxing the floors, moving furniture, replacing the high-up florescent bulbs using hydraulic lifts, and on and on. And then they were all out, split up into small teams. The crew worked so hard, Jimmy didn't have strength for much else—and that's exactly how he wanted it. Work all day just to come home and sleep.

He got home the same time each day, dirty and tired, smelling of cut grass and gasoline, and went into his bedroom to lay face down and sweat through long naps with his windows shut. He'd wake up hours later, starving, when the rest of the house was asleep or gone, and eat cold soup straight from the can in a dark kitchen. Alive just enough to be hungry. Mind for once not thinking about his disintegrating life, just pleasantly fuzzy with sleep. He enjoyed the animalness of it.

JIMMY KIRKUS, FIFTEEN YEARS OLD—ONE YEAR AND FOUR MONTHS UNTIL THE WALL.

Still, no matter how hard he threw himself into work, there were some nights when he woke up for food and found himself giving in. He took his basketball, still scribbled all over with the names of his childhood idols, and walked down to Tapiola Courts to shoot under the weak light. It was surreal how he was pulled to the courts. Almost as if his body were a vehicle and he were only along for the ride. He wondered how, even when he was too tired for anything else, he could still do the dribble, dribble, shoot. He felt guilty about it and worried for some reason that he might be seen. With the wind coming in quick off the river to sweep the cement, he'd shiver and look around. A vague fear singeing the edges. He was distrustful of Youngs River, only an outlet pass away, like at any moment it might rise up. It'd happened in the past. It would happen again. The blackness just past the edges of his peripheral vision suspect too. Sometimes he swore there was something scuttling close to the ground. A fucking sand toad. He could turn as quick as he wanted, and still see nothing.

And yet it was all worth it because on a few nights, alone, he was his old basketball self. Teeing off from all over the court, our kid Jimmy was vintage. A throwback to when everyone, including Jimmy, thought he was truly special. And it felt *good*. Good like his kid brother still adored him, like he still had his best friend, like roundball could still save and the haters didn't know what they were talking about. Then he'd go home, sick and giddy with hope, only to fall asleep and wake back up in the world where he was still *Jimmy Soft*, still a basketball bust.

Then, alarm blaring, he'd hump it to another day of work.

. . . . . .

That summer, Pedro got a good weed connect from a guy he met online named Smokey Bear. He started hanging with some older kids, smoking cigarettes, chugging beer. Watch *Star Wars* with the rule that every time Luke whined, you had to shotgun a Miller.

Drunk as a skunk before young Skywalker killed his first storm trooper. Wake up feeling sick with a need for life, spend an hour or two with his brother's box of girlie magazines in the downstairs bathroom. Finally come out for breakfast feeling weak and disgusting. Roll one up. Get high. Do up a couple more for the road, for his friends, meet with the new crew he played tagalong with. Fuck Jimmy. Fuck basketball. He wanted to get laid. Or get high. Mostly get laid while high.

Kids all around him had these stupid dreams. Stuff like wanting to be a music producer, a fashion designer, a business owner, but Pedro was the only one who knew the secret. All those people wanted those things so they'd have the money and time to chill out, relax, drink high-end scotch, and smoke tight, illegally imported cigars. He had a better idea. He'd just do it now. His dream was to have no dreams and unexpectedly, without Sunshine Jimmy and his ridiculous basketball hopes, he felt relaxed. Sad too, but he liked to linger on the relaxed part.

Jimmy could be a real pain. He was always on about basketball. Like, did you see the Vince Carter jam from last night? No, no I did not, because we're not twelve anymore and there's bigger things in this world than hoops. Hoops leaving Jimmy served him right. Still, a part of Pedro felt for our kid. Jimmy with no basketball skills was like Taco Bell fajitas—shit just seemed fake.

Sometimes when he sat at the top of Columbia City Column Hill with the other stoners, Pedro felt like his shortcut-to-happiness plan was really panning out. From his perch overlooking the entire town, pretending he was flying while he was flying, Pedro could really feel his body getting lighter, fast approaching the moment when it was light enough to take off. Made him smile, mouth the word "adios."

He tried to hang with Dex, but as the summer progressed this became more infrequent. Dex started running with kids too cool for Pedro and the stoner burnouts he'd glommed on to. Kids under the influence of being good-looking, talented, or rich—or some combination of all three. When Dex and Pedro did see each other, they bitched about Jimmy, complained about him acting like a little girl, remembered those times when he promised he'd ride the booster bus with them, but ditched last second.

More and more though, Dex was separating from Pedro too—becoming his own force.

. . . . . .

For Dex, it had been a punch in the gut to hear of Pedro and Jimmy's fight. Much of his world to that point had been those two. And while it pained him, he would have taken Jimmy's side, no doubt. Problem was, Jimmy just stopped talking to him after the fight. So he waited, scared his big bro was mad at him for some reason. Then Jimmy just kept silent like Dex was at fault in it too, and that scared feeling went sour in his belly, way past the expiration date, until he was pissed off. Then when summer really got going hot and bothered, he jumped on for the ride.

Finally away from Jimmy's pressure to play roundball twenty-four hours a day, Dex more fully inhabited his own personality. He ran with gangs of summerland kids, doing normal teenage stuff. A summer glued together with bubble gum and ripped to shreds by bottle rockets. He liked it, to be honest, just being normal. He got lit with Pedro and learned Spanish slang. Toilet-papered houses and shoplifted beer. Once spent an entire day sun burning "Fuck Off" onto his chest, only the third *f* didn't really take. He ran around with "Fuck Of" instead. He and his friends turning it into a joke, an adjective. "You want a little *fuck of* me? Now that's a *fuck of* a movie." He went to bonfire parties on the beach and touched the sweaty, pebble-hard nipples of three different girls, felt their tongues mix him up with his mouth as the cauldron, had their hair in his eyes as the wind played interference.

Sometimes Dex, on bored nights, went down to the courts in

secret and watched his big brother from the shadows. Sipped tall-boys he stole from pops and saw Jimmy just like he used to be. Smooth, fluid, and special. Here at Tapiola, it all looked so easy. Almost made it seem like Jimmy had choked on purpose. Dex watched, chucked the empty beer cans behind him, felt the blood pound in his temples.

······

With fall football coming on fast and the town getting ready for back to school, Jimmy and Mr. Berg were having lunch in the stands that overlooked the half-mown football field.

"Your Dad was like Dex, you know, all big and strong," Berg said between mouthfuls of peanut butter and banana sandwich. "Holy cow. But he could shoot a little too. Nowhere near what you can do, but he could shoot a little."

Their pants were stained green where the mower had kicked up the juicy bits. Spackles of half-digested plant stuck in their hair and on their faces. The almost tart smell of cut grass hung in the air. Jimmy picked a disfigured leaf off his forearm. "Wasn't small like me, huh?" he said.

"Wasn't *quick* like you." Berg patted our kid's arm. Jimmy flinched and Berg pulled his hand away. "Hey, he wasn't quick, what I say? And he couldn't light it up like you can. Jeez Louise, forget about it. All those chants about Daddy's better, all that stuff? That's ignorance right there, 'cause you're just as special as him."

"Wish I could do it in a real game," Jimmy said.

"You will, you will. You're special, just like your daddy. I re-member my father pestering me about how come I wasn't stepping up, making more plays, and I'd tell him, 'Hey Dad, when you got Freight Train on your team, you feed him the ball. You don't go around putting paint on the Mona Lisa and you don't play a game of basketball with Todd Kirkus and *not* give him the damn ball. Plain and simple.'" Mr. Berg laughed. "Here's the thing, though,

Jimmy. If your dad was the Mona Lisa, then you're the whole museum. You got all the keys to be great, I'm telling you."

A black sedan pulled into the parking lot. They quit their conversation to watch. The car stopped and shook slightly. Mr. Berg started talking again but the tone of his voice shifted. The words were decapitated by his breath. The door to the black sedan opened with that precise sort of quiet pop that only comes from very expensive cars. Out stepped Principal Berg—recently promoted to superintendent—in tan shorts and a loose button-up shirt. The promotion had taken his shoddy internal spring, ground down with old age, and put the bounce back in it. Jimmy had heard all the rumors. How Super Berg used the bump in salary to fuel a "midlife" crisis—coming full three quarters of the way into his life. He'd divorced his second and married his third wife, bought expensive toys, and took to wearing his silk shirts unbuttoned a few too many. He carried most of the change flabbily in his belly.

Super Berg shaded his eyes as he turned slow circles in the parking lot, trying to spot them. Jimmy looked at Mr. Berg. The man made no attempt to get his father's attention. His jaw clenched tightly. The talking stopped.

When Super Berg finally spotted them seated high up in the bleachers, he whistled shrilly and motioned with big sweeps of his arm that they, or rather just Mr. Berg, should come down. Raising his arms like that caused the bottom of his shirt to ride up and expose his hair-peppered paunch. A pale slug.

Mr. Berg stared straight ahead, not talking, not waving back.

Finally Super Berg threw his arms up in an exaggerated shrug and started the climb up the bleacher seats. As he got closer, Jimmy noticed he was wearing a pair of yellow-lens sunglasses. Round things like a rock star could maybe pull off. Guy like Super Berg though, he just looked goofy. Too old to pull it off.

"Hey," Mr. Berg said to Jimmy, the trouble palpable in the air. "Why don't you go get started on chalking the end zones, I'll be down in a second."

Jimmy, sore and curious, moved slowly. "OK."

"Hurry up now," Mr. Berg warned.

Super Berg was close, huffing. "Make. Me. Climb. Your father. Of all. The."

Jimmy could see the rage building red in his pudgy face.

"Wait a second," Super Berg called.

Jimmy's stomach tingled. "Me?" Super Berg had come to each and every game of Jimmy's disastrous freshman season, big bucket of popcorn on his knee and Mary, the new wife who said little, at his side. Talking with everyone who passed, fingers getting progressively shinier as the butter built up, until by the final buzzer, there was a yellow tint to everything on him, butter smeared on his cheeks and pant legs. He always asked Jimmy before a game with that crooked, greedy smile, if he was "feeling it tonight."

"Yeah, you," Super Berg said.

Jimmy stopped.

"Get to work, Jimbo, I'll be down in a second," Mr. Berg said. Our kid had never been called Jimbo before and it rang out untrue.

"Jimbo? Call him Jimbo now? Hey, let me ask you a question, Kirkus." Super Berg took a handkerchief and wiped his forehead. "What do they call David at school? My grandson, behind his back, what do they call him?"

Jimmy bit his lip. This wasn't about him.

"What are you talking about?" Mr. Berg asked.

"Call him Faggy Berg, don't they Jimmy? *Faggy Berg.* James, that's what your son is known as."

Mr. Berg swallowed, looked away. "So?"

"So? This is about David, son, this is about him." Super Berg coughed. "If you would just pick up the phone we could have already been over this and I wouldn't have to go trolling through town, looking like an idiot, trying to fish up MY OWN GODDAMN SON!" His voice echoed in the football bleachers. He breathed deeply, made a show of calming himself. "We could have taken care of David right when this issue popped up."

Jimmy looked at Super Berg's eyes, the true color hard to pin down behind the yellow lenses. It gave him a headache like wearing 3-D glasses outside the theater. Super Berg's eyes were a slightly off version of Mr. Berg's kind eyes. Jimmy didn't want any part of this. None of their fight, their fuss, their issues. A sense of unease curled up in a little ball at the pit of his stomach, kicking out, trying to carve more space in his life. He imagined it as a miniature sand toad that had infected him first in basketball but was now spreading into other parts of his life and the lives of those around him. Gray, rough skin. Breadcrumb tongue. Eyes big, sick, and yellow. He was carrying a very communicable infection.

Mr. Berg and his father were arguing louder, shouting.

"SO YOU THINK IT'S OK?" Super Berg bellowed. "Just let David fuck around, not join the football team, not join the *basketball* team for Christ's sake?" He held out his hands, pleading. "Not even something like *swimming*? It's good for the boy to do *something. Anything.* Builds character."

Jimmy looked at the older Berg. Is that what sports were supposed to do? Out of everyone he knew, David Berg seemed like the person to want sports, need sports, the least. Basketball? Naw. That kind of pressure wasn't him. Jimmy didn't know what David needed, but it wasn't sports.

"If he doesn't want to, I won't make him."

Super Berg kept talking. "Gives you chances you didn't normally have. Look at you. You got your chance to shine when Todd was suspended. Because of that you went on to college, right? You got a degree! Imagine if."

"YOU SHUT YOUR GODDAMN MOUTH ABOUT THAT!" Mr. Berg could not contain himself. He was spitting mad. First time Jimmy saw the competitor come out in the man. The real baller who had once been the second-best player on Columbia City's team when fact of the matter was, he'd have been the toast of any other team that didn't feature Todd Kirkus. Mr. Berg was standing, fist coiled to strike his flabby father who stood a bleacher row down.

Super Berg remembered Jimmy was still there, suddenly turned on him. "You know that, kid? My boy finally got to star in a game 'cause your father went out drinking the night before and got himself suspended. My boy finally showed everyone what I always knew—he was just as good a player as Todd ever was. Good enough to get to college for it. Good enough to get scholarship money, a degree in history."

"Shut up," Mr. Berg said. "Don't do this. Freight Train was heads and tails."

"Be a man, James, won't you? You were just as good. And if you'd just *push* David a little more."

"He'd what? Change overnight? Stop dressing in black, throwing rocks at kids? This isn't about Jimmy. Let's talk about this in private."

Jimmy touched the scar above his right eye. Where was David Berg right now?

"Isn't about Jimmy? All worked up about a Kirkus, again, when it's your son, your David . . ." Super Berg laughed bitterly. "You're right, son. People don't change." And then, to Jimmy, "Your pops got his knee busted resisting arrest. Drunk and looking to drive. Trying to run away from Genny. He was scared 'cause your

mamma was pregnant with that sweet little girl and he was looking to fly."

"Jimmy, listen, listen to me kid," Mr. Berg said. "It isn't all like
that."

Our kid felt like he was getting buried alive. What the hell was
Berg defending anyway? His pops had a rot in him, Jimmy knew,
and all this new information was doing was showing him how
deep the infestation went. He'd heard these rumors before, of
course, little pieces of the story here and there, but he didn't put
much stock in it. Rumors grew in Columbia City with equal parts
exaggeration, speculation, and malice.

"Tell him the truth, James." Super Berg smiled, at least that was
what it looked like to Jimmy. A little smile that carried more sorrow than a frown ever could. Jimmy hadn't known emotions to
twist like that. "Todd 'Too Big for the Team' Kirkus couldn't handle your mom being pregnant with that beautiful little girl. No
real adult around to teach a man responsibility and that's what
happens. James, you got to lay something down for David, some
structure."

Mr. Berg shot out with a little jab of his left fist and rapped his
father on the forehead. Jimmy wished the punch would somehow
hit him too, but physics don't work like that. The fat man stumbled backward and tripped over a bleacher seat. Super Berg rolled
twice, comical and slow, making little high-pitched "oh" noises
along the way.

Jimmy jumped to where the big man stopped three or four rows
down. Furious and grateful all at once for the truth he'd just been
told. He helped the pudgy man up while Mr. Berg ignored them.
Super Berg looked past Jimmy to his son, the yellow glasses cat-
awampus. Beneath the lens, Jimmy saw, his eyes were the same
color as all the Bergs'.

"You know, Jimmy," Super Berg said in a voice loud enough for the fuming Mr. Berg to hear, "You tell me what a grown man with a history degree is doing as a janitor." He rubbed his neck. "You clue me in on that, 'cause it sure beats me."

"You should go," Jimmy said. "We have work to do."

Super raised his palms in protest and then brought both hands down in disgust, as though it wasn't worth the effort. He turned and stomped back down the bleachers to his car, unraveled the dust on his way out.

. . . . . .

At Mona's restaurant in Tillamook—an hour and fifteen minutes just to have dinner—Genny Mori and Doc McMahan were having a conversation neither had had since they were in high school. A breakup over appetizers. Light low enough that they could risk being real. Real tears, real regrets, real ultimatums, and real failures.

"If you're with me, you're not with anyone else," Genny said. She had insisted on driving herself should things go poorly. This fact alone had probably set McMahan on notice. Her original plan had been to get a glow going with a couple glasses of wine before wading in. As soon as she sat down, though, she knew it to be impossible. He was tense, eyes darting, not risking touching her knees beneath the table as he normally would. "Not anymore, at least."

"Genny, you know it's harder than that. I have a whole family."

"And me?"

"*Genny*, why now? We love each other, so, why now?"

"You love me?"

"I do." Here he thought she was cracking. He reached across the table and found her hands. Cold, damp. She pulled her hands from under his and he was left with his fingers outstretched and alone like stars on the dark tablecloth. "I love you very much."

"Why didn't you help me? In the parking lot? Todd was drunk and angry. He could have hurt me."

He sighed, pulled his hands back into his lap. "You know why. That's not a fair question. It was so long ago."

To Genny it was more than fair. They'd been seeing each other for so long and nothing, nothing, *nothing!* was changing. It was beginning to seem like McMahan would never leave his wife for her, no matter how many times he implied he might. Hints were hints until they were taunts. Genny stood up, no wine drunk, no appetizers eaten. "If you're with me, you're not with anyone else," she said again because a rehearsed line, it couldn't change half-way through like something said from the heart. She waited for him to jump in, say something, save it. She needed for him to fight for her.

He shook his head though, whispered viciously, "You're not be-ing fair."

She left, heart still sitting at the table, aching with every step of distance she put between them on her way to the van. Swallowed hard. Burning tears pushed down. It was over. Her and the Doc. It was done.

. . . . . .

That night after Jimmy watched Mr. Berg and Super Berg fight, he couldn't sleep. Thoughts of his pops boozing so much he'd busted his knee didn't seem too far from the man he knew, but running away from his pregnant mom? That was the rub. By all accounts the man had loved Suzie, the sister Jimmy had never met. Kept that creepy cow's skull on the dash of his work rig just because it was the last thing she had collected. Jimmy rolled back and forth in the tangled sheets and the more he tried to push away the thought of his father running out on his mom, the more he couldn't get it out of his mind. Finally, he gave in and took his gray ball to Tapiola.

The air was cool on the walk down. Summer, finally, had begun to turn. It cleared the stuffiness from his head. On the courts someone else was already shooting, scooping his own rebounds, and shooting again. As Jimmy got closer, he saw it was Dex. He walked to midcourt and stopped. Watched him unveil move after move. Jimmy always knew his little brother was a solid player, but he gave most of the credit to his size. However, on that night he could see that Dexter Kirkus really was special. He'd been blind and stupid to have not noticed before. Also, it made him hungry to play.

On a long rebound, Dex noticed Jimmy standing there on the moonlit court, watching.

"Jesus," Dex said.

"I scare you?"

He laughed, bitter. "Well, creepo, you sneak up on someone."

"How you been?" The whole summer of not talking with Dex unrolled inside of him, and in his excitement he tacked on more words before his brother had a chance to respond. "You're looking good out here."

His little—*huge*—brother walked closer. "You know, sometimes I come down here and watch you. Been watching all summer. Figured you might be out tonight."

"Yeah?"

"I see you down here some nights," Dex repeated. He took the ball and bounced it twice with both hands. Sound huge in that dying summer night. Couple of gunshots. "I mean, where you been, Jimmy? Where you been all summer?"

Jimmy started dribbling his own ball. Gray thing so fuzzy the sounds came muffled. He felt light. Something in finding the whole truth about his pops was what did it. "Ah shut up, Dex. Been working for Berg, you know that." Jimmy laughed but found he did it alone.

"They call you Jimmy Soft now. You know *that*?"

Jimmy dribbled harder, went through his legs, behind his back.

JIMMY KIRKUS, FIFTEEN YEARS OLD—ONE YEAR AND FOUR MONTHS UNTIL THE WALL.

Such control the ball might as well have been on a string. "You want to play?"

"With Jimmy Soft? No. 'Cause I know the thing about you. I see you out here all summer. You still got it sometimes. Been there all along. You aren't Jimmy Soft. You been tricking the rest of us with a bogus slump for shit knows why."

Jimmy dribbled up to his brother. Huge Dex towered above him. Chest heaving. Sweating like a man while Jimmy still couldn't grow armpit hair. "I'll shoot for ball." Jimmy took a step around him and let go a shot from five feet behind the three-point line. Nailed it midstride. He turned back, smiling. "Guess I get ball."

Then Dex was there. Pushing Jimmy. Our kid tripped and tumbled. Bloody hands and knees. Rage out the ears but fear too, like an aftertaste that makes you worry about the food you just swallowed. Jimmy on his back. Dex stood over him, breathing harder than from any basketball game. Kid was backlit and so dark he looked like a shadow himself, a shadow for what Jimmy couldn't yet know, but it had to be enormous.

Jimmy went to sit up, but Dex was there too. Moving as fast as a chest pass. Down on him with full weight. Both knees on his chest. Squeezing out the air. Face a mystery with moon-glow behind it.

"Get off or—" Jimmy wheezed.

"Or what, Jimmy? What? You gonna fight me? You gonna show me something?"

"Get the fuck off." Jimmy clawed with his free right arm. His left was pinned at the bicep under Dex's kneecap, getting the shit bruised out of it. All he wanted was to be strong enough to get out from under there, but he was nowhere near. He had the cold, ridiculous fear that someone was watching. He gurgled and slapped with his free hand. Tears coming to his eyes. Tried to scream, but it was tough going with the air being pressed out of him. Whole summer of hard labor, muscles bigger every day, and still Dex moved him like food pushed around a plate. Just tried to breath. *In and out* were the only two thoughts in the world. *In* and *out*.

. . . . . .

Dex grabbed Jimmy's slapping hand, grip was iron. "Jesus, Jimmy," Dex said. He couldn't believe this wet, little, crying, breathless, spineless, lying, slumping, snakeskin kid was once his hero. He pushed off him. One last shove to take the remaining air from Jimmy's lungs. Left him mouthing like a fish. *Fish*. You could give a man a fish or you could teach a man to fish. Or, if you're really pissed, you could just give him nothing *and* not teach him a goddamn thing.

Dex walked off toward the river. With parents like Todd and Genny Mori, it didn't much matter when he came home. Maybe he'd go find Pedro, get high. Maybe he'd hit up that girl who'd been texting him. Some freshman from Seaside looking to live dangerous with the rival. Dex would get her alone someplace and see how far she'd let him go. He'd dry his eyes and see if one of the last summer nights had anything left for him.

Rule 21.
Don't Get Too High, Don't Get Too Low

Friday, February 29, 2008

JIMMY KIRKUS, SIXTEEN YEARS OLD–SEVENTY-FOUR DAYS AFTER THE WALL.

After home games, Jimmy goes straight to the parking lot without showering or changing; doesn't even stay for postgame recap from Coach Kelly.

Not since LeBron James has a high school player created such hype. From sea to shining sea college coaches are making their early pitches for Jimmy Kirkus to join their team. Be a bronco, a buc, a bumblebee. Be a blue devil, a muskrat, a tiger. Join a storied team with pedigree and fistfuls of championship rings. Be the one to bring a program to glory, national renown. Unlike LeBron—a golden boy with a big grin and easy laugh who went straight to the NBA before the rules changed and college became re-quired—to consider Jimmy is also to consider his darker history, his slump, his family. And still, these people come. These college scouts and recruiters attend games, wear bad hairdos and sun-glasses indoors. Make notes on legal pads, text in scores after each period on their cell phones. They frequent Dairy Queen and Pig'n Pancake. Bad chili and big bellies. Favor large Cokes and even big-ger mugs of coffee. They are overweight and sweaty. They are the greasy paper holding the food. They all claim to have Jimmy's best interests at heart. They call him, send e-mails to his supposed account, are seen in cars idling in parking lots just so they could say, "I've been there for you all along." All to bring him to a school so that school could win more games. Jimmy, however, ignores them all. He brushes past each buddy-buddy scout with the shoulder-draping half hug and maintains his privacy with resolve. He also never answers questions from the reporters who are growing more numerous with each game. The most they can get out of him, with a nod to Rasheed Wallace, is a "both teams played hard."

"Pretty good game," Todd always says when Jimmy climbs in the idling van.

"I played OK."

"Better 'n OK! You are the cream in the quiche!" Grandpa says from the back.

"There's no cream in quiche, you old idiot."

"Oh, there's plenty of cream in my quiche!"

"Let's eat," Jimmy says. It's their routine.

The three of them get dinner at the Dairy Queen, away from fans and reporters, and they talk of nothing, really. Whose turn it is to do the dishes, the laundry, the lawn. Anything that's not The Thing is fine. The Flying Finn's plans of opening a new restaurant. Todd's reluctance to join on. If it doesn't include a brick wall, basketball, or Dex and Genny Mori, then it's fair game.

"Come on, Toddy-boy, we call it Kirkus's Smorgasbord."

"What in the hell's a smorgasbord?" Freight Train asks.

"It's like a buffet, Pops," Jimmy says.

"How the hell do you know the word 'smorgasbord,' old man?" Todd points a chicken strip at the Flying Finn. "Wait." He turns the greasy fried chicken on Jimmy. "How the hell do *you* know?"

Jimmy shrugs. "Studying is all."

"It's a moo point," the Flying Finn says. "I don't like the name no more."

"Goddamn, Grandpa. It's 'moot point,' there's no cows involved."

"I know there's no cows involved!"

Then James Berg comes in with Sarah Parson, RN, hot new couple in town, and they order cones, hers strawberry dipped, his plain.

Berg turns and sees the Kirkus men with his tongue already deep into the first lick. He does a sort of snorted laugh, and then holds up his cone in greeting. The Flying Finn and Todd wave back.

"Sundays, four o'clock," Berg calls. It's an old man's pickup game he's setting up.

"I'll be there," Todd says.

Sarah Parson winks, and Jimmy knows it's just for him. After they leave, Todd is smiling. Good to see the man relax, let's Jimmy relax to.

"The old hound dog," he says.

The kid is close to happy when he's eating DQ with the Flying Finn and his pops. It keeps him close.

. . . . . .

Jimmy's a loner most of the time, but he tracks down Carla once the notebook is full with his life, all sprouted from her poem, thinking it's the right thing to do. She steered him toward this new, tentative thing he's doing called writing. He thinks if he can share it at all, it will be with her. She is pretty, maybe she is love. They can break this whole only-phone thing wide open. Why not?

He finds her at work behind the counter of Peter Pan Market. Already her appearance has changed since that night she spoke with him and he went out to beat ten in a row. When he grabbed her arm, it grabbed something else inside her. Activated it. She wears makeup badly. Her eye shadow arcs too high and her lipstick cakes too thick, but the effort hints at an adult sexuality, and that's enough for Jimmy to feel a pulse in his loins.

"Hi," he says when the doorbell trips and announces his arrival. The market is empty. It is always empty. It's just another mystery in small town magic. A store can survive with seemingly no business outside of the random grade school kids coming in with their grubby-palmed pennies. "Thanks for the poem. It was . . . it made me do this."

She looks confused and Jimmy looks away because of this, sees the Boston Baked Beans and MoonPies on a lower shelf and this feels nostalgic. The bloated notebook in his hand feels offensive. He wishes she'd just take it.

"I don't know. It's that." His heart is racing. It seems like she has no idea what he's talking about. He feels cheated, defeated, and a little bit horny despite it all.

"Thanks, I mean, whatever," she finally says. She looks behind him and he realizes she's making sure they're alone. All the ease of their talks on the phone has vanished. She doesn't reach for the notebook, just brushes it politely with her eyes.

Jimmy presses on, hoping he's not being made a fool, hasn't been expecting too much from this. "Your poem meant a lot to me." He looks her in the eyes, notebook rolled in his hands, trying to show her, to relate to her. The last chance.

Carla looks nervous and says the Wrong Thing. "You're so good at basketball. 6A, it seems easy to you."

Jimmy deflates. He'll not show her the notebook after all. She doesn't understand anything. "Hey, thanks," he says.

And then two honks and her pops the preacher is outside. Steaming in the driver's seat. Jimmy knows he's been labeled a Bad Seed. He's even heard that Carla's father speculates in his sermons about whether Jimmy and the brick wall smacks of possession by the devil. Jimmy wants to scream at the nervous little preacher man, "You think I'm gonna get her high, knock her out, and then knock her up? Well fuck off!" He doesn't though. Of course he doesn't.

"I got to go, but we can hang out sometime, if you want," she says, batting her eyes with their questioning makeup.

Jimmy is too stunned to makes sense of her. "OK," he says.

On the way to the car, in full view of her father, she kisses him on the mouth. She presses too hard and he feels her teeth through his lips. Blood, must be his own, comes into the equation. She

JIMMY KIRKUS, SIXTEEN YEARS OLD—SEVENTY-FOUR DAYS AFTER THE WALL.

leaves him standing there, wiping his mouth. Her father's car squeals off. The man who took over the cash register for Carla whistles. "Well, damn."

Jimmy leaves the store. She didn't want the notebook, but said they could hang out sometime. Has played coy but kissed him on the lips.

Later he calls Sarah, catches her in a hurry to go someplace.

"What's up with girls, they're so weird."

"Can't talk, Jimmy, but I'll tell you something about girls, every single one is the wrong one until you find the right one. Over the next ten, twenty years you'll shoot like point zero one percent on girls. It's not like basketball, Jimmy."

"I never said it was."

"Gotta run."

"Have fun with Berg."

"*Very* funny."

. . . . . .

Meanwhile, the town grows rapturous with basketball glory as the wins keep piling up in the wake of this new breed of basketball kid—Kamikaze Kirkus.

Hail Jimmy, full of grace . . .

They come out in droves to witness little—*not so little anymore*—Jimmy "Kamikaze" Kirkus blur across the floor. Fans will forgive anything if their team is winning and Fishermen fans are no different. They forgive the letdown of the previous two seasons and the strange way he's been acting this season. People have seen him at Tapiola Courts, screaming taunts at the river; running miles around town late at night; making circles on the counter with his coffee cup at Dooney and Steve's café, staring to the distance. And before each game, instead of participating in the "mandatory" pregame warm-ups, Jimmy sits on the sidelines—hood on, earbuds in. He holds his ancient gray ball with names written all over it. He rubs the name written biggest and darkest of all with his thumb. Three letters—D-E-X—the rest of the names he's allowed to fade.

The basketball is with thee.

His classmates start coming to games wearing helmets of all kinds as a nod to the Flying Finn and also Jimmy's encounter with the wall. They call themselves the Crash Dummies. Jimmy's reckless style of play is their drug.

Blessed art thou amongst Ballers.

So it's after a game and Jimmy sneaks out when his pops and the Flying Finn fall asleep after arguing long and hard about Kirkus's Smorgasbord: Salty Snacks and Sweet Treats. The Flying Finn saying they should have all kinds of different food. His pops being like "A restaurant should have an identity." Jimmy takes the van keys straight out of his pops's jacket pocket. Nobody knows where Jimmy is, and he likes the feeling. Windows down, headed for the beach, for the jetty. He parks in the same parking lot he remembers from so long ago. Area C. He gets out and looks around. He's alone. He climbs up the dunes and down to the water beyond.

Blessed are the games you play.

He's wrong about being alone, though. Up in the dunes, unseen, David Berg is smoking a cigarette, contemplating life. End of it mostly. He's walked from Sunset Beach, about twenty miles in total, to this violent, rock-strewn jetty. His feet bleed—he's worn the wrong shoes. His black cape flaps restlessly in the wind. He's realized lately that all his friends are just raw nerve endings searching for Novocain. That's what all the getting high and dressing in black is about. That's what he's about. He also feels bad about the security tape. He was the one who stole it, digitized it, e-mailed it around anonymously. First because he didn't think Jimmy had actually done it, later because he actually had. The grainy tape cast a spell over him. It's the reason he finally spoke up for Jimmy in front of Ray at Peter Pan Park. Jimmy's epic sprints at the wall were like everything he'd been feeling personified. For all the drugs and piercings, the black tape and metal spikes, Jimmy was pushed to do something that was real and painful. It made all David had done seem childish.

David's attention is grabbed by a dark figure walking over the dunes toward the beach. It's Jimmy. So David stops his contemplation and instead he watches over him. He doesn't know it but watching over Kamikaze is also watching over himself. He leaves him be, but makes sure he doesn't drown.

He keeps his secret safe, too.

Blessed is the life you live.

Jimmy rolls back and forth in the cold, soupy sand like he had seen his pops do so long before. Tastes the salt on each incoming wave. He tries to taste what his father tasted. He wants it to be the same, but how can he be sure? The sand is gritty, abrasive, black. It sticks in his teeth, catches under his tongue and in the hollows of his cheeks. It burns against a canker sore he has on the inside of his lip. Been there forever, it seems. *I used to have a sister*, he thinks, *a mother too. I had a brother once*, he knows this well.

The salty water feels tacky against the back of his throat and he coughs and sputters; he spits and squirms. The water that comes over him with each incoming wave, steady and strong, still feels cold, even after he's numb. *The fuck's getting numb about if I still feel it?* He gets weighted down deeper and deeper into the soupy sand. How long will he stay in this watery bed being built around him? How far will he sink? Past the sand fleas and crabs. Past the sand toad.

Hail Jimmy, player of ball.

Jimmy stays until he is too tired to stay any longer and climbs back up the dunes. Great chunks of black, wet sand fall off of him like icebergs at the end of a glacier, like the excess of a creature sloughing away as he is more minutely formed, and he walks up the sand dunes and into the parking lot. He starts the van, squeals away, heater going full blast.

Safe again.

Play for us sinners.

The stars are out like embers and David of the Dunes cashes out his cigarette. He decides to go home again, if only for the night. He starts the long walk back to Sunset Beach where the car is parked. He'd walked so far because he hadn't intended on walking back. Each step hurts.

Now and at the hour of death.

His junior season, Jimmy Kirkus—who by this point even the newspapers call Kamikaze—leads the league in steals, points, rebounds, and guts. Kid loves the floor more than staying upright. Runs into the stands, flies through the air. Busts his elbow and cracks his chin. Wears his injuries like a Boy Scout's medals. Doesn't miss a game. Lets the hurts shape him. Points are an afterthought. Pleasant side effects to the gritty part of playing he's come to love. Everyone has forgotten about Jimmy Soft.

Amen.

JIMMY KIRKUS, SIXTEEN YEARS OLD—SEVENTY-FOUR DAYS AFTER THE WALL.

Rule 22. Know That Sadness,
No Matter What, Will Come

Friday, December 8, 2006

JIMMY KIRKUS, FIFTEEN YEARS OLD—ONE YEAR UNTIL THE WALL.

The winter and fall of Jimmy's sophomore year were tough. Teachers pitied him, jocks reviled him, Goths mocked him, and everyone else just ignored him. At school he tried to disappear. He ate his lunch in the library with all the nerds—a little shrimp has-been. Pedro, who was becoming famous for his weed connect, made it his lunchtime routine to get kids high and tell embarrassing stories about his once-best friend. He was entering the terminal stages of a fanatic: collecting the kitsch of the celebrity in order to own his obsession so that he could then desecrate it, separate from it. In this case, stories. He fed the Jimmy Soft rumor mill with all the tales he'd been privileged to over the years. Freight Train and the pumpkin smashing, the Flying Finn and learning to ride a bike, Genny Mori always gone or going. These stories would come back to Jimmy, filtered through one or two kids, and at first all he would be able to see were the reasons they were wrong, how Pedro had changed them to make Jimmy come off worse. However, as these stories continued to circulate, their validity began to seem hard to question, even to Jimmy.

Meanwhile, the contrast in fortunes between Jimmy and Dex was striking. His kid brother ran through the halls with a booming laugh following his jokes. Rattling lockers, doling out high fives, an expert distributer of noogies and headlocks. Macking on chicks, pinned against them in corners and stalls, a true inheritor to his father's legacy. Huge kid with a quick charm—a freshman who was treated like a senior. A rumor started making the rounds that Jimmy was adopted.

When basketball season came, Jimmy didn't sign up. That freshman season was enough. He was happy to bequeath the team to Dex. Step further into the shadows. Hope everyone could forget him and how he had become Jimmy Soft while they discovered Dex. No one questioned this move. Jimmy and ball, naw, that was done.

One afternoon on his walk home—through the front parking lot of Columbia City High School to avoid the Goths on the hill behind the baseball field—Jimmy ran into a group of ex-teammates. It was the day before the matchup with Shooter Ackley and the Seagulls, the opening of the Cowapa League regular season. Joe Looney, a senior that year, stopped him in the middle of the parking lot.

"Yo, J. Soft, we got your sweetheart Shooter tomorrow," he said. He spit a brown spurt from his lower lip. Landed on Jimmy's feet. Our kid danced back, warm tobacco juice already turning cold as it soaked through his shoes. "Want me to give him a message for you?"

"Shut up, Joe," Jimmy said, and immediately regretted it. The other kids in the parking lot, leaning against cars or each other, oohed, pointed, clapped once or twice. It was on. Big Joe's eyes flashed red. Jimmy could easily outrun him, but did he really want that on his reputation too?

Instead he froze and let Joe catch him by the arm. "You a weak boy, Jimmy Soft. I hear you're adopted. Makes sense 'cause your brother, he's nothing like you." Another warm, brown stream, this time on Jimmy's shoulder. He could feel it soaking through his thick sweatshirt. The smell of tobacco and chicken fingers in his nose. Jimmy watched the brown stain on his shoulder instead of looking Joe in the eyes. It was true about Dex. They were nothing alike. His brother was ripping through preseason with a ferocious brutality that Jimmy lacked. He was bigger, stronger, and tougher than anyone else. Plus people seemed to like him even without ball.

Jimmy pulled back and at the same time thought about whether he should go for a punch. He'd heard of weaklings getting lucky with a desperation swing. Why not him? Then in the next moment, he knew he wouldn't ever try and hit Joe Looney and a cold fear shimmered inside him because he saw the rest of his life like this. Where were the teachers to stop this, where was Mr. Berg?

Joe slapped him across the cheek and then shoved his index finger in front of Jimmy's face. "See, you're a bitch. So I slapped you, and this," he wiggled his finger, "is me telling you." Jimmy wrinkled his nose, furrowed his eyebrows, desperate not to cry. He stopped struggling to get out of Joe's grip. It was no use and it was embarrassing to keep trying. A crowd had gathered. "'Cause with bitches," Joe rambled on, "you always got to be telling them."

Then there was a flash. Joe's hand was off his arm. Someone, somewhere, let out a little scream. Jimmy was jostled back, but managed to stay standing. He looked down and there was Joe Looney, sprawled and blubbering on the blacktop, his Black Cat baseball hat crooked. Brown snuff juice dribbled from his mouth. Mixed with blood coming from somewhere. For a moment, Jimmy thought he had done it. He flexed his fingers, looked at his hand. Then he saw Dex, fist still hanging in the follow-through, breathing harder than the big bad wolf.

"Damn, you're a fat chunk of lard," Dex said. The gathered crowd laughed uneasily and Joe got up on one knee, swaying but determined as hell not to show how much it hurt. Dex helped him stand.

"Fuck, Dex," Joe said.

"How about you lay off Jimmy."

Joe looked at Jimmy. Jimmy looked away. "Yeah, OK," Joe said. He rubbed his jaw. "Ho-ly—"

"Shit is right." Dex looked straight at Jimmy, eyes hot enough to burn. "My brother's an asshole, but see, he's kind of like my asshole, so it'll only be me doling out shit."

. . . . . .

Dex didn't come home for dinner that night. Jimmy ate microwave Hot Pockets on the couch while the Flying Finn pumped his stationary bike, watching tapes of the Tour de France. His mom was out and his pops was somewhere in the house but nowhere really. Jimmy went to bed and stared at the ceiling, waiting for the sounds of Dex coming in the front door. What kind of man lets his little brother protect him? He already had the reputation as Jimmy Soft on the basketball court, now he was going to have it for getting rescued by his baby bro too. He must have fallen asleep at some point for when he woke up, it was time to go to school and Dex was already gone.

Next day, kids steered clear of Jimmy. No snide remarks, no sharp elbows or stiff shoulders. Word had spread that Jimmy Soft was off limits. He saw Dex from afar a couple of times, always in a hurry. Running around the school, pulling basketball players aside to whisper in their ears. Then in the afternoon, Coach Kelly pulled Jimmy out of English class.

"How we doing, Jim?" he asked.

"We're fine?" It was the first time since the end of his freshman season that Coach Kelly had spoke to him.

"Glad to hear it. Dex tells me you can still shoot?"

"Sometimes I go down to Tapiola."

Coach Kelly patted him on the shoulder. "Well, you think you'd be ready? Get back on the team, maybe go through the reps?"

Jimmy squinted his eyes, mind racing ahead, nosing around for the trap. "I don't know if I'm any good."

JIMMY KIRKUS, FIFTEEN YEARS OLD—ONE YEAR UNTIL THE WALL.

"Oh, you're too young to know one way or the other." Coach Kelly walked off leaving Jimmy to wonder what the hell was going on. When he went back into the classroom, all eyes were on him. Mrs. Parson stopped her lesson on similes. Silence. Jimmy realized he was frozen in the doorway—halfway in the classroom and halfway in the hall.

"Sorry," he said, and quickly found his seat.

When the final school bell rang, Jimmy went home, lay on his bed, stared at the ceiling. The Fishermen had their game with Seaside that night. He planned to listen in on the radio. Imagine himself there. Three hours to tip off, and he wasn't even going to play, and yet his stomach was a mess of nerves.

Then his door burst open. "Get up," Dex said. "Let's ball or something."

"What?"

"We got Seaside tonight. Bus leaves in ten. Coach says you can play, so play." Then Jimmy understood all the strangeness at school. Dex had been orchestrating this all day, lobbying on his behalf.

There was a pause where both boys acknowledged the space between them they'd opened up that summer to make room for the pointy edges of their fight, Jimmy's argument with Pedro, the basketball slump, shit with Mom and Pops.

"I'm no good," Jimmy finally told him. "Not anymore."

"Well you ain't good as me anyway."

Jimmy's face flushed. "Why knock Looney down, anyway?" In the end, any shame he felt about being protected by Dex was burned out with the glow of love that came from knowing his brother was still in his corner.

"Dickhead was annoying me." Dex couldn't help but smile. "Listen, I got something I was thinking on. Know that saying, a bird in hand is better than two in the bush? What if you didn't like bird? What if all you were looking for was the fucking bush 'cause you were a vegetarian? What about that?"

Jimmy couldn't help it, he laughed. "What's it got to do with basketball?"

"Nothing, just something I was thinking about."

"Jesus, Dex."

"Just come on, huh? Don't be a jackass."

And so Jimmy went. Just because it was Dex asking. He put on his sweats, packed up his sneaks. Took his gray ball and walked down to the bus with his little—*enormous, heroic*—brother at his side, yammering on about potential nicknames for himself.

"What about Microwave?"

"What?"

"Like, I'm going to put you on three minutes high!"

"No."

"Windmill? 'Cause I got long arms?"

Jimmy laughed. Shook his head. It felt good to laugh, be cheered up. He played along. "You *do* got huge arms, but no."

"One Punch? One Punch Kirkus?"

"One Punch?"

"I knocked Joe Looney down in one punch!"

"Hell Dex, you'd knock most of the population down in one punch."

When they boarded the bus, every player looked at the two brothers as if they were extraterrestrials, nervous of how to make first contact. Jimmy would've turned and fled if Dex hadn't boarded behind him.

"So Dex talked you into it, huh?" Coach Kelly said.

"Guess so." Jimmy looked away and the music stopped. No one knew what to do next.

Dex punched through the silence in an act of gallantry on par with punching Joe Looney in the face. He shouted, "Let's go roast us some Shooter Ackley!" and the team cheered and Jimmy found a seat. They started up the bus and headed down the coast to Seaside.

......

Excitement about the Fishermen's rematch with Shooter Ackley and the Gulls ran high like a deadly fever. It would either break in a cold, satisfied sweat or someone would die. It was that simple. Genny Mori didn't hear the end of it at work. During her rounds at the hospital, other nurses, doctors, and patients found ways to bring up her two boys and their basketball fortunes. She liked having this new buzz. She enjoyed the attention, but more than that, it helped to take her mind off Doc McMahan and his beautiful eyes, his remembered touch, those hopes she had harbored for a future, shared life together.

At first after she had broken it off he had tried to find her alone in the hospital to plead his case. Walking through the tan, brightly lit corridors she came to half expect being sprung upon from a doorway by a waiting McMahan whispering entreaties to come over to his condo, have a drink, talk. He called at night, counting on Todd to be off on his night shift, and told her how he loved her and in all the different ways, until she cut him off with phone to cradle. These little run-ins and late night calls sent her heart rocketing, but she held strong. If he wanted her—this seemed more and more clear—then he needed to go in all the way.

So on the desperate nights with Todd felling forests beside her, as she clenched her teeth, hugged her pillow, and waited for the sadness, the missing, to seep out, the colder, rational part of her brain congratulated her on her resolve: if McMahan couldn't commit to her, then she'd be doing right by her family; but, also, by making him choose she was seeing if their love was a real possibility.

. . . . . .

On the day of the game, McMahan set off to find Genny Mori. He planned on cornering her in public so she couldn't blow him off. He was a new man. This was it.

For McMahan, the affair with Genny Mori had been all about passion where his marriage was all about practicality. He liked to be able to say things to Genny Mori like "I wish I could stay inside you forever" that Madeline would ridicule him for. He hadn't exactly lied all those times he told Genny Mori he was planning on running away with her, he just had a proximity problem. In Portland, in his big house with wife and kids, it was easy to promise himself he'd break it off with Genny.

Then somewhere around the turnoff for Saddle Mountain on Highway 26, on his way to a three-day stint in Seaside, everything would shift, his body would produce a chemical and pump it into his bloodstream, he would press the gas pedal farther, eager to see his sweet Genny Mori, silently vowing to leave Madeline instead.

Since Genny Mori broke it off though, he missed her all the time. Even in Portland. Especially in Portland. Madeline had gotten into cleanses. Their fridge full of different color shakes and damp, leafy greens. Never before had his wife smelled so bad. And then also she always seemed annoyed with him. Jumped up, ready to fight.

No, this was it. He'd make Genny Mori listen to him because now he had something real to say.

. . . . . .

McMahan approached Genny Mori in the lunchroom while she sat gossiping with her nursing friends. He came up to their table, clicking a pharmaceutical company pen compulsively.

"Dex is the talk of the town, Nurse Mori," McMahan said in the loud, disaffected "doctor" voice he used when talking to nurses. It came off sounding like a bad robot impression. The nurses stifled their laughter. There were plenty of McMa-bot impressions around the hospital, but Nurse Larry had the best. Genny, though she felt bad afterward, had even tried it a few times. Despite a real suaveness when he had been alone with Genny, and an undeniable physical appeal, McMahan stiffened up when addressing a group. And, she was happy to notice, he had gotten worse since the breakup.

"Yes, Dex's doing well," Genny said quietly, already sensing trouble.

"People are saying that with Dex in the middle, the Fishermen are hard to beat." His words came as though from memory and Genny thought she may have read them in the *Columbia City Standard*. He put a hand on the back of a chair, and then, finding it awkward, put it in his pocket. Then back to the chair. "Now if Jimmy can find his touch again, you could have an exceptional team."

"You seem to know your basketball, Doctor," Nurse Larry said in that suggestive lilt he saved for stuffy men and women he wasn't interested in.

McMahan didn't pick up on the sarcastic tone. He let out an expansive sigh. "Well I played a little when I was younger. I was fortunate enough to get the Country Christian Cougars into the playoffs one year."

"I think I *remember* that year." Genny Mori chimed in. "We bumped you didn't we? I mean Todd and his friends."

McMahan cocked his head. "How *is* the delivery-man business these days?" he asked.

Genny Mori stared at him in disbelief. There was a big bulging vein on his neck. She felt the other nurses watching them, sensing a bruised spot between her and McMahan. They were uncomfortable. There would be gossip over what the tension between Doctor

McMahan and Nurse Kirkus *really* meant later, she knew. One by one the nurses made their exits, Nurse Larry last.

"You two *play nice* now," he said.

......

It hadn't gone well. He'd snapped at her. Nobody could get him to a boil the way Genny Kirkus could. He was sorry for what he'd just said. He leaned in and whispered, the bigness of his news rounding out the words with hope. "Have a drink with me tonight."

"No." Genny folded her arms.

"It's just a drink. There's something I want to talk about."

"Go jump off a cliff. You want to talk? You just want to screw." She stood and stalked off into the cafeteria crowd.

He caught up to her, pulled her arm, people looking, but finally he didn't care. "I want to be with you, OK? I don't care about anything else." Genny's eyes cut to those around them, everyone staring. "I'll give you a ride to the game. We can talk."

She looked at him. He knew how she loved his eyes. He didn't dare blink. Then she looked down, and he saw through the part in her hair how her skin was turning red. Warmth. He'd got to her.

"Yeah, I do." She looked up at him, blushing, but steely too. "We can watch together, side by side. What do you think?"

She meant to test him. He swallowed, eyes breaking to the floor and then back to her face. "Yes, OK, sounds fun."

......

Meanwhile, Todd was hearing the same hype about Dex at the Van Eyck Pepsi Plant. The night of the game he was paired with Ray Atto.

"So, Mr. Kirkus, big game tonight," Ray said as they loaded up the truck.

"Sure is."

"Too bad Jimmy quit playing." Todd gave him an eye, but Ray stammered on. "Well, you never know with slumps. Alls I'm saying." Ray rubbed his fingers together: a little tic that drove Todd nuts. It came whenever the kid tried to quit smoking.

Todd sighed, tried to change the subject. "So your girlfriend's pregnant again?"

"Oh she wasn't pregnant before, or the time before that. If you remember. She just thought she was. Now, I guess she says it's for real. She's all mowing down on these dill chips all the time 'cause they're the craving."

"Better kick smoking then. For real."

"Sure, I know. I have. Flushed all my cigarettes last week. It's been a bitch. My fingers keep moving like they think there's a smoke." He set down a crate and looked at his hand. "Hey, you think Dex got a chance to be as good as me. Or you?"

"He'll be better than one of us, that's for sure."

Ray hummed while he thought it over. "You got recruited from everywhere. I heard Oregon, UCLA. So you *got* to know if Dex will make it."

"Ray."

"But if you had to guess if he got what it takes. I mean, Jimmy, he started for a while, you know, until the pressure got up."

"Drop it, Ray," Mr. Kirkus growled. "It takes one bum friend and one bum knee is all it takes."

They loaded the rest of the product in silence. Todd hated to admit it, but he *was* feeling nervous about the game. Ever since Jimmy's meltdown against Seaside last year—and his own drunken scene that followed—he had an ominous feeling in his gut that there were still more hits to come. He was actually glad he had to work and couldn't be there.

"Easy, OK, I get it," Ray said, all forced cheer.

Todd put his energy into ignoring Ray. He stiffened his face, didn't say a word. Todd was a guy who could use silence like the blunt end of a bat.

Their boss, Ronnie O'Rourke, walked by. "You two ladies in a spat?"

Todd didn't laugh so Ronnie scuttled off.

Todd kept it silent all through the drive out to Warrington where they were setting up a new display at Fred Meyer after store hours. They didn't say a word as they loaded up the hand trucks. In the parking lot, the fog hung so low it felt like they were dipping their heads into a sky-bound pool. Everything was beaded wetness. Ray fell into a coughing fit and the sound was huge, long-legged, as it ran off under white cover.

Later, while Todd and Ray were setting up the new display, they listened to the game on a little battery-powered radio. Todd was surprised to hear Jimmy was in the lineup. He thought the kid wasn't even on the team. *Nobody tells me anything.* He cracked a beer. Ray looked around, chuckled, opened his own.

As they listened to the game, Ray knew enough to keep his mouth shut and Todd was happy he did. They were in a deserted store where anything could happen if he lost his temper. Finally, when the last buzzer sounded, Ray opened his mouth, and Todd was happy he did that too.

"Your boys did pretty good, Mr. Kirkus," he said.

"Ray, you got no idea."

. . . . . .

Genny Mori and McMahan enjoyed a ripe silence on the way to the game. It had been a while since they had been like this: alone, embarking on something together. There was a giddiness to it that reminded her of when things between them were just starting. She'd do it right this time, though. No sneaking around. If he wanted her back, then take her all the way. They could get a place together in Seaside. Jimmy and Dex would come live there half the time. With the Doc's salary, they could afford a house on the beach. A big house. Glass windows, reclaimed wooden furniture.

JIMMY KIRKUS, FIFTEEN YEARS OLD—ONE YEAR UNTIL THE WALL.

She envisioned a hot tub in the back, running through the cold rain with him to that steamy, bubbly water. Any day could be like that.

"This is nice," he said. Through the skylight in his rich man's car, an early moon lit up his face. Glowed.

"Yes," she said, and resisted holding his hand. "It is."

They watched the game side by side four bleachers up from the court. The gym so jam-packed their sides touched from ankle to shoulder. Genny remembered it was one of the things she preferred about McMahan. In the tortuous months she'd spent apart from him, she'd almost forgotten this. How she felt she measured up against him. Never tiny or eclipsed. They shared an excitement at being forced into such tight physical contact in a public place.

"Need more room, Genny?" McMahan asked. What he really was asking was *Can we again?*

"No, I'm OK," she shouted over the pandemonium. *Let's try, for real this time.* She ran her eyes from his feet all the way up to his shoulders and then into his eyes.

Genny felt the heat pulsing from him. Funny how her man who was supposed to make millions in the NBA was barely paying bills stacking cans of Pepsi while little Doc McMahan, who couldn't get his team out of the first round of the Oregon High School playoffs, owned a yacht. That was life for Genny though: a slippery thing. Being with him here felt like her orbit was tied to his gravity. It was a thing she remembered about her and Todd when they were first starting out. Up until Suzie died, really. Focused so tightly onto one another that their own world came to seem so big it was hard to believe anything else existed. A complete tipping into that she hadn't come out of for so long. So close to one another that it was hard to tell when they were being ridiculous, hard to know when Todd was taking it too far, holding on too long. Slowly though, with an inevitable force, Todd pushed her out.

And here was that world-expanding feeling with McMahan. She hadn't realized how much she missed it.

. . . . . .

That Seaside game would prove to be both the first and last time the Kirkus boys played together in high school. The Gulls came ready. With all the hype surrounding Dex, and the history of Jimmy's meltdown the previous year, Shooter Ackley and his team had long had the game circled on the calendar. Shooter was loose, confident; the Gulls' fans rowdy. When Jimmy unexpectedly walked in for warm-ups—everyone had heard he *wasn't* on the team this year—Seaside's chants almost immediately shifted to the old classic.

"*Dad-dy's bet-ter!*"

"*Dad-dy's bet-ter!*"

"*Dad-dy's bet-ter!*"

Industrious lowerclassmen boys ran among the crowd selling Krispy Kreme donuts they'd driven in from outside Portland for three dollars apiece. People high on the sense that something important was *finally* happening in their area, laughed louder than normal, touched longer than usual, and lingered in bathroom doorways and on every step back up to their spot in the bleachers, hoping to get caught in conversation with someone, anyone. Everyone was an expert. The band played loud, sloppy versions of "We Will Rock You"—focusing more on their choreographed trumpet swings than on the actual notes they hit—while the crowd stamped the popcorn-crunch ground in appreciation. *Boom, boom, clap.* Wading perilously through the crowd an overweight woman wearing a Seaside basketball jersey with "Trevor's Mom" stitched on the back sold raffle tickets to the fifty-fifty drawing at halftime. Some lucky bum would leave the gym with more than $200 extra in his pocket for the investment of a dollar. Then he'd either get famously drunk with his pals, or buy a new spray-in liner for the bed of his pickup.

It was the kind of atmosphere the Flying Finn would have thrived in. Running around the gym, shaking his hips to the pep-band music, inviting and flinging back taunts. He wasn't there, though. He was home, listening on the radio, nobody willing to give him a ride to the game.

Super Berg was there, though. Wife Mary at his side. Eating popcorn and open-mouth laughing at whatever the guy next to him was saying. He was in his greasy element.

Out on the floor, our kid Jimmy felt all kinds of butterflies in his belly. No, forget butterflies. Try locust. Sound packed tight.

"Don't worry about it," Dex shouted to him, "Just a game. Don't mean much."

"OK, Dex."

Neither of them believed it, but it was still nice to hear.

"Besides, that kid," Dex pointed at Shooter Ackley in the layup line, legs so muscular his shorts seemed a few sizes small, "he's more worried about showing off those pretty legs than playing ball. Look at him wiggle his butt around!"

Jimmy chuckled. "His mom dry them on high?" The brothers laughed.

Then Dex stopped, serious. "I'll put Shooter in his place, you just shoot like Tapiola."

"OK, put your money where your mouth is. I bet Shooter shuts you down."

"I'll never put my money where my mouth is," Dex said, falling into his old joke. "Don't you know where money's been?"

"It's filthy."

And the brothers laughed some more, and it felt good. Felt like they were all the way back.

"Look at that guy," Dex said. He pointed to Pedro in the stands, so high his face looked like unfired clay, melting off his head.

"Hey you guuuuys!" Pedro shouted in an impersonation of Chunk from *The Goonies*.

"He really should get involved with DARE," Jimmy said.

"*Càllate, idiota*!" Dex yelled wildly.

Dex was a bit shorter than Shooter, but a lot wider. Plus Dex had a chip on his shoulder the size of Oregon and most other western states combined. He hated Shooter more than he thought it possible to hate someone. It scared and electrified him, took his body over like when he socked Joe Looney.

Jimmy started the game on the bench and Seaside went up early. While Dex had a pretty good handle on Shooter, the rest of Seaside's team got wide open looks and knocked them down. Dex needed outside scoring help. Stretch the floor. Couldn't do it all on his own.

Each time Dex ran up the court, he shouted to Coach Kelly, "Put Jimmy in!"

Finally, start of the third quarter and Seaside up by fifteen, Coach Kelly called for Jimmy. Our kid retied the drawstring on his shorts, stomped his feet twice, and checked in. Seaside's fans went berserk. Chants of *"Dad-dy's bet-ter!"* rained down. The whistle blew. Jimmy got the inbounds pass. First few dribbles were shaky, he had to look at the ball instead of up the court. Everyone in the stands held their breath. The Seagulls player guarding Jimmy went for a swipe. Instincts set in, Jimmy dribbled through his legs and spun around. So smooth and tricky the defender was suddenly behind our kid, confused, disoriented.

"Oh, now!" Dex yelled.

The Seaside crowd cooed, confused.

Shooter Ackley came off Dex to pick up Jimmy. A caught crab, snapping his claws, eager to take off the first finger he got hold of.

The crowd regained their lungs, sputtered, then full-out. Cheering, jeering, and shouting ensued. Jimmy saw Shooter running at him. The other game flashed in his mind. All the taunts came back fresh as the day they happened. "Your baby bro's bigger than you." BRICK. "Your Grandpa sleeps on the streets, crazy fuck." WHIFF. "Your daddy was better than you'll ever be." AIR BALL. His whole life had locked up after that game. The pressure. It was happening again. He could feel his joints calcifying.

"Jimmy, baby, how I missed you," Shooter yelled as he came.

Then Jimmy saw Dex setting up a screen to the left of Shooter. A little glint in his eye. Baby bro was going to be Jimmy's rock, and a bad second choice to Shooter's hard place. Jimmy jabbed to his right, which he knew Shooter would anticipate, knew the big, cocky farm kid would be ready to go full-steam to the left, and so Jimmy went full on to the left too. Led his man right into Dex's bricked-up body. Shooter moaned when he hit. Screen? Naw, this was a playground *pick*. It picked inside Shooter's body, jangled up his organs, stole all his wind. Left him coughing, spitting, broke. Hurt so bad his grandkids would be sore. Freed Jimmy up completely. He was practically floating. Pulled up from so far beyond the three-point line, he might as well have been shooting from a different state. Redraw the territory lines 'cause Jimmy claimed it Kirkus Country. Splash. Three points. Game on.

With Dex taking up so much attention in the middle, it freed Jimmy to skate the perimeter, free and clear. Nobody could keep up with Jimmy long enough to knock him off his rhythm. The Fishermen clawed their way back into the game. The small contingent of Fisherman Faithful were dancing in the aisles after every shot made. Shooter quit his talking to concentrate on his breathing.

Then, with ten seconds left in the game, score tied at sixty-three, Jimmy had the last shot. He had the ball. Had the open look. Then there was Shooter, barreling at him, seething. And Jimmy glanced around. Dex was tangled below the hoop. No help for him this time. And Jimmy—images of his pops's career ending, his meltdown last year, all mixed in his head—flinched. Tried a halfhearted pass. Shooter got a hand on it. Up, up, up in the air. Somehow, Dex disentangled himself. The crowd held their breath. Dex ran for the ball. Threw his body after it. Clock winding down. *Five, four, three*—he got a hand on it and tapped it back to Jimmy. Shooter, his momentum carrying him past Jimmy, screamed. Jimmy caught—*two*—and released—*one*—as time expired and Dex, getting to the ball had been too much, careened into the bleachers. The shot was a little wrist-flicker that nestled in the very bottom of the net like it lived there and was just going home.

The Columbia City fans rushed the court—Seaside's home floor—to mob Jimmy. Everyone loves a comeback story. *Hope springs eternal* and *In Jimmy we trust.* The chants of *"Dad-dy's bet-ter"* forgotten. Not only had the Kirkus boys done well enough to make it seem silly, they'd proven there would need to be an addendum in the legend surrounding the Kirkus family. Maybe, in truth, Freight Train was the second, or even third best Kirkus to ever play ball. In the center of the packed court, Coach Kelly found Jimmy and shouted in his ear, "We're gonna let this Kirkus train roll, baby, roll."

"Yeah, Coach," Jimmy said.

"You guys play like this, and we're talking state titles. That's plural. We'll be getting calls from all over the country on you two. Nike Hoops Summit invites. Draft chatter."

"Thanks, Coach."

Jimmy tried to turn away but Coach Kelly wrapped an arm around his neck, roped him in. He didn't like to be dismissed. That's the way it was with Coach Kelly. Basketball, basketball, basketball, always and forever, one more detail, always one more detail, to discuss. "We just gotta get you tough. You should've waited on that last shot. Shooter would have fouled you." It was exhausting.

JIMMY KIRKUS, FIFTEEN YEARS OLD—ONE YEAR UNTIL THE WALL.

Jimmy pulled out of his coach's grip, squinted at him like, *What the fuck, we just won, why the hell you telling me now?* "Whatever, we got them," he said.

"Listen to me, kid, the body's an amazing thing. I know, I teach health class. Your head, your skeleton, your hands, your feet. They're meant for this kind of shit. Pardon my French. You just *can't* run fast enough into a wall to really hurt yourself. Impossible. Bodies are meant for it. Look at Dex, he ran straight into the bleachers for the tip, and he's fine."

Each of Coach Kelly's words was a small amount of weight bringing him back down to earth. So Jimmy left him, filtered into the crowd, looking to reclaim some of the jump he'd felt after burying the game-winner.

. . . . . .

In the bedlam, Dex had been forgotten except by those people he pummeled through in their seats. He'd landed shoulder first on a bleacher's edge. He was bleeding and swollen and sitting in the first row. Someone had brought him a handful of concession-stand napkins. He had the bloody wad up against his bottom lip and took it away to spray water from a plastic squeeze bottle into his mouth, letting it drip pinkish down his chin, laughing in joy at the celebration.

. . . . . .

When the final buzzer sounded, Genny Mori, as if floating on a cloud, made her way through the mobbing fans to her son. She brought Jimmy into a tight hug. He pushed away at the odd display of affection from her.

"Jimmy," she said, "Jimmy."

Then Dex came up, bloody napkins still held tightly to his lip. He'd procured an icepack somewhere and this was strapped to his already purpling shoulder.

"Oh, Jesus, Dex, what happened?"

"Tough last rebound."

She turned to McMahan, little man of her dreams almost lost among the height, athleticism, and sheer joy of his surroundings. "Well we've got a doctor right here. What do you say, Doc?"

McMahan stuttered. "Well, I." He lifted the edge of the napkin wad. "Might take him to the hospital for a look, just to be completely certain." He touched the throbbing shoulder, "Yep, we should definitely check this one out."

"Dex, mind if I ride the bus?" Jimmy asked. He looked over at Naomi, the cheerleader who had ignored him for the past year but was right then staring smoldering eyes at him—game-winning shots can be *very* sexy on some people.

"Jimmy's got a girlfriend," Dex said in a high voice.

"Shut up," Jimmy said with no malice. He hugged his mom one last time, punched Dex soft in his good shoulder, and then walked over to Naomi. She led him to the team bus.

"Pretty good playing out there, Dex," Doc McMahan said. "I used to play a little out in Colton for Country Christian."

Dex straightened up to his full six-foot, three-inch height. He puffed out his chest and looked far down at little McMahan. "Guess they're pretty desperate for players that far out."

. . . . . .

There was a traffic jam in the parking lot after the game. Cars honked happily to one another. All, even the Seaside fans, still under the spell of the Kirkus boys' display of greatness. Fishermen fans because it meant another uptick in the basketball quality of life, and Seagull fans because they had just witnessed something truly transcendent. The Fishermen bus edged through the lot foot by foot as traffic allowed, while smaller vehicles slipped by and honked to the players. Jimmy sat in the back of the bus, game ball in hand, Naomi at his side, just waiting for the

JIMMY KIRKUS, FIFTEEN YEARS OLD—ONE YEAR UNTIL THE WALL.

darkness of the open road to cover them. Waiting for the future. Waiting to be the Jimmy Kirkus the town wanted him to be.

. . . . . .

In McMahan's car, Dex sat in the back and traded texts with teammates and Pedro. He was weighed down with fatigue. More so than he'd ever been in his life. And while he could have been on the bus trying to get with his own lady, doing that awkward wrestle with her on fake leather bench-seats, smelly adolescent boys all around, all he wanted to do was sleep for a million years.

The world was spinning pleasurably. The Doc had given him some wonderful pain relievers. Large, white pills that found the pain occupying his banged-up shoulder and then revoked its right to vote. Peace once more in the body of Dexter Kirkus. The start and stop traffic lulled him. He put on his headphones. Huge, black things with half-inch of donut cushion on each side. He slumped his head against the window, watched scenes play out in the cars stuck in traffic beside him. Kids and parents. Sing-alongs and fights over seats. Cell phones and radio dials.

He was about to press play on his CD player, finger on the button to import the fat beats of Pharrell into his skull, when he noticed his mom and the Doc both glance back at him through the rearview mirror at the same time. On a hunch he didn't press the button, but started to nod his head as if he had. He closed his eyes, pretending to drift off to sleep.

. . . . . .

The moon was out, and just before Arch Cape, the traffic cleared and McMahan stepped on the gas. Genny Mori and him were having a whispered conversation. Kind of thing that seemed light enough to float away on the night, but that was only because it was too dark to see all the heaviness it carried. "Come away" was said a lot. "With me," too. "Please" was everywhere and "I don't know" splattered the space between knee and stick shift and knee again.

And then finally, "Yes."

Genny Mori knew something and she smiled to herself. This was where the tide shifted. The Doc would be hers and a second act of her life was set to begin. No more highs and lows courtesy of blustery Todd Kirkus. She had made up her mind and the Doc had too. Decision reached, it seemed so easy and she wondered why they hadn't done it sooner. She had an urge to celebrate. Go somewhere and plan a whole new life. They were headed to the Columbia City hospital to have Dex's shoulder looked at, but after that, who knew?

"Hawaii, what about Hawaii?" McMahan said.

The idea seemed so big Genny just laughed, but then again, now that her two boys were back to being friends, back to their old selves on the court, she felt free to let her mind roll. "Like Hawaii, Hawaii?"

"Like aloha."

She squeezed his knee and yipped and he shushed her, Dex was in the backseat after all. Genny giggled, did a poor job of covering it up. Life was an exciting, huge thing and she had love for everyone and everything in it, but especially those monstrous headphones that she knew from experience blocked out any incoming sounds to Dex's ears. She was chiefly thankful for those.

McMahan really had the car going when he reached the curves leading up to the cove. He seemed jumped up, heady on the conversation they were having. A sort of thing that felt like it was stamped all over with LAST CHANCE and yet they'd made it just under the wire.

......

The bus—loaded with Fishermen players sleeping or listening to their iPods, or, in the case of Jimmy Kirkus, about three hundred taste buds deep into Naomi's mouth—was a few cars ahead of McMahan's and troubled with the steepness of the hill. The bus slowed as the driver shifted into a lower gear to take on the steep grade. Doc McMahan's car went boldly into the oncoming lane and around the bus, lit off like a UFO.

"Fucking hell, punk," the bus driver muttered.

. . . . . .

Tuned in to his mom's conversation with the Doc, Dex almost missed the headlights barreling down the hill at them. The Doc was leaning toward his mother, not looking at the road, entering sacred airspace, and Dex was trying to concentrate hard enough to get his hands to release their death-grip on the seat cushion and instead wrap around the scrawny little man's neck. The head-lights were too much though. They demanded notice. Through the fog of the painkillers pumping in his blood, he registered what was happening. The oncoming Toyota pickup, jacked easily a foot above regulation, came roaring down around the curve and drifted into McMahan's lane. Dex screamed in a hoarse way, his voice mostly gone from the game. It caught the Doc's attention and he tried to turn away from the truck, but it wasn't enough because it was too much. His mom's voice entered the fray. One word, re-peated again and again. The Doc's luxury car tumbled over the shoulder of the road, tripping on the guardrail, pivoting and flip-ping so the back hit the metal ribbon upside down. The in-dash navigation computer cried danger. The guardrail skinned the back end of the car and the big, muscled Dex within, flat. Then the car glanced off one tree and wrapped its nose around the next. It was so sudden, violent, and final that when the car settled and silence quickly followed, it was almost as if it had never hap-pened. Two or three seconds was it.

All three dead on the scene.

Part Three

Rule 23. Don't Ever Stop

Saturday, March 8, 2008

JIMMY KIRKUS, SIXTEEN YEARS OLD—EIGHTY-TWO DAYS AFTER THE WALL.

The radio is blaring.

> Hunter: *Welcome to Eugene, Oregon, sports fans, for the 2007 Oregon 6A state basketball championship. Columbia City versus North Bend. This is one for the record books. All because of one young Jimmy Kirkus from Columbia City, Oregon. I'm Hunter Smith, on behalf of Craig Lang, we're happy to have you with us for what will surely prove to be classic basketball tonight.*
>
> Craig: *That's right, Hunt, but you gotta get your names right. McArthur Court is The Pit and Jimmy Kirkus is Kamikaze Kirkus.*
>
> Hunter: *My partner in crime is right. Here in Eugene it's a federal offense to call it anything but The Pit, and the star of the show, Jimmy Kirkus, he's not only transformed his play this year, but his name as well.*
>
> Craig: *Transformed his play is right. He'd be a lottery pick in the NBA draft right now if they still let kids come out of high school. Guaranteed. I played against his dad, a heck of a player, heck of a player, Freight Train, and eh, well a lot of tragedy has befallen the Kirkus household and we here at 950 The Fan wish them all the best.*

Hunter: *This has truly been one for the record books, partner. A thing of beauty. Jimmy has just steamrolled a strong team out of Canby led by the Duke-bound Ian Callert, and it doesn't seem like he can be stopped.*

Craig*: OSAA might want to reconsider sending the Fishermen down to 4A! I mean, have some mercy!*

Todd Kirkus throws a half of a chewed pizza crust at the radio. He misses. "Fucking Craig Lang!" He sits up from where he'd been reclining on the couch. "Pop, you remember Craig Lang?"

The Flying Finn is on his bike in its spinning stand, fully spandexed in gear, pumping away the nerves as they listen to Jimmy play a couple hundred miles south for the state title. "No, was he in this movie *Princes of Persia*?"

Todd takes another piece of pizza, collapses back into the couch, takes a big bite and speaks through his chewing. "You're hopeless. Craig Lang was ball boy for Seaside my senior year. He never played against me." Todd balanced the piece on his mounding belly, closed his eyes, and tried to picture what it would be like at Mac Court this very instant. This is where life has led him: not being allowed to watch his own son play for a state championship. Jimmy and his no-away-game rule. Stuck at home in Columbia City with an old man who thinks ball boys could be movie stars.

"Well, I's still think this Langy fellow might be from the movies . . ."

They both fall silent. It's happening.

Hunter: *Kirkus has the ball, and he's beat the first defender, around the second, holy cow this kid can move! Almost clear for the hoop. Ted Brown from North Bend set up to take the charge and.*

Craig: *What a hit!*

Hunter*: Jimmy puts it in! Whoa Nelly, Jimmy Kirkus just laid out Ted Brown to put a cap on this game. Brown was moving his feet, and is called for the foul. A good call, although it appears Brown's the one a little worse for the wear, partner.*

Craig*: Jesus.*

Hunter: *Bingo-bango-bongo tonight the Fishermen Faithful are going to party. Break out the champagne in Columbia City, folks. Kamikaze Kirkus has just put in fifty-six brutal points on the way to the 6A state title. The North Bend Loggers want nothing more to do with it! Send it to the presses! The Fishermen win! The Fishermen win!*

Craig: *Never seen anything like it before. Never. Like he's working basketball, not playing basketball.*

Hunter: *The fans have rushed the floor! It's pandemonium in Eugene! But where's Kirkus? Where'd he go?*

Craig*: Kid vanished like a ghost!*

It's after one a.m., deep into nobody-o'clock, and Columbia City is deserted. Jimmy walks home from the high school parking lot alone. He told his pops and the Flying Finn that the team was staying the night in Eugene. Otherwise he knew they'd be waiting for him, couple of stooges in an idling van, and he wanted this walk for only himself. Still, everyone and their mother offered to take him home, but he said no. And they didn't persist. This is Kamikaze Kirkus after all. Guy you listen to if he decides to speak. Bringer of championship, silencer of critics.

It's cold, and the frost cracking under his foot as he walks along the river toward Dairy Queen, and then up the hill to Glasgow and his house, seems to be the only sound left in the world. Jimmy relishes it, walking slowly, letting the ice crack out over seconds of time. To him, his hearing still dulled from the packed gym in

Eugene—"Call it The Pit, boys"—this ice cracking is the loudest, best thing he's ever heard. It takes him an hour to get home when it should take less than five minutes. Looks like he's walking in slow motion. The few people who drive by honk their horns, shake their heads, smile. *There goes crazy Kamikaze Kirkus, one for the ages.*

The house is dark, the front door unlocked. Inside it's warm and Jimmy breathes deeply. He sets his duffle bag on the couch and sits beside it. This house smells like home. Dust, wood, and gym shoes. His earbuds, which have been around his neck, hidden beneath his hoodie, are uncomfortable. He takes them off. They're still playing. He holds one earbud to his ear. "Diamonds on the soles of her shoes." Song on repeat. He pulls out his iPod and presses stop. It's the only song on there.

He's bone tired and sitting uncomfortably on the couch. Slouched so far half his back is off the cushions. He's still not used to how big he's become. He thinks of himself as a smaller kid. A Keebler Elf, Dex would say. He is constantly racking up bruises by underestimating his size and running into things. He's awkward anywhere off the court. He shot up to a six-foot-eight beast of muscle and power in his year alone.

His soreness is a deep, rasping thing. As if each one of his muscles was taken out and stretched to the point of breaking and then put back into his body. Any movement might snap them. Leave him limp.

He stands up with the idea of eating something. He goes slowly toward the kitchen, moving with the exaggerated motions of a child pretending to be blind. He wishes he had turned on the light when he first came in, but now he doesn't want to risk finding the switch and knocking something over, waking the whole house, having to talk.

In the kitchen, Jimmy opens up the fridge and finds leftovers.

Plain cheese pizza: fair enough. He remembers how his mom used to always make them get half the pizza BLT, which Jimmy didn't mind so much until he was in situations like this—eating cold pizza in the dark. The T in the BLT pizza always let out the rest of its water into the pie as it waited to be eaten in the fridge. Then, when you went for a bite, you got all this ice-cold, watery tomato juice dripping on you. Cheese pizza, well hell, that wasn't so bad. Cheese pizza held its own. Locked up tight.

From in his pops's bedroom, he hears the bedside lamp click on. Jimmy stops trying to be quiet—the Flying Finn would sleep through a bombing—and scrapes a chair out from the kitchen table. He sits down and waits.

Big Freight Train Kirkus comes into the kitchen scratching his bed-messed hair. He flicks on the lights. Both men squint. His pops stares at him for a few moments. Jimmy feels it on the top of his head. Brightness like rain. He doesn't look up though. He's staring at the congealed yellow topography of his pizza.

His pops goes to the cabinets over the kitchen sink and takes down a bag of breath mints. He's been cracking them nonstop to keep his mind off drinking. He stopped for good on that flashing-light day he lost Dex and Genny more than a year before. Going to rot out his teeth because of it.

His pops is so big around the middle these days, he has to sit down first and then pull the table in after. The chair creaks and Jimmy watches his plate move out with the table, and then come back in. His pops settles, yanks on his shirt so it's better spread over his ample body.

"You played good tonight, kid, real good." He cracks a peppermint. "At least from what the radio told me."

Jimmy finishes his fourth slice of cheese. He nods.

"Thought the announcer was going to lose his voice." His pops cracks another peppermint. Sound crisp like a gunshot. "Let me think. Hell, I remember, fifty-six points, twenty-three rebounds, and eleven assists, I mean, Jim-my." He says his son's name in two pulled-apart syllables, hoping he can put some goddamn joy in it. "That's something else!"

"Thanks," Jimmy says quietly.

His pops drums his fingers on the table. "Hey, let me drive you somewhere, get you some warm food or something."

"No, this is fine."

"I mean it. Let's get you something special. What does a father buy a son to eat after he's just won the state championship?"

"Really, no."

Jimmy yawns and the two men consider the sound for a long while. His pops changes his position in the chair, and then Jimmy does the same. These chairs are too small for these large men. Everything in this house is too small for them, even their beds. They have to sleep diagonally with their toes off the end.

When he get so big? thinks the pops.

Am I so big? thinks the son.

"Wish I could have been there, Jimmy. Grandpa too. Would have loved to have been there."

. . . . . .

Jimmy catches something in his throat. He's coughing and he needs a glass of water, so Todd jumps up and gets some for him. He watches his son drink, his Adam's apple leapfrogging the water as it glug-glugs down his throat.

"You got a lot of basketball left in you, Jimmy. Guys on the radio said you're the top recruit in the country. Said you'd be drafted right now to the NBA." Todd pauses. Indeed the phones have been ringing off the hook. College coaches from all across the country. "Can't expect me and Grandpa to stay away from every game till kingdom come." There, wrapped inside this man-child, are elements of the kid he used to tell stories to, tried to protect. He wonders when was the last time he picked his kid up. Held him, kissed him on the forehead? There had to be a last time. There had to be. He wonders if on that day he had any idea how different the future was going to be. Had he any idea how sacred that last time was?

"Dad . . ."

"Listen, kid, what happened to Mom and Dex, was an accident, plain and simple."

"Dad."

Outside thunder cracks and a great rain rips down. The storm the news has been going on about for the past three days has finally come. It's raining cats and dogs—if cats and dogs were lions and bears. It smears itself onto the big river-facing window, water pulsing in the gusts of wind as if they were inside a chamber of the storm's heart. Todd uses the weather to pause, to gather himself because, *hell no*, he's not going to cry this night. He speaks louder over the rain and wind outside. "We're going to be safe when we drive. We just want to see you play. Nothing will happen. We'll take a bus even, if it helps. Next year, I just want to make this clear, we're coming to your games. We're not taking no for an answer."

Jimmy gets up and puts his dish away. He comes back to the table and sits. Tomorrow will be the best day in a long while. But it isn't tomorrow yet.

His pops tries a different tack. "Coach called but that was over an hour ago. You took your time coming home. I meant to stay up but . . ." He chuckles, trying for levity—no go. "Anyway, Coach said you left your medal on the bus. You can pick it up tomorrow." Todd lets out his breath. "Although I bet the way you're playing, he'll gift wrap the thing and bring it up to the house on his knees."

"Naw, me and coach got it good. He don't care if I get the medal or not."

JIMMY KIRKUS, SIXTEEN YEARS OLD–EIGHTY-TWO DAYS AFTER THE WALL.

"Oh?"

"Dad," Jimmy says with those serious, dagger eyes he's picked up from somewhere, "how come you drank that night in Eugene?"

Todd is surprised by this, and yet, not at all. It's too small town in Columbia City. It was a secret, sure, but one he never meant to keep. "Jimmy, it's a long thing and . . ."

"Just tell me." Jimmy stands up. His size is impossible.

So Todd tells him, in words more ready than he ever dared to hope. "You know how it is, Jim, you get so good at something that it's like no one can ever know, you know? And then you're alone because of that, and so it's nice to just stop feeling for a second, for one goddamn second."

"But you'd been good for a while, Pops. You'd already won the title once. Why drink on that night? You could have been playing D1. Gone to the NBA."

Todd remembers something. This guy Chuck from work came in pale and shaking because the night before he dreamed he had died with his best friend and they both went to hell. The devil came to them and said, *Each night you will die a new way, until you've died all the ways there are to die.* So the first night Chuck died falling off a cliff and his friend died being stuck in a car, fighting for air as it sank into the ocean. It was as terrifying and sad as if they were dying for the first time. On the second night, Chuck's friend had an idea. They would take turns dying twice so the other person could get a day off. Chuck went first. He died being stretched apart by horses and also choking on a piece of steak. It was terrible, but he looked forward to his night off when his friend would do the dying. However, when Chuck went to find his friend, he was gone. Chuck had been tricked and each night he had to die twice.

Todd shakes his head. The dream has stuck with him: Try and do right and you get the short end of it. Better to just do yours.

"Look, it's just . . . see, I had this argument with your grandpa. He wanted me to get drafted, go to the NBA. Get the money. I don't know if you know this, but the Nets called." He looks up into his son's eyes, sees if this impresses him. Jimmy's eyes are blank. "And Coach Kelly kept pushing for me to take the scholarship to Oregon, 'cause he'd get a coaching job out of it. But it wasn't only that. James'd be on the team too . . . I got into an argument with Dad about it. And you know. Going to Oregon wasn't just going to Oregon, it was helping coach and James too. And Dad didn't understand, wanted me to take the money and go pro, and he was kind of the one guy I wanted to understand me, you know? Your own father?"

"Were you running? From Mom? 'Cause she was pregnant?"

Todd tilts his head. How can he answer this? He was scared, sure. He was just a kid. Can he even remember how he was feeling that far back? He wasn't running from Genny, nope, he's almost sure of that. Even if he *had* been running from Genny at the time, it wouldn't have stuck. No way it would have lasted. "No, Jimmy, that's not what it was."

He sees his son swallow, getting ready to say something. "Pops, I want to get my GED. Go to college early."

He chuckles—relief—and stands up too. Rubs his eyes. "I don't think it works that way, kiddo. The NCAA is tough. You got to be a certain age for playing basketball. You can't just jump to college and play early. There are rules. I know this new league will be easy and all, but you got to wait. You're only a junior."

His son stares at him for a long, hard time. The thing about Chuck's dream is that Todd would rather die once than twice. Finally he gets what Jimmy is saying and has to look away from his son. Not playing ball—that's the whole point.

JIMMY KIRKUS, SIXTEEN YEARS OLD—EIGHTY-TWO DAYS AFTER THE WALL.

Rule 24. Facts Rarely Help

Spring and Fall, 2007

JIMMY KIRKUS, SIXTEEN YEARS OLD–SEVEN MONTHS UNTIL THE WALL.

The Fishermen team bus had tooled by the wreck at two miles an hour. Jimmy had done what the rest of the kids did. He looked, he pointed, he said, "Shit," and then he got back to the business of going too far with a girl. He hated himself for it but who could blame the kid? How the hell was he supposed to know what he was seeing? He didn't recognize the car. It was McMahan's after all. It never crossed his mind that maybe . . .

When he did find out, Jimmy didn't go back to school or the team. One night, he snuck out and threw a rock through Naomi's window. Then he sat in the bushes and watched her father patch the hole with cardboard. He listened to her crying. He waited there, his breath visible in puffs, until the coldness had infiltrated the deepest part of him.

. . . . . .

From home he caught on to a rumor going through town that everyone knew but no one would tell Jimmy. That's what rumors are, after all, secrets kept from only one person. He'd heard a part of this rumor from a neighbor lady talking overloud on the phone with her window open. Finally, one day, he cornered Pedro behind the gym, sniffing deeply of a sandwich bag full of crumbly green.

"Pedro," Jimmy said.

Glassy-eyed and slack-faced, Pedro literally jumped at Jimmy's voice. "Jesus and Mary, my man," he said, barely able to get the words past his relief, giggling, his ragged draws of breath. "What. What you doing here? You don't go to school."

"I came to find you."

"Yo. Check it, Jimmy, check it," Pedro poked around in his plastic bag and came away with a small lump pinched between index and thumb. "This is a nugget." Pedro stuck it near his flared nostrils and sniffed so hard, Jimmy was afraid he'd suck it up. "Look at this, Jimmy, it's like a little corn on the cob. I just want to put some butter on it and nibble."

Jimmy leaned in. Uncomfortable but feeling he had to play along. "That's big?" he asked. To him it looked like a cat turd.

"Hell yeah." Pedro pinched off a little into his palm, peppered it into the opened corpse of an eviscerated cigarette, and set to work twisting it back up with some new paper. Produced a little spliff that looked like it had aged in the cracks of a public bus seat. Despite all evidence to the contrary, Pedro apparently wasn't high enough. Clicked the lighter. Lit it up.

"Stinks," Jimmy said.

"Yeah, well. Smells good to me, so?" Licked the end of the joint tenderly. Inhaled again. "You know, you should really try this shit, man." His voice got squished tiny, all the smoke crowded around it. "I mean, seriously, they've done some studies and shit. Medicinal as hell. Works for, you know, depression."

"I'm not depressed."

"Whatever, man, you're not in school anymore, so." Jimmy turned away but Pedro crab-walked around so he stayed in his line of sight. "Listen, you ever think about what Dex was thinking just before he—"

"No."

"—died? I do. All the time." Another toke, his voice squished up again. "It's like, what the hell could he been possibly thinking in that little bitsy space of time? But, he was thinking something. And it's like, I don't believe in God as like a rule, but when I get thinking about what Dex was thinking, then I'm thinking damn, I hope there is a dog." Pause. Full stop. Then Pedro laughed frenziedly. "I mean *God*, not *dog . . ."* He laughed till it was unwound. Then in a whisper, "But holy *shit*, what if God *is* a dog?"

The truth was, Jimmy almost constantly thought about what Dex had been thinking, feeling, just before. It was all he could do to keep it *out* of his mind.

"Pedro, what's going around about my moms, and that doctor, huh?"

Pedro waved him off, the little joint splashing out ash. "Naw, you don't want to know. Bad energy. Bad juju!" He started laughing again, more coughing.

Jimmy slapped the joint out of his hand. It sizzled in a puddle. "Just tell me."

"Little Jimmy making a big stink. You want to fight again, cabrón? That was good weed."

"Just tell me."

"Your mom was fucking the good doctor, that enough for you?"

. . . . . .

His pops understood about him dropping school and basketball. Even supported the choice. Seemed to him that fate for the Kirkus family was to get everything ripped away and then some. The Kirkus Curse. His pops educated Jimmy at home for the rest of the year. Taught him best he could from a curriculum he ordered over the phone from a lady with a Texan accent, hoping his son would forgive him one day for any gaps in his education.

The Flying Finn never came back after the funeral for Dex and Genny Mori. He had been mumbling something about catching up on training when he rode off on his bike. Suit coat flapping. No one bothered looking for him. It wasn't the first time the man had disappeared.

. . . . . .

Jimmy stayed in gym shorts and sweatshirts day in, day out. Slept whenever he could. Thought about his brother dying so young, about his mom sleeping with some doctor from Seaside. His whole life she'd felt apart from him. Like it was a *favor* that she gave birth to him, nothing more. She pushed him away and yet died fucking some stranger. It was a bile-laced rage he felt toward her, made all the more acidic by the fact that he would never be able to call her out on it.

Day in and day out he felt himself sinking into a depression that was big and black and without a bottom. He felt as though each day was dragging him nearer to the edge and at any moment he could go over. And that would be a relief. But the edge always moved farther off. There was always a lower way to feel. He didn't touch a basketball. He ate, he slept, and he studied with his pops.

And, oh yes, he grew.

Grew huge. Enormous. A tree among grasses. A lion among cats. A Big-Gulp among eight-ounce cans. Wide like Dex but taller and quicker still. Those damn Kirkus genes. Late to the party, but ready to party nonetheless.

Then, finally, seven months into this self-exile, his pops couldn't take it anymore. Couldn't bear to see his son drifting so much. Remembered about the pain he felt walking away from basketball and not looking back. All that trouble, and for what? He tried something he thought drastic. He told the kid, "I hear basketball's

JIMMY KIRKUS, SIXTEEN YEARS OLD—SEVEN MONTHS UNTIL THE WALL.

starting up. You could go shoot around. Just go check out a practice. Just because. Just to see. You're set to go back to school tomorrow anyway. And. Well. Dex would have wanted you to. I mean,
can't just stay inside all day every day for the rest of your life,
right?"

So Jimmy went.

Just to check it out.

Rule 25. Leave on Your Terms, Never Theirs

Sunday, March 9, 2008

JIMMY KIRKUS, SIXTEEN YEARS OLD–EIGHTY-THREE DAYS AFTER THE WALL.

The rains have been on for two days straight. Jimmy's brought Columbia City their first championship in years and yet the town is threatening to slough off into the river. With good comes bad. Gray streaks across the atmosphere muddling everything the same color. Rumors are lighting through town that the Coast Guard could be called in soon to evacuate. Those alive who remember the 1938 flood prophesy doom. The rivers on both sides, Youngs and Columbia, are hopped up on rain and wind, giddy to take a stumble through town, pop off parked cars and houses like a drunk does trash cans on his walk home from the bar. Clouds that start in the sky don't end until they're hovering over mailboxes.

Jimmy, his pops, and the Flying Finn sit in the living room and watch the downpour. Power's been out, so they just talk—or not. The phone's been ringing off the hook and cars honk wildly as they drive slowly past, wading through the torrent of rain water washing down Glasgow Street. Sometimes the cars stop in front of the Kirkus house and people fire bottle rockets from the windows to explode damply in the gray air. They call out, shake their fists in pride, and blow off-key blasts from cardboard party trumpets—*charge!* Jimmy "Kamikaze" Kirkus is the toast of the town.

There was to be a party at Tapiola Park for all of Columbia City to celebrate the state title—bonfire and a band, hundreds of hot-dogs and generic-brand pop—but this is canceled due to the weather. Twenty or so people still show up. They end up dancing in the mud, drinking straight from bottles poorly hidden in paper sacks that melt away in the rain. The cops come to break it up a couple hours later. Find a handful of men and women drunk, in various states of undress, shivering and singing bits of the high school's song: "Hail to thee our alma mater . . . ."

The rain doesn't quit until it's fed Youngs River and her evil big brother the Columbia strong enough to swell up, swallow the high school and the Brick House too. Trees fall all over Peter Pan Court, and Tapiola Court simply disappears beneath the tongue of the river water. Cats are found on roofs, dogs don't stop barking, and some jokester has vandalized the sign on the edge of town so it says, WELCOME TO COLUMBIA CITY LAKE. The Kirkus house, on a hill, is spared, but there is a fear that its feet will be swept from beneath it. The sidewalk a rushing river. What a strange phenomenon. When Jimmy looks out his front window and sees all that moving water he feels as if he too is drifting.

Just three miles outside of town the clouds thin, the rain slackens, but here in town everything is veiled, drenched. As if Columbia City has finally grabbed a piece of the squirrely heavens and won't let go. She holds the clouds close to her chest and damn the rains.

On the fifth straight day of rain, school cancelled, the cabin fever is too much, and Jimmy wades out into the freezing water in enormous yellow boots his pops once bought thinking he might take up clamming. He takes his old basketball and makes his careful way down to the high school. He finds a canoe abandoned, stuck, and choking in a swing set at Tapiola Park. He bails out the water the best he can with his stocking cap. He's soaked now, shivering. He paddles on the shallow water the rest of the way to school. Surreal to glide over sidewalks and clogged storm drains. The splashing rain hitting the churned-up water is so constant in its roar it becomes an off-brand of silence. If he doesn't turn and paddles straight ahead, he would be in the Pacific Ocean before long and who knows how many days it would take to find him—catch on to a good current and be a hundred miles out before night—but he does turn in the end.

When he gets to the gym, the doors to the Brick House stand open. He has his battered, gray basketball with him, almost black with wetness. He paddles in. Each splash of his paddle echoes in this giant cave. The gym is gloomy, dim, also without power. It means there is no security camera to catch his private moment this time. The EXIT sign somehow still shines on.

He ties the canoe to the bleachers and wades into Coach Kelly's office. It's a bathtub and some of his framed pictures, old trophies, and yearbooks are toys. There, still dry on Coach Kelly's desk, is his medal. 6A Boys Basketball State Champions. He picks it up; it's cold, and heavier than he thought it would be. On the bus ride home some of the other guys had been kissing their medals, grinning with them, wearing them into pit stop gas stations, waiting to be noticed. He hadn't wanted his. Told Coach to hold on to it for a while. Now. Here. This is it. Jimmy puts it on. It taps on his chest. He thought it would be different than this. More. He feels claustrophobic and needs to leave the office. Back into the gym glowing red from the EXIT light.

He gets back into his canoe and the light guides him well enough to get to the spot on the wall he stained. To the exact place he smashed his head. The red and undulating water cast a wobble over everything. He touches the wall with an open palm. He breathes in. It's still here. His blood. The blood-red bricks of Kamikaze Kirkus. Already the canoe is drifting. A longer reach to touch these bricks. He takes the medal off his neck. Drops it into the water. Then, in the next moment, he tips his old basketball overboard. It rotates so he sees the last name he wrote on it.

JIMMY KIRKUS, SIXTEEN YEARS OLD—EIGHTY-THREE DAYS AFTER THE WALL.

Blacker, thicker than the rest. Three letters. D-E-X. It drifts slowly away, spinning, the name of his brother dunked; this time it will not come back.

Soon the rain will stop, soon the town will rebuild, but they will do so proudly. They were founded on the fur trade, built up by canning, and both have left them, but they don't stumble. They've had two fires, and two floods, and still they survive. "Is this it?" they will ask the sky. "This is all you got?" For their town is home to a champion once again—a legend.

Jimmy Kirkus unties the canoe and paddles back out into Columbia City.

Rule 26. First Time Is Rarely the Charm

Monday, December 17, 2007

JIMMY KIRKUS, SIXTEEN YEARS OLD—TWO HOURS UNTIL THE WALL.

When Jimmy finally left the house, cold air biting back on each breath, it was into what seemed like an impossibly big and crowded place. It was the first snow of the season. A white blanket spread over everything. All the cars just lumps in the snow. The Youngs River a thin, black ribbon tying the white day—down or together, no one could be sure. Snow wasn't common in Columbia City, and neither was Jimmy Kirkus anymore.

Jimmy wouldn't have been able to say how bad off he was. He was like a smudged, unclear word without the sentence written around it. He didn't know that spending almost a year in seclusion wasn't normal. It'd been bleak so long there wasn't another way. He was too young to know that no one is spared sadness or tragedy in this life and that going on, always going on, was expected. Our kid had basically spent a year—*a year!*—inside that house. Always in the same spot on the couch, trying to say as little as possible and mostly succeeding. Going over every detail of his last day with Dex and his mom. Looking for loopholes, hoping that through some technicality, it would be called back.

. . . . . .

Snow brought people out in droves. The kids rode flattened cardboard boxes down rough hills to spill out at the bottom in jumbled messes of limbs and bruises. They wore blue jeans sprayed stiff with rain repellant. They called it good enough. Till next year at least. And then when the next year came, it would be the same story. Just spray down the blue jeans, it'll work fine. And it never did. Snow always soaked through. That's so small town.

As Jimmy walked, the kids sledding, the couples making snowmen, the people walking their dogs, all stopped and stared at him.

Look, poor Jimmy Kirkus leaving the house finally.

They say he lives in the attic and won't talk to anyone.

Look! He's gotten so big.

Well, it's been a whole year . . .

In his every step, there was a scary amount of physical power right beneath the surface. Made people nervous just to see it. Like handing a loaded gun to a little kid, they were afraid some part of him might go off on accident. Take a head with it.

. . . . . .

When he got to the door of the gym, he stopped and froze, hand midway toward the push bar. He had a brief, but thoroughly terrifying vision of something quick and violent, sandy and cold. A sand toad? He would've turned around right then and gone back home—what did it matter?—and there would never have been a legend of Kamikaze Kirkus, if it weren't for Mr. Berg taking out the trash. The door bust open from the inside and Jimmy jumped.

"Well, Jimmy, been a little while, now," Mr. Berg said with a giddiness poorly hidden in his voice.

"Been a minute or two."

"Well, you *grew* didn't you?"

Our kid Jimmy didn't answer and so he and Mr. Berg each looked off at the hungry Youngs River, running by the high school, on its way to the Columbia. Anyone else and Jimmy would have left without another word. It was Berg though. Guy who was always on his side.

"Well Jimmy, let me get the door for you," Mr. Berg said, instantly vanquishing the universe where Jimmy just went home, and there was no Kamikaze, no ten opponents beat in a row, no infamous YouTube clips.

"Thanks, Mr. Berg."

"No problem."

He held the door open and the warm air rushed out. Smells that gave Jimmy goose bumps. Rubber and sweat, Gatorade and dust. A little popcorn, maybe? From the last game of the last season?

He was late to practice and when he stepped into the gym, the noise stopped. Everything hung from where it was about to leap. Words clung to kids' lips, balls stopped bouncing and stuck to hands, Coach Kelly's whistle hung crooked in his teeth.

Then—movement.

"Well, hey, all right Jimmy!" Coach Kelly yelled overloud.

And the words dropped again, "Give me a pass, bro." And the ball bounced, *thud, thud*. The whistle blew, *tweet, tweet*.

"OK, boys, OK," Coach Kelly yelled awkwardly. Spit laced around his whistle. "We'll go one more."

Jimmy took off his sweatshirt and boots. Sat on his gray ball and laced up a pair of Dex's old sneakers, the only ones in the house still big enough to fit him. He walked out on the court with shy steps. He'd grown a ton and it wasn't over, either. Our kid was bigger than Freight Train. A legitimate NBA-sized player.

"Jesus, Jimmy," Brian Johnston said. "Grew like a madman." And the others crowded around the big kid who they once had known as a tiny thing, scared to take a hit.

"Grow much, Jimbo?"

"You ate the old Jimmy, you monster!"

"Sasquatch is real!"

"You could change the lightbulbs in this place without a ladder." The team looked up at the high ceiling of the Brick House and laughed, even Jimmy a little.

"OK, stop flirting, ladies, let's go," Coach Kelly said happily. He patted Jimmy's arm. "You are *huge*! You look just like—well, never mind."

They played, but Jimmy was hesitant. Hands unsure. Feet slower than his thoughts. Worse than before, really. It was masked somewhat by his new size—kids were simply afraid to run into a guy big as he'd become—but it was still there. Jimmy was spooked about getting hit. Anytime contact might become involved, he held back, turned away, passed. He was the biggest on the court, but he still felt the smallest, the weakest. He wanted to scuttle away and hide. And this, just like before, infected everything else in his game: passing, shooting, even knowing where to be. The other team won, 11-6.

Afterward, Coach Kelly pulled Jimmy aside. "Look," he told the kid, blinking his watery eyes. "Remember what I told you? Your body can take a lot of punishment and keep ticking. No reason to play scared. You're body's built for this stuff. The running and the banging, the falling and the, the skidding . . . all of it really. The other kids should be scared of you! You're so goddamn big now! You could run headlong into a brick wall and it wouldn't do a thing. Your body's built for as fast as you can go on your own feet. Trust me, I teach health class." Coach folded his arms.

"I'll try, Coach." And in Jimmy's head, the process had already begun. Maybe not the actual idea, but the series of cranks and levers, pulleys and switches, that would eventually create The Idea that would create Kamikaze were moving.

In the locker room the other kids asked Jimmy how he'd been. They gamely didn't bring up the fact that they hadn't seen him—hardly anyone but that stoner Pedro had seen him—in almost a year. They didn't talk about the mediocre season they'd had after Dex died and Jimmy left the team. They certainly didn't say anything about Dex and Mrs. Mori getting in that car crash with that doctor from Portland—a fact that was still vibrating the gossip webs of Columbia City: AFFAIR! CHEATING! VIOLENCE! DEATH! They kidded him about his size and how they bet he had an easy time with his pops in charge of his home school. Easy As and all that. Talked about which poor freshmen kids got bushed and the seniors told him about the colleges they'd applied to.

Jimmy listened but said little as his mind worked. They were all being so nice. He couldn't really understand it. Then it came to him. He was a mess. They felt sorry for him. He was fragile. They wanted to try and protect him because he seemed like the sort that needed protection. They knew it just as he did: he was still Jimmy Soft.

He wouldn't care except for the power his failure gave them. Besides the team there was a whole town, a whole state, who had opinions on the fall from grace of the Kirkus house. If Jimmy couldn't do something to change their minds, then their opinions carried weight, no matter how falsely.

He undressed and showered slowly. The other kids left one by one until he was alone. He dried himself off in front of the mirror. He had avoided looking at himself during his time of solitude, and it surprised him now, what he saw. It was like looking at a movie poster of an action hero and then you realize that's *your* face. It's *your* goddamn face on the poster. Where'd the shoulders and muscles come from? And yet, it was still him. He found the scar where David Berg had thrown a rock at him the year before. Above his right eye. The scar was raised. He'd healed from that.

Coach Kelly came in, whistling softly, swinging the keys on his finger. Jimmy could see in his gait that he had places to go, people to see, and gossip to spread: *Jimmy Kirkus is back, bigger than life itself. But, get this: soft as ever.*

"Get outta here, Jimmy," Coach shouted playfully. "Practice is over."

JIMMY KIRKUS, SIXTEEN YEARS OLD—TWO HOURS UNTIL THE WALL.

"I'm going, Coach."

"Come on then, hurry it up."

Jimmy glanced at the door that led to the parking lot, and then over to the door that went back into the gym. "Go ahead, Coach, I'll be done in a minute."

Coach looked at his watch. "What you trying to stay around for?"

Jimmy sighed, as though he'd been caught. "Just thought a few more shots is all. I want to get in a couple more. You know. Feels good to be back."

Coach Kelly closed his eyes and rubbed his temples. Wheels clicking in there, Jimmy could tell. Guy was a glory hound, that was first of all. If Jimmy could get him thinking he was going to get good again, then Coach would do anything for him. "Fine, fine. Just make sure you close the door all the way when you leave." Coach Kelly opened the door to the parking lot. Cold air rushed in. He turned back. "And Jimmy, I'll see you tomorrow at practice."

"Sure thing, Coach, you got it."

"Close it all the way behind you, Jimmy, I mean it. I don't want any trouble leading back to me, now." He winked at the kid.

"No problem, Coach. No trouble."

So Coach Kelly left and Jimmy turned around.

The Wall was waiting.

Later. Time

There are coaches out there right now saying things like "Kid's got a Larry Bird shot." Or, "There's a player on Central, with this incredible Olajuwon footwork." Or, "A Dwayne Wade leap, a Chris Bosh upside, a Steve Nash floor vision," and on and on . . .

And then there are those young players who play with such guts and determination, such leave-it-on-the-hardwood drive, that coaches shake their heads, get that look in their eye and say, "Kid's playing with that Kamikaze heart."

Ah, Kamikaze Kirkus. You ever hear the legend of Kamikaze Kirkus?

Kid once beat fifty players in a row without giving up a point.

One time he thought the game was too easy so he played barefoot and still ran circles around them fools.

Caught a ball headed for the back of his head without even turning around.

The very first time he ever picked up a basketball, he made seventy-two shots in a row, as a kindergartener, including the last one when four or five kids dog-piled him as he released. I'm telling you, it still went in.

And most of all: *You ever hear about the time Kamikaze Kirkus went head first into a brick wall over and over again? They say you can still see the stains on the bricks. I'm serious.*

The legend of Kamikaze Kirkus grows and spreads as all true legends do. Carried close to the heart, told in whispers over campfires, in the close atmosphere of darkened cars. First it was common lore only in Columbia City, but over the years it has seeped out and became adopted by other teams, other towns, and other states.

It's impossible that all the people who claimed to have been at his final game, or truly seen him in action, actually have. But does it matter? Don't legends belong to anyone who needs them? The Flying Finn told Jimmy that to see a legend was to believe in magic, even if just a little. While that's not quite it, it's something close, and sometimes close, if the distance is small enough, is just as good. Search Kamikaze Kirkus online. See if the legend is gone. See if people no longer care.

If you go to Columbia City now, and you attend a game at the Brick House, you'll notice each player on either team takes a moment out of their warm-up to run over and touch those famous bricks. Close their eyes and feel the very texture of a boy becoming a man, a man becoming a legend. In the end we are never measured by the times we got knocked down, bowled over, smashed in. We are measured by the other times. The times when we got back up, gathered ourselves together, undid the dents, walked away. To love something without faults is an easy love. To love something just limped in, just dragged through, just got up again, that is a love to know about, to tell about. The blood-red bricks of Jimmy Kirkus.

It's raining now in Columbia City. Basketball will soon be here in full force again. The warm Brick House packed to the gills with the whole town rooting for the Fishermen. *"We are the FISHER-MEN, the mighty, mighty FISHERMEN."* What a thing! It's coming. Pump up the ball, lace up the sneaks. *Dribble, dribble, shoot.*

You ever hear of Kamikaze Kirkus? Basically wrote the rules for becoming a legend.

. . . . . .

Acknowledgments

Here's the thing about this book. It's not the first one I wrote. It's not even the third. I failed my way to this book. More times than I care to admit. And it's a testament to the friends and family I've been blessed with that every time I failed—spectacularly in some cases—I never questioned if I would try again, only when.

Thanks to:

Rachael Dillon Fried. I know most authors say their agent is the best in the world. They all lied. You are.

Maggie Riggs. You are an editor of the highest skill and you made this book so much stronger.

Eva Bacon, for convincing me to send it to Rachael.

Hal Fessenden, an early reader, and the best boss I've ever had. Sorry you're fourth down. You can take it up with Maggie.

the Penguin marketing and design team: Carla Bolte, Paul Buckley, John Thomas, Noirin Lucas, Carolyn Coleburn, and Nancy Sheppard. It's an honor to work with you all.

others at Penguin who helped make this book real (even if they didn't know they were helping): Adina Gabai, Sharon Weiss, Draga Malesevic, Ritsuko Okumura, Lorna Henry, Leigh Butler, and Balie Keown.

Alexander James Humphrey. You're a dusty old rattlesnake but I tip my hat to you.

Chris Lang for being my creative partner, early and frequent reader, and friend since third grade.

Brian "Microwave" Alfonse for being an early reader and steadfast friend.

Story Syndicate. Scott Gabriel, Eliyanna Kaiser, and Felice Kuan. You three have helped this book grow from a little short story. Your critiques and friendship were invaluable. Still waiting on our Skype session.

Mrs. Patterson, my twelfth grade English teacher, who told me, "If this is what you want to do, I think you're good enough to do it."

Mrs. Lilly, my fourth and fifth grade teacher, who let me put the stories I wrote in the school library.

those along the way who never balked and gave only support when I told them I wanted to be a writer when I grew up: Gina O'Looney, Glenda Turnbull, Brian Torres, Michelle Berny Lang, Dan Caccavano (the original Shoeless), James Pozdena, Joe Mansfield, Kathryn O'Shea Evans, Robbye Good, Alison and Steve Courchesne, and the Koval Clan (Randy, Laurie, Zach, Isaac, Nathan).

my brothers Ackley and Sydney for being my best friends and two of the most hilarious, loving people I know.

Cousin Mim and my sister, Abi, for being my earliest of readers.

my mother and father, Wendy Ackley and Scott Lane. With great love, you taught me the value and magic of story.

that girl in my Spanish class. You always believed in me, even when I didn't myself. Thanks for being my wife. I love you, Tiffany Leigh Lane.